'Dazzlingly good . . . I turned the fi[nal]
know already I shall return to [it]
Elizabeth Da[y]

'Burton is a writer fully in control of her craft . . . a triumph'
Guardian

'Gripping'
Cosmopolitan, Book of the Month

'A declaration of a woman's right to take charge of her own
destiny . . . complex and compelling'
Herald

'A clever and finely crafted tale of a woman
trying to find herself'
Daily Mail

'A beautiful novel and one that will stay with me
for a very long time'
Louise O'Neill, author of *Only Ever Yours*

'Her best yet . . . *The Confession* is clever, assured
and compelling and I am deeply jealous of every reader
who has it all ahead of them'
Daisy Buchanan, author of *The Sisterhood*

'Stunning'
Red

'Her spiky musings on motherhood, marriage and sex are
sharp and feministically funny'
The Times

'I lost myself in the story, not wanting to come up
for air. A bold, intelligent, wonderful novel'
Sarah Winman, author of *Tin Man*

'An absorbing tale of self-discovery'
Woman & Home

'Irresistible . . . She unpicks you stitch by stitch, then puts you
back together again'
Stacey Halls, author of *The Familiars*

'Burton is particularly good at evoking a sense of place,
whether a contemporary London house or a 1980s Hollywood
poolside . . . stylishly written'
Sunday Times

'I loved Burton's debut, *The Miniaturist*, but this is even better!'
Prima

'Bold and beautifully written'
iweekend

'Spellbinding . . . this is a sweeping, life-affirming tale you
won't be able to forget'
Sun on Sunday

'Powerful and moving'
Woman

'Lushly enjoyable . . . Burton writes with supple grace and easy
momentum and, as ever, evokes an intoxicating sense of place'
Metro

'A beautifully told tale of love, longing and creativity that moves between 1980s Hollywood and the present day to ask what the price of freedom might really be'
inews

'A twisting tale of betrayal, abandonment and hidden identities . . . illuminating'
Financial Times

'Beautifully written and brilliantly evocative . . . powerful and deeply absorbing'
Heat

'Captivating'
Psychologies

'My favourite yet of Jessie Burton's books . . . it asks all sorts of interesting questions about motherhood and whether it's right for everyone'
Good Housekeeping, Books of the Year

'*The Confession* reveals the extent to which women try and assume roles they have watched others play'
Irish Times

'A compelling tale of self-discovery'
Woman's Weekly

'Burton's best yet . . . a terrifically skilled storyteller'
Daily Express

'My favourite Jessie Burton novel so far'
Prima, Books of the Year

'An absorbing, intelligent piece of storytelling that succeeds in sustaining its mystery to the end'
Guardian

'Stylish and riveting . . . every bit as gripping as *The Miniaturist*'
Vogue

THE CONFESSION

Jessie Burton is the author of the *Sunday Times* number one and *New York Times* bestsellers *The Miniaturist* and *The Muse*, and the children's book *The Restless Girls*. In its year of publication *The Miniaturist* sold over a million copies, and in 2017 it was adapted into a major TV series for BBC One. Her novels have been translated into thirty-eight languages, and she is a regular essay writer for newspapers and magazines. She lives in London.

Also by Jessie Burton

Novels
THE MUSE
THE MINIATURIST

Books for Children
THE RESTLESS GIRLS

THE
CONFESSION

JESSIE BURTON

PICADOR

First published 2019 by Picador

This paperback edition first published 2020 by Picador
an imprint of Pan Macmillan
The Smithson, 6 Briset Street, London EC1M 5NR
Associated companies throughout the world
www.panmacmillan.com

ISBN 978-1-5098-8619-7

7 9 8 6

A CIP catalogue record for this book is available from the British Library.

Typeset in Dante MT Std by Palimpsest Book Production Ltd, Falkirk, Stirlingshire
Printed and bound by CPI Group (UK) Ltd, Croydon, CR0 4YY

Visit **www.picador.com** to read more about all our books
and to buy them. You will also find features, author interviews and
news of any author events, and you can sign up for e-newsletters
so that you're always first to hear about our new releases.

for my friends

MARÍA VARGAS (Ava Gardner): That's difficult
to believe, living in this day and age.

HARRY DAWES (Humphrey Bogart): What makes
you think we're living in this day and age?

JOSEPH MANKIEWICZ, *The Barefoot Contessa*, 1954

One can return from the fictive world to
the everyday world, but something alien remains
alive in the mind after the return.

PAULI PYLLKÖ

1980

1

That Saturday – an early winter's afternoon on Hampstead Heath – Elise had actually been waiting for someone else. It was a set-up through John, her flatmate and landlord. She wasn't quite sure why she was there for a man she'd never met, but she often went with other people's suggestions. In the end the bloke hadn't shown, and as she came out of a clearing into the last low beam of light, Elise saw a woman standing with a sweep of trees behind her, their leaves the colour of cinnamon on the Turkish-blue sky. The scale of the trees against the woman's body was immense but correct. They looked part of an exquisite giant headpiece, as if she was a goddess or Nature's queen. She turned to Elise across the span of land, acknowledging her with a smile, as if Elise was a page in her court, a lucky fellow being given his mistress' ear.

And maybe a man did come to the Heath for Elise, running late, in a scarf and a padded jacket, pacing through the falling leaves? Elise would never know. She smiled back at the woman, who began to move towards her – and the plan had been disturbed. Elise turned and walked away. She looked once over her shoulder, and the woman was following her. Elise was used to people following her. Aged ten, eavesdropping on the adult conversation in the kitchen, she'd heard her mother's friend say, *That one's going to be a heartbreaker!* and she'd never forgotten it. When you're a child, people will tell you what you are, how you're going to be, and often you remember it. Beauty had come to Elise; they told her it had. She never talked about it or did anything about it, although she was asked to model and all that kind of thing; being stopped on the street at thirteen, fourteen. She never did it, never called back. But there it was. Despite the scrutiny, she still felt invisible, until Constance Holden looked at her on Hampstead Heath by the cinnamon trees.

*

They left the Heath and approached the long wall of railings that bordered a cemetery, and Elise thought about what was going to happen. She'd never been with a woman before. She stopped, not turning round, waiting like she was the wolf in the game of Grandmother's Footsteps. She imagined hurling a railing like a javelin as far as an Olympian, deep into the graves where skeletons would shatter. It would show this woman that she was strong.

She turned and the woman was still there, arms folded, looking a little sheepish. She was certainly older than Elise, but Elise was twenty and most of the adults in her life were older than her. She was probably in her thirties. Elise took in her clothes: a man's shirt, long overcoat open to show slim, uncomplicated jeans, a pair of brogues. No obvious make-up, a small silver ball in the lobe of each ear. A delicate wristwatch on a beautiful wrist. Elise placed her hand round the cemetery railing and spoke because she believed she was safe in this public space. This woman couldn't molest her, nor spear her with her own railing. And after all, Elise's life-model class had been cancelled so she had nothing else to do.

'One day I'm going to die. And that'll be it,' Elise said, pointing her finger between the railings. She made no comment on the fact that the woman had been following her.

The woman hugged her arms tighter to herself and laughed, and her laugh made her look confident, a vixen upright on her hind legs. Elise looked over the woman's left shoulder to the gravestones pushing through the earth like crooked teeth. They were on the poor side of the plots here, far from the tombs of splotched marble belonging to dead pioneers of industry, and somewhere near them, their wives, angled in the soil. Beyond was a crematorium brick chimney, tall and erect, thankfully not puffing smoke.

'You're not going to die for a very long time,' said the woman, and her voice ran through Elise like a shot of iron.

They stared at each other. 'Is there something I can do for you?' said Elise.

*

They quickly found an all-hours greasy spoon but didn't eat anything. The woman said her name was Connie. Elise told her that her name was Elise Morceau. They had mugs of tea, sitting opposite each other, warming their fingers on the cheap china. The woman looked at Elise as if she wasn't real. 'I don't normally do this,' she said. 'Do you?'

'It's OK,' said Elise. Then she said, 'Do what?'

Connie looked up from her mug. 'This. Just meeting like that. Walking together.'

'No, I guess not.' Elise looked at Connie and could see her trying to hide a yearning for answers. 'I don't normally do this either,' she said, and Connie visibly relaxed.

They talked a little about where they lived – Connie, nearby, Elise in Brixton. 'Have you always been south of the river?' Connie asked.

'Yeah.'

'You were born there?'

Elise looked at her. 'Yeah.'

'How old are you?'

'Twenty-eight,' said Elise.

Connie frowned. 'I don't believe you. How old are you?'

'How old are *you*?'

'I'm thirty-six. That is my real age. And Connie is my real name.'

'I'm twenty,' said Elise. 'And I'm Elise.'

'Do you work in London?'

'I work in a cafe in Pimlico. It's called Seedling. And as an usher at the National Theatre. And a life model at the RCA.'

'A diverse portfolio,' said Connie.

'Do you work in the centre?' said Elise, and Connie straightened up a little as if she was being mocked by the strange phrasing.

'I work at home,' said Connie. 'I'm a writer.'

'What do you write?'

'Stories.'

'What kind of stories?'

'Fucking good ones,' said Connie, laughing.

'You sure about that?' said Elise.

'Sometimes.'

'Would I find you in a library?'

'You would. And bookshops.'

'That's pretty cool,' said Elise.

Connie stared into her tea again. 'I guess it is.' She looked up. 'Can I take you for dinner?'

*

The next Friday, before their Saturday dinner, Elise took herself to Brixton Library and found the *H* in fiction. There was the book: *Wax Heart*, published the year previously. Elise took it out, noting that lots of people had done so before her. A tagline on the back jacket stated: 'the book everyone's talking about.'

When John returned from work that night, she told him that she'd met Constance Holden the novelist, who wrote *Wax Heart*. She edited the bit about meeting on the Heath, not wanting to give the impression of being the sort of person who got picked up in parks. She met people at refined soirees where novelists went. John acknowledged her experience only mildly, seeing as Constance Holden didn't write novels about heists, with raised lettering on their covers, the inevitable outline of a man running from a burning building. Nor had he studied her at school. Basically, he had never heard of her.

That evening, Elise read *Wax Heart*. It was intense, harsh, passionate and full of sentences she wanted to underline. Elise found her allegiance switching from woman to man as she read it; poor Beatrice, the blighted weirdo married to a man who led her a merry dance. But how seductive, how reasonable Frederick could be. Beatrice was in love with a man who would bring her danger. But in love, nevertheless: in love, in love. Would she escape? What would happen to her daughter, Gaby, in the aftermath? It was compelling, propulsive, violent and revelatory, a sort of anti-love story that seemed full of heart.

Elise thought about love that night, with Connie's book splayed open on her chest, the spine cracked slightly under the library plastic. Love. How might it feel? Elise believed that for her whole life she had been tiptoeing round the edge of a volcanic crater whose depths she could not quantify, but which was full of something powerful, something she had never been shown before. Down in that darkness were many happy souls but many dead bodies.

*

For their dinner – their first date, really – they had gone to a restaurant on Dean Street in Soho, called Mariposa. Connie had chosen; dark booths, brass lamps and banquettes of worn red velvet whose shade you sensed but could not truly see. Elise descended the staircase into a space that spanned before her underground: busy, smoky, humming. Women with heavy eyeliner, wearing velvet dresses with warrior shoulders, rubbing against tired City boys and men whose long hair flowed from fashionable hats. Denim, leather, nicotine, money – Elise could taste them on her tongue like elementals.

Connie was already there, and had ordered a bottle of wine. She stood out of the shadows to greet her guest, and Elise was surprised to see how much of an effort she'd made. She looked sensational: plain black cocktail dress, gold chain, her red hair tousled to cavalier perfection. Elise felt a surge of envy: she would like to be thirty-six, and own a house, have published books like *Wax Heart*, to know about these places in Soho where people like this ate.

'Hello,' Connie said.

'Hello,' said Elise. She looked down at her clothes: black jeans, white T-shirt. 'If I'd known, I'd have dressed better.'

'You look wonderful.' Connie put out her hand and touched Elise's shoulder. They smiled at each other.

'I've come straight from the cafe,' said Elise, sliding into the booth.

'Seedling.'

'Yeah,' said Elise, enchanted that Connie had remembered.

Without asking if she wanted any, Connie poured Elise a glass of wine. 'And when you're at the theatre, do you get to see the shows?'

'Every time.'

'Do you ever get bored?'

'All the time.'

Connie laughed as a waiter appeared, a young man with a slender waist and eyes loaded with kohl. Elise tried not to stare at him. Connie opted for pot-au-feu with a side of greens. Elise quickly scanned the menu and chose the steak. 'Cheers,' Connie said, lifting her glass. 'So here's to waitressing, ushering and life-modelling.' She took a deep mouthful of the wine. 'Are there other things you're keen to try?'

'Other things?'

'Jobs? Countries?'

'I don't know,' said Elise.

'What do your parents think?'

'I don't know,' said Elise, and she stared at Connie as if daring her to ask more. Connie did not. 'I have ideas for plays,' Elise went on.

'Plays?'

'Yes. I'd like to write a play.'

'Then you should.'

Elise didn't know if it was strictly true that she wanted to write a play, but she thought it sounded impressive. It was true that she would sit in the darkness of the National's three theatres, her eyes heavenwards as the backdrops descended or revolved, turning blank spaces into Victorian drawing rooms, Greek tragedies transposed to post-apocalyptic worlds, rural English idylls, Japan, Manhattan, India. Sometimes she tried to write a scene, but meaning eluded her, in the end the task was too great and she was content with unwritten plans. She could not commit the world to paper. The swirl within herself, its movement, its abstract nature, made perfect sense. She thought that one day it would make its way out of her. *But*, she thought, *not yet.* 'I love being an artists' model,' she said.

'Why?' said Connie.

When Elise removed her clothes and walked out in front of those students, her body was called upon, willing and adaptable; her lips, her hands, her breasts, her throat, the insides of her legs. She sat still for hours, listening to the light scratch of pencils on thick paper, and walked through the chambers of her mind. Elise was so good at being still that the art college asked her back, again and again. And sometimes, when the students had left for the day, she would wait in the loo and creep back inside the workshop, circling the easels where the day's work had been left. She was on the hunt for herself, although she was the one who had provided the map. She would wander the paper forest of her own limbs, waiting for the moment of finding the person who had truly captured her. No one had yet succeeded; the treasure remained buried.

She didn't say any of this to Connie. 'Because it's peaceful.'

'But you stay in one position?'

'Yes.'

'For hours?' Elise shrugged and Connie grinned. 'You like to be looked at,' Connie said.

'Is that a bad thing?'

'No. Though it's quite unusual to admit it.' Connie smiled. 'Will you come here?' she said.

Elise was momentarily confused. 'Where?'

'Here,' said Connie, patting the seat next to her. Elise obeyed, feeling Connie's cool fingers upon either side of her face, as if she was trying to press Elise into a new shape. 'I could frame that face,' Connie said.

The wine made Elise feel as if she was losing control. 'It'll cost you,' she said. She closed her eyes and wondered if the other woman would understand that was a joke.

Connie cupped Elise's face more gently. She leaned in. Her breath was sweet and hot. Elise could see the bow of her slight mouth, her eyes attentive in the candlelight. 'How much will it cost?' Connie said.

'Fifty pounds a kiss.'

Connie laughed. 'I said frame, not kiss.'

Connie's palms fell away and Elise felt caught out. She picked up Connie's hands from where they sat in her lap, and placed them once again upon her face. 'I read your book,' she said. 'I read *Wax Heart*.'

'Oh?'

'You're very good,' she said, holding Connie's hands tight, and Connie laughed.

*

Elise woke up to discover she was in an unfamiliar bed. She lifted the duvet: she was still wearing her knickers and T-shirt, but her trousers were gone. When had she taken them off? There they were on the floor, like the cut-out of a murder victim. Her boots were at a crooked angle, soles facing each other, kicked off at some point that she could not recall. Where *was* she? The room was dim, but she could make out walls of green-striped wallpaper, a small wardrobe, a wastepaper basket, everything neat. A large, fluffy tortoiseshell with a big white bib and white paws sat in the middle of the room, surveying her.

'I hope Ripley isn't bothering you,' said a voice at the door.

Elise turned. 'Ripley?'

'The cat. Shh, don't try and sit up.' Connie came over with a tumbler of water and two aspirin and laid them on the bedside table by Elise's head.

'Thanks,' Elise mumbled.

Connie pulled open the bedroom curtains, and the weak November light made Elise groan. 'Sorry,' said Connie, but she did not close the curtains.

'What happened?' Elise said, her voice a croak. Connie did not immediately reply. She was looking out at the garden. 'Connie?'

'What happened when?'

'Last night.'

'Don't you remember?'

'Yes. No.'

Connie walked round and perched herself on the end of the bed, facing Elise. 'We went to dinner. We drank too much, came back here, and you passed out on the sofa.'

'I passed out on the sofa?'

'Yes. And I carried you up here.'

'You carried me?'

They gazed at each other. Connie smiled.

'I'm sorry,' said Elise. 'I should have gone home.'

Connie reached out and put her hand on Elise's forehead. 'I would never have allowed it. Not in the state you were in. Were you comfortable enough?'

'What time is it?'

Connie looked at her watch. 'Eleven-twenty.'

Elise closed her eyes. There was something wrong with the fact that eleven-twenty was the time, but she was lying here. 'Oh, fuck. *Fuck*. I've got work today.'

'Surely not. What's open on a Sunday? Don't go.'

'I have to. The cafe.'

'What if I do pay you that fifty pounds?'

'What fifty pounds?'

'Ah, you *were* drunk. Never mind.'

Elise felt uneasy.

'Forget the cafe,' Connie said.

All right for you, Elise thought. 'I *have* to go,' she said, struggling upright like a geriatric.

'Elise, darling, lie down.'

'Connie—'

'You're in no fit state to do anything. Just lie down.'

Elise lay down. She thought she might weep. 'I'm going to hypnotize you to not go to work,' Connie said.

Elise scrunched her eyes. 'Are you joking?'

'Yes. I never did get my O-level in hypnotism.'

Elise felt revolting but she laughed anyway. Connie was looking at her gently. 'Would you like me to make you a bacon sandwich?' she said.

'Please,' Elise whimpered.

Elise watched Connie disappear, and heard her speaking on the telephone. Soon the smell of frying bacon wafted up the stairs, along the corridor, under the door crack, into Elise's nose. She closed her eyes and wished for a new body. She really wanted a hot bath.

*

Connie returned with a bacon sandwich and two mugs of tea on a tray. 'There,' she said. 'My finest work.'

Elise had managed to sit up. 'Thanks,' she said. 'How long to Pimlico from here?'

'You don't need to worry,' said Connie. 'I called them.'

'You *what*?'

'Seedling. What a name! Told them I was your flatmate and that you had a virus.'

'They *believed* you?'

'Of course they did.'

'Was it Gabe?'

'It was a man. I don't know if it was *Gabe*. But he said for you to get well. I said it would take a few days and the doctor said you shouldn't over-exert yourself.'

Elise stared at the sandwich. It was an alien feeling, to have someone else work your life out for you. 'Right. Thank you.'

Connie sipped her mug of tea. Elise read the words round it: I ♥ BIRDWORLD. 'Should I not have done it?' Connie said. 'Sometimes I can cross a line—'

'No. There's no line. Work would have been nearly impossible. I just – I wasn't expecting you to call them.'

'I think I did you a favour.'

Elise wondered if she still had a job. She wondered if she really cared. She reached towards Connie's mug and their fingers brushed. 'Did you really go to Birdworld?'

'With my friend and her son. It was for the boy. But I ended up really enjoying myself. Flamingos, penguins, tits. The works.'

'I'm trying to imagine you at Birdworld.'

'I was perfectly at home at Birdworld.'

'You're too glamorous.'

'Elise, no one is more glamorous than a flamingo.'

They laughed. This was flirtation, Elise knew – wired, worried, hungover flirtation. What step to take next, what to do. Did anything happen last night? It didn't *feel* like it did. 'Would you like a bath?' Connie asked, as if she knew.

'I would,' she said, so quickly the two of them laughed again. 'I just feel so awful,' she said. 'I'm so sorry.'

'Oh, god. You look absolutely fine.'

'You're lying. My skin!'

'You're beautiful. Don't worry. I'll run you one.'

Connie left Elise alone, eating the bacon sandwich. John's flat didn't have a bath and the front door to Connie's house felt so far away. The greasy bread was manna, a restoration of some sense of flesh to Elise's bones, but she knew the day was unwinding beyond her control.

Suddenly, she thought: *Connie's going to keep me prisoner.* The paranoia of her hangover almost fed this quasi-wish to be absolved of any self-dominion, a little girl in the bosom of this powerful, talented person who didn't let stupid things like dehydration prevent her ability to impersonate someone else and get Elise off work, to keep her warm in the house on a cold November morning, to run her a bath, to give her a fresh, clean bed.

When the bath was run, Elise slid into it and thought she might cry with the purity of the hot water.

'Going to clear my head on the Heath!' Connie called.

Elise was astonished that Connie trusted her enough to just leave her in her house. *I could be a thief!* she thought. *I could have weaselled my way in here to nick some ornaments and her handbag. But then again, look at me. I can't even string a sentence together.*

She thought of Connie like a witch in the wood, going to look for more Gretels to bring back home, luring them with gingerbread and sweets. But an hour later Connie was back, pink-cheeked, the Sunday paper under her arm, saying, 'If there's one group I would happily see massacred, it's the people who let their dogs shit *anywhere* and never pick it up.'

Connie was fizzing with something that day – she was softer, more open than she'd been in the restaurant in Soho – and she was gentler with Elise. She sat on the sofa with her in the front living room, and as November's early darkness fell, Elise still didn't leave the house. They watched an episode of *We, the Accused* on BBC2, because Connie liked the 1935 novel and wanted to see what they'd done with it. Elise drifted, her head in Connie's lap, and eventually she fell asleep with Connie's fingers stroking her temples with a tenderness that she could not, in her adult life, recall.

2017

2

I was fourteen when I killed my mother. Before that, I'd always kept her in the wings, where she was doing something more interesting than everybody else's mum, only waiting for me to send her the cue to walk into my life. But she was never ready, she never appeared. Between the ages of ten and eleven, I told my classmates that she'd run off with a Russian circus, and was living in a tent made of yak pelts. I wrote postcards of mountain scenes in her handwriting and brought them into school. 'See? She's there. I told you!'

'The cards don't have stamps,' said a child called Hamilton Tanner. I hated him.

'They came in *envelopes*,' I said. 'My dad threw them away.'

I was always prepared to dig the next layer of fiction and entrench myself. From childhood onwards I went through every tale, but my mother was a story with no answers. According to my dad she left before I was one, but I only began to feel her absence more keenly when I started primary school. It was when all the other mums came to the gates, chatting to each other with their arms folded, swinging from side to side as their children tugged the hems of their puffa jackets. At birthday parties, these same mothers organized such smooth afternoons of games and food and fun, making sure I was always given extra attention, which made the other children hate me. It was nice to be looked after, but I always wondered:

Where is she right now? What is she doing? Why isn't she doing it with me?

I used to love stories about babies coming out of plants, or turning into humans from animal form. I pored over the Greek myths – how a baby could be born from a ray of light, or a thunderbolt, or from a swan. I felt an affinity with these babies, these other kinds of humans – a dangerous affinity, I should add, for in fact I was simply a very normal human being. Ovid would not write about me. I was not a god. But where had I come from, out of whose body? Whose heart had beaten for my father?

I didn't find any answers, and I began using my unseen mother to make myself seem mysterious and unusual rather than pitiable. I offered inconsistent drama, romance, wild supposition. I tried hard. From what I can remember, there was the Russian acrobat story, the criminal-on-the-run story (she'd stolen a priceless diamond necklace, but it wasn't her fault) and the ship story – her being the captain of a trading vessel that moved around the Bahamas. But children are suspicious, and fond of order, normality. My classmates thought I was weird, even careless. What kind of creature was I, that my mother would not even stick around – even if it made it difficult for her as a jewel thief? When we read those myths and fairy tales at story time, Hamilton Tanner, for whom my feelings of hatred were mutual, said to me, 'Your mum made a pact with the Devil. She's been turned into a beast.'

*

All I knew about her was what my dad had told me: her name was Elise Morceau, and she had me young, when they were living in New York. And she had left, thirty-four years ago, before I turned one. There were no photos of us together; my father had none. No trace of her on paper, or in the heft of objects once in her possession, left behind. As far as I was aware, my father had never managed to find her after her flight – either he gave up, having no inclination to chase her, or she had told him not to. He wouldn't say. I would wait for opportune moments – these were rare – to ask about her, and occasionally Dad would cede information. *She had short legs.* (Short legs! How does that contribute to a personality – or indeed, an ability to flee quickly?) *She had hair your colour.* (I liked that one.) *She was difficult. She was positive.* Once, when he'd drunk too much: *It wouldn't have worked. She had a temper.*

Dad would tell me that he didn't remember enough, or that it was so long ago – *and so much has happened to us since, Rosie – and you're OK, aren't you?* So I did not know the circumstances of how he met Elise, and I didn't know why he'd been given custody of me. I knew the stay in New York had been relatively short, because he had brought me back to England before my first birthday. He wanted to protect me from hurt, I suppose, and he threw himself into being both parents, asking me just to think of myself and of my life, not what had come before. He was always loving. He wanted to spare me. But I can't help feeling that this refusal to find the words caused more damage than anything.

It's hard for him to talk about, my Grandma Cherry, Dad's mother, would say before she died. I thought it was harder *not* to talk about, but it seemed a consensus had been reached, and I was not privy to the reasons why. Grandma Cherry was also tight-lipped about Elise, as if to talk about her was to unleash a curse.

When I asked my grandma if she'd ever met Elise, she said that she had not. 'She was a tricky woman,' my grandmother said, which I thought was an unfair thing to say about someone you'd never met. But to my grandma, how could Elise be anything other than a tricky woman, a woman executing this sleight of hand, a disappearing act where she climbed into a box and cut herself in two.

So in the end, I killed her myself. My fictional adventures for her became as embarrassing to me as they had been for my schoolmates. By fourteen, I didn't need the Hamilton Tanners of this world to tell me what had happened to my mum. She did not snap her neck on the Russian trapeze, nor waste away in a jail for emerald thieves, nor wreck her ship on Bahamian rocks. She was not a beast. She was just . . . dead. And my dad was in agreement: in fact, *he* seemed to think it was better just to pretend she'd never existed, a fairy tale to be forgotten by adulthood. He'd maintained this pattern of behaviour when I was tiny, and as I grew up the only way I can describe it is that he didn't know how to break the spell. Not having learned the mother tongue, he couldn't teach me. Absolutely better she was dead.

But as I entered my twenties, I began to know people who had real parents – people who they'd lived with their whole lives – who'd really died on them. I witnessed their devastation, the reeling disbelief, the feeling that the pain would never end. I went to a funeral of a friend's mother and watched her coffin disappearing behind a curtain, my friend watching it too, her face unrecognizable in grief. The loss of *my* mother was to me a palpable but different kind of pain. My version of grief was a locked box, a house to which I did not have a key, a place on a map I could not pronounce. One day it might be revealed to me, and duly overwhelm me, but I never told anyone about this fear. I didn't have a mum, and I'd never had her, so how could I miss something I'd never really lost?

I don't tell people about the yearning. The wonder. I tell them, *You can't miss what you never had!*

There were swathes of time when I didn't think about her. There were other periods of my life when I felt her absence intensely. Once search engines on the Internet became a thing, I used their shrinking nets of existence to trawl for her – but I could never find an Elise Morceau, during long nights alone when all I had for company was one bottle of wine too many and irresistible rabbit holes of family tree sites. My guess was that Morceau was not her real surname. Morceau is French for bit or part, and I think this must have been a joke – on her part. It was all fruitless. Nothing ever came of my virtual journeys.

I don't think she gave my father the full pieces of her puzzle – lover to lover, who does? But in her case, maybe she gave him even less. A borrowed name from a list of characters. She gave my dad only the littlest crumbs, he passed them on to me, and there seemed nothing I could do with them at all.

3

My boyfriend Joe and I spent the last week of the summer of 2017 with my dad in France, where he now lived. My father had recently recovered from prostate cancer, and had tasted his mortality; his wife, Claire, was originally from Brittany, so they'd gone there to live permanently, in a small cottage that had belonged to her parents. These days, our visits were too intermittent, sustained only by text message – and this fact, together with the remission, had made this particular trip seem important. Joe thought that me and Dad were 'constipated' with our feelings – but then again, Joe came from a family who made you feel you were in an amateur production of *Cat on a Hot Tin Roof*.

My dad loved the ocean. He'd always liked being near water, and for him, in the end, the Thames didn't really cut it. Joe and I had put most of our money into Joe's burrito business, Joerritos, so when they offered us a holiday in the spare room in their cottage, we said yes, despite Joe's reservations. It was a mistake in the short term, and in the long term it wasn't. We were all cooped up together, staring through the windows at leaden skies. The sea was dark with changing bands of grey; I yearned for sun and golden beach visions. And from the beginning of the week Dad was strange, veering between conversational and despondent. I felt almost physically ill at the thought that the cancer might have returned. 'Is he OK?' I asked

Claire the first morning after we'd arrived, when he was out at the market with Joe, fetching bread.

Claire, small in the darkness of her Breton kitchen, drew her bifocals away from her head and rubbed her eyes. 'Matt is fine – if you mean with the cancer. But I think he is worried about you,' she said.

'Worried about me? Why?'

'You will have to ask him.' Claire sighed. 'I think also he is a bit depressed.' She closed her eyes. 'It happens to old men.'

'We came all this way!' I said, as if we'd used a caravan of camels over six months to find them in a desert, rather than two drives with a P&O ferry in the middle of it.

'I know,' Claire replied equably. 'Just talk with him, Rose. I think he would like you to try.'

Dad got lucky with Claire. As for Claire, I don't know if she feels lucky, particularly, but I'm glad for her existence. They met in their mid-fifties, at a friend of a friend's summer party, and got married when I was twenty-six. Of course it does not escape me that my father has ended up with a Frenchwoman, given my own mother's surname, but I don't say anything about that to him. Claire is far from an evil step-mother. Claire understands my dad and she loves him, plain to see, but always with her terms intact. I think this is because Claire has been married before. She's made mistakes and learned, and I expect she chose a different type of man the next time round. She wields self-assurance over Dad – demonstrated by her composure, her long-sightedness about their future – but she does it cleanly, and kindly. I admire that. Dad needs that. I have come to realize he needs to know where he is.

I often wondered what he'd told Claire about his past, about how he was a man before he was my father. She never asked me anything, that's for sure. In their spare room there's a framed photo of Dad and me on the dresser. I must have been about two, a little top-knot on my head, done up with a technicolour bow. Slightly scuffing my foot, I'm holding his hand as we stand in what looks like a petting zoo. He was muscular, then. Dark-haired, legs far apart in a combative stance. Of course I'd wondered who'd taken the picture. I must have asked, until I knew not to. No one had taken it. We'd taken it ourselves.

*

'Shall we go for a walk?' I said to my dad that afternoon.

He did his customary head dip, looking through the low front window of the cottage, towards the water. 'The beach?' he said, as if there was anywhere else we could go.

We went down to the pebbled shore below the house, side-stepping crab carcasses, reaching down for a razor shell or a faded oyster, the debris of marine life that could not survive once out of water. The gulls wheeled above our heads, mewling. I thought: *Claire's got it wrong. This is the conversation where he tells me it's come back, terminal.*

'Do you start back straightaway?' he said, lowering himself to the pebbles.

'Yeah. Soon as we're home.'

My dad stared out at the unending line of the Atlantic Ocean. I looked at his profile, the slim angles of his face, the large nose, the cheekbones sharp as the edge of a cuttlefish, the scruffy grey hair. He was sixty-four, and I was thirty-four. It had always been just us. I knew that he hated how I worked in a coffee shop, even though it was a nice, popular one, called Clean Bean. How many times had I heard the phrase 'first-rate brain' when he talked about me. I suppose I did have a good brain in many ways, and I should be doing more, even though I could never say what 'more' was. Even my best friend, Kelly, had started to say something about this, hinting that I'd outgrown Clean Bean. *You can do anything, Rosie! You're so bloody clever. Just believe you can do it. Please.*

Dad couldn't seem to understand how things had gone, even though he'd been my longest, closest witness. I'd given up defending myself, but I still defended Joe. We were going to make Joerritos a success. We didn't talk about Joerritos to Dad. It was something of a touchpaper.

'Rosie,' he said. 'I could – give you some money, you know. Not much, but some. Isn't there a course, or something you'd like to do? A language? Or a skill?'

'Dad.'

He put his hands up. 'Sorry. Sorry.' He paused. 'And you already have a degree.'

'Yes, I have a degree,' I said. We'd been having this conversation on and off for a decade. Ten years can go fast when you're not looking. After graduating in my early twenties with an English degree, I'd worked in a mainly secretarial capacity at quite decent, interesting companies. But I never pushed myself. I was essentially an enabler, a facilitator, an administrator of other people's plans and ambitions. When Joe had suggested the burrito venture two years ago, I decided to resign from my job and join him in planning our own business. I figured: *I'm a good cook.* And I was scared of being a subordinate for the rest of my working life.

'Are you happy?' my dad said suddenly.

I looked at him in alarm. *No*, was the word I wanted to say. And hearing that word in my head, I felt that it was not the answer a woman of my age and good health should be giving. In the beat of my blood, in the swallow of a glass of water, in the glance of a stranger, I could see happiness. I have known happiness – but I feel as if I can taste other people's happiness much more strongly than I can my own. I couldn't have told you what makes me happy, yet I was tired of constantly trying to improve myself. To find, amongst my many shitty selves, my *best* self. Joe would just roll out of bed and be Joe, but I could not escape my failing self or the potential selves inside me. The Internet told me, daily, that there were many routes to happiness: good yoga leggings, a scented candle. A plant we call the succulent. But the Internet also loosed a second message, a subliminal arrow that still breaks the flesh: by thirty-five, you ought to have it sorted.

I felt a slight collapse. 'I've been a bit stressed, I guess.'

'I talked to Joe at the market,' Dad went on. 'He told me you two were thinking about starting a family.'

I turned to him in disbelief. 'Joe said that to you?'

'Just in passing. Just in terms of the long term.'

'Right.'

'Which I guess is normal, for a woman of your age, to be thinking about.'

'Yep,' I said tightly.

'It might be the making of you,' he said.

'*What?*'

'It might be—'

'I heard you the first time.'

My father looked pained. 'It's coming out wrong. I'm just saying, Rosie. A baby is no bad thing.'

'Depends on whose baby it is.'

'It's worked for Kelly, hasn't it?' he said, ignoring this. I'd known Kelly since my first week of secondary school; so had my dad, because we were inseparable from the off, always in and out of each other's flats. Now she had one daughter, Mol, aged four, and had recently shared with me, not without some shock in her voice, her discovery that she was in the very early stages of a second pregnancy. She wasn't the only one – most of the friends that I had held on to from school or university were baby-producing, marrying, house-buying pragmatists. I said nothing.

My dad cleared his throat. 'When I thought I was going to – you know – *die* – I just, all I wanted was to know you were going to have a good life when I was gone.'

'But you're not gone. So I can carry on having a shit life!'

'Rosie, be serious. I know it hasn't always been easy for you. But I want to say – that I think you'd be an excellent mum.'

I couldn't say anything for a moment. 'Dad,' I said, my voice husky. *'Don't.'*

He fell silent, and we said nothing for a few moments. I turned and turned a pebble in my palm. 'How can you say it would be the making of me?' I said suddenly. 'What was I *doing* the last three decades?'

'I didn't mean it like that.'

'You sort of did. You don't get to say that.'

'I'm sorry,' he said. 'I fucked this up, didn't I?'

It was late afternoon, and a wind was coming over the sea, whipping small waves of white foam. Autumn was somewhere near. I thought of London, of what was there and what was missing. 'You didn't, Daddy,' I said. 'It's fine.'

4

On the last day, about an hour before Joe and I were due to go back to London, Dad and I were sitting at the kitchen table, waiting for the morning coffee to be ready. Joe was still asleep and Claire had gone for a run. I'd slept badly, tossing and turning, my mind uneasy. It was the fresh air, I told myself. People always say they sleep better when they get out of a city, but I found the cleaner air and the endless sound of water almost psychically disturbing, because I couldn't hide my habits of thought from them in the same way I could from the stupor of London's fumes and flashing lights. My selfhood lurked in London's layers, hidden under the millions. Here, by the sea, I felt naked.

Dad's face was pale and tense. His lips pressed tight together as if he was trying not to breathe. He reached down to the bench he was sitting on and brought up two books, placing them on the scarred table Claire had sourced years back from a local flea market. The books sat between us, a pair of innocuous paperbacks.

'Have you ever read these?' he said. 'Ever read them in your degree?'

'What?'

He pushed them towards me, and reluctantly I picked them up. The first one was called *Wax Heart*, and the second was *Green Rabbit*. The covers were dated but imaginative, the fonts simple but the pictures elaborate. *Wax Heart* had a giant heart on the front, made from an old-fashioned woodcut. The heart had been divided like the twelve signs of the zodiac, but instead of the usual symbols – the goat, the crab, the bull – there were seemingly traditional feminine pursuits; a saucepan, a needle, a ball of wool, a pressed flower, all in that heavy Elizabethan black ink. *Green Rabbit* was wilder, a freehand, masterfully dashed-off single green ink line drawing of a rabbit's outline, except if you looked at it again, the rabbit could also have been a silhouette of a woman. They were both written by a woman called Constance Holden.

'No,' I said. 'I focused on the Victorians.'

'She's a very good writer, actually. Was.'

'Is she dead?'

'I don't know. You've really never read them?'

'No, Dad,' I said with exasperation. 'Why are you asking me?'

'You should read them,' he said. 'They were very popular when they came out.'

I wondered if this was the beginning of senility; the non sequiturs of conversation, the sudden retrieval of the past's objects, lifting water from the well of your own life and finding no one wants to look inside the bucket.

'The covers are beautiful,' I said, leafing through the pages of *Green Rabbit*. They were faded on their edges, the type small and dated. 'But why have *you* got them?'

He didn't say anything. I looked up. 'Are you just trying to get rid of them? You haven't read them, have you?'

'Your mum—' he began, then stopped. He took a breath.

I was alert now, my fingers gripped hard on the yielding paperback. 'What? What about my mum?'

The air between us thickened. My dad pointed at the name on the cover. 'Your mother knew Constance Holden,' he said.

'Dad, I don't understand.'

He looked away from me, through the kitchen window towards the sea. 'I should have just come out with this years ago,' he said.

I could feel my heart thump harder. 'What should you have just come out with years ago?'

He looked back at me. 'Before I met your mother,' he said, his fingers twisting to a fist, 'she and Constance – they were together.'

I stared at him. 'My mum?' I placed my hand on the top of *Wax Heart*. 'My mum was with this woman?'

'Yes.'

'My mum was a lesbian?'

'I don't know, Rosie. She might have been. For a time, they were inseparable. I mean – we had you, so I can't . . . qualify it.'

'So she was bisexual?'

'I guess that's what you might call it.' My dad looked like he wanted to curl up in a ball and never unfold himself.

I took a deep breath, clutching *Green Rabbit* like a talisman. 'Wow,' I said.

'I need some air,' said my dad, exhaling heavily. 'Let's take the coffee outside.'

*

So there we were, side by side on the pebbles again. I still hadn't let go of the book, but now I laid it on the top of my thigh. The tide lapped a few feet away, and this time a crab moved mechanically along the edge, its front pincers raised. I looked at the sky, an unshifting haze of cloud. My head was pounding, but all I wanted was more. 'Why are you telling me this now?' I said. My father didn't reply, just stared out at the flat grey line of the horizon. 'Dad? You're not . . . *ill*, are you?'

'No, no. I'm fine. I just – I don't know. It's been on my mind. You. Your mum.'

He made it sound like he'd been worrying about Arsenal's performance in the league, but I knew, on the very rare occasions when he was expansive like this, that the best thing was to let him find his way. 'It was when Joe talked to me,' he said. 'I just thought, this isn't right, you know? You not knowing anything about her, and thinking about becoming a mum yourself.'

Without any warning, tears sprang into my eyes. Sometimes it would come at me, how much he tried, how ill-equipped he was, but how he had done everything for me. How much I meant to him, how powerfully bound to him I could sometimes feel. I said nothing and wiped my eyes.

'You've always asked me, Rosie. You've got angry with me.'

'I know. I—'

'And quite right too. And I never said much, because the truth is – I just don't know what happened to her.'

I turned to him. 'Dad, is that really the truth?'

He swallowed, gripping his tin mug in one fist. 'Yes. She vanished. That's the truth.'

'In a puff of smoke?'

He gave me a hard look. 'One day she was there, Rose, and the next she was gone. I *looked* for her. Not for my sake. For yours. Do you think I could understand what happened?'

'You'd understand it better than me.'

He sighed. 'Your mum, she . . . we weren't together by then. She left. Took you with her. And Connie – Constance – was there.'

'In New York?'

'Yes.' He sighed. 'But your mum went to live with a friend. A woman called Yolanda.'

'*Yolanda?* But what about this Constance woman?'

My dad batted the air with his hand impatiently. 'Just wait, Rose. Listen. Your mum and Yolanda worked together in a diner in Manhattan. Yolanda was as clueless as me about what happened. After your mum disappeared, Yolanda rang me, and I came to get you. I'd had enough.'

I'd never heard any of this before. I took it in, staring at the sea. 'How hard did you look for her?' I said quietly.

He turned to me, angry. 'I spent *months* looking for her. I was even brought in for questioning.' He paused. 'But your mum didn't want to be found. She'd gone.' He stared back out to the water. 'What I want to say, Rose, is that if you want to know what happened to your mum – if that's what you really want – then it isn't me you need to talk to. I don't have the answers. And the only person who might know is Connie.'

'Why are you calling her *Connie*? How well did you know her?'

'Well enough,' he said with a grim expression. 'But we weren't the best of friends.'

'Why not?'

By now, my father was looking as if he wanted the sea to drag him under. 'It's hard to talk about. We all make mistakes. It was – a very difficult time. All I've ever cared about is you, Rose.'

'If you cared about me, you would have told me this years ago.' I felt the tears rising again and I jumped to my feet. The paperback of *Green Rabbit* tumbled to the pebbles. I kicked it and my dad scrambled to rescue it. 'Why did you let me make up stupid stories about her?' I went on. 'How could you keep this from me? This is *information*.'

Dad tried to encircle me with his arms. I pushed him away and staggered a little down to the edge of the shore. 'I'm sorry,' he said. 'I just thought it wouldn't help. It was all such a mess! We were back in England, your mum was God knows where. I just wanted things to be *stable*.'

Gingerly, he took a few steps towards me, and I didn't move away. 'If you still want to know about your mother,' he said gently—

'I do,' I said. 'You know I do.'

'I know. Constance Holden was there, just before she disappeared. She was the last one to see her.' My dad paused, his face as pale as a winter bulb. 'All I know is that Connie went to visit Elise at Yolanda's, and we never saw your mother again. I don't know where Connie is, Rose. All I've got left of that time are these bloody paperbacks.'

'I want them.'

'You can have them. That's why I pulled them out of the cardboard box. But Rosie, the chances are she won't want to speak to you.'

'Why not?'

My dad sighed again, pinching the bridge of his nose as he always did in moments of discomfort. 'It wasn't a happy time. So if you do find her, you'll have to be careful.'

'*Why?*'

He looked miserable. 'Your mum was – easily led. You're strong.'

'I'm not strong.'

'You're stronger than you think.' He turned towards the water. 'Sometimes, Rose, we say things and do things, and we don't for one second imagine the consequences of our actions.'

'I just can't believe you never talked to me about this.'

'Believe me, I thought about it. But what could you have done? I'd have been imposing it on you when you were too young to be able to do anything about it, or to see it from all angles.'

'Dad. I'm *thirty-four*.'

'It wouldn't have been fair. It would have been too much of a burden.'

'You don't think I've been burdened anyway, this whole time?'

'Maybe me telling you now is still unfair. *I* don't know all the angles, Rosie, and I was there. But I've told you what I know. Connie was a charming woman and your mother was in her thrall.' He placed the novel in my hands and turned away, heading back to the cottage, arcing the dregs from our coffee cups against the uneven stones.

'What the hell am I supposed to do, Dad?' I said.

He stopped, but he didn't turn round. 'Find Constance Holden if you want answers. I don't know any more.'

1982

5

All twenty-six of Frida Kahlo's principal paintings had come from Mexico to be displayed in the Whitechapel Gallery, the stipulation being that they travelled together, or not at all. Connie and Elise wandered the rooms, looking into the small and vivid portals. Foliage, babies, blood and beauty, a prayer book of a different order, its pages torn and hung against the wall. Illumination by a woman, her mouth closed on silent screaming prayers, a poetry they couldn't teach in church. Always, that gaze: a suspended, knowledgeable survey of herself that managed to include you too.

Electrified by these images, Elise watched Connie's lovely neck, the tendrils fallen from her messy attempt to tame her hair – her hair the colour of a fox's pelt, the scoop of her shirt revealing a pattern of freckles across that collarbone. Her fingers upon that collarbone, then pointing at this painting or that, moving, always moving, so slender and pale like the fingers of a maiden in a tapestry. Her cologne of citrus and smoked wood. Her small chin that widened up into a heart-shaped face, with grey-green eyes and neat brows like the wings of a settling dove. She was so russet and English compared to the Mexican enigma she was facing. Frida and Constance could be creatures from two different planets and yet they both inspired something similar inside Elise. Nearly two years they'd been together, and Elise felt she'd come to the point of loving Connie so much that she wouldn't last long in this world if Connie died first. Her body would give in, knowing Con's had been handed to the gods.

Elise had never experienced this before: the mind with the flesh. Her father still didn't know she was in love with a woman; he would never know. She'd left his house when she was sixteen, her mum dead long before that. Now Elise had entered the most beautiful chapter of her life – perhaps the only beautiful chapter she'd ever had.

*

Connie had invited Elise to come and live with her some six months after that first hungover morning in Hampstead, and Elise had sat on the floor of John's flat with nothing more than two duffel bags, her heart jumpy as she'd waited for the sound of the tiny red Citroën. *This is the right thing*, she'd told herself, going down the stairs, the bags bumping her hips like the buckets of a milkmaid. She'd left a month's rent in an envelope on the kitchen table, which Connie had paid. *It feels like the right thing.*

That drive from Brixton to Hampstead had taken a long time. Elise admired the deftness with which Connie switched gears and never hesitated to zoom through an amber light. 'This city's wonderful,' she said to Connie. 'Can you imagine what the Blitz was like? The Great Fire?'

'I'd rather have the wanker bankers,' said Connie laughing, lifting her hand off the steering wheel to put it on top of Elise's. She had dry, strong fingers. And she was such a confident driver! They sat at the traffic lights, touching hands, and Elise kept looking out until the lights turned green and Connie left her hand alone, shooting them up the Euston Road, past St Pancras, past the women standing in the street on York Way, then further north, to Hampstead.

*

After the Kahlo exhibition, Elise and Connie stood next to each other outside, watching the traffic go up and down the street. They walked towards Whitechapel Station in silence, not holding hands. 'She really ran the gamut,' Connie said eventually, as if talking of a friend. It was April, and breezy, and Connie's pale red curls were blowing all over the place.

'Gamut?' Elise repeated. She had no idea what a gamut was. It sounded vaguely Yiddish. She was still reeling from the intimacy of the paintings. She wanted to be like Kahlo, to know every smashed moment of herself and accept it anyway. She looked at Connie and wanted to touch her, but you never knew who was looking. Soon, everything they had together was going to change. Soon, *Wax Heart* was going to be turned into a Hollywood movie called *Heartlands*. They were going to Los Angeles to see it happen. Suddenly, Elise wanted to kneel on the East End pavement and hold it close against her palms. This was her city, wasn't it?

'Well, you know,' said Connie. 'The childhood illness. Then the accident – the operations. How much she wanted children. The miscarriages. That *marriage*.'

Elise shrugged. 'I don't know,' she said.

'Only forty-seven when she died,' said Connie. 'What a waste to die so young!'

'Not always,' Elise said. 'And forty-seven isn't *young*.'

Looking disconcerted, Connie carried on. 'It's hard to put my finger on why I feel so sorry for her.'

'I don't feel sorry for Frida Kahlo,' said Elise. 'I don't think Frida Kahlo wants your pity. She was angry, looking at some of those paintings. She was quite determined to show you what she wanted to show you.'

Connie laughed. Elise hated it when she did this, like a glass of water dousing a burning candle. She couldn't help it if she felt strongly about these things. Art wasn't truth, it was a lie told to tell the truth. That's what the drawing master said at the RCA where she modelled. And truth held different qualities to a fact. It was a question of angle, where you were standing and what view you needed to see. Art was being always on the hunt for something to which you could cling.

'Frida Kahlo,' Elise went on, fishing for her Tube ticket in her purse, thinking of herself as the drawing master – 'she worked on everyone she knew, by the looks of it. She did it to herself. But she used everyone else, too. She put everyone in the soup.'

*

The Tube pulled alongside the platform at Whitechapel and they got on, sitting side by side on the District Line to Monument. Connie looked tired. She rested the side of her head against the carriage window. Elise rolled and unrolled the exhibition programme as the carriage swayed them, the lights of the tunnels flashing past. Since meeting Connie, she had felt her heart maturing at speed like a peach in a heated laboratory. It had swelled out, gathered heft, pushing away from the stone that had lived inside her always. Even as Elise got to the door of Connie's Citroën on the day she moved in, she felt older than she had five minutes previously, and did not realize this could only be a symptom of being so young.

Connie had said: *I want you to flourish.* Why did Connie want this for her? Elise wondered, as they hurtled their way back into the city on the Tube. What did Connie ever want from her? *I just want to love you*, she would say. *It is the greatest privilege to love you. Now, why don't you write that play?*

Elise no longer ached daily for Connie, as she crossed the city to her various jobs. Her face was still as a pond, her cunt a warm coal. But the love she felt was still growing, pressing her down; it was pushing roots into the ground. She knew she hadn't done much since being with Connie. She was twenty-two years old now and everything was still inside her. Dippy moorhen, that's what Connie had made her. Ripples in the water; small-headed bird, desire reducing her to black and white. She felt so powerless, and so happy.

6

Elise stood on the threshold of Connie's study, silently watching. She never went in. Connie was so deep in concentration that she did not notice, her head bent slightly over the desk, her arm moving across the notepaper. Ripley lifted his head from the carpet and laid it back down. He rolled over and stared. Connie was a witch with her familiar, writing up her spells, Elise thought. When she was near Connie, she felt just like Ripley, luxuriating in the warmth and safety of Connie's presence. She wanted to be the one curled up on the carpet at Connie's feet. Connie had been working longer and longer days, looking occasionally pained at the end of them, distracted at breakfast, lunch and dinner, but also emanating a kind of elation which Elise found exciting to be near.

'Con?'

'Hmm?'

'Would you like a cup of tea?'

'No thanks.'

'Biscuit?'

'No.'

Elise continued to hover. Connie's cleaner, Mary O'Reilly, was downstairs. Elise didn't like it when Mary was there. The first time she'd met Mary, early on in their relationship, Connie was working upstairs and Elise was reading the paper in the kitchen. Elise had heard the door unlock, and tensed as whoever it was came in – own key! Then footsteps, a woman's back, woolly hat, placing her rucksack easily on a kitchen chair, walking to the cleaning products under the sink. Only then did Mary turn and see Elise sitting at the table. Mary, in her fifties, slender, a bored and solemn mandarin who understood her cabinet minister's secrets. 'Hello,' Mary had said, clutching her hat by the tips of her fingers. 'So. You're the one who's stopping by.'

'I am,' said Elise. 'I'm stopping by.'

*

'What are you writing?' Elise said. Connie's back stiffened. She stopped writing, but didn't turn round.

'Something.'

'*Something?*' said Elise.

Connie placed her pen down, but still did not turn round. 'El.'

'I'm sorry.'

Connie was writing; that was all anybody would ever know. Elise knew she should not ask these questions, that they were juvenile and invasive, but she felt annoyed that day. Los Angeles was less than two weeks away – she'd handed in her notice at the cafe, she'd done her last shift at the National. She told the art school she was going to America for a while, so she wouldn't be able to pose for life class. She made it sound like she had plans over there, and then she'd sat for the last time in the draughty workshop, listening to the pencil scratches. Elise was closing down everything she'd made here and thought she might like to keep, except for Connie – because they were going to Los Angeles, because there was no way they were going to be apart. And now Connie would not turn round.

'I've told you everything *I* do,' Elise said, leaning against the door frame, trying to be casual. 'Everything you ask me, I tell you.'

Connie swung round on her office chair. She looked exasperated. 'I'm writing about a green rabbit,' she said.

'A what?'

'A green rabbit.'

'OK.'

Connie's jaw tightened. 'Please. Don't do that.'

'Don't do what?'

Connie rubbed her forehead. 'I'm sorry. I just – let me show you it when it's finished.'

'OK.' But Elise still hesitated. 'What d'you think it'll be like?'

'The book?'

So she was writing a book. 'No. Los Angeles.'

'Oh. A Hockney swimming pool,' said Connie. 'Sunshine. Make-believe.'

'And will Sorcha really look after Ripley?'

Sorcha was a friend of Connie's from her days as a student at Manchester. Now she was a professor in modern history. But like many of Connie's friends, Elise had never met her.

'Of course she will.' Connie scrutinized her. 'Is something wrong, El? You want to keep on at Seedling? You don't want to go? What is it?'

'No. Nothing. Don't worry.'

Elise went up to their bedroom and lay back and thought about LA. She knew little about it. It seemed a place of dreams, a place where the inheritances of fame were grotesque. Film stars through the century, killing themselves with drugs and alcohol, falling prey to the humiliation of obsolescence or the hubris of too much exposure. It seemed a place where the race was for dollars, where an actress was valued not for her talent but for her receipts. *A bad film topples you*, Connie had said. *I hope to god we don't make a bad film.*

*

Despite Mary banging cupboards downstairs, Elise loved Connie's house for its peace, a peace which she had never known before and was proud she'd managed to find for herself. Connie had lured her in, and Elise longed not to escape, but to stay. This was the first place that had felt like it could be home. She had been free to project her daydreams onto Connie's over-loaded bookshelves and mismatched furniture, like a stage-set in an amateur theatre after the actors had left.

That night as they were lying in bed, Elise told Connie she was like an almond. It felt as if they'd had an argument earlier, and something needed to be righted. Some silliness needed to be introduced. 'If you were a nut, that's the nut you'd be,' Elise said.

Connie was on her side with her back to Elise, and Elise put her hand on her lover's neat-shaped skull, inhaling Connie's hair, as sweet as marzipan. 'I could grind you up and put you in a cake,' Elise said. Connie laughed, and Elise watched the flex-ing of her pointed shoulder blades, feeling desire rise up inside her.

'I don't feel like an almond,' said Connie. 'Aren't I more of a cashew?' She rolled to face Elise and tucked her into the arch of her armpit. 'What nut are you?'

Elise loved the fact that Connie did not reject these bedtime meanders, as they carried each other in the ebb and flow of words and ideas, as they talked a world into being together, a riverbed of time that was theirs alone. 'I'm a Brazil,' she said.

'You creamy Brazil.' Connie made a hungry rumble noise. 'My favourite.'

This is what Connie did. She turned them from being nuts into a reflection of their love, a magician of metaphysics who left Elise enraptured. She placed her hand on Connie's cheek, moving it down to that collarbone, those pale shoulders flecked with freckles. Connie drew your eye; but once your eye was drawn, you didn't know what to do next. You didn't necessarily want to go much nearer, for fear of not being permitted. Connie never seemed aware of how strong she was. She didn't register how dismissive her voice could be. But now, she was silent, waiting. She would not move until Elise did something more.

Elise kissed her on the mouth, gently, hearing Connie's exquisite sigh of pleasure as she did, feeling Connie's hands reach for her and draw her to her own body, the most natural thing in the world.

*

Elise woke early. Connie was a beautiful sleeper, so still and quiet, like a woodland creature come in from the trees to shelter next to Elise's human heart, unaware that any minute Elise might skin and eat her alive. Connie was a miracle, but Los Angeles was coming, and Elise feared it. She buried this fear, a corrosive thing that had led to many problems before. It was rust in her soul and it was always there.

'I love you,' she whispered, and the words hovered on the air, waiting to be taken up.

Connie woke, her face a page of surprise. Her limbs underneath the bedsheets sounded like the rustle of leaves. 'El,' she said, smiling, burying her face in Elise's neck. 'El. I love you too.'

2017

7

I started *Wax Heart* on the ferry back to Portsmouth, barely exchanging a word with Joe. I hadn't told him what Dad had told me. I was angry with him for discussing our imaginary babies with Dad. I suppose I felt that stuff – the inner workings of our relationship, of my body – shouldn't be discussed over a casual coffee in a French bistro. Joe seemed to read my mood and knew to leave me be, mooching around the deck, before plonking himself down on a seat and scrolling the Instagram accounts of food bloggers and chefs.

Wax Heart had been published in 1979, followed by *Green Rabbit* in 1983. *Wax Heart* was slim and elegiac, with hints of a seventies setting yet strangely timeless. It was about a woman called Beatrice Jones, whose husband conducts a long series of affairs, after the discovery of which she ends up alone yet victorious. *Green Rabbit* was an angry, more rooted and sensual book – but still a variation on the first. It told the tale of a woman in love, although in the case of *Green Rabbit*, one who does not wish to be alone. I tried to imagine my father reading these books, and found the vision of it disorientating. But if I was going to hunt for secrets about Elise and Constance, then I had to accept that he had his secrets, too. Finally, he'd given me what I'd always wanted – a window on his life with my mother, albeit one that was still half-closed, a room with a compromised view – and I didn't know if I liked it.

Nevertheless, I persisted. Now that Dad had – reluctantly, painfully – given me Constance Holden, I was hardly going to hand her back. I particularly loved *Green Rabbit*, the lives lived and lost inside it, and those allowed to bloom beyond the final paragraph without definitive answers. Back in London I stood on the bus to the coffee shop, swaying side to side reading it. I sat on the loo with it. I waited for the kettle to boil with it, turning for two days into a one-handed woman, whose head and heart had integrated with the heads and hearts of Connie's characters. Of course I sought my mother in these pages, but how was I to know her if I saw her? She was invisible, but crowding me at the back of my mind nevertheless, like a clutch of funfair balloons, buffeting me out of space and time, their strings about to lift me off my feet.

Constance Holden didn't seem to exist in that group of writers whose names you know, even if you haven't read their books. She wasn't a Spark or an Angelou or a Lessing or an Atwood. She'd faded – like so many women's writing lives, eclipsed by other names. And yet Connie's style was inimitable – though people, I realize, have subsequently tried. *Green Rabbit* is a book about the solitariness of life, the devastation of love gone wrong. It's a book about the ever-enduring need to be with others, and the ever-present desire to push them all away. But how much, standing on that bus, did I want it to come out well for Rabbit, a green woman, a woman of hope and jealousy and new beginnings.

How much did I want for a book to come into my heart and change my life? As I read Connie's words, it was a terrifying delight to me that according to my father, this woman had known my mother so intimately, and might know exactly what had happened to her. It was painful to me to be aware of this connection, yet not to know what to do with it, except read her fiction. I didn't want the fiction: I wanted somebody to tell me the truth.

★

I asked Zoë, Clean Bean's resident English undergraduate and bookworm, whether she'd heard of Constance Holden. Zoë's eyes widened as she pulled down the steam nozzle into a customer's cappuccino. 'Oh, man,' she said. '*Green Rabbit*'s one of my *favourite* books.'

'I've just read it,' I said.

'I'm just sad she only wrote two,' said Zoë.

'Do you know why she didn't write more?'

Zoë, who was twenty, with her septum pierced and her fine blonde hair dyed blue, took everything very seriously, from novelists to Netflix, and I adored her for it. 'There are some theories,' she said. 'She wrote this really famous essay a year after *Green Rabbit* came out, and it's literally included in every feminist theory class I've ever taken.'

'Did she say in it that she wasn't going to write again?'

'Not exactly. But it was the last thing she ever published. It's called *The Locust Plague*. I can bring you in my copy if you like?'

'That would be really cool. Thanks, Zoë.'

'No worries.'

'Do you know if she's still alive?'

Zoë frowned. 'I'm pretty sure there'd have been an obituary in the papers for her. I don't think she's dead. She was a big deal. She still is, in a culty, weird recluse way.'

'Weird recluse way?'

'Well, why would she stop writing like that at the height of her success? She needed to write *more*. We needed her! But she stopped. It's such a shame.'

Zoë shuddered; she felt things deeply. I felt ashamed, because I, being fourteen years older, had forgotten how.

*

Back at our flat, sitting at the kitchen table, I looked Constance up on the Internet. Zoë was right: whether it was the case that Constance Holden wanted to be forgotten, or whether other people chose to forget her – or whether it was nothing so deliberate at all – she wrote those two books, then *The Locust Plague*, then nothing more. The only photos I could find were grainy headshots from the eighties: black and white, pumped-up messy hair, baggy blouse, prim but lipsticked mouth. She looked young, and I began to think of her like that – though by now she'd be into her seventies. The biography on the back of Dad's books was wildly out of date, but there was no new information online to supplant it. Where was she now?

'Who's *that*?' said Joe, looking over my shoulder at the laptop screen.

'Constance Holden,' I said.

'*Who?*'

'A writer. I've just read her books.'

'She's a fox,' he said.

'These are old photos,' I said. 'But she might be an old fox.' I swivelled round to face him. 'Joey,' I said. 'Dad told me something when we were in France. This woman knew my mother.'

Immediately, Joe looked wary. Any mention of my mother made him look like that; he couldn't help it. He'd witnessed too many tears, had waded through too many of my black fogs. 'Right,' he said.

'And I'm going to find her.'

'Rosie—'

'I am.'

'Are you sure that's a good idea?'

'Of course I'm not. But I have to try. It's the first time—'

'No, I understand. OK.'

'What?'

'Well, just don't get your hopes up, OK?'

'I won't.'

We both knew that wasn't true.

'We've got to leave for my parents' now,' he said. 'Are you ready?'

I sighed and closed the laptop, unwilling to be drawn back to reality. 'How did last night go?' I asked. Joe had taken an investor 'angel' for drinks to see if he'd be interested in funding our new business idea for the burrito van.

'Good!' he said brightly.

'And?'

'These things take time,' I heard as he walked away.

Inside I was screaming. My mouth, whilst seemingly closed, was fully ajar, a preternatural hurricane bawling out of it. For two years, I'd done the heavy lifting in our team of two. I closed my eyes, crushed by his lack of enthusiasm over the discovery of Constance Holden and her potential connection to my mother. These things took time and they never gave it back.

Two years ago Joe had wanted to turn his love for Mexican food, new music and travel into something solid, and an internationally roaming festival burrito van was to be the intersection where these three loves met. I had agreed it was a great idea – it *was* a great idea, it was romantic! – and as we submerged into our thirties it felt important to cling to any visible signifiers of romance and adventure. It made Joe happy, and initially he was enthusiastic about getting vendor licences, reaching out to festival organizers.

It was not a great idea, however, to quit his job as a broker in the City at the same time, and to use his inheritance from his dead grandfather to buy a van, and live off the remainder. He needed to convert the interior into a state-of-the-art kitchen, but that, too, 'would take time'. Joe was stubborn and he did not realize – or would not acknowledge – how brutal and competitive the festival food van business actually was. You had to want it, but Joe only loved it. He was completely unequipped, or unwilling, to push himself.

Joe's parents had bought him the flat we shared, and I lived there rent-free. This fact always held my tongue (unless alcohol had been involved) on the lack of progress with Joerritos – I had no stake in his property, so for some reason I had no stake in his behaviour with his business and how it affected our relationship. It was far from ideal. The flat protected Joe like some sort of fairy circle, and in my opinion had left him without much of an appreciation for what hard work really was, and what it felt like not to have a safety net.

We'd been together nine years. We did have good times, of course we did. Lots of them. Otherwise why else would we have been together? I did love him. I just sometimes wondered if other couples dragged themselves across the seabed like this, and why they did it. Because they all believed in love? Because there was nothing else to do? When we argued, I would know a heaviness to my arms, my stomach, my shoulders, that was not an afternoon slump. Fights with Joe weighted down my body. But more recently, I felt no longer furious at him: it was too exhausting. It was a sulk; it was nothing. Instead, perhaps a new sense of resignation was coming; this subaquatic feeling being mine to keep. Every day I felt I had to carry it. To break up with him was inconceivable. We'd seen each other through half our twenties, and that is no mean feat. Kelly had had many boyfriends, many lovers; so did several of the girls from school. Not me: I'd found my rock and I had clung.

Joe wasn't an archetypal wastrel; he didn't spend lots of money he didn't have, but what he did have went on 'investing' in the business. And love was less appealing when I was the only one remembering to keep us in loo roll, the provider of intermittent dinners out, the means of a holiday for two weeks in the summer, and the only one who ever thought to buy a nice candle or a cushion as some pathetic marker of adulthood in our shared existence. My own grandparents had left me a bit in their wills, and I'd put half of it into Joerritos, without telling my dad. It was unlikely *he* would ever be able to hand me down a property.

My anger was sharpening, becoming more easily accessible to me. No one else could tell. I was good at keeping it to myself. But any time I saw a chef on the TV sampling the delights of Mexican cuisine (where there was never even a mention of a burrito), or talking about Mayan civilization or walking round Aztec ruins, I would have to switch over. I had begun to loathe burritos. I had felt the failure of the business to launch every morning when I left for a shift at Clean Bean and when I came back. The van continued to rust on the drive of Joe's parents' house, where his mother Dorothy had agreed to house it, providing it was under a canvas cover so that no one could see its hideous burnt-orange colour. She also paid the road tax and insurance. I don't think Joe's father knew this.

The year turned into two, and now Joe's inheritance from his grandfather was almost gone, and we were in the same state: testing burrito recipes and saying that we would try this county fair or that village fete. It was an astonishing blind spot, and we only argued about it when we were very drunk, because for me to insult the existence of the van was as if I were attacking Joe's very being, and everything he hoped for – as if I were stamping on his dreams and laughing at his attempts to achieve. He was manipulatively sensitive about the whole thing, and I knew that one false move might turn back the burrito clock even more than it had been turned already.

*

I was not apprehensive about our forthcoming lunch at Joe's parents', because although I never enjoyed myself particularly, it was all familiar. Joe had a sister, Daisy, who was three years younger than us, but married with two children, who diverted the bulk of attention and enabled me to avoid too much scrutiny. It had long been a source of tension for Daisy that she'd got everything right: school grades, gap year before university, graduate-training scheme, charity bungee jumps, a marathon, a solvent spouse, two kids, lost the baby weight – and Joe, who had done literally none of those things, was imperceptibly but nevertheless undoubtedly their parents' favourite. I'd met Daisy's friends at her wedding to her husband, Radek, and they were as competitive as she was. Compared to them, Daisy fancied herself as a little outré, because she smoked a bit of weed and had a small tattoo of a peace sign on her inner arm. She was not outré, and the peace sign looked like a Mercedes Benz badge. She'd been in the City like her father, before having her children. Radek was still there, working every hour God sent. I figured I might be out all the time too, if I was Daisy's spouse.

At these Sunday lunches, we often talked about six-year-old Lucia's schooling or baby Wilf's 'fevers'. Joe's mum was a GP. His dad, Ben, was due within the year to retire from some sort of CEO-ship of something financial I'd never quite understood. Ben was easier to deal with, a lifetime of networking and delivering his own voice across boardrooms made him predictable, manipulable company. Dorothy was more difficult. I always had the impression that she felt Joe had not reached his 'potential', and that somehow it was me who had failed to make it happen for him. It was possible that she thought it was entirely my fault. More recently it was making me feel rebellious and irritated. *She's his mother: she was there first!* I thought.

*

Approaching Dorothy and Ben's house, there was the burrito van, hidden under its tarpaulin. I pulled the roses I had purchased from the Shell garage out of my handbag, and peeled off the label. We passed the van, saying nothing, and made straight for the front door, lifting the brass knocker.

Lucia opened it. She was wearing her riding helmet. 'You're the right height for a jockey,' I said to her, stepping inside.

'I know!' she cried, galloping down the hallway on her invisible horse, into the large extension that contained the kitchen. 'They're here!' she shouted.

'Hullo!' called Ben, from the front room.

'Hi, Ben!' I said brightly. He appeared at the doorway and we kissed each other on the cheek.

'Can I get you two a drink?' he asked, patting his son on the shoulder.

'A glass of red would be lovely,' I said.

'Yeah, me too,' said Joe, slouching off to the kitchen like he was fourteen.

'Coming up,' said Ben, making his way to the cellar stairs. They had a wine cellar, but they wouldn't have called it that. They would have just said they had a couple of wine racks down there.

I followed Joe, passing the pretentious grandfather clock and the studio portrait of Daisy as a young teenager. There were endless school pictures, and the deliberate-casual engineered photo collages of the family on holiday through the nineties, everyone cut out in their stripy swimsuits, Dorothy with an ill-advised perm. I could feel a cloak of claustrophobia envelop me and paused a moment to breathe.

'Ah!' said Dorothy. 'The wanderers return!'

I smiled at her and gave her a kiss. 'These are for you,' I said, handing her the roses.

'Oh, thank you darling,' she said. 'Oh, they're from Morocco! I wondered how a rose would grow this time of year. Luce, do you want to put them in a vase for me?'

'I'm riding,' said Lucia.

'It won't take a minute,' said Dorothy.

'I'll do it,' I said. I took the roses back, feeling their North African identity had courted Dotty's disapproval: carbon footprint or racism? It was hard to tell.

'How are you?' she said.

'Good, thanks,' I replied, feeling a malaise melding with the claustrophobia and settling rapidly into the centre of my stomach. Daisy appeared at the kitchen door. 'Hello!' I said.

She too kissed me on the cheek. 'Hi, Rose.'

'Where's Rad?'

Daisy rolled her eyes. 'Stag do. You'd think they'd all be married by now.'

'Yeah.'

'Actually, this is a second marriage. They're far more suited.'

Dorothy sighed. 'Will you tell your father to come and cut this beef? What on earth is he doing in there?'

'I think he's getting wine,' I said.

'No, he's trying to set the Sky player to record,' said Lucia.

'Again? Go and do it for him, Luce. I don't want everything to get cold. You two made it just in time,' Dorothy added, but she only looked at me.

*

At lunch, we talked mainly about the impending wedding of a couple none of us knew except Daisy. I watched her mouth moving, and thought how utterly exhausted she looked. I tried to tune out, thinking of Constance Holden and how she might have fallen for my mother, but Daisy had a persistent voice, and as she went on and on, I began to yearn for a change of subject. A new update on Wilf's phlegmy lung, or Lucia's curriculum, and the latest way Daisy's daughter had excelled beyond her classmates – ('although it's a far better idea to *keep* her with them, because it's really important that she knows how to deal with people her age?'). I had a vision, suddenly, of what Lucia might be like in fifteen years' time. I saw her, friendless, cluelessly brainy. It was bleak. I stared round the blandly decorated dining room, at the aspirational portraits of Dorothy's distant Victorian relatives. The grandfather clock chimed in the hall.

'And talking of weddings, what about you two?' Daisy said as I cleared away the plates.

Joe stiffened and I smiled blankly. 'You've been in that flat so long!' said Daisy gaily. I wasn't fooled. 'When are you going to make an honest woman out of her, Joe?'

'Oh, god,' said Joe.

'It's just a *question*.'

'It's a shit question!' Joe said. 'What if I'm happy with the way things are?'

Daisy snorted. 'Mummy's a pig!' said Lucia, and I couldn't help laughing.

'Don't you two believe in marriage, then?' said Daisy. 'It's fine if you don't!'

'Oh my god. *Thank* you, Daisy. I was *so* worried for a moment there about your thoughts on the matter,' said Joe. Yet, regardless of Daisy's invasive tactlessness, I was disturbed by how furious he was. 'Mum,' he said. 'Tell her to shut up. She always does this. It's ridiculous.'

'But don't you want the *security*, Rose?' said Daisy.

I looked at her. What, if anything, did she really know about her brother's life? Could she not see that aside from the flat with its four walls and roof, Joe brought me no security whatsoever?

That these days, his emotional offerings were hazy, sketchy things, underlined by his own preoccupations? Perhaps not. Perhaps it was well hidden to those who did not care to look. I laughed, not knowing what else to say or do.

'Rose, why are you always laughing at me?' said Daisy.

'I'm not,' I said. 'I promise.'

Daisy looked at me with dislike. Dorothy intervened. 'Daisy, for Christ's sake, put that wine down. You're tired. She's so *tired*,' she said to me directly, as if I had provoked this garbled projection of insecurity and bile from her adult child. 'Young children are exhausting.'

'She wouldn't know,' said Daisy.

'*Daisy*,' said Dorothy sharply. 'Go and sit in the front room.'

'For *fuck's* sake,' said Joe.

Ben remained silent. Daisy got up and walked out of the dining room with the air of a hurt duchess. I knew from my friends that young children were exhausting, but none of them acted like this when they were tired. I wondered if Daisy was depressed.

'They're having problems,' Dorothy said quietly.

'Dot,' said her husband, finally speaking up with a warning in his voice, his eyes in the direction of Lucia.

'Oh well,' said Dorothy, sighing. 'Everyone has their ups and downs.'

There was something of the prairie matriarch in her voice, and it irritated me. Daisy should not have been let off the hook for what she said to me, but she was – she always was.

'Dad, shall we go and look at the van?' said Joe.

Dorothy, Wilf, Lucia and I were left behind, sitting in the aftermath of another Sunday lunch. 'Luce, poppet, go to the playroom and find a puzzle for us to do,' said Dorothy.

'I hate puzzles, Granny.'

'Don't we all, darling. But go and do as Granny asks.'

Robotically, Lucia laid down her pencil and slunk out of her chair like she was pouring herself onto the floor.

Dorothy sighed again. 'How's your father, Rose?' She always said it like that – never, 'How's Matt?'

'He's well, thank you. He's in Brittany.'

Dorothy ran her finger round and round an embroidered peony on the tablecloth. 'I expect he misses you.'

'He's got Claire.'

'Will you go there for Christmas?'

I felt alarm. Dorothy liked to plan Christmas early. Did she *want* me to go to France for Christmas? Was this some sort of attempt to get me away from her son? 'No, I don't think so,' I said. 'I'll stay with Joe. Wherever Joe is.'

Dorothy looked up at me. Her expression! It was so strange. I felt bereft as I looked into it, as if a halo of defeat was framing her head. It seemed to be slipping over her eyes and drawing them shut. 'Christmas,' she whispered.

My eyes flicked to her wine glass. Was she drunk? *Christmas* – the way she said the word, I saw that season roll round again, as we headed towards the last quarter of the year. All the same dynamics that Dorothy had witnessed for over thirty years would play out once again – the same arguments, the same carols, the same turkey. I felt it in her voice. I wanted to reach out and take her hand, and tell her she didn't have to do it all – let Joe cook, let Daisy sort it! – but I didn't. She didn't invite that kind of intimacy. Even after all these years I was a guest; I never felt like family.

'Are you all right, Dorothy?' I said. 'Can I get you a glass of water?'

'No, no, thank you.' Dorothy looked up at me, and I saw her mentally rearrange herself. 'Oh, Rose,' she said. 'I do hope they haven't found any more rust on the van.'

8

Zoë came good on *The Locust Plague*, and I devoured it. *All women deserve the privilege of failure, but very few get it*, Constance wrote. *It is a privilege to get something catastrophically wrong, and be given another chance as if nothing really happened. Men do it all the time, and afterwards, are castigated as individuals. Politicians spring to mind. Businessmen. Killers. The white devils who ruin our world. Women are devils too, of course. But when a woman screws it up, it's usually on behalf of all women, as if we move inside one breast. And yet we should be allowed to screw it up! Self-consciousness in a woman's life is a plague of locusts!*

I liked the boldness with the exclamation marks. I loved the entire thing. But Constance was being universally political here. I wanted the personal. *Women are devils too, of course.* I wanted to know what mistakes of *hers* she was talking about – what had she done in her own life that was so catastrophically wrong, and how might it be connected to my mother? I thought about what my dad had told me, about Elise being in her thrall.

I had also been doing some deeper digging on the Internet. Constance Holden was ex-directory: her address had been removed from the public domain, so I couldn't just turn up at her house. Her books had a presence on the web, however. According to one essay, *Green Rabbit* showed 'a woman in the prime of her writing self: fluid, alarming, switching effortlessly between raw pain and aching diffidence'. It had won several prizes in its year of publication, and since then had sold well over a million copies. In both books, Holden seemed preoccupied with mothers and daughters, love, the nature and conditions of emotional punishments, and missed opportunity. *Wax Heart* had been turned into a perennially popular film called *Heartlands*. It had won an Oscar for its lead actress – the legendary Barbara Lowden. Neither book was ever out of print, but Constance hadn't written another novel since *Green Rabbit*. Some of the press-cuttings posited not that she had suffered writer's block, but that she had simply opted for a percentage of the box-office takings for *Heartlands* and decided to retire. This didn't seem likely to me, but then again: there were no other novels.

I discovered that there had been an attempt, in 1997, to interview Constance. A journalist for the *Observer* had tried to do the same as me – to understand why someone would want to vanish at the peak of her powers. Her agent, a woman called Deborah Clarke, had refused to cooperate – at Holden's request, apparently. The journalist described how Holden had always been 'cagey' about her upbringing, often questioning the point of peeling back her layers when the books existed as sufficient codes for a life lived. According to the journalist's profile, in a previous interview given when *Wax Heart* was published, but not available online, Constance had mentioned a father who had been in the army, a peripatetic life moving to wherever he was stationed, not staying there long enough to plant roots in the soil. 'But roots are conservative, anyway,' the journalist quoted her from the earlier piece: 'The concept of them is to put us, and keep us, in our places.' As far as the journalist could tell, Connie was unmarried, and there was never a mention of a partner or children. All the journalist could find out was that for a period of time, Holden went to live in America, then perhaps Greece, then a mooted cottage somewhere in the south-England countryside. He couldn't find friends, he couldn't find family. The local shopkeeper in the village where Connie was allegedly living was 'blunt' and 'protective', which convinced the journalist she was somewhere near. And then the trail went cold. No one would help him. The journalist made a virtue out of this and turned his piece into one of those literary mysteries. But he offered no solutions.

That was twenty years ago, and no one had bothered since.

*

I was re-reading the opening of *The Locust Plague* at Clean Bean, waiting for Kelly to turn up, when Kelly bundled herself and her daughter, Molly, through the door. My heart lifted at the sight of them, so familiar, so warm.

Kelly had not been the most bookish at our school, but she was by far the most adaptable and smart. We were an odd couple, because I was very academic and much shyer, but we loved each other. She derived joy from my weirdness, and I from her capabilities. When the rest of us were having doom-laden panics about getting into the right university, Kel suspected that in ten years' time those letters wouldn't matter quite as much as what might follow after. *But!* as some of our other friends had pointed out when Kelly wasn't there, *it's all right for Kel. She's got CHARM.*

In fact, charming as she was, Kelly had worked very hard to keep her head above the water, no help from family, no connections. She climbed up and up, before landing on the paradise island that had been her working mid-twenties: job as a junior stylist, then art director on an influential magazine. Then she became an Instagram marvel – @thestellakella: taste queen, collaboration maven, with thousands of follow-ers. Clothing shops and furniture stores started to look like the inside of @thestellakella's house – it was hard to tell exactly how the line had blurred, but it had. Unlike so many chancers on the Internet, at least Kel had the weight of experience and proof behind her. And then came Dan, now her husband, one of those Instagrammable people who seemed self-motivated since he was five years old – although Kelly would always say that when she'd met him, *Man couldn't even cook a potato.* And then came Molly. *I'm never having another kid,* Kelly said, when Mol was born. *Ever again.*

Now Mol was four, and Kelly was due another baby next March.

Mol settled herself into a chair, got out her pens and pad, and proceeded to descend into her own world. She was drawing a box of a house and filling it with merciless, ravishing streaks of fuchsia. She did not keep to the borders of the house, and the colour spilled out of its walls, every which way. We could easily have not been there, two adult women she was so certain of that we could have turned to pillars of salt without her noticing.

'Been crotchety earlier,' Kelly mouthed, taking a seat.

'Would you like anything, Mol?' I said. I'd already ordered two flat whites from Zoë, remembering that Kelly was on decaff.

'No, thank you, Rose,' Mol replied.

I looked at Mol, her bowed head. I liked being with Mol – walking through parks in particular. Mol, always running ahead, squatting easily to pick up twigs splodged with lichen, or an especially splendid leaf. Her centre of gravity was so low, she was up and down like a pop-up toy. Already, she had Kelly's eye; my friend had encouraged in her growing mind the power of observation, the wonder and pleasure to be found in looking for the interesting in the everyday, hauling them out of context, turning them into magic wands, fairy blankets, good fodder for a collage when they got back home. I knew these collages, because I followed them all on Instagram when I didn't make it to the park. I'd seen leaves splattered in gold paint that got over 25,000 likes.

Zoë came over with the flat whites and beamed at Kelly and her daughter. People often did that with the pair of them – they looked so wholesome, just how a mother and child should be. I went to pick up my coffee. 'Hold on,' said Kel, and I knew what was coming. Mol's head was neatly positioned peeping between the two cups, and Kelly already had her phone out. 'Just carry on drawing, love,' said Kelly, but it was as if Mol hadn't even heard her: she was so used to the phone as to be oblivious. The photo taken, Kel swiped through three or four filters before finding the one that clearly captured the moment more than the moment itself. ' *"Brat whites,"* ' she said out loud as she typed these words in the photo caption, pressed *send* and slipped her phone back into her bag. I wondered idly if she had entered her location, and if she had, whether Clean Bean's takings would see an uptick.

Mol and Dan were regular, if passive, contributors to the addictive story Kelly wove online. Privately I still felt it was weird to monetize your child and partner, putting them in a place where strangers were looking at them every day, and all of it without Mol being able to give her permission – but Kelly was still my best friend, and doing a hell of a lot more with her life than Joe or I. And one thing was indisputable: Mol was superlative content. *It's a community*, Kel would say – *of support and interest! The girls who started following me a few years back are beginning to have kids too. It just works!* Mol was sweetly, deeply, entertaining, and Kelly didn't ever seem to be in the mood to discuss the philosophical, ethical angles of her decision. I guess

it was just her choice, and there was no doubt, with her endorse-
ment deals, her free hotel stays, the fact that I had seen several
women in one week wear a jumper that Kel had debuted from
a tiny line in Stockholm – @thestellakella was a pop culture
phenomenon.

'How's Joe?' Kelly said, drawing her cup towards her. 'How's
Joerritos?'

I sensed the weight in her words, but couldn't tell their temperature. I knew, in many ways, that Kelly was fed up with Joe,
but she still held it in.

'He's good,' I said. 'He's talking to an investor.'

Kelly stirred her coffee. 'An investor,' she repeated, leaching
the word of any magic.

I found it weird she was asking about Joe first, but I let it go.
'And how's it all going with you? You feeling OK?'

Kelly looked down at Mol. 'Yeah, it's not bad. The morning
sickness is wearing off, thank god.'

I shook my head in wonder. 'I don't know how you do it.'

She laughed. 'You could do it too, Rosie, if you had to.'

'Do you really think so?'

She looked at me with surprise. '*Course.* Look, if I can do it,
anyone can.' We both knew this wasn't true, but I let it go. 'Oh
yes, I wanted to tell you – I'm gonna ramp up @thestellakella
into a double maternity thing. See how that goes.' She waved
her hands decisively in the air. 'A journey of moving from being
a mother of one to a mother of two.'

Mesmerized, I watched my oldest friend. Kelly was so good
at this kind of thing: making stories simple for the greatest
number of people. Kelly was relatable yet confident; the reason
her preposterous plans worked was because she believed in
them, and because she understood that many people were lost
these days, and needed a guide. Me included.

'That sounds good,' I said. 'I wanted to ask you about something, actually,' I went on. 'About my mum.'

'Your mum?'

As with Joe, alarm entered Kelly's eyes, but I carried on. 'Do you remember, growing up, whether my dad ever said anything to you about her? Or ever mentioned anything, in your presence, about her?'

Kelly turned her head to look out of the cafe window. I could see she was thinking how best to answer. She'd spent many hours in our flat after school or at weekends, sleeping over, my dad driving us to the cinema or dropping us off at the shopping centre. Kelly knew my life as well as I did, if not better. 'Why are you asking now?' she said.

'When we were in France, my dad told me there was this woman my mum knew. I think they were lovers.'

'OK.' Kelly folded her arms on the table. 'This is interesting.'

'Listen. You were round the flat so much. Did my dad ever say anything about someone called Connie? Constance Holden? She wrote this book.' I tapped the cover of *The Locust Plague*.

Kelly looked at it with interest. 'I'm sorry, Rosie. No. It was so long ago.' She gazed at me tenderly. 'Are you OK?'

'Yes, I'm OK. I mean, I was a bit shocked.'

'Have you told Joe?'

'Yeah. Well, not everything. I told him Constance Holden was a writer that my mum knew.'

'And?'

I shrugged. 'It wasn't a big deal.'

She sighed.

'Anyway. He doesn't like it when I go on about my mum.'

'Well, I guess it's just 'cos none of us know what to say or do, Rosie.'

I looked down at the table. I was sitting with my father again, on that Brittany beach. I closed my eyes, thinking I might cry.

'Are you sure you're all right?' said Kelly.

'Oh, god. Yeah,' I said. I reached out and gave her hand a squeeze, feeling the tectonic plates of our love, shifting once again.

'Mummy, when are we going?' said Mol.

I looked away towards the counter, where Zoë was cleaning the coffee machine, her young face set in concentration, the fine spray of acne on her forehead that only seemed to enhance her lovely, youthful beauty. My life felt insubstantial, yet my body was weighted and I was wading deep.

*

After we said our goodbyes, I decided not to go straight home. I left the cafe and sat down on a bench in a nearby park, thinking about the conversation with my father. I thought not of his ominous commentary on Constance Holden, but more of the way he had urged me to think of a language or a skill, as if what I was right now was not enough. *I remember you were set for great things!* was a refrain I'd often heard. In fact, only one seismic thing had ever happened to me. I hadn't been enough for my mum to want to stay.

The fact of this had finally caught up with me. It had been gnawing and gnawing at me until I couldn't find the strength to fight the message that had wrapped itself around my heart for thirty-odd years. And now I didn't know who I was any more, or what on earth I was supposed to do with myself. I felt no kindness towards myself. I was ashamed at my stasis and ineptitude – because the truth is, everyone has their losses, their shames, their obsessive thoughts, and these people seem to manage it. Somehow they do it – they get on, they make a life for themselves. I hadn't managed it. I was in thrall to a ghost of a woman, and a boyfriend who seemed to live in his own fantasy, and I hadn't made anything for myself. I didn't have a Mol, or a gigantic Instagram following, or a book in my name, or a wife to live with by the sea.

Fuck it, I thought. *Fuck it*. I got out my phone and typed into the search bar: *Deborah Clarke, literary agent*.

Self-consciousness in a woman's life is a plague of locusts.

1982

9

Driving from the airport over the LA freeway in the taxi the film agency had sent, Elise, jet-lagged, longed to leave already. *But the lifestyle there!* people had said, so she remained by Connie's side in search of lifestyle. Back in London, Constance had also claimed to be unsure. But looking at her now, in her sunglasses, gazing at the sprawl of LA, turning to Elise every now and then with a grin, Elise wondered quite how unsure Connie really was. They'd had a call from her agent, Deborah, shortly before they left England. Barbara Lowden – *the* Barbara Lowden, two-times Oscar winner, grande dame not just of this town, but of every cinema screen in the Western world – had said yes to playing Beatrice Jones. Connie and Elise had simply stared at each other agog at the news, before erupting into hoots and whoops and getting incredibly drunk at the pub at four p.m.

Elise had read an article on LA in the hairdresser's, which had described the city as 'a place of strange dreams and drinks called *Brain On*, algae shots and reefer and blood-test diets, bungalow buildings hiding truths behind dark doors.' *Can I live there?* she had wondered. She kept thinking of the scene in the novel *The Godfather*, when Tom Hagen comes to LA to see the head of a movie studio, and witnesses a prepubescent girl tottering from the man's office like a broken fawn. She thought now of broken fawn legs, of Bette Davis, of Joan Crawford, how long eyelashes masked a starlet's poverty, and how despite all that, the glamour never faded.

Beyond, beach; yes, sunshine; yes, the sense of opportunity. But up close, Elise just wanted Connie. She wanted peace and calm, and small acts of living. Connie was strong at the moment: flying into LA with her famous novel embedded in both her physical body and her abstract self. Like an amulet, it would protect her in a place like LA, where once she would have felt so pointless. Elise did not have an amulet. She only had Connie.

*

Like all cities, parts of it they drove past looked abhorrent; there was the layer of smog, the air of enslavement, the endless streams of cars. *Healtheeeeeeee 4 U!* screamed a billboard. The taxi had its radio on: 'Buy! Buy! BUY!' it yelled. The advertisement seemed never to stop; the word threatened to overwhelm her. They drove past a huge metal ringed doughnut, erected outside a diner. The doughnut, ingeniously bulbous, easily the height of an average elephant, had rusted on its rotator. Paralysed but very present, it loomed past; Elise tried to take a photo, but the taxi had moved on, the doughnut diminished to a Polo mint. The taxi drove past another giant billboard, perched above the road. All you saw of it was a woman's face, huge and immaculate, with ravenous eyes, and the words, THE PRESIDENT'S WIFE.

'Oh my god!' squealed Connie. Elise winced. She didn't associate squealing with Connie. 'It's *her*. Can you believe it? It's Barbara Lowden!'

'Should we go and see her in it?' said Elise.

'We should,' said Connie. 'I can't believe it. She's – I mean, is there actually anyone more famous?'

'The Queen. The Pope?'

Connie grinned, readjusting her sunglasses. 'I bet more people want to sleep with Barbara Lowden.'

Barbara Lowden. Soon, they would meet her. How ridiculous it seemed.

Silvercrest, the studio making *Heartlands*, had rented a bungalow for Connie. The taxi reached West Hollywood and meandered round silent floral streets, finally stopping at a low-slung building in a Spanish-colonial style, still and quiet, surrounded by jungle-like foliage discreetly tamed, sentinels of cacti adeptly lining the borders, the windows dark and unyielding. It astonished Elise how far away the house in Hampstead felt, which in turn had felt so far away from the tiny flat in Brixton. All the places she had called home, but which never really belonged to her.

'Are you ready?' asked Connie.

'I'm ready,' she said, although she didn't know what she was ready for.

Connie rang the doorbell and somewhere deep in the bungalow, they heard a chime. Within a minute, a woman answered, dressed as a maid. Her name, improbably, was Maria. Maria was shy and young, and nothing like Mary O'Reilly back home.

*

Elise knew, really, that the city owed her nothing. The mountains were there, the beach, the light. She liked the light, this lavender sky at dusk. She and Constance sat opposite each other in the front room as Maria organized them tea. They were slightly stunned, in silence. They had done this; they were here.

Later, wide awake in the gigantic bed at the back of the house, Elise listened to the automatic watering of the grass. Connie slept deeply, but Elise was chilled by the recollection of Maria's face, her mask of politeness that failed to hide the fatigue behind her eyes.

10

'Everywhere in Hollywood the marriages are breaking up,' said Barbara Lowden. 'The men here are monsters.'

'Are they?' said Elise.

'We are,' said Matt.

'And the women,' said Barbara, laughing.

'That's just not *true*,' said Shara.

'My friends say that Los Angeles will eat your brain,' said Connie, tipping back her gin.

'I know a dealer who'll help you with that,' said Matt and everybody laughed.

Connie probably thought she was acting naturally in front of Barbara, but Elise thought she was just being weird. They were at a welcome dinner to celebrate the impending commencement of filming on *Heartlands*, in a restaurant called Gino's, a legendary Beverly Hills spot high up on North Crescent Drive – a two-storey, white-stuccoed villa, with ruby-pink froths of bougainvillea climbing up the walls into the night. Candles lit the path towards the entrance, a plain green door which swung open as they'd approached, as if by its own volition. Their table was secluded, near a small courtyard pool, an illuminated lozenge of turquoise upon which stray petals floated with no direction.

They were a party of seven. Connie, Elise; Connie's American friend from university, Shara, and her English husband, Matt;

then one of the movie's producers, Bill Gazzara; the director, Eric Williamson, and the pièce de résistance: Barbara Lowden.

Elise had said to Connie before they left the bungalow, that she couldn't believe that Barbara was actually going to turn up.

'I expect she likes to be seen,' Connie had replied.

And now that Barbara *had* actually turned up, was actually in front of them, Connie was feigning a coolness that didn't convince Elise. For Elise – with all those nights she'd spent in the theatre, the practical, dignified, hardworking theatre, which should have immunized her to glamour – Barbara was everything she could have hoped for. The woman was miraculous, but not over-cooked. Not carved up, not just a pair of cheekbones walking on air, nor just the fact of her eyes, infamously dark and huge. She was more than beautiful: she was *Barbara Lowden*.

Beatrice Jones, the character she was playing in *Heartlands*, was a mess of a matriarch. It was a part with wit and libido, fabulous set-pieces of cruelty, both inflicted and received, that would make all forty-something actresses weep with desire. These parts were all too few and far between.

Barbara Lowden was not forty-something. She must have been in her early fifties, given the longevity of her career, the sweet and grainy nostalgia of her early films, but her elastic beauty had grown only more permanent as the decades passed.

To Elise, watching as Barbara came towards the table in the restaurant, it was as if they were in the presence of an archangel. Here she was, sitting with humans! Barbara's head was small but leonine, and her forehead was high. Her teeth, when she smiled – and she smiled quickly at Elise – were large. And that extraordinary mouth! The smile pleaded honesty. Her accent still held hints of the South: warm and deep and rolling, wry and musical. The blue-collar twang it was rumoured she'd started with had long evaporated. When she sat down, the air seemed to ripple outwards from the space she'd taken up. Her aura posed an interesting question in Elise's mind as to whom this dinner was really for.

'So how are you finding LA?' Matt said as everyone took their seats. It was a moment before Elise realized he was talking to her.

She'd become familiar with Matt and Shara over the last three weeks. The two couples were spending a lot of time together, with Shara and Connie eager to catch up. Shara had two modes: acting high on the sight of her old friend, or exhausted by everything. She had said she would take them shopping on Melrose, if they wanted. She rarely went these days, but she knew the perfect places for a manicure, a massage, a kiwi-juice cleanse. Shara wasn't just American; Shara was *Californian*. She was a painter with family money, and had a huge airy studio overlooking the sea. She seemed a kind person, whose own history threaded six generations deep into this state, when the sun and the land and the water had glinted in the rush of gold, and wooden houses had nothing to do with drinks called *Brain On* and strip malls. Elise couldn't imagine that past was any easier, but she was glad to meet Shara and Matt, and to get to know Connie's friends, a fragment of her past. It made her feel more legitimate.

She thought about Matt's question. Truthfully, she found the place bizarre. How strange this place could be, a locus of work, not life, where even going to a pool party was about laying the ground for a job! There were the sinister undertones of insincerity from waitresses, more than average idiocies on billboards, and a plurality of everything, dizzying, deeply uncomfortable to her. *You either hate it or love it!* Shara had told Connie and Elise when they'd visited Matt and Shara's Malibu home; the inference being that if they hated it, they were square and uppity, European.

'It's a bit different,' she said to him.

Matt laughed. 'To London?'

'To everywhere.'

'Have you ever been to New York?' he said.

'Never.'

He looked at her seriously. 'I think you'd like it there.'

At Matt and Shara's beach house, when they all sat on the shore, looking at the ocean, Elise secretly believed she'd seen better coastlines in the south of France, and the sand on Malibu was gritty. Elise was glad for Connie's acts of storytelling that had brought them here, but it seemed that everything was a plan for tomorrow, with nothing for the moment in hand.

Shara was Connie's age, but Matt was younger, probably about thirty. He was shortish, slender, with a wiry, sprung energy to him, a slim, attractive face, a shadow of stubble and dark circles under his eyes. His hair was a nest, scruffy and tawny-coloured. Apparently he wrote screenplays. Connie said that Shara had met him in a bar in Manchester, and he'd followed her over here to pursue his dreams. So far, none of his screenplays had been picked up. According to Connie, Shara's parents had thought their only daughter had married some sort of English lord, but had rapidly been disappointed. Matt was very . . . normal. *It hurts him*, Connie said. *Americans can be even snobbier than the Brits. All men are created equal? Some chance.* Tonight, he was wearing a white blazer, and he'd rolled up the sleeves. He seemed twitchy. *It's Shara's money*, Connie said. *He doesn't know what to do with himself.*

Cicadas whirred in the background of the hills as the party filled their glasses, and Elise was disappointed to find she was not seated next to Barbara, but placed between Matt and Eric

Williamson, who had Barbara on his left. She caught Connie's eye, and they held a conspiratorial moment.

Eric Williamson was small and intense, like a vibrating crystal at the table. He had grey hair and a taut, tanned face. He did not look like the kind of man who would wear a baseball cap and sit in a director's chair. He looked more like a philosopher in a fitness instructor's body. He did not seem interested in talking to her.

'You think they're all boneheads, don't you?' Matt whispered.

Elise felt exposed. 'No,' she said defensively. 'I don't.'

'I did too, at first. When I arrived. But actually, you have to be clever to survive here,' he said. 'I've met more bright men and women here than any other place on earth. And I've been to a lot of places on earth. Sure, *some* of them are as thick as shit,' he went on, grinning. 'But you've got to have ideas, enthusiasm, tenacity like you would not believe.'

'You've also gotta make sure you don't drink the Kool-Aid,' Barbara interrupted, emerging suddenly from behind them, putting her hand on the back of Matt's chair. Elise felt herself go rigid with the proximity. 'You know, go travelling up your own ass?' Barbara went on. Her cigarette was balanced between two fingers and the smoke was curling into Matt's hair.

Matt turned his face up to her, acting relaxed. 'I'll remember that,' he said.

'I just wanted to get that clear,' Barbara said. 'Felt I should.'

'Don't you think Elise should do a screen test?' Matt said, turning back to address the table.

'Me?' said Elise.

'With your face,' he said.

'Just with my face?' she said, and everybody laughed. Barbara moved on, back to her own seat. 'I'm not an actress,' said Elise.

'You just have to be a good liar,' said Matt.

'Hey!' said Barbara, but she was smiling.

'I'd say the writers have to be good liars, and the actors are the ones who have to be truthful,' said Connie.

Shara sucked on a slice of lemon and bobbed it back into her vodka tonic.

'You're a good liar, then, Con?' said Elise.

Connie looked at her. 'Most of the time. I'm also good at the truth.'

'Would you call London home, Elise?' said Shara. The softly lit courtyard lent itself to her cream shoulder pads and the amber necklace on her tanned décolletage. The insistent way Shara uttered the word *home*, and the talk of Connie being a good liar, made Elise uncomfortable.

'I run away a lot,' she said.

Matt laughed, and Elise thought she saw a flicker of disappointment in Shara's eyes. Elise wasn't sure Shara would understand her lifelong experience of constant moving, nor absent parents, nor the perverse comfort of pitying yourself for not yet arriving where you're supposed to be. 'I mean, I used to run away. Before Connie,' she said.

*

The setting of *Heartlands* had been moved to America. London had become New York and the English countryside was now the Catskill Mountains. The exterior shots – Beatrice's village, its surrounding woods, her daughter Gaby's walk-up in Greenwich Village – were to be filmed in situ. All interior shots were to be filmed on the Silvercrest lot. Thus Connie's novel was to be anatomized, broken apart over the stretch of a huge continent, to be put back together at the end in a coherent whole.

'Does it matter to you, Connie?' said Barbara. 'That it's American now?'

Connie considered this. 'I'll rub my cheque into the wound,' she said, and everyone laughed.

'So are you two ladies gonna hang around for the whole shoot?' said Bill Gazzara. 'You'd be more than welcome.'

Connie's expression was unreadable to Elise – a first – and she did not like it.

'We're not sure yet,' said Connie. 'We don't want to get in the way.'

*

Barbara was a good actress that night. She was no fool. Elise supposed Matt was right: you wouldn't last long in LA if you were. She must have known what her presence would do for this film. It was part of Barbara's mythology that she'd had four husbands so far – the truth was, she was as famous for her marriages as her acting. She was often quoted as saying, *I love men, I just couldn't eat a whole one* – but no one knew if she'd really said it. Elise watched how delicately she ate her prawn cocktail. Like Shara, she had a vodka tonic bubbling before her: Elise hadn't seen any of this arrive; she felt blind to detail, yet paranoiacally aware of everything larger. A waiter poured her a white wine, and she watched the cold liquid form a film of condensation on the glass, wishing someone would give her some food. Barbara, Connie and Eric were now talking about *Wax Heart* and the book's theme of how one can be reborn without having to die.

'I believe in that kind of reincarnation,' said Barbara. 'Except we don't even *need* to be reborn to make the same mistakes again and again. There's something in us that just goes on repeat.'

'When it comes to me and tequila I'd be inclined to agree,' said Bill.

'It's about where the coin falls,' said Eric. 'You gotta get lucky.'

'The bit by the coffin, Constance. When Bea says to Gaby she's a disappointment? Jesus *Christ*,' said Barbara.

'Oh, call me Connie, please.'

Bill cackled. 'It's *amazing*. But why doesn't she just say something back?'

'Bea's just more interesting than her daughter,' said Shara. 'Gaby – that woman! Oh, I could not *bear* her.'

'She's just a girl,' said Matt. 'Cut her some slack.'

'Me and Eric have worked together four times,' said Barbara, raising her glass in Eric's direction. 'We *know* each other. I know you, Eric. This is gonna be exciting. It's gonna be such a great movie. Though it's a shame you couldn't get Derek Yelland to shoot it for you.'

'Barb, he's eighty-four,' said Eric. 'He had a stroke last year. Give the guy a break.'

'Derek wouldn't have done it anyway,' said Bill. 'I offered him *Glory Days*, but his wife wouldn't let him work again. She won't even let him off his ranch. I think he's in a bridle.'

'It's likely,' said Eric. 'But this wasn't right for him, anyway. I love the guy, but when was the last time Derek did a picture with intimate scenes like this material requires? Everyone's either grunting or kicking the shit out of each other.'

'I don't go to the cinema very often,' said Connie.

Barbara winced theatrically on her behalf, covering her eyes with her hands. 'Is this an *attack*?' she said, but she put one hand to her temple and pointed her other hand ridiculously at Connie, so everyone knew it was a joke. 'You sounded so *English*!'

'English people don't make *movies*,' said Connie. 'We prefer to tell stories by a spitting fire as sheets of rain travel over bogs.'

'That's probably a good thing,' Barbara said. 'So many movies are just a crock of shit.'

'What I was looking for,' said Bill, trying to draw the attention back to himself, 'and what I *got*, is someone who can tell a story, who actors like, but who has a sense of the epic beyond the individuals moving in the drama. Someone with a wild vision, but who knows how that translates to a housewife in Ohio or a nurse in Detroit or a business guy in London.' He pressed his hand to the tablecloth as if it was an altar. 'We needed someone with a heart. But instead, we got Eric!' Everyone laughed. 'Kidding, buddy. What an absolute coup you are, to be doing this. Everyone at Silvercrest is so delighted.'

The company appeared moved by this conviction, and let the moment sink in: a movie director who had a heart. Glasses were clinked.

'Wrong town to have a heart,' said Barbara, with a dry laugh as she lit a cigarette. The catch of the flame, the quotidian ease of her inhale – *Is this a line from a movie?* thought Elise. Her timing was just too good.

They raised their glasses to Barbara's observation. Then to Barbara, then to *Heartlands*, and finally to Connie – the heartiest toast, 'because without you, Connie,' said Bill, 'none of this would be happening.'

'Oh, I'm sure you'd find another novel, Bill,' said Connie, but Elise could tell she was touched and happy.

The appetizers arrived. Elise wasn't sure who ordered them, but here they were – terrines and tiny salads and over-the-top architectures of mousse that could be snaffled in a mouthful. She thought about pasta. Maybe this would come next? Barbara declined it all: the prawn cocktail and the vodka tonic were apparently all she required.

'Ursula Inning was keen to play your daughter,' said Eric. 'I didn't think she was right.'

Barbara frowned. 'Urse? She wanted to play my *daughter*?'

'I'm glad we got Lucy Crenshaw.'

'Who's she again?' said Barbara.

'Oh, she's *beautiful*,' said Shara.

'How old is *she*?' said Barbara.

'Eighteen,' said Eric.

'Going on twenty-eight,' murmured Bill.

'Have I seen her in anything?' said Barbara.

Eric rolled his eyes. 'You *know*, Barb,' he said. 'She's Chubby Crenshaw's kid. Left Juilliard early to film *Red Destiny*.'

'Chubby Crenshaw?' Connie snorted, covering her mouth to stop herself hooting.

Shara looked at her. '*Charlotte* Crenshaw – the model?'

'No, I'm sorry. No idea,' said Connie.

'Married the movie composer, Tom Crenshaw?' Shara persisted. 'Retired years ago, runs a llama sanctuary in Topanga. Now her daughter's making waves.'

'How the hell do you know all that?' said Matt.

'Magazines,' said Shara.

'I'm just the one who writes the novels,' said Connie heavily.

Elise felt as if they'd been sitting at this table for fifteen years.

'So why isn't Lucy here tonight?' said Barbara. 'If she's my daughter?'

'She's finishing shooting out east. She'll be back next week.'

'And the men?' said Barbara. 'Have I got a lead yet, fellers? What's the delay?'

'You could take your pick,' said Eric.

'Baby, I always do.' Barbara seemed congenitally incapable of not making her conversation sound like lines from a screwball comedy. 'Let's get some of the theatre men in,' she said. 'Please not the meatheads. It's too much.'

'Agree with you,' said Eric. 'I totally agree.'

'It's impossible to find everything in one man. I never can. I want one guy's dick and another one's mind, and I can never find those two things in the same damn place.'

*

To Elise's delight, the main course was pasta; beef shin ragu farfalle or courgette and cannellini tagliatelle. She took portions of both. So did the men, and so did Connie. Shara took some of the vegetarian option and forked small discs of courgette into her mouth, twisting the strands of pasta round and round on the plate, as if she was preparing the meal, not eating it. The talk of actors faded, people moved places, lit cigarettes, ordered brandies and random desserts. They discussed Reagan and Thatcher in slightly detached tones, as if the food had sedated them and no one could be bothered.

'Wasn't he an actor once, too?' said Elise.

'He was better in his former job,' said Barbara.

The evening began to lose structure. Connie and Barbara went towards the pool, arm in arm like ladies from an Austen novel. Elise watched as Connie said something to make Barbara laugh. Bill and Eric were still at the table, leaning back from the soiled tablecloth, discussing the script, which had been written by a new wunderkind called Daniel Stein, who lived out in New York. Matt was listening to them, and Elise wondered how he felt. Daniel Stein was twenty-six and already being feted. 'He's gifted,' said Bill. 'He's taken Connie's novel – he *gets* it, and he's turned it into this script I wanna kiss. You know, Barb loved the novel, but she'd never have done it if it wasn't for Danny's script. He's made it sing.'

Shara excused herself and went to the ladies'. 'Honey,' she said, placing her hand on Matt's shoulder. But she didn't say anything more.

Matt and Elise watched Shara disappear into the main building. 'Do you write?' he asked her, turning away from Bill and Eric.

'No,' she replied. 'Are you working on anything at the moment?'

'Recently, it's been mainly poetry,' he said.

'Wow. Have you been published?'

'Small presses, based out here. You should come surfing one Sunday,' he said. 'If you're bored.'

'I'm not bored.'

'You might get bored.'

'I've never surfed.'

'I'll teach you.'

'OK.'

Matt was not looking at Elise now, but across the pool to the stately progress of Barbara and Connie. The women were indifferent to everyone, their heads together, until a waiter came to whisper in Barbara's ear. 'My driver's here,' Barbara said loudly. The evening was over and it had only just turned nine o'clock. Shara returned from the ladies', a smile laid on her mouth. They all stood to say goodbye to each other, but it felt natural that Barbara should be the first addressed. Each of them embraced the movie star lightly, like family members used to a certain ritual. Elise did it too, feeling the slightly damp touch of Barbara's cheek, the scent of vanilla, the wisp of Marlboro.

'Call me,' Barbara said to Eric. 'Connie!' she cried, taking Connie's hand. 'It's like meeting a soul sister.'

Connie smiled. 'The pleasure's all mine.'

'I can't wait to give Beatrice the passion she deserves.'

'Thank you.'

'And we'll see each other soon.'

Barbara let go of Connie's hand. She smiled at Elise. Then she was gone.

*

In the taxi home, Connie and Elise dissected the evening. 'I think that was one of the most insane nights of my life,' said Connie.

'I didn't know Matt was a poet,' said Elise.

Connie laughed. 'Matt and his fucking poetry.'

Elise recoiled at Connie's tone, and Connie seemed to sense she'd gone too far. 'Elise, you haven't read them. He reads them out at *dinner*, sometimes. You literally have to put down your knife and fork and listen to him. Can you imagine if I did that?'

'Shara seemed a bit strange,' Elise said. 'She seemed annoyed with Matt.'

'She hasn't been out that much,' said Connie.

'Oh? Why?'

Connie continued to stare out of the taxi window. 'She had a miscarriage last year,' she said. 'The baby was six months.'

'Oh my god.'

'It wasn't good. Matt couldn't handle it.'

'What do you mean?'

Connie sighed. 'I don't know exactly what happened. But he wasn't there for her.'

'But why should he be able to handle something like that any more than she could?'

Connie was quiet for a moment. 'True. But from what I gather, he didn't try to understand what it did to her. Shara . . .

closed down and he didn't persist. And now I think she's punishing him for it.'

'You would never know, from the way she is.'

'Guess Barbara's not the only good actress,' said Connie. She put her arm round Elise and Elise nestled into her shoulder.

'Neither of them are to blame for something like that,' said Elise.

'No, of course not. It must have been awful. But it's how you handle it afterwards. She's my age, El. She's thirty-eight. He's got light years ahead of him. Reading between the lines, I think this pregnancy was a rare occurrence.'

Elise closed her eyes and thought about how, at dinner parties, there are always other conversations not being shared. Matt and Shara and their unseen baby, lost like a ghost inside their marriage. Elise wondered whether there was any pain left in Shara's body now, or whether it was just in her head, an occasional guest who led her down a staircase that only she could tread.

11

The next day, Elise sat by the pool of their bungalow with her legs in the water, and thought about her mother. She was seven when Patricia Morceau had leant against their kitchen counter and told her daughter she had a funny lump in her brain. The surgeons cut it out along with the power of speech, and although Patricia did learn to speak again, it was erratically, not as her former self. She had no guard on her tongue any more. Neither Elise nor her father knew what might come tripping; poison words or sweetness.

A few weeks after the operation, the family attended a party to celebrate the end of a show for which Patricia had designed the costumes. The change in Patricia was not immediately obvious, until she looked straight at Elise. Her eyes were different. They had always been a dark blueish grey, and now they were pale, as if someone had bleached them. Her pupils were tiny, and didn't seem level. Her mother had gone.

Elise dragged her legs back and forth in the bright blue water, remembering how Patricia had kept pinning her with those pale eyes at the party, as if she had to impress upon her daughter this change she didn't want. Elise had not known how to respond to her mother, who now held the murk of a drained rock pool inside her skull. She had been wanting for some time to be able to say something – anything – helpful, but Patricia made it harshly clear that there was nothing to be said or done.

The removal of the tumour had blown the hinges off the maternal gate. There was no small talk, all that was pointless. Elise became the one at a loss for words, and all she could do was keep her undesired sympathy to herself.

Whenever Connie asked Elise about her dead mother – and she did so quite frequently – Elise felt she could tell Connie the truth, which she had never told anyone else. She told Connie how the tumour had grown back two years later, and that the second time it was too damaging, too much, and it had killed her mother. *I'm so, so sorry*, Connie had said. *You must miss her.*

At this point, Elise had lied and said you got used to it. She said everything was OK now, these things happened. To Elise's astonishment, Connie seemed to have accepted these statements, allowing their flimsiness to remain in place.

I must be a good liar too, she thought, kicking her legs in the water.

'My mother would have liked it here,' she said out loud. As soon as she said it, Elise felt her voice wobble. What was happening to her in this place?

Connie who was hiding her pale skin under a parasol and writing in a notebook at the table looked in Elise's direction. 'Sorry?'

'I was just thinking about Shara,' Elise said.

'Poor Shara,' said Connie.

'Did she want the baby very much?'

'Yes, I'm certain. Her sister has about four, I think.'

'Do you ever think about babies?' said Elise.

'You mean my own babies?' Connie put down her pen. 'Not so much now. Once, I did. I'd quite like my periods to stop so that it can never even be an issue. Where's all this come from?'

'I told you,' Elise snapped. 'Shara.'

'OK,' said Connie, gently. 'Well, seeing as you've asked. I don't want to be a mother, El. I don't have time. It seems like a lot of hard work. I'm not that interested. I never have been, really. I do like their little feet and their little ears. I like the beauty of them. But they grow up, and their whole purpose is to leave you. It's how it has to be. Quite frankly, El, I find that devastating. To think someone might do to me as I've done to my own parents.'

'So really, you're a softie who doesn't want her heart broken.'

'Ha. I don't know.' Connie paused, as if she was thinking. 'There's another thing, that's not so easy to explain.'

'What is it?'

'Well, from what I've seen of it, from the people I know who've had children – certainly when the children are young, it's that one very much has to live in the present. It's a sort of constant vigilance. You are very focused on the moment, on the matter in hand.'

'I guess that's right.'

'And I'm sure they do think about the future. But the thing is, writing is sort of the opposite. I live in different temporal spaces. I live in a fabricated present, and I'm constantly making up a future as well – and reimagining the past.'

'Don't you think people with children do all that too?'

'Maybe. But they do have to hop back to a mundane present. I don't, or at least I don't have to do it as much. And I've spent such a long time where I live, in my head, that I don't know whether I'm prepared to give up my citizen's rights.'

She is so brilliant, thought Elise. *And she would be a good mother.*

'Also,' said Connie, 'I like the beauty of many things. The beauty of children doesn't, for me, outweigh the beauty and reward of other things.'

'Would you ever say any of that publicly?'

Connie pulled a face. 'God, no. I'd never be able to talk about anything else. Same as them not knowing about me being gay. Can you imagine? Not fucking worth it.'

'It makes sense you don't want them.' Elise slipped into the water and began swimming lengths. She did breast-stroke, keeping her head above the surface.

'I don't know whether to be offended or pleased,' said Connie. 'Why does it make sense?'

'Because you're you.'

Elise went under and opened her eyes. The world beneath was bulbous and blurred, even more bright blue. She imagined being able to breathe underwater. Would she live there if she could – not here, in a trapped chlorine rectangle, but out in the ocean like a mermaid, huge-finned, moving between reefs? Her lungs were hurting; and she came up. Connie was kneeling by the side of the pool, wearing a concerned expression. 'Do *you*?' she said.

'Do I what?'

'Do you want to have children?'

'I don't know, Con.' This was true.

'You're too young, anyway,' Connie said.

'I'm not.'

Connie sighed, which irritated Elise more. 'You shouldn't say things like that to me,' she said. 'That I'm too young. You say it a lot. I'm nearly twenty-three.'

Connie looked like she was going to say something, but stopped herself. Then she said: 'You *are* young, but you're not *too* young. I'm sorry,' she added, and went back to her notebook in the shade.

12

They decided to stay on in West Hollywood whilst all the interior shots for *Heartlands* were being filmed. Another fortnight had passed; they had now been in Los Angeles for six weeks. In that time, they'd spent three days in San Francisco and a long weekend in Monterey, including a trip to Salinas because Connie wanted to see where Steinbeck had lived. 'Are you going for inspiration?' Elise asked.

'No, I'm going because I'm nosy,' said Connie.

The places they saw were mind-blowing. The size of the redwoods, the clifftop ocean views, the sun a July goddess, gilding the tips of waves and human shoulders, before the night fell and the owls and other creatures came calling. Elise wanted to stay longer in the woods, but they followed a motor route, staying in motels, and Connie drove them everywhere, fast. Elise imagined they were a pair of frontierswomen, panning for gold despite the opprobrium from the menfolk who'd also come to make their fortune.

Sometimes, when Connie was writing, Elise would take out a notebook too, and try to write. Nothing came. This fact almost physically hurt. How did Connie do it? She was doing so well here, writing all the time, probably about that green rabbit, but she'd never say. She'd even become actual friends with Barbara Lowden. The two women would meet – to discuss Barbara's character, Connie said. She intimated that it was, at times, exhausting, but when Elise said she didn't have to pander to the film star's every whim, Connie said she wasn't pandering at all.

'Don't you find it weird,' Elise said. 'Looking at her?'

Connie laughed. 'No. She's a human being. A very funny one. She's been so famous for so long that she behaves differently to other people. I find that fascinating.'

They had not yet agreed as to whether they would decamp with the film production to the Catskills, but the stay in Los Angeles, in America as a whole, certainly seemed open-ended. They often went out to Malibu to see Shara and Matt. The four of them would sit round a fire, their faces warm from the flames, shawls round their backs as the stars pricked the sky, and Elise would watch the married couple, imagining their secret pain.

It was Matt who suggested that they make an overnight outdoor stay in Joshua Tree Park. 'It's only three hours,' he said. 'You wait for *those* stars. And the rocks.'

Elise listened with admiration as he spoke about the shapes they formed, their colours changing in the setting sun.

'No way,' said Connie. 'I don't want to die in the jaws of a coyote.'

'Don't you like the tranquillity of forests, Con?' asked Shara.

Connie made a face. 'It's like space. No one will hear you screaming if you die.'

'That's a bit of an exaggeration,' said Matt.

'There's nothing to *do* in nature, essentially,' said Connie. 'Except be horribly aware of how easily you get bored.'

'I'd love to go,' said Elise. But the conversation had moved on, and no one seemed to hear her.

*

Elise had noted that Connie and Matt barely talked as a pair – when they did, it was never frosty or difficult, as such, but Connie seemed to cauterize his attempts at generating conversation.

'Have you got a problem with Matt?' she asked Connie, on the way home from Malibu one day. They'd hired a car on a long-term basis by this point, and the footwell carpet was full of sand that shook off Elise's soles and seemed impossible to get rid of.

'Matt? He's fine,' said Connie. 'I just don't think Shara should have married him.'

'Why?'

'He's mediocre.'

'He is?'

'Don't you think? What does he ever talk about except places we should visit, or that he's visited himself? I hate that.'

'He wants to *share* it, Con.'

'He wants to *show* it. I can go to bloody Joshua Tree without him.'

Connie, Elise thought, had become more unforgiving in their new social situations: impressive and dazzling, yes, but too critical of others' foibles. Maybe it was the other company she was keeping – some sort of confidence transplant from Barbara Lowden, via osmosis. Or possibly it stemmed from Connie's belief that Matt didn't support Shara enough after the miscarriage. Perhaps she was right, thought Elise: perhaps peace was not to be found in the centre of the peyote plant, but rather in looking after your wife. But what about Matt? What had he felt, during that time? Had anyone bothered to ask him?

'Did you know that Shara's name is actually Sahara, but she took out the first "a" to annoy her hippy mum and try and seem more normal?' said Connie, laughing. 'She was a shock to Manchester as an undergraduate, I can tell you.'

'Why the hell did she go to Manchester to do her degree?'

'Her dad's work. She grew up half the time in England. But here is where she belongs.'

'And does Matt belong here?'

Connie gave her a wry look. 'You tell me.'

Connie hadn't needed to spell it out. There was a tangible fracture line between Matt and Shara – Elise could see it, as the child of a difficult marriage so often can. Shara was hard and fixed, and Matt seemed restless, forcibly eager, over-invested in plans that ranged from watering their cacti under a full moon to planning road trips. Then he would become moody, meditating on the unfairness of the world, of the difficulties in being alive. Elise could sympathize; she felt Matt was out-smarted by Connie, like she herself often was – and neither could she connect much with Shara. She liked Matt's enthusiasms, and the fact he made an effort with her when so few did.

One day, Shara invited Elise and Connie into her studio to see her paintings. The women walked in with some trepidation. The space was large and light-filled, and canvases were propped up everywhere around the walls. They were large, abstract in the main, often covered with a semi-tangible amalgam of circles.

'These,' said Shara, pointing. 'I wanted to make a comment on the immanence of motherhood.'

Elise didn't know what to say, but Connie nodded. *What the fuck does Connie know about the immanence of motherhood?* Elise wondered, but then remembered that half of Connie's job was to be curious and the other half was to give the appearance of authority.

'That one, Shar,' said Connie. 'I love that one.' She pointed at one of the largest pieces. Elise stared at the endless shading of the circles, like eyes staring back at her, but avoiding her scrutiny at the same time: a void luring her in.

'Have it,' said Shara.

'Get away with you,' said Connie. 'I'll buy it.'

'No,' said Shara. 'I want you to have it.'

'Really?'

'Really.'

Elise mooched around the studio, feeling she should leave them in peace. She thought about when she'd turned twenty-one, and she and Connie had had a picnic on the Heath, near the spot where they'd first laid eyes upon each other. Among a pork pie and cold sausages from the butcher, Connie had even made a chocolate cake. Elise recalled the unprecedented sensation of being cared for, finally – mixed with an overflowing lust despite the Blytonesque picnic hamper and bottles of ginger beer that Connie had packed. For her next birthday, Connie had bought them tickets to see *Much Ado About Nothing* at the National Theatre. 'So you can have a night off and be ushered to a seat yourself,' Connie had said. Penelope Wilton had played Beatrice and Michael Gambon was Benedick, and Connie and Elise had laughed and held each other's hands in the dark.

Elise felt, now, an irrational surge of hate for Connie, to be so trapped by her. She would like to be thirty-eight, and be given paintings by American friends. She would like to go driving off in a car towards West Hollywood. She would like to live by the beach in Malibu. Instead, she was watching it all happen. None of this was hers. And Connie could take away the little she had, in an instant.

2017

13

I sat in the living room of our flat, staring at the scrunched-up Post-it note where I'd written the number for Deborah Clarke's literary agency. *Hi, I'm a huge fan of Constance Holden!* That wouldn't work – that was the last sort of person Constance's representatives would let anywhere near her. I didn't imagine Deborah Clarke was still working, given the amount of time that had passed, and I thought that might play in my favour – but nevertheless, whoever now worked for Constance was unlikely to pass on any details. *Hi! I think Constance may have had a hand in my mum's disappearance, I'd love to talk to her – think she'd be free?*

I thought, briefly, that I could tell the truth. Give the name of my dad, say that I just wanted to put the pieces of my early life together. Imagine that – just being honest. I never seriously considered it. All I could think of was my dad telling me to go carefully with her, that she was strong where my mother had been weak, and that Constance might not even want to talk to me about Elise Morceau.

I would make up a name, I decided. A quiet, simple identity, that could easily be lost on the Internet. Laura and Brown, a ubiquitous enough pair of bookends between which a real life could hide. Of course, it was tempting to give myself an exquisite alias, Miranda, Isabella, Penelope, tied up with a surname like Storm or Montgomery, but that would have been rather risky. I looked up the agency website. They had one assistant, Rebecca Forrester, and luckily, in these days of such transparency, her email address and phone number were right there.

I was Laura Brown, and I wanted to write a letter to Ms Holden. Where might I send it? I pressed the digits on my phone and waited. After three rings, someone picked up. 'Clarke and Davies, Rebecca speaking, can I help?' said a woman with a flustered voice.

'Hi, Rebecca.' I sounded foolish, informal. I panicked, and my mind went blank. 'It's about Constance.'

'Oh, thank *god* you rang me back,' she said breathlessly. 'I—'

'Hold on a sec.' There was a rustling sound on the other end of the line. 'Have you got anyone yet?' said Rebecca. 'She's getting quite impatient.'

'Impatient?'

'Well, don't say I told you that,' this Rebecca went on. 'But she's turned down all your other candidates and we don't really know what to do next.'

'No, of course,' I said, feeling vertiginous.

'So have you got anyone? We need someone urgently.'

My mind was working as fast as it could. I had no idea what this Rebecca was talking about, but I knew that to deny her what she wanted could lead to myself being denied too. 'Yes,' I said.

'Fantastic. Can you send me her details?'

'Can I send you her details?' I repeated, trying to buy time to get my thoughts in order.

'Ye-es?'

I tried to pull myself together. 'Sure. Sure. I'll email you?'

'Yes,' said Rebecca, sounding slightly impatient. 'Are you able to do it now?'

'Of course I am. One thing – I'm working from home. It'll come in from my personal email. From—' I stopped. On the small dining-room table was a bottle of McIntyre's Hot Sauce, left there because Joe hadn't tidied it away. 'It'll come from mcintyre0553@gmail.com.' My head was pounding. 'Is that OK?'

'Sure,' said Rebecca. 'I'll look out for it. Call you back after I've read it. I've got to jump into a meeting now.'

'Actually – would you be able to reply by email instead? It's just, I've got a sleeping baby here and she wakes if the phone rings.'

Fuck, I thought. *What the fuck am I doing?*

'No worries. Let's be in touch soon,' said Rebecca. She was sounding more and more harried, as if she had fifty-five other things to think about that day. She hung up the phone.

I'd started something, but I wasn't sure what. It needed water and light. I was astonished at how quickly I'd made up the lie. I flipped open my laptop and began to construct a CV for Laura Brown. I couldn't believe I was doing this, but here I was, fluently making it all up.

Laura Brown was my age. She'd studied at the same university as me, same subject. As tempting as it was to give her an unusual, high-flying career history, I figured it would be better to keep as much as possible in the non-fiction realm so I didn't get caught out as a physics graduate who'd won a junior Nobel Prize, or as someone who knew how to translate Russian novels.

That said, I upped her degree class to a first.

Then it dawned on me that in my shock at how quickly I'd concocted this charade over the telephone, I didn't even find out what the candidates were candidates *for*. I'd have to guess, in which case everything might come crashing down before I'd even started. Care work for Constance? Secretarial? This was ridiculous. I took a deep breath. *Let's go for a mix*, I thought, feeling more alive than I had in months.

Laura Brown had done some charity work and volunteering, three years working in a bookshop, and she'd worked as a teaching assistant in Costa Rica. It was astonishing to me how quickly my fabrications came. I could find adjectives to describe Laura quicker than I could for myself. She was diligent, enthusiastic, positive, had great attention to detail. And yet she took long walks in her spare time, just like me.

In the end, the fake CV wasn't the problem, it was making the fake email account. I was heading deeper into the forest towards Connie, this would look terrible if I was caught – but I didn't want to leave a trail of breadcrumbs. I prayed that no one already owned the mcintyre0553@gmail.com account. I was in luck, if anything about this scenario could be called lucky.

From: mcintyre0553@gmail.com
To: rebecca@clarkeanddavies.com

Rebecca,

Thanks for taking my call. Herewith, as discussed, the CV for Laura Brown. Laura's very keen to meet Constance for this position, and to discuss all the requirements Constance has. She's a fabulous candidate, only recently become available for new work, as her previous employer has moved country. He was very sad to lose her! Laura is extremely dependable, personable and an all-rounder, and we think she'd make an excellent, adaptable fit for your client.

Kind regards, and looking forward to hearing from you.

I didn't sign it. Rebecca might put it down to distraction on my part thanks to my fictional fractious baby, and before I could back out of it, I pressed *send*. What easy madness. I pushed the laptop shut and went out for a walk, as if to leave the incriminating equipment behind might exonerate my deception and desperation. I wandered round the small park at the end of our road for fifteen minutes, and when I got back to the flat, Joe was sitting on the sofa, flicking through a monthly food magazine. 'Hey,' he said. 'Have you got any thoughts on dinner?'

'Hello,' I said, sitting next to him and giving him a kiss on the cheek. 'Nope.'

Joe didn't react. 'Did you meet up with Kelly?' he said. 'Is she going to stream the birth on Instagram?'

'Of course not,' I said. But then I wondered. 'Mad she's having another baby. They always say it happens at thirty. But I definitely didn't want a kid at thirty.'

'No, you didn't,' said Joe.

'You didn't either.'

'*They*,' said Joe. 'Who are *they*? It happens when it happens.'

I knew he didn't understand what I was talking about, not really. Joe's body had never truly changed for him. Yes, it had got hairier, bigger – but inside and out, it had more or less stayed the same. For me, who had been shocked by the first, unfamiliar melting ache in my lower abdomen when I was twelve, by the blood that came, completing my A-levels five years later, bent double in agony – I, who had waxed and waned like the moon, month in, month out, who knew the differing levels of wetness inside her could supposedly predict her fertility – I knew the inside of my body so much better than he knew his. Strangers on the street hadn't scrutinized his body like they had mine. And now I was at a point where my body might fail in its performance of the act of producing another person before it was too late.

'I miss the passion, Joe,' I said suddenly. 'Between you and me.'

'Yeah,' he replied, but I couldn't tell whether in agreement, defeat, or both. 'But you can't keep that up.'

'Are you serious?'

'I don't know how anyone does.'

'People do, though,' I said. I wondered what a lot of sex actually was, in terms of quantity.

'If you had a baby, what would you call it?' Joe said, closing the magazine.

We'd had this conversation before, and usually it was very abstract in its tone, hypothetical, distant. But there was something in his voice that alarmed me.

'It's hard thinking of a name when you haven't met the person,' I said. 'But it would have to be something that wouldn't get them teased. Something that isn't about me. I just don't get why people give weird names to their kids. Giving your child a batshit name is so unfair.' Joe looked amused. 'What? I feel strongly about it.'

'So I see.'

'Oh, people can name their kids whatever they want. Yellow, Hamburger, Dandelion. Who am I to judge?'

'Hamburger's nice.'

'Hammie! Get off that swing!'

'It's got a ring to it.'

We laughed. We could get on. We did. Anyone looking at us right then, on our sofa, might have thought, *Yes, they've got it nailed.* And maybe we had. Maybe the perpetual acts of compromise and the feelings of frustration, a chronic sense that somewhere round the corner – or behind you on the path where you missed the turning – your real life was waiting, was simply a condition of being alive, and moreover, trying to be alive with someone else?

If you'd asked me, *Do you love Joe?* I would have answered yes. But I did not love the person I was when I was with him. I did not like how I'd . . . *slid*, over the years. I was convinced that there were many other selves belonging to me that were locked inside and would be forever locked if I stayed on this path – this steady path, my hand in his. My dad had never put himself to any long-term test before Claire, so I had no precedent of how people negotiated the peaks and slumps of an entire lifetime together – the dulling acts, the imperative to find grace in repetition, in flaws, in boredom.

I loved my past with Joe, but inside this present we'd reduced ourselves in order to fit its shape. I felt the tinge of sabotage in my blood. If I let it, would it spread? And at the same time, I wanted to apologize – for not being enthusiastic any more about Joerritos, for never knowing what I wanted, for not being someone even a bit like Kelly.

'Joey, how are you feeling about the whole baby thing?' I said.

'I don't know,' he replied. He paused. 'Is it a good time?' he went on. 'With me and the business?'

What fucking business? I wanted to scream. I couldn't believe how deep we were into the delusion. It felt like there was no way out.

He looked hard at the carpet, as if to divine his future in the microscopic tufts. 'How are you feeling about it?' he said. 'Do you want to have a baby?'

I looked at him. I knew that I had begun to play a guessing game with Nature, like a walk on Escher's staircase, where you might wander and never end up anywhere concrete. Older women would often say to me, *You can't mess with Nature!* as if

Nature was a prickly colleague called Janet, with pernickety rules, but who they grudgingly admitted was good at her job. Those women could afford to be complacent, old-wivey, slightly hectoring. They saw it as the right of those who were stuck with their decisions, wanted or otherwise, and had done their best.

'A baby is the one thing I can't take back to the shop, Joey,' I said. 'The one thing I will have done in my life which is utterly irreversible.'

'I know that, babe.'

'It's also expensive. We're lucky, with the fact that we have the flat, but it's only got one bedroom.'

'You can put a baby in a drawer,' he said.

'Be serious. London costs a fortune.'

But cost was not the reason I was worried. When I was a schoolgirl the talk was determinedly not about babies. It was about other kinds of achievement, those from outside the body. Degrees, usefulness, wings attached with wax, soaring up towards the sun. Most of my friends had been like me, mythical women, wax-winged. But one by one they'd become pregnant and had their children – so beautiful, all of them – and they had used the old feathers on their wings for nests. I had never felt jealous or sorrowful when the news came. I'd always felt delight and excitement – and a not insubstantial relief that this time, it wasn't me. I could enjoy these children and then go home at the end of the day.

I was intelligent enough to know you could never be certain of the body's next twist, but also optimistic enough to think it might be possible, in one's mid-thirties, to arrive at a sense of solidity. But I had not. I didn't want to talk about it any more. I couldn't bring myself to say the words. I probably wanted him to express the desire and conviction that was required for both of us, which was unfair, I suppose. Instead, I opened my laptop, and there, shiny and new, was an email from Rebecca.

'Oh, my god,' I said.

'What?' said Joe.

'I applied for this job.'

'Were you applying for jobs?'

'Hold on.'

I opened the email, my heart thumping. Joe tried to read it too but I moved off the sofa and went to the bedroom. 'What's going on?' he called after me, but I didn't reply.

Laura sounds great! Rebecca had written. *I've discussed with Deborah, and she chatted with Constance. Could Laura get to Constance's for an interview tomorrow at 2pm?*

Holy mother of god.

Hi Rebecca. Yes, I typed – *she should be free most of this week in the daytime. I'll just confirm this time with her and get back to you. Could you send me the address again?*

Risky, but I had no choice.

Sure, Rebecca emailed back. Clearly she was rushing this one through, keen to impress her boss, or simply to get the matter off her desk. *It's 17 Dacres Road, NW3 5RP.*

Perfect, I wrote.

I sat on the edge of the bed and texted Zoë. Hi Z, can we swap shifts tomorrow? Sorry for last minute. I'd be so grateful.

Zoë texted back immediately. Sure thing x.

Thanks, I wrote back.

I waited for five minutes to pass on my watch. I opened the laptop again and replied to Rebecca's last email. *Laura can do tomorrow at 2pm*, I wrote. *Let me know any feedback, and we can take it from there.*

Thanks, wrote Rebecca. *Fingers crossed!*

And that was it. I lay back on the duvet. *This cannot work*, I thought. *It simply can't. At some point, the literary agency is going to be in touch with whoever was suggesting the candidates to them. I cannot get away with this.*

But at the very least, I reckoned I had about twenty-four hours before I was caught out. And before that happened, I was going to make sure I got inside 17 Dacres Road, and put myself in front of Constance Holden.

14

Not having lived north of the great dividing river, I never much went to Hampstead Heath. If I wanted vast open space, I went to Richmond Park, revelling in its huge skies and autumn golds, thinking of Henry VIII hunting his deer – their descendants still grazing underneath the oaks. But here I was, striding over Parliament Hill. I made my way to the famous view of central London, the whole of the sky from east to west, Gherkin, Walkie-Talkie, Shard, the dome of St Paul's, the hollow of the Eye – a witch's broken incantation into Soho, the modern geography glinting in the sun. It was a warm October; people walking in shirts and sunglasses, with a carelessness that belied the fact that in eight weeks we'd be deep in the grip of a London winter. In a daze, I passed small cloudy poodles, and watched a blue-eyed husky drag a woman along, her thin arms jerking on the lead with a hint of savagery. I saw men, their white legs in sports shorts; children on scooters, whizzing.

I was there on that hill, and I was not. I felt as if I was floating above myself, watching the fast pace of my own feet as they made their way off the Heath. I was Rose Simmons, and I was Laura Brown. I was north, I was south, and I was no point on the compass. Somehow, I was walking down the hill that led to Dacres Road, to meet a person who'd known my mother. A woman who my father said might have something to tell me. I tried to gather myself together, to remember all the things Laura Brown had achieved in her life.

I hadn't told Joe what I was doing. I didn't want his opprobrium or doubt. I wanted to do this entirely on my own. And yet, it occurred to me as I turned into Dacres Road, that no one knew I was here. What if Constance recognized my mother's face in mine, and made a prisoner of me, feeding me through a cage, fattening me for her stove? I would die here, answerless, and no one would know how to find Rose Simmons ever again.

*

The houses on Dacres Road were four storeys tall, with little gable windows at the top and basements visible if you looked down as you ascended the steps to the raised front doors. Their brickwork was good quality, and had endured well over a hundred years of London air. They were deep reddish brown and neatly built, and the window bays were painted in creamy white. Trimmed tight hedges and plump rose bushes complemented the ivy that tumbled over stained-glass porches. Expensive serenity – although by the looks of them, many were now divided into flats. There seemed something inevitable that Constance, a writer, lived in one of these grand Hampstead houses – but actually I was glad of it, because this would probably be the only manner by which I would ever get to see inside one.

Numbers 11, 13, 15 – I was nearing her house, my pulse racing. *Just knock on the door*, I said to myself. *What's the worst that can happen?*

I thought – in fact, I was convinced – that she would open the door and recognize me immediately, that the traces of Elise Morceau would be so obvious to her. I pictured Constance, taking me to New York, finding the apartment I'd spent my early days in. A closing of a circle, to find my mother's story: that was worth this risk.

I reached number 17. The front of the house was covered with ivy, which cloaked the lintel of the porch. The tiles beneath my feet were small black and white diamonds, cracked here and there with age. The door was a dark bottle green, with two panels of glass in deep red and yellow, blue and violet. The knocker was a cast-iron shape of a woman's hand, emerging delicately from a cuff. I lifted the hand and dropped it on the iron ball beneath, and waited. After a good ten or so seconds, through the warped glass panes I saw a figure moving down the hall, tall and dark, mutating as it came forward, its outline like a ripple of black water.

You could run, I thought. *You could pretend none of this ever happened.*

But I was sick of pretending. I wanted to know the truth.

Then Constance was before me, the door wide open, her face and body framed by the mouth of her house. She stopped short when she saw me. Her eyes rested on mine fractionally too long.

Now, I thought. *Now! Everything's going to fall into place.*

'Can I help you?' she said.

I'd been expecting someone slightly haggish, I'll admit. A reclusive novelist was supposed to be an old lady, a wyrd sister with poor personal hygiene, hoarding cereal boxes, a mad oestrogen-deprived biddy with her hair matted on her head, but the brain inside it a work of genius. Constance Holden did not look like that.

She looked hard, I would say: her body looked *hard*. Her body was a lesson. There was no spare flesh on her, jumper tight and neat about her, black trousers fitted yet loosening out towards the ankles. A single gold bangle on her wrist. White hair, up in a chignon. Tortoiseshell half-glasses hanging round her neck. Her eyes were light, her cheekbones broad. Those eighties headshots flashed past like a series of matryoshka dolls rising up from within her.

In the flesh she was more upright. Had she really known my mother, kissed her, held her, hurt her? Had she ever wondered what had happened to the child that Elise once had? My breath stopped in my throat; I couldn't speak. I shifted on the tiles, trying not to grab her by the arms and say, *It's me, Rose. I grew up.* I remembered what my father had told me; that I needed to be careful.

'Are you all right?' she said, interrupting my thoughts.

'Oh – yes. Sorry. You're Constance Holden?' I said. My voice tightened. *I shouldn't have come*, I thought. *Better never to have come.*

Constance's clever eyes looked in my face. 'You're here for the interview,' she said.

'Yes.'

'Come in.' She did not smile, nor offer her hand. She simply stepped to one side.

I went into the hall, feeling sick. I turned to watch her close the door, fumbling slightly with the latch. That was when I noticed her fingers. Her knuckles were swollen, her thumb jutted awkwardly from the side of her hand, and her other fingers didn't span upwards neatly in the right direction. Her hands looked as if they belonged to someone else, sewn on in a cruel experiment, possessing a mind of their own.

She saw me staring at them, and I looked hastily away at the walls. She had pitted dusky pink against old green furniture, and a low, long shelf on one side of the hall was lined with at least twenty misshapen pots. 'These are lovely,' I said, too brightly, gesturing.

'From the Yucatán peninsula,' she replied. Her voice was strong, unwearied. Present.

'Have you lived here long?' I asked.

'I've owned this house for nearly forty years,' she said. 'But I haven't always lived here.' She narrowed her eyes. 'What's your name again?'

'Laura Brown,' I said. The name tripped off my tongue as easily as if it were my own.

Who dusted those pots? I wondered. What would happen if a coat hem knocked one off? Death, probably. My eyes began to roam, drinking in everything I could see. I felt like I was hunting this woman – but clumsily, and she would know exactly what to do to avoid me.

I asked if I could use the bathroom, and Constance pointed with her unruly fingers towards a door under the staircase.

It was just a small water closet, tastefully devoid of any maritime theme. I clicked the lock, and sat on the loo with my head in my hands. The space was dark and gold and velvet, a little room inside tall walls. I sat in this gem of a cubby hole, trying to wee quietly. I had done a crazy thing to get into this house. But I was scared of it. I splashed water on my face and told myself to get a grip.

'Shall we do this in the front?' Constance said, after I emerged. She was still standing in the hall, like a guard in her own house.

'Thank you.'

'Do you understand what I'm looking for?' she said over her shoulder, leading me into the front room. The October afternoon light played through the huge bay window. Beneath our feet were Turkish rugs, and around us, the unusually high walls were painted in gunmetal blue. Prints were hung quite higgledy-piggledy; I wanted to examine every one but knew I couldn't. The armchairs and sofa were covered in velvet roses and looked tired but comfortable.

'They didn't tell me a huge amount,' I said. Constance rolled her eyes. 'But I've read *Green Rabbit*.' She stopped in her tracks. 'It's—'

'You're not a Ph.D. student, are you?'

'No.'

'Thank god.'

She looked at me again. My face felt like it had lost a layer of skin. Then she moved to an armchair and lowered herself into it. It partially swallowed her up. 'Please sit down, Miss Brown.'

'Laura, please.'

'How old are you, Laura?' she asked.

'I'm thirty-five next July.'

'A crab?'

I looked at her with surprise. I did not take her for one who had an interest in the stars. 'I am.'

'Do you like to hide?'

'I hope not,' I replied.

I couldn't get at her. Constance had got to me first and I didn't know the rules. I didn't have any weapons, I didn't feel bright or sharp or whatever it was I suspected Constance wanted me to be. Constance was too strong, too rude, too used to bending the world to her will. I'd never been spoken to like this by anyone before. The normal rules of politesse clearly did not bother her.

She held up her hands. 'It's these,' she said. 'Severe osteo-arthritis. They keep pussy-footing round the whole thing, so when the girls turn up – and it's always girls – they don't realize how much help I really need.'

'And how much help do you need?' I said.

She looked at me appreciatively. 'I live alone,' she said. 'There is no significant or insignificant other. I can dress myself. At the moment. As long as the clothes are put together with zips, not lots of little buttons. I can turn on a kettle. Pour a cup. I can open a book, and I can read it. But it's the neater motor mechanics I'm finding hard. It's pull-on loafers for my feet these days. Spaghetti bolognese is a fucking disaster. I will probably never peel my own prawns or drink a bowl of soup in public again.'

'I'm sorry,' I said.

'Thank you.'

'Can you write?' I asked.

Constance looked at me hawkishly. Then something in her face seemed to give way.

'Shall I make us a cup of tea?' I said.

*

She directed me to the kitchen, and I walked through to the back of the house, which opened out into a medium-sized, beautifully designed kitchen that looked onto a small courtyard garden lined with junior-sized fruit trees and large planters full of mint. I opened cupboard after cupboard until I found Constance's mugs. Her collection belied any sense of elegance and power evident in the rest of the house. They were from the school of the tired velvet armchairs, faded mugs from Cadbury that had probably come with Easter eggs wedged inside them long ago, alongside SAVE THE CHILDREN, SAVE THE WHALE, and I ♥ BIRDWORLD, with an emu on the side who'd seen better days.

'Are you picking the tea leaves too?' Constance called.

'Coming,' I said, grabbing I ♥ BIRDWORLD.

I returned to the front room bearing her tea. 'I'll just put it on the side to cool down.'

She looked at it dubiously. Her hands sat in her lap, and I wondered how often she drank, or ate, in front of others. 'I'm finishing a novel,' she said. 'It'll probably be the last one I write.' I felt unease pushing from the middle of my body like a black dove against my ribs. 'I can type, but very slowly,' she went on. 'I hate computers. I prefer to write by hand. But my handwriting's atrocious. So I'm in a bit of a bind.'

'I see.'

'I don't get up early,' she said. 'So I wouldn't expect you to come in before ten. I have coffee, then I write till one o'clock in the afternoon, stopping for lunch.' She sighed. 'I don't exactly know how this will work.'

'What's your novel about?' I said, and immediately regretted it. I saw it in her face; the displeasure and resignation fighting with the desire to tell me – or to try, at least.

'Would you be interested in helping me?' she said.

'Yes,' I said. 'And I wouldn't ask a question like that again.'

She smiled, holding up her hands. 'Aside from all this boring business, can you manage a diary?'

'Yes,' I said.

'Can you work some evenings? Cook for me? *Can* you cook?'

'Yes, I can.'

'And what are you really looking for, out of this position?'

I found myself lost for words.

'I see,' said Constance, looking dubious. 'I'll be frank, Laura. You're the oldest candidate the recruitment agency and Rebecca organized for me to meet. I don't think you're remotely *old*, obviously. It's just all the others are in their early twenties. They look like they want to get on somewhere, you know? This is an *interim* thing for them. A limbo. And to be quite frank, I think most of them were scared. Would you be able to tell me why you're here?'

'Have you read my CV?' I said.

She batted the air with her hands. 'I took a glimpse. They all look the same, to be honest. And people always make half of it up, anyway. I'd prefer to talk to a person. I'm a good judge of character, you know.'

'Of course.'

'So why do you want this job? Are you just looking for anything at the moment?'

'No. Something specific,' I said.

'Oh? What?'

'I would like – to be useful,' I said.

Constance laughed. 'You would be very useful.' She leaned back in the armchair and surveyed me. 'But would I be useful to you?'

'I'm sorry?'

'You're telling me that working here would be an entirely altruistic pleasure?'

'Well – no. I mean, I need a job. There's that. And I think this would be an interesting position. And I need a change,' I added. Feeling some truth upon the air, at last, I felt my cheeks turn hot.

It was as if she smelled it too. 'A change?' she said. 'You're not happy where you are?'

'I've taken some shifts in a coffee shop. It's not – stimulating.'

'But if you worked here, there would be no one else to talk to, except me. And I wouldn't call making cups of tea any more stimulating than making cups of coffee.'

'You sound like you're trying to talk me out of it,' I said.

'I just want you to understand. I'm not here to entertain you, to tell you stories. I need – essentially – a maid who can type.'

Her abruptness, her asperity – I understood why many might have been put off by Constance, or might have wilted under her glare. 'I'm not expecting anything from you,' I said, and I had to look away, hot-faced from my lie. When I turned back to her, she was waiting for me to speak again. 'Miss Holden—'

'Connie, please.'

'Connie. I would love this job. That's the truth. I will do what you want. I will leave you alone when you want to be alone. I will cook for you. I will type for you. Your hands are yours, and they always will be. But you can have mine too, if you would like them.'

Constance looked taken aback. Possibly no one had offered themselves to her for a long time, in any shape or form. Her eyes even briefly moistened, but she blinked, and I looked away to save her embarrassment. I suspected she could not countenance the idea of weeping in front of me. In truth, I had not expected such an outburst from myself, but perhaps some unconscious part of me knew that this moment couldn't be let go. I didn't know how it would work with the recruitment agency, but I was on the cusp of something that might be here today and never seen again. I was already in too deep – I needed her to want me more than the others. I needed her to want to make this work.

She scrutinized my face, as if she was divining a mystery or looking at a confusing work of art. 'There's another thing,' she said.

'Yes?'

'The recruitment agency Rebecca used.'

A sick feeling swooped into my stomach. 'Yes?'

'What percentage of your earnings will they take?'

'Er, twenty per cent?'

'Mmm,' said Constance. 'For doing what, exactly? Every

other person they sent me was a wet blanket. They've wasted my time.'

'I guess that's part of the search, though,' I said. 'The match-making process,' I added jokingly, and immediately regretted it.

'This is what I'm going to do. I'm going to call the recruitment agency and tell them the search is off.'

'Oh?' My heart beat faster. If Connie mentioned my name to this recruitment agency, my cover would be blown. They would have no record of Laura Brown. The only person who knew my name was Rebecca.

Connie misunderstood my hesitation and raised an eyebrow. 'Do your principles forbid you to agree?' she said.

My mind was racing. 'I'll call the recruiters myself,' I said. 'Tell them I'm not interested in the job any more. To take me off their books. I could tell them I've found something else?'

Connie nodded. A paranoid part of me wondered if some suspicion she held about me had been confirmed. But if this was the case, why was she so keen to take me on? 'You should probably do that,' she said. 'But I'm going to let them know I'm not looking any more.'

'OK,' I said. This couldn't end well.

'And then come to me privately,' Connie went on. 'I'll pay you direct, in cash. And I'll tell Rebecca that the recruitment agency has found me someone and I'm finalizing the details myself.'

I felt slightly lightheaded. 'But – won't Rebecca want to sort it for you herself?'

Connie shrugged. 'Unlikely. It's hardly her remit, and she was a bit miffed having to deal with it in the first place. She thinks I'm cantankerous and I'm sure she's scared of me.'

I thought back to Rebecca's harried manner on the phone, her desire to get this matter off her hands as soon as possible.

We need someone urgently. There was every chance these two facts might work in my favour.

Connie smiled. 'All right. It's settled. Good to save a bit of money, don't you think?'

'Yes,' I said, feeling the adrenaline drop through me. 'I suppose it is.'

I was worried, but I decided not to over-think it, and to see instead how far my luck would take me. I imagined the rooms above our heads right now, cupboards and drawers full of letters and diaries – even photos – that might contain a portrait of my mother, and by extension, me. If finding them meant cooking some vats of bolognese, I would take the risk..

'Excellent, Laura,' said Constance. 'Right then. I've got a good feeling about you. When can you start?'

*

We said goodbye, agreeing that I would come at ten a.m. in two weeks on the Monday. I walked to the station feeling extraordinary. Connie's invitation to go inside her world had wrapped its shining bonds around me as if I were a chrysalis she'd spun with her crooked fingers. For thirty-four years, I had offered the world one version of myself. Within minutes of Connie's company, I'd cast it off.

15

Joe's reaction to my job news was decidedly underwhelming. 'I don't think this is a good idea,' he said.

'Why not?' I snapped. 'You're always telling me the coffee shop has no room for development.'

'Oh come on, Rose. You know why not. This is *weird*. Are you going to tell this woman what you know about her from your dad?'

'Not yet.'

He tipped his head back and closed his eyes. 'You're in her house. And you're going to lie to her.'

'No, I'm just not going to tell her.'

'Won't she see your surname and ask questions?'

'I'm not using my real name,' I said.

Joe put his head in his hands. 'Oh, god. Rosie, no. This is dangerous.'

'It's fine. I needed – to protect myself.'

'It's not fine. It's not fine at all. What are you *doing*?'

'I don't know!' I shouted. 'I just – I just wanted to do it, OK? I needed to do something. To change something.'

He looked at me in alarm. 'To change something?'

I could feel tears coming. 'Yes.' The last thing I wanted was for him to voice the very doubts I had myself. I didn't want someone I trusted thinking this was a bad idea, a sort of madness. 'I just wanted to *see*,' I said. 'You wouldn't understand.'

'You could be arrested for this.'

'I'm not going to be arrested.'

He sighed. 'Well, I don't want you to be disappointed.'

'Trust me, Joe. When it comes to my mother I couldn't be any more disappointed than I already am.'

He put his hand on my shoulder. It felt like a lead weight and I wanted to shake it off, but I knew that would shoot us into the next level of an argument and I couldn't face it. 'You might get hurt,' he said.

'She's an old woman, Joe. What's she going to do – batter me to death with her walking stick?'

'Rosie, you know that's not what I mean. I know I can't ever understand what it must be like for you, to know your mum left. And to not have any answers. But I really don't think this is a good idea.'

'Well, I'm doing it. And you can hardly talk about good ideas.'

'What's that supposed to mean?'

'Joe, I have supported you with your burritos and your van, and all of it, for *so long*.'

'Rose, they are very different things—'

'—And I'm asking you to support me. In this one thing. No questions asked. Just support me.'

'OK,' he said, but I felt it was only to defuse the situation, to draw my voice back down the vocal scale where it had been creeping up to 'shrill'.

'Does your dad know?' he said.

'No, and I don't want him to. It's just too complicated. This is my thing.'

'OK,' said Joe, looking miserable. 'OK.'

*

That night, I texted Kel: can we have dinner? Got something to tell you.

She replied: ??? I can do Tuesday night?

I waited to see if this would actually be the case, because there would often be last-minute cancellations as she and Dan juggled childcare. We agreed to meet at our favourite place, a ramen restaurant down a tiny passage in Soho, where the windows were always steamed up and the *bao* were always sublime.

'So?' she said, sliding onto her bar stool, and breaking open a pair of chopsticks, even though we hadn't ordered yet.

'I've got a new job,' I said.

I saw it, the moment – so brief, but so finite in her eyes – of disappointment. It pricked my heart, and I realized then how much I'd been pinning my hopes on her. But Kelly had been waiting for me to tell her that I was pregnant; that was the hope she'd been pinning on me. I just knew it. She knew my ups and downs around the issue of motherhood, and she wanted them conclusively solved. News of a baby would have brought her more joy than news of a job. My best friend, who loved *her* work so much, who knew how hard I was fighting to find my path.

'Oh my god!' she said. 'Good on you. What is it?'

'I'm working as an assistant to that novelist I mentioned to you.'

'The novelist?'

I sighed inwardly. This often happened. These days, Kel would be very present in our meet-ups, enthusiastic and open – but she would not absorb all the information we exchanged, like in the old days. We used to be each other's existential encyclopaedias, no chapter of the other not covered in notes and marginalia. But the holes in her attention had been widening since Mol was born. I didn't usually mind; I knew it was part of our evolution, and I loved Mol, dearly. I knew we couldn't be fourteen for ever, and I didn't presume that the flotsam and jetsam of my life were compulsively memorable. But this oversight of hers that day bothered me. This job was really important. It signified the beginning of something new for me – a new *me*, potentially.

'The novelist, Constance Holden?' I said. She still looked blank. 'The one that Dad says knew my mum. The *lover*.'

Then it dawned on her. 'Oh, my god,' she said. 'Are you serious?'

I nodded.

'Fuck. That's pretty meta.'

'Is it?'

She looked at me with one eyebrow firmly raised. 'Yeah. It is. Does she know who you are?'

'No. I've used an alias.'

At that point, Kelly just stared at me. 'You've *what*?'

'You heard me. I've used another name.'

I wanted Kelly to laugh at my audacity, my unwillingness to leave my past, my potential future, in the hands of someone else. I was taking destiny by the horns, something she was always telling her Instagram followers to do. But she didn't say a bloody thing. She just carried on staring at me. The waiter came up to us and we both ordered *tonkotsu*.

'Are you going to say something?' I said.

'I don't know what to say. How did Joe react?'

'He wasn't particularly enthusiastic,' I said. 'I want a beer.' I got the waiter's attention. 'Do you want one?' I said. She patted her bump. 'Oh, sorry. Course.'

'He's probably worried,' said Kelly.

'I'm just a bit bummed out that nobody seems to want to support me in this.'

'It's just a bit . . . it's a bit out there, Rose. What's the name you're using?'

'Laura Brown.'

She took this in. 'Rose, isn't this a bit of a – fantasy?'

I swallowed the urge to snap at her. 'That's exactly why I'm doing it. Because everything's been too much of a fantasy. I'm trying to get to the truth.'

'But if you're trying to get to the truth, why don't you just tell her who you are? You've waited all your life for this.'

'Exactly,' I said. 'I can't go straight in there and tell her. My dad said she's quite a strong personality, and from what I've seen of her, he's right. I don't know what happened between her and my mum, and apparently neither does he. If I tell her who I really am, Connie might kick me out. She might deny it. And then I'll have lost that one link to my mum. For ever.'

'If, indeed, she *is* a link,' said Kelly gently.

'They definitely knew each other. Dad was pretty adamant about that. And if she is the only surviving link, I need to get to know her. I need to keep her close. I need her to trust me.'

'How's she going to trust you if she finds out you've used another name?'

'Because she's not going to find out,' I said.

'OK,' she said. 'OK. Just bloody text me when you're there, all right? She might poison you or something.'

'Why would she do that?'

'I don't know! You don't know her!'

'That's just a really weird thing to say,' I said.

We sat in uncomfortable silence, and to our relief the ramen arrived.

'How's Dan?' I said, taking a spoonful of the broth. 'Oh, god, this stuff is so good.'

'Working all the time,' Kelly said. 'How's Joe?'

'The opposite.'

This could have been funny – it could have been an opportunity to rescue our evening, but Kelly wasn't having any of it. 'You can break up with him, you know,' she said. I looked at her, my chopsticks aloft. Her jaw was set in a dangerously determined way I'd been witness to for nearly twenty-five years. 'He won't *die*, Rose,' she said.

'I know that, Kel. I know he won't die.'

'No, I don't think you do, Rosie. I actually don't think you do. Somewhere, deep inside of you is this . . . *belief* that this is *it*. This is the *bond*. That it's better to be in this twosome of yours. Even if – you might not be happy.'

'Kelly.' I could feel my hackles rising.

'He doesn't even have a job,' she said.

'He's got the burri—'

She held up her chopsticks as if to ward off evil. 'Oh my gosh. Do not even say that word to me again.'

'Fine.'

'And what about the sex?'

'What *about* the sex?'

'Well, from what you've told me recently, it's not been great. I mean I'm not one to talk, 'cos I'm not even having sex right now. We're just too tired.' She sighed. 'I'm sorry. I don't know, Rosie. It's just – you don't look at him after nine years and think, *"be the father of my children"*?'

I stared at her. 'Wow,' I said, my voice rough, my face hot. I knew there was some sense in what she was saying, but I wasn't going to give up. 'What have children got to do with this?'

'I just – someone needs to *tell* you this. I'm trying to help. Really. I'm sorry. And the thing is – you always seem to think that everyone else is in a better boat than you. And it's bullshit.'

'I—'

'I'm *exhausted*,' Kelly said. 'I am more tired than I've ever been in my entire life. And I sometimes feel like I'm carrying *all* of us.' Her voice started to break. 'And Dan's just lapping up the rewards of it. He goes off to work every day and doesn't see even a quarter of what I do. And I think so much that I can hardly sleep. And this baby is cracking up my skin all over me, and I'm not ready for that. I'm not ready.' She stopped, breathing heavily. To my astonishment, she was crying. Kelly never cried.

I shot my hand out towards hers. 'Kel,' I said. 'You're right. Oh, god, I'm so sorry.'

She took my hand and squeezed it. 'It's OK,' she said. 'I get it. It's OK.'

1982

16

Barbara had developed a habit of telephoning Connie and Elise's bungalow on a regular basis. It irritated Elise the way Connie leapt up like a girl on prom night whose date has rung the doorbell. She would carry the telephone into the bedroom, and it was understood between them that Elise should not follow: this was work, this was important. Elise loathed the curling cord that stretched like a dead snake up the hallway. To compound her frustration, there was so little for her to do. She could have picked up her own notepad, of course, but she felt overwhelmed by a sort of stupor in this place. The activity and bustle and fast-talking of the other people she had met made her feel as if her limbs were clay.

She and Connie were lying side by side at the pool, immobile on their sun loungers, when the telephone rang again. Connie jumped up.

'Did you know that Lowden isn't really Barbara's surname?' Elise called after her. 'Born Betty Sheinkovitz.'

'Who told you that?' said Connie, but she didn't stop to hear the answer.

It was Matt, in fact, who had told Elise. Matt who had told her that it was no wonder, with a name like that, that Barbara had wanted to escape the South. *Does anyone in this town use their real name?* she had asked, and he'd laughed.

★

About fifteen minutes later, Connie returned. 'Barb wants this film to win her an Oscar,' she said, grinning.

Elise grimaced. 'That was why she was calling?'

'Yep.' Connie sounded defensive. She plonked herself down on her lounger.

'And will it?'

'I've no clue, darling. But that's what Barb wants. She says Don will make healthy box-office figures, so it'll definitely sell tickets.' Don Gullick was the actor who had been cast to play Frederick, opposite Barbara. He was, alas for Barbara, more on the meathead side than the sensitive Hamlet type. For all Eric's protests of agreement with her, they had turned out to be platitudes.

'Barb says there's no way she and Lucy can pull off receipts like his, even as a pair,' said Connie. 'Can you believe that?'

Barb, Barb, Barb. If she wasn't so annoyed, Elise would have smiled at the painful irony of Barbara's nickname in her side. 'Well, it's not *Barb*'s film,' she said. 'It's not a one-woman show.'

'It is, in a way,' said Connie. 'I feel for her. I don't know if Don can actually *act*.'

Connie cared about the film; that was understandable. She was alive inside it: invested, important. But Elise felt lost. She was trying very hard not to feel like the odd one out, but she couldn't help it.

'Do they all know we're together?' she asked Connie. 'I mean, Shara and Matt know – but does Barbara? Do the rest of them? Do they . . . understand?'

'Of course they do.'

'And what do they think about it?'

'I should think they couldn't care less. Why on earth do you ask?'

'I just – I don't know. You never actually introduced me as your girlfriend.'

'I didn't think there was a need. I thought it was perfectly obvious who you are.'

'So who am I?' Elise said, sitting up.

'I'm sorry?'

'Who am I?'

Connie lifted her sunglasses and squinted, before quickly putting them back on her face. 'Are you all right?' she said.

Elise didn't want to cry. She didn't want to need anything, or anyone. But it was too late: she wanted Connie – her strength, her love and the giddy pleasure of being the central object of such a person's affections. She slapped her sun lounger with both palms. 'Why am I here?'

Connie, alarmed, sat up and swung her legs round to face Elise. She swiftly changed sun loungers and embraced her. 'You're here because I love you,' she said. 'Because I need you. Because you're special. No one I've ever met has made me think these things.'

'So I'm here for you.'

Connie thought about this. 'Well, yes. I suppose you are. But you're more than welcome to make of the experience what you will. I didn't *drag* you here, El. I want you to enjoy it.'

'But you never say those things to me any more,' Elise replied, mumbling into the top of Connie's arm. 'The things you said at the beginning.'

'What things?'

'That you needed me. That I'm special.'

'I'm sorry,' Connie said, holding her tightly and kissing the top of her head. 'I do need you. You are special.'

*

The storm between them blew out of the garden without breaking over their heads. Elise felt both vindicated, and chastened. Connie was neglectful at times, it was true, and Elise didn't want to be pitied like Shara. Nevertheless, she still felt that the expression of any autonomy, of self-confidence or demand, would make her position precarious. When she expressed what she wanted – Connie's attention, which really meant Connie's respect and love – she sounded childish, and felt as if she was being indulged. Elise stared at the water. She did not want to be a mermaid any more. She wanted to feel part of the earth.

*

Connie took her to a day of filming. Inside the hangar, Barbara strode towards them in a billowing kimono, a cotton bonnet tied tightly over her head. Elise's heart sank. Only weeks before, she'd been so excited to meet Barbara, but now it was as if the woman approached her and she couldn't think, couldn't breathe. She was too much. Barbara was wearing no make-up, but her skin was perfect, giving her the appearance of a luminescent boiled egg. Her breasts had been spectacularly trussed together in a corset. 'I know,' said Barbara, pointing to them. 'I should wear this get-up every day. But any higher and I'd have problems getting cutlery in my mouth.'

Through the open doors, Elise saw a crocodile of lumpen extras being walked along the side of the road, all of them in Hollywood's peasant palette; dun, a little cranberry, shifting shades of dirty cream. 'Who are they?' she asked.

'They're making a film about the founding fathers,' Barbara snorted as Connie craned her head to watch them go. 'Welcome to the New World. Come and wait in my dressing room, ladies. I've got ages before my scene.'

Out in the July sunshine, Barbara hoicked herself up onto a waiting golf buggy, and Elise and Connie sat on either side of her. Her kimono was so enormous that it crept over Connie's and Elise's laps, mushrooming over the sides of the vehicle. The hem shimmered under the sun like the edge of a gigantic manta ray. Barbara reached down into the line between her breasts, accidentally elbowing Elise in the ribs as she pulled out a cigarette and a lighter, jamming the cigarette in her mouth like a cowboy, a clash with her Calvinist hair-protector.

'My emergency smoke,' said Barbara. 'Do you feel it, Elise?'

'Feel what?'

Barbara dragged on her cigarette and blew out a grey plume. 'The *beginning*. I love beginnings.'

'So do I,' said Connie.

Barbara prodded Connie's forearm. 'It's the middle and the end that are the fuckers.'

Connie laughed, squinting up at the cerulean sky. 'Maybe just the middle.'

Barbara shaded her eyes as they trundled along. 'I'm exhausted.'

'Don't you want to be alone to prepare yourself?' asked Elise.

Barbara sniffed. 'No, no.' She paused. 'My ex-husband is being a total bastard,' she said, out of nowhere. Her voice was raw, her hands quivered in her lap before she stilled them. She looked at Connie. 'He came round again at one a.m., Con.'

'Oh, god. I'm sorry,' said Connie.

Con. Con and Barb. Barbara seemed so at ease spilling herself out to Connie – or maybe it was just because Barbara was so used to reading about herself, seeing herself outside of the immediate, intimate circle of her life – outside of *herself*, in fact – that she did not think talking so openly in this way would ever harm her. Elise thought Barbara's life experiences under public exposure would have sealed her mouth by now, but perhaps you forgot how to live any other way.

'He wants money,' said Barbara. 'He knows I'm doing this film so that's when he comes truffling.'

'Did you give him any?' asked Elise, trying to keep inside the flow of conversation.

Barbara swivelled to face Elise. 'Never get married, honey. If that's the one piece of advice I've got for you, that's it.'

'Why would I get married?' Elise said.

Barbara did not reply. Elise reflected that Barbara, with her four ex-husbands, had never seemed to heed that particular nugget of advice herself. Barbara and Connie talked on and on, and Elise tuned out, her eyes closed in the sun.

Privately, she considered the idea of marriage – in which you became one joined person, one *new* person – to be utterly irresistible. To think: you could annihilate yourself like that, and everyone approved! It was so hard to continually *be* a person. Imagine finding a better self of thoughtfulness and kindness, your own heart transformed in the night, just by lying next to theirs! Imagine letting them take the lead in a way that *still felt* as if you were shoulder to shoulder! That it could be so easy!

With Connie these days, it was not that easy.

Elise thought as the buggy still trundled: *I could get a plane to New York City.* She'd never been, but she did not need to ask Connie about New York City as she had enquired about LA – because everyone knew what New York was: yellow taxis, Greenwich Village, bagels and Tiffany's. The blue of Hockney's swimming pool dissolved into a vision of the russet leaves of Central Park. Elise thought of *The Great Gatsby*, and the song 'I'd be rich as Rockefeller!' and pizza cooked by immigrants from Naples, like Bill Gazzara's father. She willed herself there like Dorothy, but when she opened her eyes again, the three of them were on the golf buggy, still trundling the lots.

★

Barbara's dressing room was surprisingly spare in terms of furniture; a long shelf attached to the wall, surrounded by a huge mirror lined with many little glowing lightbulbs, a low-slung red velvet sofa, an incongruous wooden farmhouse chair, and a clothes rail, upon which hung the outfits for Beatrice Jones. On the shelf Elise saw make-up brushes, pots and potions, a heavily folded and pencilled script, a bottle of water, one of vodka, three used glasses and a smattering of good-luck cards. Next to these, a huge bouquet of lilies, a fruit basket and an overflowing ashtray. A small fridge hummed in the corner.

Barbara delicately scrunched the cellophane of the fruit basket with her forefinger and thumb. 'You girls want an apple?'

They both declined.

'They always send me fruit but the acid's such a bitch. A beer, then? Take a seat.'

Connie and Elise sat on the sofa. It was deceptively uncomfortable. This all felt strange. Again, Elise didn't think it was *normal* for a star of Barbara's status to invite them into her inner sanctuary. Surely such a person should be guarded and dismissive? Why was this happening? Barbara rustled to the fridge and pulled out two bottles of beer. She opened them with a sharp blow and handed them over. Bewildered, Elise took hers and sipped. 'Thank you,' she said. Connie was already drinking hers.

Barbara collapsed on the wooden chair. 'So are you two decided yet whether you're gonna come with us to the Catskills?'

Neither woman said anything, and Barbara laughed. 'Oh, jeez. It's like that, is it?' Elise wanted to hit her. 'Lucy's right.'

'Lucy Crenshaw?' said Connie. 'What's it got to do with her?'

'We were just wondering,' said Barbara, looking at Elise. 'We thought you might have had enough of it here.'

Connie took another swig of her beer. 'Why would you think that? We're staying.'

'Great,' said Barbara. 'How's the beer?'

'It's cold,' said Elise.

Barbara patted her corset sides. 'I'd kill for one,' she said. 'But I won't. Imagine being gassy in this contraption. My tits would inflate even more and they'd have to pull me out of the lighting rig.'

Elise felt mildly stupefied. The surface elements of Barbara's personality were pressing her down, but it was the sudden news that they were going to be staying in America that knocked her sideways. She gripped her beer bottle. When, exactly, had Connie been planning to tell her this? Provoked by Barbara, had she just made up her mind, *now*? Elise began to bristle. As Connie's younger partner, with no discernible talent herself, she felt she had to be always solicitous, alert, smiling – and she was beginning to find it very difficult. She just wanted Connie to look at her with the same levels of admiration she looked at Barbara – to talk to her with the same confidence she spoke to Bill or Matt.

Suddenly, Elise wished she'd taken Matt up on his offer of surfing. To be on the water now, even to be walking along the shore – rather than here, in this airless room with its basket of unwanted fruit and intense lightbulbs. Exhausted, she shuffled to the back of the sofa, clutching the beer bottle tightly.

'You OK, honey?' Barbara said, undoing the knot of her white cotton bonnet and revealing a head of rollers. She looked more human, but her face still vacuumed up attention like something supernatural.

'I'm a little faint, but OK, thank you.'

'Do you need fresh air?' said Barbara.

'Do you need to go home?' asked Connie.

*

Barbara called for the production manager to get her a car back to the bungalow. Elise protested that she didn't need it, that she was fine. Connie said she looked pale, and an afternoon by the pool would be better. She gave up trying to protest, and left Connie and Barbara in the dressing room.

'Is she really OK?' she heard Barbara say to Connie, through the door. 'Did she really want to be alone?'

'She'll be fine.'

'Con, you should go with her. She's just a kid.'

'If I treated her like a kid, Barb, she'd hate that even more.'

Elise wasn't really ill, but she'd wanted to get away from Barbara and have Connie come with her. Alone with Connie was where she wanted to be. Wandering the corridor towards the rectangle of light at the end, Elise stepped slowly along the linoleum. She wanted nothing more than to leave – to go back to London, just her and Connie. She felt, with a painful, exhilarating awareness, that the new life she had gripped onto was sliding through her fingers. She stood outside in the sunshine and waited to be picked up, watching the extras filing out of another hangar; centurions from Rome, their helmets glinting in the sun.

*

Elise knew she could not control Connie. She could not know everything about her, and she never could. She did not know whether the words Connie spoke to her were words she'd said before, or words she would say again, to another. There was no anchor here.

When she got home, she went straight to the telephone and dialled Matt and Shara's number in Malibu. It was Matt who answered.

'It's me,' she said.

'Elise,' he replied. 'How are you?'

'I'm OK,' she said. 'I was wondering – is Shara there?'

'Shara?'

'Yes.'

'Hold on.'

There was a pause, the sound of footsteps. Elise waited. Finally, Shara picked up the handset. 'Hi, Elise,' she said. 'What's up?'

'Can I model for you?' Elise said.

'I'm sorry?'

'For a painting. Do you need a model?'

There was a pause. 'Oh – well. I mean, the work I've been doing is more abstract, Elise. I'm really sorry, but I'm not using models at the moment.'

Elise felt an inexplicable wall of rage rise up inside her. 'Of course,' she said. 'I'm sorry. It was a stupid idea.'

'No – it's a lovely offer. I'm just sorry that how I'm working at the moment doesn't—'

'You don't have to explain,' said Elise. 'I'm really sorry I asked, Shara. I shouldn't have asked. I guess we'll see you soon.'

'Hey—'

But Elise put down the telephone before she could hear any more.

2017

17

The first Monday working for Connie, in the middle of October, I arrived shortly after ten in the morning. She gave me a key immediately, because she couldn't be bothered to walk all the way downstairs to open the front door every day. As far as I knew she didn't eat breakfast, because I went straight to the kitchen to make coffee and the place was spotless.

'I like it from this stove-top pot,' Connie said. 'But you must watch very carefully to make sure it doesn't boil over on the hob.'

'Got it.'

'Also, Laura, please open my post for me.'

'Are you sure?'

Connie blinked at me owlishly. 'I never get sent anything of much interest, and I can't be bothered faffing for thirty minutes trying to open an envelope telling me I could get better broadband with someone else.'

It was a second element of her privacy which Connie ceded without a thought. I wondered if she wasn't bothered much by my being able to walk into her house and open her letters, because the real privacy was in her head, a place I could never access. 'Also, Laura,' she added, as if she was reading my mind, 'I barely get any post.'

*

At one o'clock, Connie came down for a lunch that I'd made. She liked nursery food, apparently: ham sandwiches, carrot sticks, a packet of crisps, easy on the fingers. When I looked in the biscuit tin, I found out one secret at least: Constance loved chocolate.

'I told the recruitment agency I found something else,' I said.

'Ah.'

'Did you tell Rebecca that you'd – taken someone on?'

'I did,' said Connie, finishing the last of her sandwich with acute concentration. I waited for her to stop eating, to place the crust back on the plate, to ask me what kind of impostor I was, to get out of her house for ever. I felt like I was waiting for an axe to fall.

'She didn't want to know any more?' I ventured.

Connie made a small grunting sound. 'Not until I'm found dead at the bottom of the stairs, three weeks after not returning her calls, would Rebecca ever exert herself for me beyond the bare minimum. Speaking of which, did you see Fiona Wilkins died at the weekend?' she went on, ripping into a Lion bar.

'No,' I replied, pulling out a tray of carrot muffins I'd decided to make. 'How awful.'

'She's been dying for about thirty years. I thought she was already dead.'

Fiona Wilkins; a novelist who was not as good as Connie, but immensely popular and absolutely loaded, thanks to a series of novels based on a nun-detective called Giovanna, battling the Pope and his assassins in sixteenth-century Rome. It had been a long-running TV series. I hadn't seen the TV version, but I'd loved every one of the books. Fiona Wilkins; who had lived near to Connie, had probably tried to be friends, and clearly failed, miserably.

'I wish I'd written a nun-detective,' said Connie. 'Still, you can't take your royalties to Heaven. Or maybe you can? Poor Fiona Wilkins. We're all bloody dying.'

'You're not.'

'I am. Still, she was older than me, at least. Could you make some tea? Did you get yourself a chocolate bar from the tin?'

'No.'

'Oh, for god's sake, Laura.'

'I don't like chocolate.'

'Who doesn't like chocolate? Did I know this about you?'

'It wasn't in the interview,' I said, and she chuckled.

I turned on the kettle. 'Do you know she had six children?' said Connie. She'd finished the Lion bar, and had moved on to a Bounty. I worried briefly about the risk of diabetes. 'Six fucking children. And where are they now?'

'Probably at her bedside?'

'And her husband was *useless*. No wonder every novel was the same.'

'I liked them.'

'What?'

'I thought they were very readable! And well researched,' I said. 'And actually they were all quite different.'

'The nun solved everything in the end?'

'Yes.'

'And got into scrapes, but always made it?'

'Of course.'

Connie sniffed. 'Repetition does take talent. Perhaps we should send flowers.'

'I can organize that,' I said.

'All right. You do that.'

Connie sighed. She could be an old lady when she was tired. Almost. Her eyes couldn't keep their brightness, her caustic wit was quiet. I felt suddenly guilty as to why I had sought her out, the answers I was planning to extract from her. And I wondered: how many books were left inside that mind? I realized I would like to read Connie's version of Giovanna the nun-detective. It would have been spectacular. But it was probably too late.

'She wrote that dreadful memoir,' Connie said. 'What was it called? *Writing My Wrongs*, or something. Christ. What's your take on memoirs?' she asked. 'Do you like reading them?'

'Depends whose memoir it is,' I said, bringing the mugs of tea to the kitchen table. 'I don't like the "long life lived" kind.' I placed Connie's steaming mug of tea before her.

'Oh,' she said. 'Please use coasters. I *hate* watermarks.'

'Of course,' I said, hastily laying out two cork coasters. She hates watermarks, but every mug is tatty as hell, I thought.

'Aren't they all dreadfully confessional?' she said. 'Self-absorbed?'

'It's sort of a requirement that they're self-absorbed, but I don't think that's a bad thing. Not if they say something to the reader.'

'I don't think people would identify with what I'd have to share,' she said.

I gripped my mug. 'Why not?'

'Well. I suppose I don't really mean that. What I really mean is that I don't want to share.'

'I'm sure you've been through a lot,' I said. 'Met a lot of people.'

Connie narrowed her eyes. 'I'd never write about it. It's why I'm writing a novel.'

I hesitated, but decided to speak. 'I suppose there's the problem you might get sued if you write from real life. Things could come out of the woodwork.'

'Oh, that wouldn't happen to me,' said Connie. 'Everyone I want to write about is probably dead.'

A shiver went through my stomach. 'You're the last one standing?' I said.

Connie looked at me. 'Something like that.'

*

She wanted us to move to the front room, to go through her invoices. Connie did not do Internet banking; unbelievably, she was still sending cheques. I built up a fire – *Oh, I haven't had one of these in over two years!* – and it felt practically Dickensian. I enjoyed poring over her purchases, the simple bills she paid as a citizen of the United Kingdom: telephone, water, council, gas. I noted with interest that she gave generously to homelessness charities, literacy programmes and guide-dog training. I tried to divine from these facts some clue about my mother – had Elise been without a home once? Had Connie found her on the streets and taught her how to read? Had my mother then gone blind and found the change untenable? *Stop*, I said to myself. *Patience. Realism. Take your time.*

Connie, it seemed, liked good wine and good solid shoes, but she didn't spend her money much otherwise. I looked at her, her face deep in concentration as she tried her best to do a decent signature in her chequebook, and wondered how on earth this situation was going to play out. Was I actually going to sit and take her dictation, like some sort of clerk from the 1940s? I thought of Zoë's disappointed face when I told her I was leaving the coffee shop; Joe's and Kelly's looks of unease as I told them the details of this new job. *The woman who knew your mum? Are you sure that's a good idea?*

Of course I wasn't sure whether it was a good idea. But I

knew that despite the precariousness of my deception, one day in Connie's house felt more exciting and full of potential than three months' worth of shifts at a coffee shop. When I stepped into Connie's house, wasn't I a woman called Laura Brown – who, once upon a time, had worked in Costa Rica and had dreams of returning there one day? Laura had seen a jaguar, Laura had been to a sloth sanctuary. Laura was going to be energetic, confident, a brilliant baker of carrot muffins. Joe was just being disapproving because for once, *I* had had the crazy idea, *I* was the one who had dared to step outside our normal boundaries of behaviour.

*

That first week I hoovered, polished, dusted and cleaned, gaining access to all the other spaces I normally wouldn't go in. In the drawing room I picked up burnished photo frames, the pictures inside them quaint sepia windows onto another time – a mother in a forties blazer, a sprig pinned to her breast. A father, I supposed, in military garb. Connie as an infant, another small boy by her side. Their eyes soft, their minds unfathomable. In Connie's bathroom I eyed her masks, the bounty of creams and serums; her expensive mascara and lipstick cases that looked like ammunition in a personal war. One morning, I gently dabbed my own mouth with the shades of *Apricot Dream* and *Harlot's Red* – before wiping away the evidence with a piece of loo roll.

I ran my hands over her bathrobe; silk but nearly worn through in places, which simply added to its charm. Then her jewels, carelessly mounded in a large ceramic dish rimmed with a coiling serpent: beads of coral, Mexican silver, Edwardian gold studded with small rubies, silver earrings in the shape of laurel leaves. I felt as if I had been blind – or deprived of some sort of sense, at least – and was learning to see again, to smell, to touch my way into my mother's past. Yet I had not come across any photographs of an adult Connie, or another woman, and neither could I find any letters or documentation. I held fast to the hope, or perhaps the belief, that I would eventually find something in this house that would lead me to Elise.

The only two places I wasn't allowed were the bedroom in which Connie slept at the very top of the house, and her office. I don't think this was because Connie thought I might be a thief. I think it was because these spaces were psychologically off-limits to anyone but her, and I must be seen to respect that. And even if I was a thief, what was I here to rob? Something that had once belonged to me too, but might in the end prove impossible to steal.

We were having coffee on the first Friday morning when Connie asked me about Costa Rica. 'What attracted you to the place?' she said.

My skin went cold and my stomach loosened. Then I remembered: I was Laura, not Rose. Laura was not the type to get flustered. Laura had adventures, and skilfully recounted them. 'The jungle,' I said. 'I was looking for jaguars.'

To my astonishment, Connie's eyes lit up. It gave me a good feeling. 'Did you find any?' she said.

'No. They were very elusive. Lots of sloths, though.'

Connie laughed. 'And how were the children?'

'Oh, they were lovely. I miss them,' I said.

'Did they like learning English?'

'They did. Have you – travelled much?' I asked her.

She seemed to consider the question. 'I have.'

'Have you ever lived anywhere else?' I went on. 'I mean – out of England?'

'I have,' said Connie again, but despite her affirmative, her tone did not invite more response. Perhaps Laura Brown had been too bold.

*

At home, Joe asked me how it was. 'It's . . . very different to Clean Bean,' I said.

'Has there been any mention of your mum?'

'Not yet.'

'You haven't brought it up?'

'No!'

'I thought you wanted to know?'

'I do, Joe.'

'Then—'

'Just don't push it.'

'So what are you going to do now?'

I placed the envelope Connie had given me onto the kitchen table. 'Cash. Five hundred quid.'

'Wow.' He frowned. 'She goes to the bank to take this out?'

'She's not a recluse, Joe. She goes out.'

'I thought she was like a hundred years old?'

That night in bed, Joe rolled over to face me and started stroking my arm. 'What are you listening to?' he said.

I pulled out an earphone bud. 'An audiobook.'

'Good?'

'Yeah.'

He nuzzled my neck and didn't ask what audiobook. I was listening to *Green Rabbit*.

I loved her before I even met her, the narrator's voice was saying. *I loved her as an idea, and when she came into my life, she made me more myself.*

Joe continued to nuzzle me, and I let him. He must have

been thinking about my plea for the rescue of our lost passion, and he moved his mouth over my collarbone, over the starting curve of my breast. I closed my eyes and pulled out both earphones, pressing pause on the story in order to do what we'd done so many times before. As he entered me, I imagined I was made of a different body. Legs I'd had seen so many times in magazines. I imagined that Joe was not Joe, but a shadow in the back of my mind. That this was not South London, but a cool room in a hot country where outside everything was humid. A bed, with a curtain billowing, my life unhooked from any past or present, and the future not even a glimmer. Everything suspended, almost animated, nothing like the real.

I was Rose, but I was Laura. I didn't know which woman I wanted to be.

18

I did not know how long my being in Connie's house would work. Connie might press me more to open up about my life, and I would press too, and both of us would attempt to find out more about the other than she was willing to share. Her questions about Costa Rica were innocuous enough, but I wondered if we were embarking on a game that could only have one winner. I had another fear, too – that my father could be completely wrong about Connie. Connie might not know anything about what happened to my mother – Elise could have cut her out, just as she did my father. Maybe Connie was as much in the dark as he was. The only thing to do was stay in the position and see how things unfolded.

You've got to believe in yourself, Kelly would always say to me. I was trying, but I didn't know whether to believe more in Rose Simmons or Laura Brown. I liked being Laura. She was bolder, more efficient and funnier than Rose. Rose was a very different creature indeed. Less confident, more frightened. She had never travelled very far: she wanted to stay in the house. She didn't know what her life was supposed to be.

I couldn't decide how far to develop my deception. Could I, if I wanted, invent a whole new biography for myself? I could eradicate Joe. I could invent a mother who I'd always known and loved. A different address. A new life – as I day-dreamed about it, it shocked me how quickly I could find alternatives. I was currently single, though there was someone I was seeing casually – a museum curator, from New York whose name was Leo. I was seeing a woman, Carenza, a lawyer I met in a bar one night, who liked rock-climbing and was pestering me to go on some godawful action holiday that involved sheer cliff faces – oh, Carenza! – when I would rather sit by the hotel pool. I was a homebody, Carenza an adventuress, but somehow it worked. My parents lived in Bath, in Glasgow; they lived in a village near Dorking. They were happy, they were divorced, my mother, Sally, lived in Madrid, after falling in love with a Spanish real-estate developer. Let's call him Geraldo. I often went there for weekends, and Sally and Geraldo would load my hand luggage with the best *jamón*.

It came smoothly to me, this loosening the threads of my own identity, weaving a new one. How had it become this easy to let go of myself, to pour words and fantasy into these gaping holes?

But if this was what I was good at, why not do it? No one would get hurt because no one would know. I assumed Connie would probably ask me about Laura's life, and the more time we spent together the harder it would be for me to remain mute about it. And even if I made a story up, it wouldn't affect my being in Connie's house. If anything, it would act as a sort of protective shield, hiding my true self behind the verbal fortifications formed by a more exciting self. And, once I had the story of my mother I would depart, taking the trail of my fictions with me and leaving Connie with hers.

*

When it came to our next personal conversation, it seemed Connie had been thinking about all this too. About me, who I was, where I was from. Who I loved, what I wanted. Maybe Fiona Wilkins' death had made her more expansive and ruminating, leaving her wanting to reach out to the closest human in her vicinity. Maybe she was just warming to me. But I still resisted telling her my life story, real or imagined. I only wanted hers.

She asked me to go for a walk on the Heath with her, so we found her a scarf and hat and a thick padded jacket. Her fingers grabbed awkwardly at the edges of the woolly hat almost as if they belonged to a child, and again I was surprised at the contrast between the rest of Connie's elegant self and the snatchy, twitchy character of her hands.

It was a grey day, the sun hiding, but at least there was no rain.

'Laura Brown,' Connie said, as we crested the hill, playing with my name in her mouth. 'Are you married, Laura Brown?'

I laughed. 'Am I married? No.'

'Do you have a partner?'

'I do,' I said, and I thought of Joe, of Leo, of Carenza. I wondered what name would come out of my mouth, and was glad that Connie moved on.

'Children?'

'No.'

'Want them?'

I said nothing. 'I see,' said Connie.

'You see what?' I said.

She didn't say anything to that.

We carried on walking. I felt bruised and prodded and wanted to go back to the house, where it felt safer than being outside with her. Outside, the ludicrousness of my behaviour – the lying, the fact I was now her companion of sorts – felt magnified. I felt that at any moment I might be arrested. 'When I was twenty,' Connie said, breaking my thoughts, 'I wrote a set of poems for a girlfriend's birthday.'

'That was kind of you.'

Connie snorted. 'I was broke, that's why I wrote them. Couldn't afford a proper present. It's not because I thought I was a poet.' She stopped by a bench and lowered herself down. 'Although perhaps I did? After all, I wrote them. I don't remember any embarrassment in giving them to her.'

'What were they about?'

'I don't remember. Love, probably. My approximation of it. Of her, of myself. They weren't "twenty-one poems for a twenty-first birthday", nothing like that. But they were an effort, I do remember.'

'You didn't publish them?'

'God, no. No. Then we broke up, again. She left them in the boot of her car. An old jalopy that she wanted to be nicked, rather than have to deal with it. But it was nicked, and the poems were still in the boot, so they went too.'

'That's a bit shit of her.'

Connie shrugged. 'They were hers. She could do what she wanted with them. She wanted no reminder of me, so my poetry could be stolen too. But *then*, she decided she regretted this decision. When we were talking again, she asked if I could rewrite them, because despite the fact she'd deliberately left them in the boot, she wanted them back.'

'Did you rewrite them?'

'Absolutely not.'

'Good.'

'Her car was named after Sirius, the constellation,' Connie said, burying her chin in the top of her scarf. 'A few years after all this, I wrote another poem about it. *Sirius*, you know – the starry name, the idea of fate.' She rolled her eyes. '*So* clever. It was about the theft of the first poems. Her quite frankly arrogant request to have them re-written.'

'What did you do with the new poem?' I asked.

'Nothing. It wasn't very good. But here's the thing. My new girlfriend found it, and was upset that I was writing a poem about former lovers.'

I thought of my father's words: *For a time, they were inseparable.* 'She was the jealous type, the new one?' I asked, my heart thumping a little harder.

Connie looked away. *Say her name,* I thought. *Tell me her name.* 'You could say that,' she said. 'Bit of a firework. I threw the poem in the bin. I should have been more careful.'

'You were entitled to write the poem.'

Connie carried on idly observing the passers-by. 'I played out old mistakes on new people. Don't ever do that, Laura. I say that as someone who's been there.'

'Right,' I said, uneasily.

'Although it's what we all do,' Connie went on. 'You only get your heart broken for the first time once. But the pain always makes itself known in subsequent encounters, even if you don't realize it. Have you ever been heartbroken?'

I thought about this question for such a long time that Connie ended up turning round fully to me. 'Yes,' I said, but I was not thinking of lovers.

Perhaps there was something true in my voice, or heartfelt at least. 'It hurts, doesn't it?' she said gently.

'Yes.'

'This new novel is about responsibility,' she said suddenly, and it felt as if she was offering me a gift. 'It's called *The Mercurial.*'

'*The Mercurial?*'

'What I wanted to explain to that girlfriend of mine—'

'The one who was a firework?'

Connie smiled. 'Yes, the firework – or perhaps to myself – was that I was tracing a scar that never vanishes. Old lines under new skin. But the *writing* of it gives it a reconfigured present. What I would call art, as we experience it. It also helps us imagine our ideal futures.'

'Are you sure that's wise?'

Connie laughed. 'No. I'm twisting it all, but it's what I do. And being a person with no faith except in artistic culture – in fiction, say – doesn't make you better than someone who doesn't read books. In some ways, it makes you terrifying. Or terrified. Depends on the day. Isn't it an abnegation of reality? A person who needs to see an actor crying crocodile tears to understand the depths of grief, a person who needs a love poem to circle closer to the feeling – *she* might find it hard to live in the real world. She's arguably deficient.'

Connie was surprising me. She was getting emotional. 'Aren't we all a bit like that?' I said. 'The real world . . . can be too much.'

She batted the air with a claw-like hand. 'I'm not criticizing. I'm sure I'm in the majority. I need those actors. I need those love poems. I've found it hard, I've needed stories. Which I assume is patently obvious.'

'Except you haven't written for so long.'

Connie didn't like that. She sniffed and looked away. 'When you came to my house the first time, you said you'd read *Green Rabbit*.'

'I have.'

'And did you think I was Rabbit?'

'No. I thought she was a fiction.'

This wasn't strictly true.

Connie smiled. 'Good. Because that's the point. It's never

reality. That's the aim. But the problem is, no one can really say what reality actually is. It's just so slippery.'

'I know.'

She stood up. 'I'm ready. Let's go back. I need a cup of tea.'

19

A few days after this conversation, I was making pizza at Connie's kitchen table when she appeared at the door. 'Laura,' she said. 'Can you stay late? I've invited a guest and I was wondering whether you'd cook.'

'A guest?'

My voice was perceptibly tight. *Imagine*, I thought. *My mother, walking through that front door.*

'That's allowed, isn't it?' said Connie, raising an eyebrow.

'I'm sorry. Of course.'

'It's my agent. Deborah.'

'Your agent,' I repeated, feeling something inside me shrivel. I turned away to the kitchen counter. I was going mad – why did I think my mother would be coming round for dinner?

'Laura, is something wrong?'

'Not at all.' I gestured to the ball of pizza dough I'd been kneading. 'But I was just planning on leaving you a pizza.'

'Pizza will be lovely, thank you. And do you want to invite your partner?' Connie said.

'I'm sorry?'

'Your *partner*? Goodness, what's wrong with you?'

'Nothing. Honestly, I'm fine.'

'I don't even know your partner's name,' she said.

'It's Joe,' I replied, too flustered to think of a lie. Leo and

Carenza vanished in the face of Connie's curiosity. 'He's working tonight,' I said.

'What does he do?'

'He's – an antiques dealer.'

'How fabulous,' said Connie, sounding genuinely delighted. My face flushed red and I kept my back turned. I took a deep breath and thought about what Laura might say. 'What period?' Connie asked.

'Mainly early twentieth century,' I replied.

Connie made a noise of happiness. 'But why's he working tonight?'

'He's up in Yorkshire. There's a big house auction tomorrow and he wants to get first dibs.'

'Well, maybe he can come next time.'

'Thank you, Connie. That would be lovely.'

'Can you fancy up the pizza a bit? Not just pepperoni?'

'Of course I can. I did an Italian cookery course, actually. When I – went to Padua. Does Deborah have any allergies?'

'Padua? How marvellous. She hates anchovies. Everything else is fine.'

*

Connie wandered off, and I heard her office door close one floor up. I sat down at her kitchen table, grateful for the pizza dough under my fingers, the spongy mass yielding under pressure. I imagined Laura, living in a romantic garret in Padua, learning how to make tortellini parcels, proper ricotta and pizza, the best and simplest Italian way. I yearned to be that girl, who took herself off and did that kind of thing. I pulled away my hand and the dough swelled up like a bleached and bloated organ, resisting the imprints of my fingers to leave no trace. Joe the antiques dealer. I imagined him, wandering the endless aisles of an antiques market, looking for the perfect Deco table. Why couldn't I have said something easier, like a lawyer, or an accountant? No one was interested in asking more questions about them.

I just wanted Joe to seem interesting. I guess the same could be applied to myself.

Whether he was rifling through antiques or making burritos, there was no way I could have Joe here, but even worse than him was Deborah. Rapidly, I went through the scenarios. What if Connie told her I'd been sent from the recruitment agency, and Deborah said she'd never heard of me? They'd want answers. They might even call the police. What if Joe's warning about being arrested came true? It felt to me as if I'd gained a tiny foothold in this house – that my mother was a few millimetres closer than she'd ever been – and I couldn't lose this chance. I couldn't be here when Deborah came. I needed to move through Connie's rooms unchallenged by outsiders.

I left the dough in a bowl under some clingfilm, and went upstairs to speak to Connie. To my surprise, her office door was open. She was sitting at a narrow desk by the window which overlooked the garden and the backs of other houses. Connie hadn't heard me approach. She was bent over a yellow writing pad, the profile of her face fixed in concentration, but what I noticed most of all was that she was holding her pen much like a novice Westerner might a chopstick. Her grip was ungainly, unmasterful, lost in a series of actions and contexts that meant nothing to her.

I froze a few feet from the door: I knew I should not be witness to this.

'Fuck, fuck, *fuck*,' she said quietly, before throwing the pen down and putting her head in her hands.

I felt such pity. Whilst I cooked for her and sorted her paperwork, made her cups of tea and doled out her Lion bars, she was not up here writing endless reams of marvellous words, but instead was trying to keep hold of her pen.

I backed away. 'Laura,' she said.

I turned round, ashamed, and as our eyes met, I saw her shame too, which she quickly masked, sitting upright, resting one elbow elegantly on the edge of the desk.

'How long have you been standing there?' she said, her voice harsh. 'Do you make a habit of spying?'

'I'm very sorry,' I said. I wanted to tell her how brave I thought she was, but I suspected she'd hate that. She'd told me, of course – more than once – that her hands were bad, but seeing in the flesh how difficult writing was for her had a very different effect on me than seeing her fumble with a bottle of champagne.

I pretended none of it had happened. Laura Brown would be smooth about things like this: tactful, effortless. 'I only came to say I'm not feeling too good,' I said. 'Is it OK if I make the pizza and then leave tonight?

'Are you not well?' Connie replied. 'You seemed distracted downstairs. Is everything all right?'

'It's my period.' I was unable to think of anything else.

Her face softened. 'Bloody things. No pun intended. Of course, Laura – don't worry at all about the food. Go home. Rest. I'll call Deborah and tell her to pick something up in M&S. Do you need some paracetamol? There's some in my bathroom cabinet.'

I felt something release inside me; an invisible muscle I'd been holding tense without realizing. I wanted to rush over to Connie and hug her, even though I thought of her as not remotely huggable. I thought about my manager at Clean Bean, a man called Giles. When either me or Zoë had our periods, he couldn't give a shit that one of us was bent over double, or even, in Zoë's case, vomiting in the staff loo. *If men had periods*, Zoë had said under her breath, *there'd be twelve weeks' statutory leave a year, and tampons would be free.*

I felt guilty for enjoying Connie's care even though I was just a coward, hiding. 'I'll make your pizza,' I said. 'You can't serve your agent pre-made M&S.'

'I've done it before and no one died,' said Connie.

'But that's what I'm here for. So you can still have nice things.'

Connie looked touched, and as she turned to her notepad and gripped her pen once more, I saw the colour rising in her pale cheek. And again the question occurred to me – when was the last time Connie had someone think about her like this, care about her, existing in close quarters with her? Her readiness to care about me was a surprise, and I wondered how long the impulse, human and natural as it was, had been lying dormant.

'Yes,' said Connie. 'I suppose that's true. But go and have a lie down in the spare room. Take a paracetamol and have a nap, and if you're no better in a couple of hours, then please don't stay on my account.'

*

I decided to swallow the paracetamol, because that's what Laura would do, given that she said she had her period. I did have a bit of a headache, it was true. I went to the raised first-floor bedroom, which was small, with a single bed and striped mint-green wallpaper; prints in clip frames all round the walls of theatre posters dating as far back as 1975. There was a bookcase full of Connie's novels in different languages, but I didn't take them out, feeling yet again that Connie was being so generous, so unwitting, that I should not take advantage. My regard for Connie was fighting my desire to know more about my mother.

I lay on top of the bed, feeling it would be wrong to get

under the sheets. I wondered if Elise had ever come into this house, maybe even lain on this bed – and if so, how that had come to be, and when, and how it had all turned out? But almost as soon as my head touched the pillow, I fell asleep – immediately, deeply, the way a child can on a long car journey, or in their parents' arms.

When I woke up, Connie was standing over me. The light outside had faded to dusk, and the tentative, concerned expression on her face surprised me. 'Ah, she's awake,' she said. 'Deborah's here.'

'What?'

'You've been asleep for three hours.'

I sat bolt upright. '*Three hours?*'

'You were under an enchantment,' said Connie. 'Or periods do that to you. I can never sleep like that any more. The young are so lucky.'

'Oh, god,' I said. 'I'm so sorry.'

'Don't be silly. Pizzas don't take long. Come and meet Deb.'

*

I followed Connie into the front room. Deborah was standing by the mantelpiece. She was short, in her sixties, I thought, and her bright hard eyes gave little away. She was wearing a huge grey shawl, and her face was subservient to a pair of large green-framed glasses. Her hair was a tufty crop, sympathetically tinted, and she had a lot of expensive-looking perspex jewellery in assorted abstract shapes which hung round her neck and clicked on her fingers. She looked like an owl and was round like one too.

'Deb, this is Laura. She's my angel,' said Connie.

'Hello, Deborah,' I said, moving towards her. I was still groggy, but realized I would have to think on my feet. 'I'm Laura.' I shook her hand.

'The new assistant,' said Deborah, looking up at me with a not particularly friendly smile. 'Are you an angel, or a devil?'

'Ignore her, Laura,' said Connie.

Deborah shook my hand and assayed my face closely. 'Would both of you like a glass of champagne?' I said.

'Yes, please,' said Connie.

'No wonder Con likes you. Go on then,' said Deborah. 'Why not?'

I left them and went to the kitchen to pour the champagne. I took a few deep breaths, leaning on the kitchen counter, and when I came back Deborah was still by the mantelpiece, unwinding the shawl from her body. 'It's such a giant thing!' she said, billowing it out. 'Like a bloody picnic blanket. Davy bought it for my birthday. The dog'll only cover it in hairs.' She folded it in a neat rectangle on the side of the sofa. Connie excused herself and the door to the understairs loo clicked shut.

'How is she, then?' Deborah said to me. 'Hasn't frightened you off yet?'

I laughed. 'Not at all. I love working for Connie. I'm very lucky.'

'Connie thinks she's the lucky one,' said Deborah, sitting down with her glass of champagne. 'The previous one only lasted a week, so you definitely have the magic touch.'

'The previous one?' I said.

Deborah gave me a bland smile. I felt embarrassed, that I should be so naive to think I was the first of my kind, that because Laura's life had begun the moment I crossed her threshold, so had Connie's. Connie's life had been lived many times over compared to mine, and Deborah's words made me uneasy. I pictured a ghostly line of assistants past, lured in, all failing to live up to some undefined, impossible task.

'Oh well,' said Deborah with a wave of her hand. 'You're

here and Con likes you. That's all that matters. How did you find out about the position?'

My heart began to pound. 'I was sent here by my recruitment agency,' I said.

'Ah, yes. My assistant, Rebecca, was dealing with them.'

'They said Connie needed some help around the house and with her work,' I said quickly, in the hope she wouldn't ask me what they were called, knowing there was one flimsy Gmail account between me and a police cell. The thought of not just having to explain my lies, but to push the spectre of my mother into the laps of these women, was too much to bear.

'It's so exciting that Connie's writing a new novel,' I said, desperate to change the course of our conversation. 'After all this time.'

'I know,' said Deborah, frowning. 'But her hands aren't good.'

'That's why I'm here,' I said. Deborah looked at me sharply. 'She says it's about responsibility.'

Connie appeared again at the door. 'What's about responsibility?'

'*The Mercurial*, apparently,' said Deborah. 'According to your angel.'

'Oh, yes,' said Connie, sitting back down in her old armchair, as if she wasn't about to break a thirty-year hiatus from publishing a word. 'I told Laura that it's about responsibility,' she went on. 'But that's not all of it. I want to tell you the plot, Deb. OK?'

'OK,' said Deborah.

'There's a woman. There's always a woman,' said Connie, giving Deborah a wry look. 'She's called Margaret Gillespie.'

'Good name,' said Deborah, taking a judicious swig of champagne.

'It's London, 1626,' said Connie. 'Margaret's husband is a

devout Calvinist Puritan, so she sails with him to Massachusetts on a ship with their daughter, Christina. They join a colony there called Peabody. It's a real place. But Margaret's husband dies, and disease affects the entire colony, killing nearly half of it. She survives, as does Christina. Their life is hard. I wanted . . . dirt,' Connie said, folding her arms, and tucking her hands away, even as she expanded upon her inner world. 'They shouldn't be there in the first place, of course. But the man who drove them there is gone and they don't have the means to return. I wanted to write about what it means to love someone at the cost of yourself. Whether it's a good thing. Whether it's the point of everything. I think that propensity sometimes cripples Margaret. Love as difficulty. Now I don't want to be predictable, and people will say I'm being predictable, but there's an obnoxious presence.'

'An obnoxious presence?' I repeated.

'The obstacle,' said Connie. Her eyes were shining. 'He's a brute, under his guise of religious conviction. Davy Roper, Christina's new husband.'

'Davy?' said Deborah. 'That's my son's name, Con.'

'I know,' said Connie equably. 'I liked it. You don't mind?'

'No, I suppose not,' said Deborah, with a weariness in her voice that suggested she was quite used to this kind of thing.

'Davy is a bomb for Margaret and Christina,' Connie went on. 'He's a junior member of the colony elders, but he's on the up. Behind closed doors, he beats and rapes Christina. He even tries to beat Margaret to keep her in line, because she doesn't like the fact that he married her daughter. Margaret's beginning to bridle at her isolated status as an unprotected widow, and she and Davy often lock horns. She always argues with her daughter about Davy. She wants Christina to leave him, but Christina won't do it. Because Davy's their veneer of respectability. Then he starts spreading rumours about Margaret, and people become suspicious.'

'Why do they believe him?' I said.

Connie looked at me. 'Why would they not? He's one of the authorities. He's a man. Margaret's an outsider. And she's a good cook,' Connie went on. 'Which means she's good with herbs. So, Davy starts with his rhetoric. How did her husband really die? he asks the community. How did all the others in the colony *really* die? What are all those bits of dried bark and mushroom hanging in Margaret's cabin? Is she flirting with the name of witch?' Connie paused, taking a breath. 'When Christina becomes pregnant,' she said, 'Margaret offers to her that she can get rid of the child if she doesn't want it to have a life like they have under Davy. Christina decides she does not want the child. Margaret tries to help her. And then it all goes wrong.'

There was a silence in the room. 'What do you mean?' Deborah said eventually.

'The thing is,' said Connie. 'Everyone is always abandoning Margaret Gillespie. This is both her pleasure and her pain.'

'What does Margaret do, Connie?' said Deborah.

'She makes an abortifacient for Christina,' said Connie.

Deborah swallowed the last of her champagne. 'Right.'

'Christina takes it, and it kills her,' said Connie. Slowly, Deborah placed her champagne glass on the coffee table. 'And so Margaret has to start again.'

Sitting in this elegant living room in Hampstead, I felt an energy crackling into life: strange and cold and unfamiliar where all had been convivial. The hairs on the backs of my arms rose up, as if, in the corner, Margaret Gillespie and her daughter were manifesting from almost imperceptible shadows into a solid shape.

'Does . . . Margaret manage it?' I asked.

'Manage what?' said Connie.

'To start again?'

She smiled. 'You'll have to wait and see.'

'Is it fair to say that *The Mercurial* is a window onto difficult family dynamics?' said Deborah. 'Can I tell interested publishers that's what the novel offers?'

Connie wrinkled her nose. 'That sounds diminishing, Deb. What about when a man writes about family? People don't think he's really talking about his *family*. If a man writes about hoovering dust from the carpet they think he's talking about cleansing one's soul. But when a woman does the same, she's talking about the housework. This novel could be about the soul.'

'I know,' said Deb. 'But—'

'They think we're incapable of making stuff up. Seeing the bigger picture – when actually we've had to be the best liars in town, the best impersonators.'

I choked on my champagne and Connie turned to me. 'Are you all right?' she said.

'I'm fine.' I could hardly bear to look at her.

'All right,' said Deborah with a touch of exasperation. 'I won't be saying it's a window onto the nature of family. Although I do believe there's nothing wrong with writing about family.'

'Of course there isn't,' said Connie. 'Except the way it's received.'

Deborah lifted her empty glass off the table and we clinked glasses, toasting Connie's novel. 'I'd better check on the pizza,' I said.

'Thank you,' said Connie. 'All homemade, Deb. Do you know, Laura made the *base*.' She widened her eyes, as if I'd split the atom.

Deborah raised her glass in my direction, her face mask-like. 'Congratulations,' she said.

*

I was dying to go back, to eavesdrop on what they were talking about in my absence, but I focused on putting all the toppings on the pizza, throwing together a salad, and laying the table. This done, I tiptoed quietly along the corridor and waited outside the door. They were talking in low, insistent voices.

'Do you really want to drag all that up again?' Deborah was saying.

I felt my jaw go slack. I closed my eyes, willing the floor-boards not to give me away.

'It's just a novel, Deb,' Connie said. 'My business is to bridge reality with the presentation of reality. The important thing is what the bridge looks like, how it feels underfoot, where it takes us. Not why I in particular am the builder.'

'Con, I'm not stupid.'

'You don't understand, Deb.' Connie seemed to hesitate. 'You never did.'

There was a pause. 'You think I don't recognize where this has all come from?' said Deborah.

'It's fiction,' said Connie, an edge to her voice. 'Did everybody think Charlotte Brontë had been locked up in a red room when she was nine years old? That she secretly wanted to marry a sociopath who kept his first wife in an attic?'

They fell to silence. I could hear the fire crackle in the grate. 'You never meant any harm, Con,' Deborah said eventually.

Connie was still silent, and Deborah made a puffing sound of impatience. 'You don't know all of it,' Connie said.

'I was there. Half of it was in your head, Con. In your *head*.

I know it was a bad time, but he never blamed you. No one did. So why should you blame yourself?'

My heart began to pound. Was Deborah talking about my dad? The thought that Connie might be putting my mother in her new novel – and I might be the one to type it up, was unbearable yet irresistible. I bunched fists up to stop my hands from shaking.

'He didn't know the half of it, Deb. But if he had, he'd have blamed me.'

'Well, everyone had a part to play. Including him. Con, you were too hard on yourself. You didn't write for so long and it was such a waste. What's changed?'

Connie sighed. 'The fact that in a year or two I might not even be able to write my bloody name? Fiction doesn't put anything right, but at least it tries.'

'And now you've got this new girl in, getting her involved—'

'Laura's wonderful,' said Connie. On hearing those words, I felt so guilty. I was not wonderful. I had invaded Connie's house in the search for my mother. I was here for Elise, not Connie. And yet, hearing Connie say those words, I couldn't help feeling a rush of affection for her. Connie had seen value in me – or a version of me, at least. I wanted to cry.

'What are her qualifications?' said Deborah.

'She's got a degree. She's travelled, taught – she's been to Costa Rica.'

'But what does she get out of being here?' Deborah persisted.

'Jesus Christ, Deb. Not everyone has an ulterior motive. She needed a *job*. She wanted a change. I think she's had a difficult time. A bright girl like her, working in a coffee shop.'

'Oh, you and your girls with their difficult times. They fall at your feet and look where it leads you. I'm sorry. It's just – I care about you, Con. I want you to be all right.'

'I'm running out of time, Deb. One more story.'

Deborah exhaled: a long, drawn-out sigh of someone who has spent her whole life dealing with unorthodox, stubborn people. Shaken, exhilarated, I tiptoed slowly and silently down the corridor. Then I retraced my steps – loudly, this time, so the women could easily hear me. I went in and announced that in ten minutes the pizza would be ready.

*

They said nothing more of interest once I was in the room with them. Deborah made small talk and Connie was little more than monosyllabic. The evening felt ruined.

'Would you say *The Mercurial* is finished?' said Deborah.

'Not quite yet,' said Connie.

'Who's going to type it all up? I presume it's in longhand.'

'That's why I'm here,' I said. I turned to Connie. 'I'll type it up.'

'My handwriting's appalling,' said Connie.

'I'm the patient type.'

Connie smiled. 'I'll call you the patient typist.'

'OK,' said Deborah. 'When Laura's finished typing up the manuscript, we'll be good to go. Everyone at Artemis Press who worked on your books has long gone, Connie. Which means we could go anywhere. There's no contract. Could be a completely new approach. There's a lot playing in your favour. People think of you as an icon. You *are* an icon. This is the long-awaited third novel from a literary genius who hid away.'

'Oh *god*,' said Connie.

'But also the market's very different from when we were starting out, Con. Publishers are different. You'll have to be prepared for that. So will I.' Deborah pushed her glasses onto her head. 'After you called me about this, I did mention that you were writing a novel to a select few. You know, to get them excited. Word spread as it always does, and I've had interest from a couple of film producers to look at the manuscript. One at Paramount and one at Silvercrest.'

'Silvercrest,' Connie said. 'You went to *Silvercrest*?'

'I didn't *go* to them, Con. I just said. They called me.'

But Connie looked furious. I had no idea why having the interest of one of the most famous movie studios in the world would be so enraging.

'Let's just get the manuscript typed up, and finished, and see what they say, eh?' said Deborah placatingly.

'Just not Silvercrest.'

'All right.' Deborah chewed her lip. 'Georgina Hyatt might be interested in this book,' she said.

'Who the hell's Georgina Hyatt?' said Connie.

'She's an editor at Griffin Books. A little older than you, Laura. She'd love this. She's a huge fan of yours, Con.'

'I don't know whether that's a good thing or a bad thing,' said Connie.

'Why?'

'Well, this one's different.' Connie paused. 'Do you think people will actually be interested in this?' she said. 'Will people actually *want* it?'

'Of course, Con. I know they will.'

'I just don't want to be one of those poor bloody women resurrected as a "forgotten masterpiece". It's this awful sort of righteous kid-glovery. A book's qualities are never elevated by the word "forgotten". It makes it seem like it's your fault, as if you deserved obsolescence in the first place.'

'Tell that to the forgotten women,' said Deborah.

*

Deborah did not stay for pudding: she claimed she had to get home to take the dog for a walk. I offered to see her out. She and I stood on the doorstep as Connie pottered in the kitchen, gingerly trying to load the dishwasher. It felt as if Deborah and I were both waiting for the sound of a smashing plate.

'Her hands really aren't good,' murmured Deborah.

'I know.'

She pulled the front door almost closed. 'Over the years, Connie's had a lot of girls and women drawn to her,' she said. 'It's a Plath thing.'

'A what?'

'Except Connie made it through alive, of course. Instead of visiting a grave, these women want to get into her *life*. Are you one of them?'

Even as I was taken aback by her forthrightness, I was so tempted to ask Deborah whether one of those girls was called Elise Morceau. Had my mother been lured into Connie's orbit, or had it been the other way round? Who had fallen first? And was I one of those girls too? Not here for romantic reasons, but still desirous nevertheless to peel back the layers of Connie's life, hoping to find my mother underneath.

'I'm not,' I said. 'I just wanted an interesting job.'

Deborah sighed. 'Fine. You know, when she was writing the last time, she wasn't always easy to deal with. She didn't like talking to journalists, and I don't see why that would be any different now.'

'Why didn't she like it?' I said, feigning concern in order to seize my chance. 'Won't they just be delighted she's back?'

Deborah looked uncomfortable. 'They like to fill gaps with their own stories. Connie's not a recluse. She just wants to live privately. But the more she hid away the more they wanted to sniff her out.'

'But why did she want to hide?' I said. 'She was so popular.'

Deborah smiled. 'Well, there's your answer. It's a curse, but it's also a game. You give a little, they leave you alone. I gave up in the end trying to make Con see that. She likes you, I can see that. She may even trust you. So you'll have your work cut out for you if this book's a hit. I *want* it to be a hit, don't misunderstand me. But it won't be easy, for either of us.'

'That's good to know.'

'I thought you should just be aware, is all. It was good to meet you, Laura.'

'You too—'

Before I could say any more, Deborah began to walk down the short front garden path and didn't look back. She disappeared past the hedge, and I remained on the doorstep, mystified and getting cold. I tried to comfort myself by thinking about the people I was soon to meet – Margaret Gillespie, Christina, Davy Roper – potentially as real to me as my mother – or even, in this strange limbo I was in, myself. I thought about *Green Rabbit* and *Wax Heart*, and *The Locust Plague*, and how much those books had stuck in me, however much the author of them had wanted to flee. *Oh, you and your girls with their difficult times. They fall at your feet and look where it leads you.* That's what Deborah had said. I thought about what my dad had told me: *Your mum was easily led.* I was convinced that Connie and Deborah had been talking about my mother, and the thought that she might be committed to a fiction that I was going to read before anyone else felt almost too much to bear.

1982

20

Connie dropped Elise off at the roadside of Shara and Matt's beach house. 'I'll come and get you in four hours, OK?'

'What are you going to do?' Elise asked, holding her hand up to shield her eyes from the sun. She'd forgotten her sunglasses. Connie was wearing hers, and Elise couldn't see her expression.

'I'm going to work,' said Connie.

'Where?'

'*Where?* Why are you asking that?'

'I just wondered.'

'I'm going to be at the house, El.' Connie smiled at her. 'Call there if you need me.'

'Con—?'

But Connie had driven off. Elise watched her disappear into the blazing day. *Con*, she wanted to say. *Today's my birthday. I'm twenty-three.*

*

Shara led Elise straight to the studio. Elise followed the other woman's gait, her ample backside like half a cello underneath her sundress. Shara was physically everything Elise was not: full-breasted, wide-hipped, with long blonde hair and tanned skin. She reminded Elise of something hauled from the water, a sea lion, perhaps – a beautiful sea lion, half-turning into a woman, with bells on her flippers.

'What's funny?' said Shara, smiling, as she sorted out her brushes.

'Nothing,' said Elise.

'Are you OK to sit there?' Shara said, gesturing to an old bottle-green chaise longue with tassels round its base.

'Of course.'

*

The telephone call had come about a week after Elise asked Shara if she needed a model. Shara had apparently changed her mind: she did want a model – and would Elise still like to oblige? It all felt a little suspicious to Elise, and she wondered if a conversation had happened behind her back. Shara, calling Connie with the news that Elise had offered herself. Connie saying, *Amuse her, Shar – she needs a distraction.*

It was possible. Elise nourished the dark nub of resentment that Connie might want her out of the way. She had felt ashamed of her request to be painted, as if she'd exposed herself in some pathetic way – this desire of hers to be observed, reconfigured, made special. And yet, when the request was passed on to her by Connie, she immediately said yes.

She looked through the large open window towards the sea. It was a stunning California day. The sky was a bright, almost royal blue, and sea grass fringed the bottom of her vision in shades of sage and gold. She could hear waves crashing beyond, but couldn't see them. The scene felt unreal, as if Elise was admiring something she could never truly access.

She closed her eyes and the vision turned orange, dust motes moving on the insides of her lids. That Connie had failed to remember her birthday burned once again. To not say a word, to not produce a card, to not suggest a nice lunch – to not *remember* – it was devastating.

'I'm so happy you said yes to this,' said Shara, breaking her thoughts.

Elise opened her eyes and looked at Shara. It was Shara who had said yes to this, not Elise – it had been Elise's idea in the first place. 'Do you often do portraits?' she said.

'I used to do self-portraits, but I stopped.' Shara gave an empty smile.

'Why did you stop?' said Elise.

'I might paint my eyes, now and then.'

'Just your eyes?'

Shara busied herself with the paints, the canvas and her brushes.

★

Elise removed her shorts, T-shirt and underwear. She felt a fury coursing through her veins; she wanted Shara to see her. 'It's my birthday today,' she said. 'So I've come in my birthday suit.'

Shara turned back, her eyes skimming the cuttlefish edges of Elise's shoulders, her dark pubic hair, her small breasts, her flat stomach and slight hips. 'Happy birthday,' she said. 'Can you sit on the chaise longue?'

'You want me on the chaise longue?' said Elise.

'Are you happy not to wear clothes?' said Shara.

'Do you want me in my clothes?'

A flicker of impatience passed across Shara's face. 'Not if you'd prefer to be nude,' she said.

'Fine.'

'Can you lie sideways, on your hip, facing me?'

Elise settled onto the chaise longue, and into herself. It began to calm her, to be in this familiar situation, where there were no demands on her other than to be still. To be present but also absent, as her real self vanished into the canvas. She liked to watch Shara's fluid movement of her arm – up to the canvas, away again, up and away – the brush making marks Elise couldn't see. She liked Shara's concentration, her air of respect.

The studio door opened and Matt burst in. 'Where did you put the—' He stopped. His eyes widened, staring at Elise's outstretched form before he turned away to face the wall. 'Shit. I didn't know—'

'I've asked you to knock,' said Shara.

Matt turned to his wife, and the couple were looking at each other as if Elise wasn't there, as if she wasn't glowing white and naked on the sofa, like a dangerous fruit Shara had plucked from the garden, unsure of how to prepare her, how to peel and eat her. Shara moved into the space between Matt and Elise – shielding Elise, or blocking Matt? Elise couldn't tell.

'What are you looking for?' said Shara.

'You asked me to renew the house insurance. So I'm doing it.'

'Right.'

'But I can't find the folder.'

'It's where it always is, Matt.' Shara sighed. 'In the study, third drawer of the filing cabinet.' Shara's shoulders were tensed up round her ears. The peace of the room was sluicing through the open door.

'Fine,' he said, and walked back through the door, closing it behind him.

Shara turned to Elise, her expression unreadable. 'Let's make coffee.'

'Don't you want to keep going?'

'I need a coffee.'

Elise wrapped herself in a large beach towel while Shara prepared a couple of mugs of instant. Once it was ready, the two of them pushed open the back door of the studio and sat on the deck that ran round the building with steps down to the sand dunes.

'Do you have birthday plans?' said Shara.

'I don't really celebrate it.'

'If I'd known I'd have bought you a present. You're sure you don't mind being here?'

'I'm sure.'

'Have you spoken to your folks back home?'

'I – my dad – no. My mum's dead.'

'Oh, gosh. I'm sorry. Me and my big mouth.'

'It's fine.'

Shara sipped her coffee, the corn-coloured strands around her open face billowing in the breeze. 'When did your mother pass?' she said.

Elise scoffed at this phrasing. It sounded loopy, new age. But the truth was, Shara's kindness and respect was almost unbearable, making Elise aware that her own reactions to things were constricted, artificial, not mature enough. What Elise felt in that moment was true pain, because Shara was treating her mother's death with care and importance.

'She died when I was nine.'

'Oh, honey. *Nine*. I'm so sorry.' Shara put her hand on Elise's and squeezed it.

'It's fine,' said Elise. She pulled the towel tighter around herself. 'Her name was Patricia,' she said.

'That's a lovely name.'

'It's old-fashioned,' said Elise.

They didn't say anything for a few minutes. Shara looked across the sand dunes. 'And you and Connie?' she said. 'That going well?'

This insistence of Shara's with these intimate questions! Elise felt dizzy. She couldn't handle Shara's assumption that because *she* felt able to ask these questions, Elise should feel able to answer them. 'Good, thanks,' she said. 'And you and Matt?'

Shara sighed. 'We're having problems. Con's probably told you. She's never really liked Matt. Did she tell you I lost a baby?'

'No,' Elise lied, not so much to maintain the illusion of Connie's discretion, but because she wanted to learn more from Shara, without Shara feeling that she'd been betrayed. 'I'm so sorry,' she said. 'That must have been really horrible.'

Shara didn't say anything for a while. Elise swung her legs underneath the deck, feeling the fine splinters of the wood pressing on her thighs. In the low distance, a pod of pelicans sailed through the sky, on the lookout for fish.

'It's the worst thing that has ever happened to me,' said Shara. 'It was all going fine. And then it wasn't.'

Elise didn't know what to say. Shara seemed to sense this, and she turned to her. 'It *is* horrible,' she said. 'It's a good word for it. I'd never been pregnant before. And then I was. I'd waited so long. And it was this joyous thing. And the weeks kept passing. And I mean, you worry about it – the usual things. Has it got a heartbeat, is it growing, will it be healthy? But you know that the odds it'll be OK are usually better. But then – one day, just a normal day, all my worst fears came true at once. You don't really understand, because you need time to understand it, and it's difficult to live in the moments of it. I don't really remember those weeks and months after I lost the baby very well. Every morning, every evening, just waiting to see whether you're going to be OK that day, or a mess. Whether the pain is going to last for ever.' She inhaled sharply. 'That's exactly what it is. A fucking horror.'

Elise felt overwhelmed with the responsibility of listening to this. 'I'm really sorry,' she said. 'I really am.'

'I just wish he would think to insure the house without me having to ask him,' Shara said suddenly. 'I expect he's gone out surfing instead.' She sighed. 'Shit. You really don't need to hear all this.'

'No, it's fine. I just wish there was something I could do.'

'It's just good to say this stuff. I feel—' Shara stopped. 'It's like the thing that happened, losing the baby – revealed us to each other. We didn't know each other in distress. I didn't realize I was gonna be such a deficient person – emotionally, intellectually – in the face of it. I mean, it's not like it's the rarest thing in the world. And he's fucked it up, too. I want him to make me feel better, and he doesn't ever seem to know what to say to me, how to help me. It's like our whole marriage was just this . . . game we were playing. It was all fine when we were thinking about the future as just words. But then the future turned up on our doorstep and we went to pieces.'

Elise felt hot in the face. Shara's emotional articulacy, her frankness – it was so un-English, so unlike any conversation she would ever have with Connie. She had not lived long enough or deeply enough with the idea of motherhood to draw from any well within and lift up an offering for Shara.

'It's a really awful thing to happen, Shara,' she said. 'But – maybe none of this is permanent, the way you're feeling?'

'I know. But it's *happened*, Elise. And it's there, between us. I was six months pregnant. Six months. He doesn't understand. He thinks another one will just come along.'

'It might.'

'But I wanted that one. I wanted that one.' Shara's voice went rough, the words were tumbling out of her, her breath and mouth unable to keep up. 'And we're not having sex. So *that's* a problem,' she added, a touch of irony in her voice that relieved Elise. 'And I don't want to have sex with him. I don't want anyone near my body.'

'That's understandable,' Elise said. She was getting cold and she wanted to go back in, but she knew she couldn't move from the deck until Shara decided.

Shara turned to her. 'Do you feel like that sometimes, too? Like, how pure and nice it is to just know your body is yours, for you? As if you're inside yourself?'

Elise thought about this. 'No,' she said. 'I've never felt like that.'

Shara looked disbelieving. 'Really?'

'Yeah,' said Elise.

Shara nodded. 'You're young, that's why.' She hesitated. 'You don't have to make yourself . . . available, Elise. If you don't want to.'

Elise thought this was a presumptuous and patronizing thing to say. It sounded like Connie. What had these women gone through in the sixteen years before Elise came along, that she did not also know for herself? What was it that happened to a woman in the intervening decade between twenty and thirty – and did it happen to all women?

'I know I don't,' she said.

Shara hesitated. 'You and Con are serious, huh?'

'Yes.'

'I see that. And are you happy out here, in California?'

Elise shrugged. 'I guess.'

'You think Connie will want to stay here?'

'Do *you*?'

Shara thought about it. 'Truthfully, I don't know. It's not like her to be away from London this long.'

'Right.'

'Elise?'

'Yes?'

'If you ever find that you're pregnant, have the baby.'

'*What?*'

'I know, I know,' said Shara. 'But even so. Have it. Because whatever people tell you, nothing will compare.'

Shara's voice broke, and she stood up and stepped off the deck into the dunes. Elise watched her walking away through the waist-high grass. The painting seemed forgotten. She wanted to shout: *But the baby isn't here, the baby never made it — how could you know?* – but she knew she could not say these things. She understood that grief could make you dogmatic. She understood that in some way, Shara was trying to warn her – be strong, be yourself, don't follow Connie around like an obedient little pup.

In Shara's mind, her lost baby was a real person – it was *hers*. It was a life that she'd been growing, and a life that had been lost. It wasn't just a concept. Shara's order to her was both subjective and ridiculous, and yet it held within it an unprecedented, atavistic conviction that Elise had never heard before. She wanted to help Shara, she wanted to respond positively. She stood up and called to the grass.

'If I ever get pregnant, I will. I promise.'

Shara turned and looked at Elise, and both of them laughed.

21

Elise decided to take Matt up on his offer of teaching her how to surf.

'Is that OK?' she said to Shara. 'I'll sit for you first, then go to the water for my lesson. If we're staying here for a while I might as well get used to the ocean.'

'Of course,' said Shara. 'It's a great idea.'

She told Connie about the lessons and Connie was pleased. She said it was a shame to have the water there and not try and conquer it.

'I'm not trying to *conquer* it, Con,' said Elise. 'You can't conquer the ocean.'

'True,' said Connie. 'But you can try.'

Shara dug out an old wetsuit that she'd had when she was barely out of her teens. At first it made Elise shudder, looking at it. She thought it looked like a dead person with the bones and head removed. But then she put it on, and she was covered in a slick rubber that made her feel strong and aquatic like a seal, not a girl flailing in a swimming pool.

She went to Shara and Matt's every other day, exiting the back door of Shara's studio and jumping onto the dunes, running down to the water's edge where Matt would be waiting for her, his board sticking upright in the sand.

The ocean, Elise discovered, had an obliterating effect. She didn't mind when she missed a wave and it crashed on top of her body, when she was spiralled inside the water, or when it slammed her to the seabed. She wanted to slam something out of herself. She wanted no missed birthday again, she wanted no age. She wanted to see what the water would give her. She learned quickly, having a natural aptitude – perhaps because she had a low centre of gravity and could hold herself well on the board. She could feel the currents of wind, she could twist and turn and take it all lightly, moving through the tunnel of a wave, like a carefree bug too out of proportion to let a monsoon bother her. She was reckless. And yet Matt fell into the breakers more often than she did.

*

Shara never came down to the beach. She was nursing a grief that no one knew how to label or assuage, because what was being grieved had never made its presence known to anyone but her.

Matt never talked about Shara, only that she'd never been much of a surfer; it was him who loved the act of getting in the water. He was the classic case of the outsider-convert evangelist, a British man brought up on the browns and greys of English rivers and coastal walks, diving into sapphire water. Together, Matt and Elise would paddle out of reach of the shore, waiting for the water to pull them along, as if it was taking them away from the unanswered questions inside the house on the beach. At first, they never talked about anything except how to stay on the board, how to fall off safely, how to gauge when the wave was coming.

Afterwards, it was Shara who would drive her home into West Hollywood back to Connie. Elise would walk into the bungalow, exhausted but in an undefinable way still unsatisfied. She would lie on the bed, thinking of all the shores in the world and the bodies of water in between them. Huge, infinite con-glomerations of ocean and sea, rivers, rock pools and lagoons, the real and imagined terrors, the beauty of their surfaces and the mystery of their life beneath.

*

As she sat by the side of their bungalow swimming pool, Elise would press the bruises from the ocean. They were buttons of consciousness in a reality where nothing made sense except her body. Connie saw the bruises. 'What are those?' she said. 'What are you doing?'

'It's just the surfing,' said Elise.

*

In August, a month after her birthday, she decided to tell Connie that she'd forgotten the day she'd turned twenty-three. She stood in the doorway of the spare bedroom, which Connie had turned into a writing room. Again, as with the house in London, it felt there was an invisible line hovering on its thresh-old that Elise felt she could not, and should not, penetrate.

Connie looked confused, almost stricken. 'Oh my god. Your birthday. Oh, Elise. I am so sorry.'

'It's OK,' said Elise. 'You're busy.'

'That's no excuse. Oh, this is awful. How could this happen?'

Elise felt the familiar tug of abandonment inside her – both of being abandoned, and of wishing to walk away herself. It was an alluring feeling, a fair justification for behaving badly. She tried to ignore it. 'It just happened,' she said. 'I'll have other birthdays.'

'What can I do?' said Connie. 'I know. Let's have a party.'

'I don't need a party.'

The telephone rang on the bedside table. The women looked

at each other. They didn't even need to speak. 'Her ex beat her up yesterday,' said Connie as the phone continued to trill. 'She's got a black eye. A tooth came out. They thought she might have concussion.'

'*Fuck.*'

'They've had to suspend filming, and we were nearly at the end of the schedule.'

'Oh my god, Connie. Answer it.'

'She wanted to come round, but I can put her off.'

'No, it's fine. Of course.'

Connie rushed to the receiver and lifted it up. 'Hello? Hi, Barb.' She put her hand over the mouthpiece. 'I will do something about your birthday, darling,' she said quietly. 'That's a promise.'

*

An hour later, a car pulled up outside the bungalow. Elise peeped from behind the living-room curtain. Gingerly, Barbara stepped out of the back seat. She was stooping, with a pair of huge sunglasses on her face, her handbag slung over the crook of her elbow. It was a strange sight – Barbara looked slighter and too bony, dressed in a powder-pink pantsuit, like a tropical bird with unreliable knees, stalking slowly back to her nest.

Connie was already at the door. 'Oh, darling,' Elise heard her say. 'Come on in, now.'

The three of them sat in the calm cool of the living room. Barbara, with seeming unselfconsciousness, removed the glasses from her face. Elise swallowed, staring. 'Hi, ladies,' Barbara said. Her right eye was almost completely swollen shut, and was shiny, weeping in the thin line between the upper and lower lids. The skin was a range of vivid plums and blues, fading to a reddish brown around the edges of the bruising. The other, lower side of her jaw was slightly swollen.

To Elise's shock, Barbara dropped her sunglasses, put her head in her hands and let out a deep sob. Her shoulders were shaking up and down. Elise felt pinioned to her armchair, knowing it was not her place – in whatever pecking order they were in – to go and touch the goddess and lift her upwards to her former glory.

Connie rose instantly and put her arms round Barbara. Barbara slumped inside her embrace. 'Connie,' she said, her voice muffled.

'It's OK, Barb.'

'I had to come to you,' said Barbara, pulling away slightly. 'I'm sorry. I just – I couldn't be in that house on my own—'

'Barb, you're always welcome,' said Connie.

'He could have done it anywhere on me. He always used to. But he went for the face.' Suddenly, Barbara reared back from Connie to her full sitting height. 'Just fucking *look at me*. How the fuck am I supposed to work?'

'I'm sure Bill and Eric can figure it out.'

'They don't care.' Barbara let out a moan. 'They just tell me to change the locks!'

'Barb, I promise you we will figure this out.'

'This is gonna cost the production thousands of dollars in lost time. And then everyone will know that Barbara Lowden is the kind of woman who lets men knock her around. If they don't know that already, in this gossip sieve of a town.'

'That isn't true. This isn't your fault. And anyway, it doesn't matter what they think. You're Barbara Lowden.'

'And who the fuck is she?' cried Barbara. 'I need a drink, Con. And a Valium.'

She began to rifle through her bag. 'That fucking *cunt!*' she screamed, and the other two women jumped. Barbara thrust a small pill bottle aloft, like an explorer who has just discovered the Holy Grail – and bizarre and awful as the situation was, Elise was happy to hear the old spirit in her voice.

*

Half an hour later, Barbara was calmer, and they sat around the pool.

'Arnica's good for bruises,' said Elise. She lifted up her top and rotated on the spot, showing her ribcage, her back, and then lifting her shorts so the other two could see the sides of her thighs. 'See? I use it all the time. I'll get it for you.'

Before Barbara could say anything, she went to the bedroom and got the cream. When she came back to the poolside the other two women abruptly stopped their conversation. 'Here,' she said, handing the arnica cream to Barbara.

'Thank you, honey,' Barbara said, placing it beside her gin and tonic. 'I think at the moment I can't even bear to touch it.'

'Maybe in a couple of days,' said Elise.

'Sure,' said Barbara. 'You – er, bruise easily too, huh?'

'Surfing,' Elise said. 'I'm taking on the ocean. I'm losing.'

'Well, you never know,' said Barbara, but Elise wasn't sure what she meant. 'Realistically,' Barbara went on, pointing at her eye, 'this is gonna take a month to disappear. But I reckon in a couple of weeks the make-up girls will be able to cover it up.'

'Is there no way they can do Lucy and Don's scenes in that time?' said Elise. 'Just rearrange the schedule?'

Barbara picked up her gin and tonic and took a sip. 'Actually, that's a good idea. What would I do without you two?'

'Well done, El,' said Connie.

Elise didn't feel proud. She felt resentful that she was being sucked into this drama that didn't really involve her, and knew that once it was resolved, Barbara would carry on overlooking her.

'El's sitting for a portrait for Shara,' Connie said.

'Oh, that's wonderful, honey,' said Barbara. 'Have you done that before?'

Elise glanced at Connie, who refused to look at her. Elise's experience at the Royal College of Art had been discussed with Barbara more than once previously. 'Yes I have,' she said.

'I'd love to see the finished picture,' Barbara said.

'Shara works slowly,' said Connie.

'I'm having a party,' Elise said. 'To celebrate my birthday.'

'Oh! When's your birthday?'

'It was last month. Connie forgot, so we're doing it now.'

Barbara looked between the two women, clearly unsure of what to say. Connie stared at Elise, an awkward smile on her face. 'I said I was sorry, darling.'

'You did. And it's forgiven.'

'Can I come?' said Barbara.

'Of course,' said Elise. 'That's why I mentioned it. You'll be guest of honour.'

'Make it fancy dress for me? I'll come as an Egyptian mummy.'

'We can wait,' said Elise. 'I mean, my birthday's already been and gone, so what's another month?'

*

That night, Barbara stayed over. They put her in one of Elise's nightgowns, tucked her in the spare bed and gave her another sleeping pill. She drifted away quite quickly. As night fell and the cicadas started up, Connie sat by the pool under the stars, nursing a tumbler with a small tot of whisky in it. Elise came and sat next to her.

'Are you OK?' Connie said. 'You made your point to Barbara about your birthday.'

'I was angry,' said Elise. She sat down next to Connie and put her head on Connie's shoulder.

'I know,' said Connie. 'Quite rightly. I deserve to be embarrassed.'

'Barbara'll wake up tomorrow still thinking you're the best thing ever.'

Connie sighed. 'She's lost, El. I'm just helping her.'

'I know.'

'It's awful. All that money, all that status, and she's still vulnerable. I wonder if that ever changes?'

'I doubt it.' Elise took the glass from Connie's hand and sipped. 'You find it hard, seeing her like this.'

'Of course I do.'

'I mean, she'll never be the movie star for us again. She'll never have the same mystique. She's a battered woman.'

'Hey,' said Connie sharply. 'She's not a "movie star", or a "battered woman".'

'She's both.'

'You're being deliberately reductive. You know better than that.'

'Don't you think it's weird, the way she's ended up here? Doesn't she have other friends? People she can trust? She barely knows us.'

Connie shrugged. 'I don't think she really trusts anyone, and I don't blame her. There's a connection. There was from the start.'

'You don't think it's just because you're on the outside, so you're not as problematic?'

'Thanks for the vote of confidence.'

'I wasn't—'

'I don't think she thinks of me as "on the outside",' said Connie.

Elise hesitated. 'Do you – are you – attracted to her, Con?'

'Am I attracted to her?'

'Well, you just talked about a connection.'

'She's a beautiful woman, I'd be blind if I said otherwise, but no. No, no. I don't think of her like that.'

'OK.'

'You are the most beautiful of them all. Come here,' said Connie.

Elise came near, and a tingle ran down her middle into her groin as Connie touched the side of her face with her delicate fingers. She lifted Elise's mouth to hers and kissed it slowly. Their lips held together for a long while, before they broke apart. Then they sat side by side for a time in silence, staring at the neon stillness of the water.

2017

22

Every day, I sat at Connie's kitchen table and typed up her story on my laptop. I had no idea how it ended, because she would hand it over in stages, five or six yellow rectangular pages at a time, the writing large and scrawled but still legible, each sentence requiring two lines of the paper. I was diligent, at times awestruck. Her prose was still as good as it had been thirty years ago. There were similar cadences that had appeared in the previous two novels, images repeated, and the themes of learning how to be alone, to manage loss, to enjoy freedom.

As I typed, I began to be convinced that Connie had cast herself in the role of Margaret Gillespie. This was because Margaret Gillespie was a woman with agency. She was a woman who did things to other women – in this case, her daughter, barely out of girlhood, trapped by her circumstances. It was an ambivalent novel because it was not clear – or at least, not yet – as to whether Margaret wanted to hurt her daughter, to punish her for something.

It tantalized me that Connie had set this novel on the east coast of America, albeit in the years of the pilgrim fathers rather than when, according to my father, she was there in the early 1980s. The otherworldliness of the place, the elements of sea and woodland, and the harsh conditions seemed to appeal to her. Her colonists were deaf to the fact that this was not virgin land, that there had been natives living on these shores and in

these forests for thousands of years, in harmony with their sur-
roundings. Margaret's discomfort in being there, the patriarchal
erasure of natural justice as embodied by Davy Roper and his
cronies, and the women around them who cleaved themselves
to power in order to maintain an illusion of dominance, provided evidence to me that Connie was critical of colonization,
in whatever form it took. Margaret was a progressive, potentially an anachronism, as much as she was an outsider. She didn't
fit into this society Connie had created, and I think Christina did,
which was why Margaret felt so desperate.

Christina herself was an enigma: she could be seen as prag-
matic in one light, spineless in another. She wanted an easy life,
to submit to its vicissitudes and hope for the best. But Margaret
wouldn't let her. *We've come too far*, she told her daughter, *for you
to shrink back down to a tiny size.*

I'm not a mad dreamer, usually. If I do dream, it will be that
strange, unrecoverable symphony of weirdness and banality,
which dissipates in the morning, soon to be forgotten. But at
night, Margaret Gillespie began to carry me off until her twisted
capabilities might have been mine. I would stand on the beach
where Margaret stood in Connie's imagination, the shore a
curved white blade with a line of firs from where the barks of
hunting dogs emerged. I knew the woody glory of Margaret's
foraged cooking. I saw minnows turn pink in the water from a
character's blood – though whose it was had not yet been
revealed to me in Connie's pages. Davy's charisma had been
revealed by now – as well as his fists, his misogyny and insecurity, stalking my night times. Christina's belly swelled, but death
was dormant in that symbol of hope, and I would wake up with
a jolt.

Since overhearing her and Deborah's conversation on the
night of the pizza, I had become hungrier for more clues about

my mother, yet simultaneously more fearful of what I might discover. So far, Connie had proven prickly when questioned about her life, and only liked to talk about things when she could control the information she imparted. And yet, here she was, handing over her innermost thoughts and workings. All I could do was hope that these pages would give me an understanding of who Connie really was, and through that, who my mother had been. I believed that writers wrote themselves into their fictions, that however they twisted the original idea into a new shape, there was some truth inside it, still. If it was true that Connie had known my mother as closely as my father claimed she had, then surely she was somewhere in these pages? So as I typed, I read, and as I read, I saw my mother as Christina, cowed by the dominance of Margaret, trapped in a marriage she didn't want but which at least offered her some independence. But how could I be that selective? If I was assigning my mother a role in Connie's fictions, then I had to give my father one too. And I could not see him in Davy Roper. My father was a caring man, not a monster. I rejected the idea that I was dipping into Connie's box of letters and spelling any word I pleased, but maybe it was true.

My dad texted me. HOW R U? he wrote. WE R FINE. As if there was a group of people over there in France, not just him and Claire, a late-middle-aged couple standing on the shore, set loose from his adult daughter, who in turn had set herself upon the wind.

I'm pretending to be someone else in order to work for a woman who may or may not know what happened to my mother. I'm wandering the woods of her mind in order to find clues. My best friend's having another baby and although I love her very much, my life is totally at odds with hers, and I am frustrated, how, despite my best intentions, I keep buying into this dichotomy dictated by society that we're so very different to each other now, even though she doesn't do that at all. My boyfriend and I are acting like flatmates who occasionally have sex, and I don't know if that's normal. I don't know what's going to happen to me in the near future, let alone where I might be in ten years' time. I'm climbing up a ladder into a cloud, but my foot has slipped off the rung and I'm dangling upside down. Is this what life is, and they just didn't tell you at school? Am I supposed to be dangling upside down?

I'm good! ☺ I wrote.

DID YOU READ THOSE BOOKS I GAVE YOU?

I hesitated. To say I'd read them would lead to endless complication. He would ask me what I thought about them, whether I'd looked Connie up.

I lied to him. I was getting good at lying. I haven't read them yet, I wrote.

YOU DON'T HAVE 2 READ THEM

I know. But I appreciate you giving them to me

IT HAS BEEN VERY UNFAIR ON YOU, he wrote.

The bridge of my nose began to sting. His care and sympathy, and the inadequacy of his words, and his awful text speak in trying to express this, contained too much pathos.

I'm ok, Dad.

OK. BUT YOU JUST CALL ME, OK? IF YOU NEED ME. OR CLAIRE. WE R HERE.

Thank you.

*

The end of October turned into November, and for four weeks as the temperature steadily dropped outside and supermarkets emptied their shelves of edible chocolate ghosts and bloated pumpkins, and refilled them with premature yule logs and mince pies, I continued to type up Connie's novel at her kitchen table. It pleased and even empowered me that this traditionally feminine site of domesticity had been co-opted by our intellectual exercise.

I'd been working for Connie for six weeks, but it felt longer – as if I had been there for years, as if I knew her from before, and we'd both been waiting for the right time to come together, that we'd trusted the timing of our lives in order for this to happen. This was nonsense, because I'd engineered the whole thing. It was nice for me to think that my getting the job with her contained some sort of inevitability, or destiny, but I had undeniably manipulated the situation to be here. But we did get on well. I seemed to fit easily into the energy of her days, and the offering of her novel to me was something extraordinary that softened the boundaries between us. On the 1st of December I bought her an advent calendar with chocolate behind its doors, and was so happy to see her delight.

*

I'd never had a woman like her in my life before. Within just two months, I had experienced Connie's directness, her interesting selfishness that was not really selfishness. It was more a *selfness*. Catlike, she just let you be near, and as a result it made you want to stay.

But I was in a dilemma. The longer I was silent, the longer I could live inside this sanctuary, but also the longer I would spoil in ignorance of who I truly was.

'Did you show anyone your work like this, before?' I asked her one afternoon after I had finished typing up her pages for the day.

'No,' said Connie, sighing as she slid herself into the chair opposite mine and began to slowly open and close her fists as if getting the blood back into them. 'I usually keep it a closely guarded secret.'

I closed the laptop. 'What's different this time?'

She frowned. 'Different? Well, I'd quite like to get this book published. Last time, I had a contract. I suppose that's what's different.'

'I guess secrets are sometimes necessary,' I said. 'As protection.'

'True.'

'So – you really don't mind, that I can read it like this? That you're sharing this secret with me?'

She looked at me enquiringly. 'I want to finish this book, Laura. My fingers are killing me, and you do half the labour for me. The compromise is, you get to see it before it's ready. We all have to make compromises.'

'Are you – scared about what people might think of the book?'

The corners of Connie's mouth turned down and she peered into the nicks and whorls of the old oak table between us. 'It is what it is,' she said.

I swallowed, gripping the edge of my laptop. 'I think it's excellent, by the way. The character of Christina is fascinating to me.'

Connie looked up. 'Really? You see her? She's believable?'

'Very. Very believable.' My heart began to thump fast in my chest. 'It's weird, actually. I feel almost as if I've met her before.'

Connie stared at me. 'Good. She was the hardest to write.'

I was about to ask why, when Connie suddenly pushed back her chair, her gnarled fingers hooked round the edge of the table for balance. I faltered, desperate to keep her in the room, but knowing that to do so might reveal more than was wise. 'Her dynamic with Margaret's quite toxic, but strangely loving,' I said. She narrowed her eyes at me and I began to gabble. 'I mean – I'm sorry – I'm not trying to offer you a critique.'

Connie looked down at me. 'Thank goodness. Because then I'd probably offer you the door.'

I was stunned. I couldn't tell if she was joking. Connie walked out of the kitchen, and I stared at the lid of my laptop, listening to her soft retreat upstairs.

23

I hadn't seen Kelly since our awkward ramen date in Soho. We never usually had a bad feeling between us, and I knew that Kelly would be as upset by it as I was, so I was glad when she texted asking to see me. We agreed to meet at one of our favourite cafes in Spitalfields and she said she was bringing Mol. I bagged us the best table at the back with the squishy armchairs, away from the steamed-up windows and the cold draught of the door being opened and closed. The PA system was playing classic Christmas songs and when they walked through the door to Bing Crosby's 'It's Beginning to Look a Lot Like Christmas', I thought I could see Kelly's bump had started to show quite obviously, even though she was so bundled up against the winter cold. My heart lifted at the sight of Mol in some excellent miniature knitwear. She saw me too, and her face lit up. 'Rosie!' she said, skipping through the chairs and tables towards me.

'Hi, Molcheeks. I got you a slice of cake,' I said, giving her a hug. Her little shoulders felt so bony and fragile. 'Chocolate.'

Mol beamed in ecstasy. She sat down, and the velvet armchair was so huge for her she looked as if she had been shrunk. 'I think my face is actually freezing off,' said Kelly, unwinding Mol's scarf, pulling off her daughter's hat like a knitted tea cosy. Mol's hair was a fuzzed crown. Kelly looked at her daughter. 'Do I still have a nose?' she asked.

Mol hooted as she lifted her legs up and down in delight. 'Of course you do, Mummy. Do I?' She fumbled with her elasticated mittens in a rush to get to the cake.

'You OK?' Kelly said to me, still standing beside the table.

'Yeah,' I said. 'You?'

'Come here,' she said. I did as I was told and we hugged. I thought I might cry – I wanted to, to let it out – but the presence of Mol and the public setting prevented a full-blown sob. I just gave my best friend an extra squeeze.

We sat down, Kelly sighing heavily as if she had just walked fifty miles and could finally take the weight off her feet. 'I ordered you a decaf and an apple juice for Mol,' I said.

She grinned. 'Thoughtful. You all ready for Christmas, then?'

'Nope,' I said. 'You know how I love Christmas.'

'We're off to Dan's mum and dad tomorrow. I've had to be super-organized. You know they don't have any phone coverage? You go there and it's like you're dead.'

'You're *always* super-organized. And it'll be good to have some time off the Internet.'

'This is true. Although you will remember who I am, won't you? When I come back from the dead?'

'I'll remember you.'

'You going to Joe's parents'?'

'Yeah,' I said.

'Good old Dorothy.'

'Oh, don't. And Daisy – oh, my god.'

Kelly laughed. 'Don't go. Skip the trustafarians. Go and see your dad.'

'Too late to buy a flight or a ferry now.'

Kelly sighed. 'No it isn't. Rosebud, why don't you just do what *you* want to do? You can, you know.'

'What do I want to do, though?' I said.

'Well, that is the question on everyone's lips.'

'It's all right for you,' I said. 'Dan's mum and dad are lovely. You're sorted.'

Kelly lifted the fork from her daughter's hand, and with the ferocity of a crazed dictator carving up a map, she divided the slice of chocolate cake into bitesize chunks. The fork tinked aggressively on the plate. Mol looked slightly frightened, knowing her mother was electrified about something. 'It's so claustrophobic there,' Kelly said, her voice now more under control as she handed Mol back the fork. 'I end up offering to chop logs for their wood-burner – in sub-zero temperatures for fuck's sake. I do it every year. Just so I can *breathe*. And then by day three I've cracked and I go and stand on a hill with my phone aloft hoping to make some outside contact.'

I tried not to laugh. 'You chop logs?'

'I'm fucking excellent at chopping logs, thank you. How do you not know this about me? I'm a bloody lumberjack. I'll be chopping logs all day long if I have to.'

Kelly had begun to laugh too, and it was such a relief to let go of the worries about our friendship that I think we'd both brought with us through the door. 'Oh, my *god*,' she said, shaking her head, bravely trying to summon good cheer. 'I *still* have so much to do, you know? I don't want to go, but his parents want to see Mol so badly. I've got this huge project coming up with a really cool brand I've been cultivating for months.' She didn't mention the actual brand, because we both knew I would never have heard of it. 'Mol's only with me because Dan said *he* had some last-minute work he had to sign off, as if my schedule wasn't just as important. But you and me had this coffee date planned for days. I was going to come on my own, then go and do some work, but *no*.'

Her smile had gone, and she sat back, radiantly furious.

'I'm sorry,' I said. 'I got wrapped up in my own thing. As usual. I didn't know about this project.'

'I probably didn't even mention it. I can't even remember my own name most days.' She raised her eyebrow at me. 'Bit like you, *Laura*.'

I ignored her. 'How's all that going?' she pushed.

'Actually,' I said, 'I really like Connie.'

'Uh-oh. What do you actually do every day?'

'Well, at the moment, I'm typing up her manuscript. She's written a new novel.'

'Is it any good?'

'It's *amazing*. It's set in Massachusetts in the 1620s. There's this woman, and she has a daughter. And the community start accusing the woman of being a witch. And then her daughter gets pregnant and it starts going wrong for them.'

'Why the 1620s in America?'

The waitress brought us our coffees and the juice for Mol. Now it was my turn to raise an eyebrow at Kelly. 'You don't ask questions like that. You just take what she gives you, and join the dots up later.'

'And are you? Joining up the dots?'

I sighed. 'Maybe.'

'What does that mean?'

I told Kelly about the conversation I'd overheard between Deborah and Connie. Kelly frowned. 'But she didn't mention the name Elise?' she said.

'Well, no. But she did talk about a man, and how he never blamed Connie for what happened.'

Kelly looked dubious. 'Rosie, that could be about anyone. Why don't you just talk to her about it?'

I took a sip of coffee. 'It's weird, Kel. I just feel – *comfortable* there. I like being with her.' Kelly looked dismayed, so I pressed on. 'I just feel useful. And she's a really interesting woman.'

'Do you think she has any idea who you are?'

I put the coffee down and picked up some of Mol's chocolate cake crumbs from the edge of her plate. 'Well. Sometimes, I think she looks at me funny. She stares at me.'

'What, like she *recognizes* you?' said Kelly, her eyes widening.

'Sort of? Or that she knows exactly who I am and she's just playing with me.'

'Oh man. That's *weird*.'

'And then I think that's just my wishful thinking.'

'But she hasn't tried to poison you yet?'

'I'm here, aren't I?'

'So you are. You're a real weirdo sometimes, Rose, but I'm glad it's working out for you. Just take care. Old ladies, man, they're dangerous.'

'Thanks, Kel.' I decided, on reflection, not to tell her how I had recast my boyfriend in the role of an antiques dealer. 'Do you – talk to Dan about how you feel – the work balance, and stuff?'

Kelly sighed. 'I've learned to pick my battles. I'll just get the work done later when Mol's in bed.'

'I just seem to wander into my battles,' I said.

'You do a bit, but that's OK. You've got good armour. You're Laura Brown.' Kelly laughed and leaned back in the armchair. 'No, but seriously, the real difference between me and you, Rosie, is that I know I'm not going to win every battle and it drives me crazy, and you never think you're gonna win any. And I hate that for you. You've got to believe in yourself. You know I only get angry because I love you and I want the best for you.'

'I know. I'm sorry.'

There was an awkward beat. 'Don't say sorry. I'll always love you,' said Kelly.

'And I'll always love you,' I replied.

We sat there, luxuriating in our robustness as Eartha Kitt sang 'Santa Baby' and Mol polished off her chocolate cake. Kelly sighed, resting her hand on the back of her daughter's small head.

'So what would you do for Christmas, if you had the choice?' I asked.

Kelly closed her eyes. 'Rosie-Rose, I would sleep for a thousand years.'

24

After my grandparents died it felt almost ridiculous for my dad and me to celebrate Christmas, to share a turkey, the biggest, driest bird that two people would have to tackle well into January – or even bother with a tree. I was always happy when it was over and life returned to normal. For the last five years, I'd spent Christmas at Joe's parents' house, and never really enjoyed it. Dad had been invited several times but always declined, asking me to come to France instead. I never did.

Christmas was getting nearer, but our flat bore none of the evidence. Joe was out a lot, catching up with his friends from school and university, and I was at Connie's a great deal, often not leaving before ten at night. I was blocking Christmas out, so was taken by surprise when I got to Connie's one morning in mid-December to see a Christmas tree, deep and green and unadorned, waiting in the bay of her front-room window.

'They've just delivered it,' she said. 'Will you decorate it for me?'

I stood in front of it – about seven foot, a quite majestic spruce. There was a large box on the armchair. 'My baubles,' Connie said. 'I was flustered with their threads. I can't pull them apart. You're going to have to do it.'

I surveyed the tree, inhaling the smell of sap. 'That's OK,' I said.

'Thank you,' said Connie. 'Don't bother about work today. Let's do this instead.'

'But we're so close to the end.'

'Exactly. We don't need to panic.'

Since our awkward conversation about Connie choosing to share the contents of her novel with me, I hadn't dared to ask her any further questions. It wasn't as if she had overtly warned me off that afternoon, but a rebuke was in the air between us: *You have a job to do. Type it up and stop asking me about it.* As much as I wanted to satisfy my own desire for answers about Connie's relationship with my mother, I felt that trying to do this might actually push Connie – and the spectre of Elise – further away. Then I would be completely lost. And it wasn't just this. I liked Connie. I liked the fact that somehow, because it was her, I didn't mind decorating a Christmas tree.

*

I set a fire going and Connie brought out a bottled of chilled champagne. 'It's ten in the morning,' I said.

'And? Can you open it? Jesus, my fingers.'

I poured us a couple of glasses. I'd never met *anyone* like her, a woman who made champagne at ten a.m. feel perfectly acceptable, almost necessary. I opened her bauble box: Connie had gone all out. Inside were white fairy lights, tinsel, old and frail-looking tin globes in cerise and turquoise, pillar-box red, bright orange. Their shades surprised me: I did not think Connie was one for all that glitter. Again, I had to recalibrate her in my mind. Just when I thought I'd got a hold on her, she wriggled away.

'Are you having guests on the big day?' I asked, trying to keep my balance on the armchair, my hand plunging into the fresh dark branches. 'Is that why you've bought such a large tree?'

'No,' said Connie, puzzled. 'Are you?'

I laughed. 'In our flat?'

'So where will you go?'

'Joe's parents',' I said.

'You make it sound like you're going to Fagin's.'

'Fagin's would be preferable.'

'But I bet you get glorious presents from him.'

'Sometimes.'

'What's the best thing he's found for you?' she said, her eyes alight.

I ran my memory over the many Christmases we'd had together. Joe had never really tailored my presents particularly tightly. Nice picture frames, a cashmere shawl, candles, books. All lovely, but not the considered thoughtfulness one might hope from an antique-dealer boyfriend. 'There've been so many,' I said. 'I can't pick one.'

'I see,' said Connie. 'And who will cook?'

'His mother.'

'Of course.'

'She never makes it a very relaxing experience.'

Connie placed her glass down, and began to comb a stretch of gold tinsel. It looked like a giant caterpillar shimmering from the light of the fire. 'Then why are you going?' she said.

'That's what my best friend says.'

'Oh?'

'I'm going because I love him.'

Connie turned her focus to the tinsel, continuing to comb it out with a shaking finger. I sorted through the box to look for the next bauble to attach, feeling my cheeks go red, grateful for the fact I had to lean over, thereby avoiding Connie's gaze. 'The lights are what I like most about Christmas,' she said.

'I'm sorry?'

'The twinkling. They bring me peace.'

I closed my eyes and suddenly felt my mother falling away inside me, unclaimed, unspoken. 'You're lucky, being able to be on your own,' I said. 'I'll probably be sat next to Lucia.'

'Lucia?'

I looked up, my fingers round another bauble. Connie was sitting very still and upright, as if she was waiting for something. 'Joe's niece. She's six,' I said. I'd given away another real name, and it felt to me as if I was shedding the skin of my made-up self.

'You don't like children?' Connie said.

'I don't like Lucia.'

Connie chuckled, coming over with the tinsel and clumsily attempting to push it deep into the tree. 'I'll do that,' I said.

She sighed, handing over the tinsel and returning to her arm-chair where she slowly yet determinedly took another sip of champagne. I saw the glass shake, and looked away. 'Why don't you like Lucia?' Connie said.

'Because she's precocious.'

'Maybe she's just confident and you don't like it.'

This was a radical thought and I didn't like *that*. But maybe it was true? Maybe I did see a self-confidence in Lucia, a happiness in her self that I'd never known. Was I jealous of a six-year-old? I felt pathetic. 'She's actually just irritating,' I said defensively. 'It is possible to be six years old and unlikeable, Connie.'

'Oh, I'm sure.'

'How many children do you know?' I said.

'Not that many. Any children I did know are all grown up.'

'Do you buy them presents and things?'

'No. I send money to my brother's children. Phoebe and Jack.' She rubbed her face. 'I last saw them when they were teenagers. They'll be in their thirties now.'

'That's – quite a gap.'

'Yes!' she said, her voice hard and bright. I was unsure of the undercurrents swirling, but the champagne had made me bolder, and I wanted to keep her talking.

'Did you grow up in London?' I asked her.

'All over the place. My father was a senior officer in the army. When he left the army, we settled in Essex. On the border with Suffolk.'

'Did you like it?'

Connie exhaled heavily. '*Like* isn't the word I'd use. My father was away a lot, particularly when I was little. He was one of the first to arrive at Bergen-Belsen in '45.'

'Oh my god.'

'Yes. For the rest of his life, whenever anything to do with the Holocaust was mentioned on the wireless or the television, he'd turn it off. My mother was distant. Maternally under-developed. Here, do you want another bauble? This one's beautiful.'

I took the deep fuchsia bauble she'd lifted from the box. 'Does one *develop*, maternally?' I said.

'Of course,' said Connie, as if I'd said a very stupid thing. 'One has to. From the little I know of it, I imagine it's all rather a shock.' She paused. 'It was the times, of course. She'd pass her children over to the nanny. I'd see her for an hour after bath time. She wouldn't read stories. She'd sit me in our drawing room. God, it was cold. Ask me questions about my day. My day! I was six!'

I thought about Lucia. 'Oh, I think six-year-olds have things to say,' I said. 'And at least your mother asked you questions.'

'I don't remember what I ever answered. I don't like questions,' Connie said.

Feeling rebuked again, I didn't reply. Connie sighed and

leaned back in her armchair. 'There's something very meditative about watching someone else undertaking a manual task,' she said. She held up her hands and examined them. 'Even if these days it's laced with a sense of regret.'

'How are they at the moment?'

'They're all right. I hate being outside in the cold, because they really start to ache. Sometimes to the point that I'd quite like them to be chopped off. They're so useless. But then it's warmer, like now, and I feel less frustrated.'

'You got such a big tree,' I said.

Connie laughed. I continued to dress the tree, selecting baubles as she watched me, the two of us in companionable silence. Outside, cars drove past intermittently, the sound of a front door closing, harried voices of those trying to get their shopping in whilst wrangling children. It was a white, bleak sky above, a bland day, a day to be indoors. Suddenly, I was very grateful for the tree.

'I was very attached to my father,' Connie said suddenly. 'He'd come back from being away, and I used to feel such a thrill hearing his car pull up in the drive. There was always this smell of starched khaki and cigarette smoke. They always say army men don't know how to express affection, but it isn't true. He was very present with me. That's what your generation say, isn't it? *Present?*'

'I guess so.'

'But when I thought about it later on, I realized for a lot of the time, he was treating me like a boy. A son. Talking to me as an equal. Letting me hold his guns. With my short hair and my skinny frame, pre-puberty, I suppose I could have been a boy. But it didn't last. My little brother Michael started to fill those shoes, and I turned into a woman. A woman who wouldn't even do the normal thing and find a nice chap and get married.

That would have been something he could have understood. But I was never going to do that. I let him down.'

'Surely not.' I went over to the fireplace and placed another log on top of the flames, luxuriating in the heat coming from the centre.

Connie smiled. 'Of course I did. It wasn't flower-power on the Essex borders, I assure you. This was the early sixties. Same-sex relationships were still illegal for men, and they didn't even think about women having them. It wasn't really a concept to the average Englishman.'

Connie leant over the armchair and plucked out another bauble, this time a clear glass ball that had been lightly glued with a smattering of fake snow. 'I honestly don't think my father knew what a lesbian was,' she said. 'He'd studied Classics, so you'd hope he'd have some sympathy for same-sex romance, but that respect was reserved for Homer. When I finally told him I was never going to get married, he looked at me like I was from another planet. I didn't bother spelling it out for him.'

'That must have been hard.'

'Oh, it was ridiculous, really. That's what I think now. Although at the time, I was naive enough to be surprised.'

'You'd assumed his love was unconditional.'

She wrinkled her nose. 'I think it was more that I thought what he'd seen in Germany might have changed him. Take love where you find it, that sort of thing. And he disappointed me. He *loved* me, I knew that.' Connie stared into the depths of the tree. 'And I loved him back, that was the awful thing. I loved him so much. But then I began to think of him as pathetic, and that's when you're really lost with a parent. A sense of defeat leaks in.'

'Did you have to leave home?'

'No. But I wanted to. I'd been at Manchester, then I moved to London. Sofa to sofa, relying upon the largesse of friends.'

She sighed. 'Did three hundred jobs, all appalling in their different ways. Wrote in any free hours I had. Nearly eight years of that. Christ. It's so long ago, now.'

'Did you ever go back?'

'Sometimes. I began to visit home less, when I realized my father was never going to be capable of dealing with who I was. He'd probably guessed by then, of course. But he never acknowledged it.' She paused. 'I felt . . . invisible.'

By now, I'd taken a seat in the opposite armchair. To see and hear Connie in full flow like this felt like an enormous privilege. It felt rare. In that moment, I forgot about mining her for my mother; I just wanted Connie's story, to be closer to her, to understand who Connie really was. 'What about your mother in all this?' I said.

'Oh, she just followed suit,' said Connie, staring into the flames of the fire. 'She didn't ever really have it out with me. My parents seemed . . . *put off* by me in a way they couldn't verbalize or possibly even understand themselves. They never said anything abusive, but it was alienating. I know it's not always the case, of course. I know often there's love. Acceptance. But it was a different time. I couldn't stand being near them.'

'I'm sorry.'

'Ah well.'

'Was it – always women for you, Connie?' I said.

She looked up at me. 'I expect so. But there were dances I went to, as a teen. The strutting boys, the preening girls, the pairing off on the dance floor – all that. I danced, too. All very heterosexual. But I did prefer to look at the girls. The back of a neck, the shape of a hand, the way a smile caught my eye. We were all of us a bit of a hormonal jumble, I suppose. None of us had the education about it, or were taught words for it. But maybe I knew even then. My first time I was fifteen. A girl called Virginia.' Connie smiled and looked back at the fire. 'What a name for a first time. Virginia Lawrenson was three years older than me and she kissed me by the drains behind the youth club in Manningtree. I still remember it. A month later we ended up in her bedroom. And a month after that, she was married.'

'Poor Virginia,' I said.

'Oh, I don't know. The Virginia Lawrensons of the world had it easier in many ways. Her husband was a decent chap.'

'I am really sorry,' I said again. 'If it's been – hard for you.'

Connie looked uncomfortable. 'Oh, I don't need you to be sorry, Laura,' she said, taking another slow sip of champagne. 'You manage. Find friends. Protection. Not many people thought I was a lesbian. I passed as a straight person, I suppose.'

'Did you . . . do that on purpose?'

She took a deep breath. 'I've not cared to think about it much. I never felt the need to go on marches, shave my head, hate all men, any of that. But maybe I buried it. I suppose I was always more interested in getting the things I wanted for my myself. The personal over the political.'

'Aren't they supposed to be the same thing?' I said.

Connie laughed. 'Of course, and I suppose that makes me a selfish narcissist.' She looked away. 'I liked to think the fact of being who I was as a radical act in itself. But maybe that was lazy. Maybe I did hide. I don't know. If anything, I always felt worse for the women I was in love with than for myself.'

My heart felt strange. 'Why did you feel worse for them?' I said.

Connie sighed. 'I could never love them easily. I *knew* I loved them, I just didn't show it very well. I think they felt they were in love with a ghost.'

I didn't know what to say to that. I'd probed enough, and I didn't want her to turn on me, clam up. Connie's eyes were moist, her gnarled fingers resting on either arm of the chair as if it was a throne. She'd spoken so much, unpacking herself, and she looked exhausted. I watched as her face folded slowly into a picture of sadness. I wanted to go to her, to comfort her, to tell her that my mother was in this room, an old love, an invisible thread, tying together the ones she'd left behind. But I stayed where I was by the Christmas tree.

25

I kept thinking about the way Connie called herself a ghost. Up until this point, I'd considered that the only ghost in this house was Elise Morceau. Connie had, for reasons known only to her, opened up to me about her childhood – her father the army officer, who she idolized, and who would probably be diagnosed with PTSD if he was around now; her mother, who Connie claimed as the mistress of detachedness. Her brother Michael and his children: absent. And above all, I suppose, the fact of how her sexuality, and therefore her self, had been passively erased by those closest to her. What she'd done by talking to me – it felt like friendship, I suppose. An offering, given in trust. I glowed with the honour of it, and my heart ached for the young woman Connie once was, who felt she couldn't be herself. I wondered if those feelings of alienation and the need for detachment had continued into her adult life as well, and I suspected they might have.

I had come to Connie's with a clear intention, but now it felt my path was muddied and uncertain. As much as I wanted Connie to share herself with me, hoping that in doing so she would either deliberately or inadvertently bring me nearer to my mother – the vulnerability she had displayed underneath that urbane, intellectual toughness was making me feel guilty and protective. Perhaps I should just be here to look after her, I thought. Perhaps I should just focus on the woman who is here, and not the woman floating around in my head?

*

By the morning of Christmas Eve, Kelly was well entrenched in the English countryside, no doubt chopping logs. I loved the image of her with her swelling stomach, splitting dead trees with an axe. I was in the living room of our flat, wrapping all the presents for Joe's family, tying them with excellent bows. I'd done my best to get nice things – body lotions and bottles of wine, a face cloth for Daisy, with apparent magical exfoliating properties that she'd probably take as an insult – but none of them were particularly special. My shoulders ached from leaning over on the carpet, trying to get neat lines on the parcel wrapping, in case Dorothy suspected, correctly, that this was all last-minute. My plan was to go up to Connie's, give her her present (which I *had* spent considerable time on and was pleased with), stay for a glass of champagne, then leave her to it. This had been what she'd indicated she wanted. Then I would go down to Wimbledon to spend Christmas with Joe and his family.

Joe had gone for an early Christmas pint with a new friend of his I hadn't met. His name was Charles, apparently, and he was very influential on social media in the London food scene.

It felt like more than one pint. Eventually, the front door opened and Joe wandered into the living room. 'Hey,' he said, looking down at the presents, the wrapping paper, the Sellotape, me, sitting in the middle. 'You did it all,' he said.

I couldn't look at him. 'I did. I went to Selfridges last night,' I said.

'Thanks so much. Was it busy?'

'Very.'

'I feel like I should have come with you.'

I continued to gaze down at the neat mound of presents. 'How was the pub?' I said.

Joe sat on the sofa and pulled out his phone. 'Good. Charles is cool. He said there might be some opportunities for us with some pop-ups in the New Year. Once the stupid detox stuff is over. He's going to put in a word for me at this new food festival in February in London Bridge. He's doing all the PR for it.'

'That's great,' I said. 'Actually,' I went on, 'you should have helped me with the presents. These are presents for your family.'

Joe looked up at me. 'Yeah. I'm really sorry,' he said. 'But Charles was only available today—'

'And last night, when I was in Selfridges?'

'I didn't know you were going to go,' he said. 'I was planning on going to get their presents this morning. You know that's how I do it.' He went back to his phone.

'Yeah, and last year, we ended up spending far too much in a panic on things they didn't even want.'

I stopped. I could hear myself. My pure, justified displeasure that would be so easy for Joe to turn into an accusation of nagging. It enraged me that my anger could so easily be deflected, deviated from its true path just by some deftly delivered defences from his corner.

'But you're so good at that kind of thing, Rosie,' he said.

'I'm not. I'm no better than you. But I can't turn up to their house without—'

'I never know what to buy,' he said.

'Why don't you ever ask them?'

He finally put his phone down. 'Because that spoils the surprise of Christmas,' he said, and I thought I was going to scream.

'Then why don't you think about it for half a minute?' I said.

'I'll give you the money for them,' he replied, and picked up his phone again.

That was what did it. It was so careless, so lacking in any sense of responsibility. I thought of all the presents I'd bought for his family on his behalf over the years. A white rage flickered in my gut, every limb in my body a branching fury. I closed my eyes, willing it to stop, trying to keep it in. Then I realized I did not want to keep it in. I thought of Kelly. I thought of Connie. I thought of Connie's mother, my mother. Dorothy. I thought suddenly about how much I hated money. I thought about how refreshed Kelly had looked after her rant. How tight our hug had been on our goodbye. I thought of her in a cottage hemmed by hedgerows, walking to the fields with an axe.

'Connie needs me to stay with her this Christmas,' I said.

Joe put his phone down again. 'What?'

'So I'm going to do that.'

'But you can't.'

'Yes, I can.'

'No. Mum thinks you're coming. She'll have made the food. She'll have laid a place.' His face was a picture of confusion.

'She can probably remove the place,' I said. 'Unless she's stuck it down with glue.'

'That's not funny,' Joe said. 'It's Christmas.'

I DON'T CARE I DON'T CARE I DON'T CARE I DON'T CARE, I thought, the words running over and over in my head like one of those screens in a stock exchange.

'Do you have to make fun of my mum all the time?' he said suddenly.

'What?' I said. 'I never make fun of your mum.'

'It's just – for once, Rose – it would be really nice to know that you're on our side, you know?'

'What are you talking about? I am on your side, Joe.'

'I just wish you could apply the same enthusiasm to you and me and our life together as you do to that old hag.'

'Shut up,' I said.

Joe looked shocked. I gestured with a sweep of my arm to the presents. 'I've even done the name labels,' I went on. 'All of them. You just need to put them in a bag.'

'This is crazy,' he said. 'You're just angry. You'll calm down and it'll all be fine.'

'No, Joe. You don't understand. You just don't.'

He sucked his teeth. 'Do you know what? You're right. Actually, I don't understand. I don't know what the fuck's happened to you.'

'What?'

'Ever since you took that job.'

'Don't blame my job, Joe. Don't you dare.'

'But it's fucked up. It's changing you.'

'Oh, don't be ridiculous,' I said.

'It's just been so shit between us—'

'It was shit before I took the job, let me assure you.' I got to my feet and stood in front of him.

'Rose, what's happened to you?' he said, adopting this expression of bemusement which enraged me. Joe loved to appear like the rational one, the one who has tried his best to reason with me, to get on my level, but who has good-naturedly had to conclude that I am beyond help.

'What do you mean, *what's happened*?' I said.

'You've changed. It's scaring me. You're scaring me.'

'I'm scaring you?' I said.

Joe leaned back against the sofa and surveyed me with pity. 'I can't deal with you when you're like this,' he said.

'Grow up, Joe. Just grow the fuck up,' I said. I wanted to go and kick the wall but I held myself together.

Joe's eyes widened. 'I can't have a conversation with you when you're hysterical,' he said.

'I'm not hysterical. I'm just angry. And I have a right to be.'

'Keep your voice down, for God's sake. You'll wake up the neighbour's baby.'

'Good. I hope I do,' I hissed. The loft-extension works from one side of our flat had kept us sleepless for about six months, and on the other, there was a baby with colic. I was feeling such ire towards Joe, I wanted all the children to wake up and piss their parents off for hours – to piss him off, too – to march up the street on their little sausage legs, tiny fists waving banners, to storm through our flat and circle him, screaming, WHAT ARE YOU DOING IN THIS LIFE, MISTER?

'Being in this flat with you is like talking to a child,' he said, refusing to raise his voice. I could tell he was just acting at being reasonable and I wanted to punch him. 'Just . . . don't be tiring, Rose.'

'You're asking *me* not to be tiring?'

'Yeah. You are so fucking tiring,' he said. 'We all think it.'

I was stunned. 'You know what, Joe? Fuck your Christmas.'

'What did you just say?'

'I just said – *fuck* your Christmas. Go on your own to fucking Wimbledon with your *fucking* family.' I kicked the presents and they scattered everywhere.

Joe looked at me with a mix of disgust and by now, a grim satisfaction. 'I knew it,' he said. 'You're a fucking psycho.'

*

Joe went back out – to where, I neither knew nor cared. I packed a duffel bag, feeling high and weird and certain.

I left the presents, except for Connie's, and locked the flat. I rubbed my eyes at the front door, took two very deep, detoxifying breaths, and stepped outside.

First, I went to Sainsbury's to purchase a big ham. I loved

Connie for her lack of snobbery over food; Sainsbury's would be just as good for her as Fortnum's. She probably had a ready-made turkey sandwich for Christmas lunch. I picked up lots of cheeses, vegetables, a chicken to roast, wines, a chocolate pudding, double cream – everything a reflection of the intensity and quantity of selfhood I felt inside, the giddiness and freedom to be doing this instead of *that*, with *him*.

But as I made my way up to North London, doubt began to seep in. Would Connie let me in? Would she have me, offer sanctuary? Or would I be crossing a line too far? I decided I would still risk it: Connie was like a siren call – the promise of a warm fire, good food. I was even looking forward to seeing the Christmas tree.

I didn't let myself in, but rang the doorbell. Her eyebrows shot up when she saw me standing there with my many bags of shopping and my duffel.

'I thought we could have a nice dinner?' I said. 'I'll cook.'

'Aren't you supposed to be at Joe's parents'?' She narrowed her eyes. 'You're not here out of pity, are you? You're not doing a Bob Cratchit on me?'

'No, Connie.'

'Mmm,' she said, but she turned into the house and I knew it was a sign to follow.

*

'I was just going to have soup and bread,' she said in the kitchen.

'Oh! Well, of course,' I said. 'But—'

'But a nice dinner will do just as well,' she said.

I started rummaging in the shopping bags. I knew she was looking at me. 'Is everything all right?' she said.

'Of course.'

'Good. Because I wouldn't like it if it wasn't. For you, I mean.'

'Have I interrupted you badly?' I said. 'I can always go back after a glass of something—'

'No, no,' she said, poking amongst the bags. 'Get a bottle from the fridge. Did you buy any chocolate?'

'I got you a bag of gold coins,' I said, and she laughed. I went to the fridge and found a chilled bottle of champagne.

'Open it, then,' she said.

I obeyed her, pouring it into two glasses. 'Cheers,' I said.

'Cheers,' Connie replied. 'Happy Christmas, Laura.'

'Happy Christmas, Connie,' I said, and I drank it like it was a magic potion.

*

I roasted the chicken and prepared everything else whilst Connie went upstairs to work. When it was ready, we sat opposite each other at the kitchen table. 'You're such a tremendous cook,' she said, sighing happily.

'Thank you.'

'Your talents are wasted here.'

I said nothing. 'Laura,' Connie went on, reaching across the table and putting her hand over mine. Feeling the warm, confident weight of it, my body nearly sagged.

'Yes?'

'You are more than welcome to stay for Christmas.' Connie kept her hand where it was and looked into my eyes. 'That room is yours. For however long you like.'

*

Connie tried to make up my bed in the spare room on the first floor, but her hands were bad so I finished the job. Closed curtains, fresh covers, the little lamp on the bedside table switched on, that dim-glowing yellow of childhood, next to a small vase of holly on the side, that she had held sheepishly between two hands as she stood at the bedroom door. I was touched, and even more so that Connie had not asked me why I was here and not with Joe. She did not probe, she did not pry. I felt very guilty, though, for not being the person she thought I was.

That Christmas night in Connie's spare room, time felt suspended. She was up very late, and I heard her quiet footstep on the stair towards her bed. Eventually, I caught sleep. I dreamed of my mother and me on a beach – not in Brittany, where my father had conjured her, but rather on the shoreline of Connie's new book. The sands of Massachusetts felt as real to me as I wandered them, following my mother's back. We were both of us looking for something, but she would not turn to me. I could not see her face. I'd done something wrong. I hadn't been truthful, and she would not turn to me.

26

For a moment the next morning, I had no idea where I was. My bed had shrunk from a double to a single, the configuration of the room was alien, and the faint morning light so different. Everything was quiet. I turned on my side, then yesterday came. The argument in the flat, the presents all over the floor, champagne and roasting a chicken. Connie's. The spare room. The vase of holly. Christmas Day.

Today there would be no stocking for me. No Lucia and Wilf incandescent with excitement, no Ben pottering for a corkscrew, no Dotty or Daisy – god, their names as a pairing were so ridiculous – and most of all, no Joe. Immediately, I felt relief, followed swiftly by disarray and fear. I kept waiting for the moment I would cry, but I couldn't feel it coming.

I checked my phone on the little bedside table. My dad had texted: JOYEUX CHRISTMAS OUR SWEET ROSE. LUV TO ALL, LUV DAD AND CLAIRE.

Happy Christmas, Dad! I texted back. Hope you're both having a lovely day. xxx

I put the phone down and pressed the pad of my index finger lightly onto a sharp prick of holly. Nothing from Joe. I wondered what he'd told his family – probably that I'd gone to Brittany. That was the safest lie. Not even Dorothy would let me sit in the flat on my own on Christmas Day.

To my surprise, my dad replied immediately. DID U LIKE YOUR PRESENT?

I realized I'd left my present from him in the flat. The only present I'd brought with me was the one for Connie. I'd noticed around the house during my sporadic dusting stints that Connie was an avid collector of ashtrays, although she didn't smoke. For her Christmas present I'd found a humdinger, a beautiful Deco number from a charity shop. It looked genuine enough to have come from somewhere proper, from a real dealer of antiques.

Haven't opened yet! I texted.

☹ DID U GET A NICE PRESSIE FROM JOE?

Haven't opened any presents yet. Just having breakfast.

CLAIRE SAYS ARE U OK?

I'm fine. Are you having a nice time?

YES. OK DARLING, I'LL CALL U IN A BITE?

*

Connie had placed two towels on the chair by the window and I put on my jeans and blouse, scooped the smallest towel and went to the gold and black bathroom to wash my face and brush my teeth. When I came out, Connie was waiting outside the bedroom door. 'I heard you were up,' she said. 'Happy Christmas.' She was dressed in her usual black, and looked tired.

'Happy Christmas!' I said.

'What do you normally do on Christmas Day?' she asked.

'I'm happy to do whatever you do.'

'I don't really do anything.' She looked nervous.

'Well, there are no rules, then,' I replied.

'You could boil that ham?' she said.

'I'll boil that ham.'

'Would you like a cup of tea?' she asked.

'That's my job. Are you sure—'

'It's Christmas. No rules,' Connie said, stomping off along the landing. From inside the bedroom, my phone started to ring. She turned. 'Will that be Joe?' she said.

'It's probably my dad.'

'Then you'd better answer it.'

I went in and picked up the phone. 'Hi, Dad.'

'Hello, my love. Happy Christmas.'

I felt immediately heavy at the sound of him, and sank into the side of the bed. I liked hearing my father's voice, but it unlocked a younger self, and jarred with the person I was in this house, right now. Tears came to my eyes, and a big rush of heat ran over me. This was the first time I'd heard his voice since our conversation on the beach, since he'd brought the concept of Constance Holden into my life.

'Are you there?' he said.

'I'm here.'

'Are you all right?'

I shuffled back on the mattress and leaned against the wall. 'I'm fine,' I said. 'You know I'm a bit *meh* about Christmas.'

He paused. 'I've been thinking about what I told you. About your mother.'

I closed my eyes. 'Oh?'

'I shouldn't – I shouldn't have left you with that.'

I opened my eyes again and looked around the room – Connie's theatre posters, her green-striped wallpaper, the bookcase full of her books. Downstairs, I could hear her clanking tea mugs onto the kitchen counter. I imagined telling my father the truth about where I was. What would happen if I did? He might not even believe me.

'It was all a long time ago,' he went on, sounding uncertain in the face of my silence.

'I know it was,' I said. 'It's OK, Dad. I'm glad you told me.'

'You should have come here this year.'

'Yeah.' I leaned forward and rubbed the hard curve of a holly leaf between my thumb and forefinger. It was so robust. 'Perhaps I should.'

'Claire's saying we should come and visit you and Joe in the New Year. Would you like that?'

I tried to taste the truth behind my dad's question. Was he reluctant? Was he really waiting hopefully for me to tell him such a journey wasn't necessary? If *he'd* been the one to suggest a visit, expressing pleasure at its possibility, that would be different. But it had been Claire's idea. I imagined it: him and Claire arriving in Portsmouth off the ferry, getting to Joe's flat and realizing I wasn't there – realizing that in fact, I'd left my job and had probably left Joe, and was now working for, of all people, Constance Holden.

'It's really OK,' I said brightly. It's so cold in January. You don't have to. I'm fine.'

'We can talk about it. Any time you like.' He hesitated again. 'Do you – need me to do anything?'

'No.'

'OK. Well, I'll text later. But have a good day, OK? Have a glass of something. Hope Dorothy's made you something good.'

'She's boiling a ham,' I said.

My dad laughed. 'Of course she is.' There was a pause. 'I love you,' he said.

'I love you too.'

We rang off, and I sat for a few moments, feeling raw. Then Connie called me down for tea.

*

Later that morning I started to boil the ham and got on with making a parsley sauce, alongside roasted potatoes, carrots, parsnips and sprouts. Connie sat at the kitchen table, having perked up since our early morning encounter. 'I'm taking the day off,' she said. 'Happy bloody Christmas!'

She proffered me a cracker from a box which she must have purchased along with her yards of tinsel. We pulled two, reading out the bad jokes, fiddling with the small plastic pouches that revealed a keyring with a bottle-opener for me, and a miniature puzzle for Connie that she didn't even bother to open, discarding it to one side immediately. We placed the paper crowns on our heads, hers purple, mine green, queen and princess for the day. I gave Connie her present, and she unwrapped it self-consciously, her fingers struggling with the string and tape. I wanted to reach out, make it easier for her, but I knew she'd hate that. When she finally got through the tissue-paper layers and saw the ashtray within, she was delighted. The sight of her turning it round in her hands with pleasure, gave me a true happiness I hadn't known in ages. 'But it's perfect!' she said, looking at me with true astonishment.

'So you like it?'

She placed it down gently. 'Is it jade? It looks like jade. Maybe from the twenties?'

'Maybe,' I said.

'My god. It's so . . . *thoughtful!*'

Again, I got the impression that it had been a long time since anyone had been thoughtful about Connie. I don't think she even realized how grateful she seemed. 'Did Joe help you with it?' she said.

'Joe?'

'Well, it must be antique.'

'Oh – yes. Yes, he did a bit.'

'Please thank him for me.'

'I will.'

Connie disappeared, coming back a minute later, bashfully handing over a small bag. 'Happy Christmas,' she said.

'Connie, you didn't—'

'I wanted to,' she said.

Inside the bag was a box. Inside the box was a gold necklace, with a gold initial L hanging off it. 'It's Victorian,' Connie said. 'Do you like it?'

I did like it. It was beautiful and delicate, but I felt such sorrow as I rested it in the palm of my hand. It was a physical reminder of my lie, and whilst part of me wanted nothing more than to wear it, another part wanted nothing more than to kneel before Connie, tell her my real name, and explain to her that in no way did I deserve a present like this.

'What's wrong?' Connie said, looking worried. 'You don't like it?'

'God, no. No. I love it, Connie. It's beautiful. But you shouldn't have.'

'Are you going to put it on?'

I obeyed her, half expecting – half hoping – that the necklace might be charmed, that as soon as it touched my skin, it might burn the false person inside it. But nothing happened. The L sat in the dip between my collarbones and fitted perfectly. It felt right.

'Sublime,' Connie said. 'I knew it would be.'

'Thank you.'

'No. Thank *you*, Laura.' She paused, looking a little shy. 'I'm very glad I found you.'

'I'm very glad I found you too,' I said.

Connie moved away, as if embarrassed. Battling with my own conflicting feelings, I went back to the stove and stirred the parsley sauce. I felt as if I belonged in this peaceful moment, with my L round my neck, in my paper crown, warm inside Connie's kitchen. I was safe within all these circles, and the outside world was cold and shapeless. To spill out my truths, to hand this necklace back, would mean possible rejection, and I simply couldn't bear it.

'Does Joe know you're with me?' Connie asked.

'No.'

'Won't he be worried?'

'Probably not.' I kept stirring the sauce. 'He thinks I'm cold,' I said suddenly. 'Connie, do you think I'm cold?'

'No, I don't. You're not cold,' she said.

I felt a sob rising up inside me, and I swallowed it down. I wanted Connie's kindness, but when she gave it to me, I didn't feel like I deserved it. 'Sometimes I think I must be,' I said, turning to her with my wooden spoon aloft. 'The things I'm capable of.' I swallowed, surprised at what I was saying.

Connie frowned. 'What are you capable of?'

A drop of parsley sauce fell to the floor. I couldn't say the words.

'Don't be so hard on yourself, Laura,' Connie said. 'You're dropping the sauce, by the way.'

'Connie,' I said, my voice croaky, replacing the spoon back in the pan. 'I don't mean to bring bad feeling into Christmas Day. Honestly, I don't.'

She waved away my concern with a crooked hand. 'You're not,' she said. 'I'm just a bit worried about you, that's all. You've looked pale recently.'

'Have I?'

'You and Joe seem to have had a falling out?'

'I didn't think I'd be here,' I said suddenly.

'You mean in my house?'

'In my life. I'm nearly thirty-five.' I felt an unnameable grief threatening to rise in my throat. 'I – thought I'd know what I needed to do.'

'It takes a long time to know what you need to do, Laura. Longer than thirty-five years.'

My tears were coming now. 'I don't think I love him,' I said, my voice strangled with sadness. 'Connie. I don't know what to do.'

I stood by the stove as the sobs began. Connie approached and put her arms around me, tentative but warm. I dipped my head and laid it on her shoulders, and let the tears fall.

*

Fifteen minutes or so later, we sat in the front room. I felt like I'd been hit by a truck, but I was calmer for crying, better for forming those words – that sentence I'd dreaded speaking aloud. 'It's never happened to me before,' I said.

'What hasn't?' asked Connie gently.

I stared into the carpet, feeling hollow, light, as if I might take off. 'I've had people stop loving me when I didn't want them to,' I said. 'That was brutal. I thought I was going to go mad. But I've never experienced this. How it feels when the love you've had for someone . . . *leaks* out of you. Like you're slowly being drip-dried, and you can't tell whether it's right or wrong, whether it's something you want or not. Whether you really want to break the contract, to say it's not enough. I've stopped *feeling*, Connie. I don't know who I am. I don't care about anything except—' I stopped myself.

'Except what?' said Connie.

'Except being here,' I said.

Connie looked thoughtful. 'I think you have actually felt a lot of things,' she said. 'But you didn't trust them. Maybe you've got to the point where you really have to trust yourself. You haven't stopped *feeling*, Laura. You're just scared of what you're feeling because it's new. There's no alternative in this world, you know, other than to trust yourself.'

I swallowed. 'I don't know if I can.'

'Think of it like stepping into another room you've never been in before, but you suspected it existed. Getting into the room is easy, once you have the key. But the reality of the room, the new dimensions, the new furnishings, the way the light sits – it will never be how you imagined it. But it is the room you're supposed to be in, because the other door has closed.'

'I feel . . . *small*,' I said.

'You're not small,' said Connie. 'You're the opposite. But just as there's always a price to pay for accepting love, so is there for stepping away from it.'

Something in her voice made me look up. 'And what's that price, in your experience?'

Connie sighed, thinking hard. 'That either way, you forgo your right to innocence. When you walk away from someone you used to love, you're stepping closer to the person you really are.'

27

Between Christmas and New Year I stayed close to Connie. I
didn't call Joe, and Kelly was still in the no-man's-land of her
in-laws. I slept at Connie's, wearing the necklace she had bought
me, never taking it off. Joe texted me on the 27th of December,
no doubt when he'd returned to the flat to find me gone.

Where are you? he wrote.

Happy Christmas to you too. I'm at Connie's.

Still looking for your mother? Found her yet?

I didn't reply.

On New Year's Eve, he texted again to apologize for his last
text: his tone was uncalled for, and he was sorry. He hoped I was
all right, and that maybe we should talk soon. What are your
plans for New Year's Eve? he asked. I'll be at Connie's, I replied,
and this time, it was me who didn't hear back. I was still looking
for my mother, but I was almost sabotaging the search. I spent
most of my time cooking for Connie. She'd asked for more
Italian foods since discovering my alleged Paduan cookery experience, so daily I was searching on my phone for articles such as
'How to Make the Best Handmade Pasta'. Connie and I took
slow walks on the Heath, coming back for crumpets and tea –
my carrot muffins being only a briefly tolerated hit – and in
between all this, I typed. I did think about my mother, but in an
increasingly abstract sense again, more as I had when I was little.
A dream woman – a woman who did not want to be found – or

someone I was truly too scared to locate? She had felt more palpable to me when I'd first entered Connie's house, as if she was definitely going to manifest, and things would be resolved. *Fiction doesn't put anything right*, Connie had said to Deborah. *But at least it tries.* But as we neared the end of typing up *The Mercurial*, I felt less enlightened about my mother than when I started.

The book would be ready by New Year's Day, Connie announced, at which point I would send it by email to Deborah.

The more time I spent as Laura Brown, the more I drifted away from Rose Simmons and all her worries. I was safe as Laura Brown in this house. I was trusted, I was needed. I took on Connie's worries as if they were my own; her life and the fate of the book were more vivid, more exciting, than anything that had been happening before I met her. I shared her concerns: that no publisher would want it, that no one would buy it, that Connie would be seen as a has-been who'd deserved to be forgotten in the first place. I reassured her, inserting myself in her quandary because I felt that my own fate was bound up with that of this new and vulnerable book. With every page I typed I'd gone deeper not just into the world of Margaret Gillespie, but that of Laura Brown as well, a lost girl in the wood of words, waiting for the epiphany of Connie's last full stop.

*

Connie was either a true artist who understood her internal rhythms before they made themselves heard to the rest of the world, or she was a control freak. Maybe it was both, because just as she predicted, on New Year's Day, alone in the kitchen, I typed up her novel's final sentences.

> *They didn't know she'd been swimming all this decade, nor half of the things she could do. They thought she could fly, become a goat,*

a hare, a virgin of perilous beauty. But they did not think much about her actual arms and her actual legs, her lungs and her boredom. They'd see the pile of clothes and think she'd turned into a gnat.

Instead she was going to turn into a fish. Margaret took off her boots and stood in the cold water, watching her toes bleach and fatten in its distorting coverage. Her skirts and apron, the stained cuffs of her shirt – she began to cast them off, the fabric expanding in the ocean. Her skin turned to gooseflesh even though it was a sunny day.

If it hadn't been for the sun, Christina had once said about their arrival, we'd have swum in the wrong direction and fallen off the world!

But Margaret knew where she was going. She knew that as long as you could breathe in it, the world went on. And after that, it wasn't your concern.

Her waist, her ribs, her breasts, underneath the water. Eastward now, submerged, breathless from the cold on her skin, Margaret kicked. Began to swim.

I sat there for a few moments. Outside in the garden it was a bright morning, and I watched a male blackbird hopping from planter to planter, his yellow beak a saffron dash against the barren soil. I closed my eyes, thinking of the story I'd just been in. Christina was dead. She'd died in her mother's arms, a scene that chilled me. It had been her blood swirling pinkly with the minnows, not Davy's. And after that, did Margaret wish to die? Not according to Connie. Did Margaret wail and beat her breast? No. She had no desire to exterminate herself, but her life was indeed now compromised. She was *compos mentis* enough to understand that she had to get away. Connie had given her character a second chance: Margaret Gillespie had escaped.

I closed the laptop. Connie's fiction held no fixed answers for me; so what choice now did I have? I could be bold. I could just tell Connie who I was – Connie liked me, she said she was glad she'd found me. And was I not both these women, Laura and Rose: their attributes living cheek by jowl within me?

'Connie,' I called from the foot of the stairs. After a few beats, I heard her office door open. 'It's finished,' I said. 'I'm done.'

'Oh!' she shouted. I stood vigilant in the hallway to make sure she didn't trip as she descended the stairs. 'So?' she said, stomping down towards me. 'What do you think?'

'The witch flees,' I said.

'The witch succeeds,' Connie replied with an elated grin. 'We've *done* it! It's done!'

We went into the kitchen and I sat back in front of the laptop screen. 'Congratulations, Con,' I said. 'How do you feel?'

'Tired,' she said. 'Relieved. What do you think about the ending?'

In truth, when it came to the ending I had anticipated a more explicit conclusion as to Margaret's guilt or responsibility. Some clarity as to whether she did actually *intend* to do away with her daughter. I thought that would be the culmination of the book. Instead, one woman was dead, and the other was still on the run. Connie's book had given me more questions than answers.

I said nothing, and sensed Connie's unease. 'At least it makes a change from drowning,' she said. 'I'm sick of women drowning in art.'

I still said nothing. 'You don't like it,' she said.

'I do,' I said. 'Of course I do. But, Connie – is Margaret guilty or not?'

She looked confused. 'Guilty of what?' she said.

I tried to mask my impatience. 'Christina's dead. Was that Margaret's intention?'

Connie frowned. 'Have I not made her intentions sufficiently obvious?'

'Maybe I'm being stupid, Con.'

'No, you're not. I'm interested in what you think.'

Emboldened, I pushed on. 'I just thought – given that it's a book about responsibility—'

'*Oh,*' she said, elongating the word, her eyes wide. 'You thought there'd be some justice. A sort of reparative chapter at the end.'

'I just thought we'd – understand Margaret's intentions. Whether she had any remorse, for example.'

'*Huh.*'

'People – are going to want to know.'

'Well,' said Connie brusquely. 'They're going to have to work it out for themselves. This is a book about how people damage each other inadvertently. I'm not going to *spoon*-feed them. Bash them over the head with it. That'll kill it.' She looked thoughtful. 'Although maybe I need to amp up Margaret's pain a bit. Show some odd behaviour or something. I don't want her to be aware of it, you see. Because she *is* hurting.'

I fought back the tears that were threatening. 'So Margaret did love her daughter?' I said.

'Yes,' said Connie, looking at me in disbelief. 'Of course.'

'And did she mean her to die?'

'No,' said Connie. 'But that's between you and me.' She paused. 'I'm sorry, Laura. I didn't realize you were going to react so strongly to it.'

'I suppose that's what happens when you become so intensely involved.'

'I suppose. And I'm glad you are.'

'And Margaret – is she going to die in the sea? I mean, it's the Atlantic Ocean,' I said.

'Well, if she didn't go into the water, they were going to set the dogs on her. She had no choice, Laura. But don't worry: she isn't going to die in the sea.' Connie put her hand on my shoulder. I felt the bone and sinew of it. 'Margaret Gillespie never dies.'

'Why not?'

'Because I haven't written that, that's why not.' I shrugged her hand off. It was the most transgressive thing I'd done to her: it felt teenaged and taboo, and Connie looked shocked. 'What on earth's wrong?' she said. 'It's just a story.'

'It *isn't*,' I said. 'I know it isn't.'

'What on earth do you mean?'

'It's your life.'

Connie's eyes narrowed. 'No, it isn't my life, Laura. It's my work.'

'But it's come from inside you. Who is Christina? Who is Margaret?'

Connie looked alarmed. 'Christina is Christina. Margaret is Margaret. Who do *you* think they are?'

'They're people you know.'

Connie stiffened. 'In a manner of speaking, yes. As figments of my imagination.'

'Just figments?'

'Where has all this come from?'

'I just – I'm confused, Connie.'

'I see that. Confused about what?'

I struggled to find the right words. 'Nothing,' I said eventually, miserably, feeling a fool.

'Laura,' said Connie more gently. 'Come away from the computer for a moment.'

I obeyed her, turning round to face her fully. She looked down at me, her expression one of concern. 'Are you angry that we've finished? Do you think I won't need you any more?'

'No,' I said, but I realized as I spoke that the thought of not being near Connie, not being wanted by her, would devastate me. 'Connie,' I said, looking pleadingly up at her. 'You haven't written anything for thirty years. Why did you want to write this now?'

She gave me a long look. From the slight twitch at the side of her mouth, I could tell she was irritated and had had enough of questions. 'Because it was what was inside me, Laura. And it had to come out.' She put her hand up to stop me saying more. 'Now, can you go and send it off to Deborah?'

*

Chastened, frustrated, I went to the corner cafe – more of a teashop than a greasy spoon, this was Hampstead, after all – to use the Wi-Fi and email the manuscript to Deborah from another account I'd had to make up for Laura Brown. I texted Deborah to tell her to expect it waiting in her inbox when she got back to work.

Deborah texted back immediately. Thanks, she wrote. What a way to start the new year! Can't believe it really. Having a brief glance now, it seems very clean. Excited!

I was interested in the word *clean. Clean* – as if Connie had threatened Deborah weeks previously with something dirty and messy, a tangle of the past unthreaded and re-woven for the present. This book had a sleek, authoritative power to it, and its characters emanated guilt and mystery. Deborah would find that out.

I didn't reply, because I was worried I'd get sucked into writing something that could be used against me if anyone ever discovered who I was. Deborah had the manuscript, and that was all that mattered. When I got back from the cafe, Connie was standing in the hallway, wrapped in a long scarf and coat. 'I'm going to the Heath,' she said.

'I might go for a nap,' I said, 'I'm exhausted.'

She stopped in the hallway. 'You're often exhausted, Laura,' she said. 'Are you eating enough?' Then she was gone.

I wandered into the front room, drained yet slightly wired from Connie's energy. I pictured her pacing the common land, sparked and restless, anticipating her agent's verdict after such a monumental break in time. But what I should have been doing was paying more attention to myself. Not to Connie. Not even to my invisible mother. Not to Margaret Gillespie or her daughter Christina. But to myself.

1982

28

Everyone from the last few months of their LA life came to Elise's belated birthday party. Connie had hired waiting staff, who moved in and out of the groups with trays of canapés. The waiting staff all looked like models – young men and women, extra-tall and extra-beautiful, their minds only half on their serving duties, waiting to get back to their small apartments in case today was the day for the magic phone call from their agent that might change their lives. The canapés they took around the patio were delicate and colourful, little blobs of avocado, curls of smoked salmon, puffs of pastry filled with Californian vegetables that nobody wanted to eat. There was tequila and vodka, and wine and beer and soft drinks. Music pumped from speakers that Connie had placed facing the garden from the living room: Roxy Music, The Sweet, The Stranglers, The Clash.

The cast and crew of *Heartlands*, Matt and Shara, plus friends of friends were there, and even Connie's agent, Deborah, who had flown out to see how things were going – but who really, Elise suspected, just fancied a holiday. Elise had heard about Deborah but never met her, and she was curious. Judging by the intensity of Deborah's gaze upon her, the feeling was mutual. Everyone had dressed up, and although looks-wise, most of them couldn't compete with the waiting staff, it seemed big shoulders, plumes of earrings, rings the size of Roman medals and fuchsia and turquoise prints were the order of the day. Connie was wearing a burnt-orange pantsuit. Elise did not think she'd ever see Connie in burnt orange, let alone a pantsuit, yet here they were.

'Deborah, this is Elise. El, this is Deborah,' said Connie. 'She runs my life.'

'I'd *like* to run her life, but she won't let me,' said Deborah, putting out her hand to shake Elise's. 'Happy birthday, Elise. We finally meet. I've heard a lot about you.'

'And I you.'

'Elise is sitting for a portrait by Shara,' said Connie. 'You remember Shara, my friend from university?'

Deborah looked unsure. 'It's going to be spectacular,' Connie went on.

'You've got a lot of people here,' said Deborah.

'They're mainly Connie's,' said Elise. 'She knows all these people better than I do.'

It was true; Connie was greeting and waving at five people for every one that Elise managed to muster a hi for. Elise felt a mixture of anger and defeat over the situation; Connie had meant well, hadn't she? She constantly tried to introduce Elise to everyone she thought Elise might like. But Elise just wanted to get away.

Connie put her hand on Elise's arm and said more gently: 'Relax. People like you. You'll have fun.'

Elise wished Connie wouldn't speak to her like this in front of other people. It was as if Connie thought she didn't have feelings on the same level of sophistication as others, that she could be spoken to like a child.

Deborah was watching them both. Despite the late-August heat making her hair frizz, and the beads of sweat on her temples, she carried herself with a natural air of authority. Elise had always assumed the woman would be older than Connie, but she wasn't: she was younger, shorter, plump and dark. She wore glasses and her eyes darted constantly, an agitated habit of looking all around her as if sizing up the emergency exits and the most useful people in the room. 'Do you like it out here, Elise?' Deborah asked. 'Would you recommend it?'

'What are you looking for, exactly?' said Elise.

Deborah seemed disconcerted. 'I'm not looking for anything.'

'Well, then. You'll probably be fine,' said Elise. 'There's nothing here except make-believe.'

Deborah didn't bother to conceal her look of alarm at Connie, but Connie only laughed. 'Ignore her, Deb. I know you're not scared of make-believe. You can't afford to be.'

'Actually, she's got a point, Con,' said Deborah. 'You could lose yourself here. Plenty of people have. I thought I should come over and check you were still sane.'

'I'm not going to lose myself, Deb,' said Connie. 'You know I'm not.'

Deborah jumped as a waiter with brown curly hair and the looks of Gregory Peck appeared at her side bearing a plate of smoked-salmon blinis.

'Ma'am?' he said.

'Are they for me?' she replied, giggling. Elise could hardly stop rolling her eyes to the back of her head.

'If you want them to be, ma'am, you can take the whole plate.'

Deborah went puce. 'Just one,' she managed to utter, and he smiled and melted away.

'*Anyway*,' said Connie. 'It's all wrapping up. Filming's heading east. We're like reverse pioneers.'

'You've stayed out here so much longer than I thought you

would,' said Deborah, looking over her shoulder to see if she could spot the waiter. 'I can see why, but you are coming *back*, aren't you?'

Connie didn't say anything. 'Con?' said Elise. 'Did you hear her? We are going back, right?'

'I heard her,' said Connie.

'Everyone's too positive here,' said Deborah. 'It's like a disease.'

'People will be just as rude to you in Los Angeles if you want them to be,' said Connie. 'In some cases, even ruder.'

The women laughed. Elise thought it was interesting to see the place through a new pair of eyes. *Have I got used to this?* she wondered to herself. *I surf in the Pacific. I say 'have a nice day'.* But this wasn't enough, and she knew it.

'Oh my god. Is that *Don Gullick*?' said Deborah, pointing to a man standing by the barbecue. 'Con, you have to introduce me. Just don't tell Robert.'

'Come on, you,' said Connie, taking Deborah by the arm. 'Don's a teddy bear.'

They left Elise standing on her own by the pool. She watched the little groups of people coming together, drifting apart again. She did not long to join them, but she longed for someone to notice her and come to her rescue.

*

The heat of Los Angeles by this time of year was insufferable, but they had started the party at six p.m., when it was hoped the earth had cooled a little. Elise couldn't bear to stand alone any more, so she walked to the border of cacti round the pool, and placed one bare sole on the soil, feeling its retained warmth, wondering what would happen if she tripped and fell into one of the huge and spiny succulents. She imagined herself skewered there, for ever. Connie had bought her a present, a gold necklace with her initial dangling from it. 'An apology present?' Elise had said, holding the shining letter E between her fingers, pleased at the annoyance flickering in Connie's face.

'It's a *birthday* present,' said Connie. 'I did say I was sorry. I found it in an old shop in Los Feliz.'

'It's really pretty.'

'I'm glad you like it, darling. Things have gone crazy here. You see that. My life – our life – you know this is what I've wanted, for a long time. It's just been a bit of a whirlwind.'

'But what is it that you wanted, Con? To live in a bungalow with a pool?'

'No. To be acknowledged.'

'You were acknowledged in England.'

Connie had ignored this. 'To do good work,' she said. 'With interesting people.'

Good work, with interesting people, thought Elise, remembering the conversation now, recalling Connie's distracted manner, her defensiveness. *Heartlands* did have a spectacular cast and production team, that couldn't be denied.

As she watched the party guests, Elise trailed her new necklace through her fingers, the E made of gold like the chain. It had been battered very thin and flat, a reminder both of who she was, and to whom she belonged.

She didn't want to be melancholic, but she couldn't shake it off. From the cacti, she kept her eyes on Connie, who'd reappeared from out of the crowd, a glowing and unmissable beacon in her burnt-orange pantsuit. Where had she even *bought* it? She was a defiant act of a redhead, a walking streak of autumn in August's closing stage. Elise had chosen to wear black.

'Hello,' said a voice. Matt was standing on the edge of the border. 'You trying to get some peyote?'

'That isn't such a bad idea,' she said. 'I want to get out of my head tonight.'

He looked concerned. 'What's wrong?'

'Nothing. I just . . . this party.' Elise gestured with a limp arm towards the doors of the bungalow. 'Who are they all?'

'Connie, right?'

'I don't know what I'm doing here,' said Elise. 'Half of these people don't either.'

'Well I know why I'm here. Happy birthday.'

'It was weeks ago, Matt. And you know it.'

He put out his hand and Elise took it, treading lightly over the soil. She felt in her body a second of not wanting to let go. He dropped her hand like it was boiling.

'Where's Shara?' she said.

'Inside.'

'Is she OK?'

'Do you want the honest answer?'

'Of course.'

'Shara doesn't like it here either. She wants to go home.'

'Well, then. You should take her.'

'But that's the thing. She wants to be alone.'

'I'm sorry. I know things aren't going well.'

'Don't be sorry. It's how it is. You know, the only time it's good is when she's painting you. Because she's doing the thing she loves, and I'm not around.' Matt ran his fingers through his hair. 'I shouldn't be telling you this. I don't know why I am.'

Elise thought she might know, but said nothing. In her sittings in Shara's studio, Shara had not talked at length about her marriage, but she had, to Elise's surprise, talked about the lost baby. Sometimes, she would only allude to it, as if the baby was wreathed in vaporous circles that Shara could not, or would not, penetrate. Other times, she talked as if the baby had survived.

She said she wanted to name the girl Dinah, though she hadn't told Matt this. After sitting for Shara, Elise would take her surfboard and head to the ocean with Matt, and she would enter the water, and think of Dinah, the lost baby.

'We're just experiencing this so differently,' Shara had said, her brush aloft, the paint dripping off it onto the studio floor. 'He thinks I'm dwelling on purpose, that I'm not willing to move on.'

'Are you willing to move on?' Elise had asked.

'I want to. But I'm not ready,' Shara had replied. 'I just want to be here, with a brush in my hand. I can't see the decades ahead with him,' she'd said suddenly. 'But I suppose that doesn't mean they aren't there.'

'Does Shara ever say anything to you?' Matt said. The volume of the music from the bungalow had suddenly been raised.

'Soft Cell,' said Elise.

'What? Oh, the music. Well, does she?'

'No. She just works.'

He exhaled heavily. 'I better go,' he said. 'Drive her home.'

'Yeah.' Elise began to walk away, wondering how feasible it might be for her to slip inside the bungalow and crawl into bed.

'Come surfing tomorrow?' he called.

She turned back. 'I don't have a sitting with Shara tomorrow.'

'I know.'

They looked at each other. 'You'll want the water,' he said. 'With the hangover you're planning. I'll come at twelve.'

Matt turned and walked away towards the patio and through the back doors. *You cool customer*, Elise thought, despite the fact that Connie would have him for breakfast. What was this – the idle flirtations of an unhappily married man – or was it her own desires, projected? He was handsome, no doubt – in a scruffy,

English way. He was young, too – but he didn't have the energy or hunger for his life that Shara had for her painting, or Connie for her writing. There was something aimless about him that many women would find unattractive.

But Elise recognized it in herself too – the capacity to blow with the winds. She felt an affinity with Matt, and thought he felt the same. Whenever she was out in the water with him she always felt wonderfully free. She felt safe about her own confusions and insecurities when he was around, because he was normal and humane. When they were in the water, Matt was always there for her, keeping an eye, making sure nothing happened to her. But he was lost like she was, of that she had no doubt.

*

Suddenly, there was a flurry at the patio doors. Barbara had arrived, carrying a huge bouquet of flowers that repulsed Elise with their hot pinkness. But she was still amazed by Barbara's presence, by the sheer fact that Barbara Lowden was bringing garish blooms to her twenty-third-birthday party.

The movie star came through the crowd, appearing to look for someone. She spotted Elise, and to Elise's surprise, made a beeline for her, laughing off the claims for attention from at least seven people in the process. She came up to Elise and embraced her. Barbara was wearing a heavy ylang-ylang perfume; her barriers were up tonight. 'Why are you skulking by the cactus?' she said loudly. 'Happy birthday, honey. It only gets better.' She embraced Elise again, and Elise took in a mouthful of hairspray. 'How's my eye?' Barbara whispered behind the bouquet. They separated a little, still hidden from the rest of the party by the giant flower arrangement, and stared at each other closely. Barbara's hair was enormous. She was wearing a pantsuit in one shade of blue, a jacket in another shade of blue over the top of it with large, angular shoulder pads, and a gold necklace, the centrepiece of which was cast in the shape of a lion.

'It's good, Barb,' Elise whispered. 'You can hardly see it. And the shimmer eyeshadow looks great.'

'*Thank you*,' Barbara whispered. 'You are an angel. You just need to show us your wings.'

*

The night darkened. Everyone hugged Elise, kissed her on the cheeks, held her arms or her hand – and with every touch, every paw on her, and exhortation to enjoy herself, how lucky she was to be so young, Elise felt more and more alone. Connie had arranged for a cake with slices of kiwi and purple flower petals fanned across it. The guests at the party sang 'Happy Birthday' as Elise held the knife aloft. Barbara told her to make a secret wish the moment she made it to the bottom of the sponge; Elise wished that Connie would want to go home. The cake looked bizarre but tasted good.

'Did you make this?' Elise asked Connie.

'God no. Barbara gave me the name of a fabulous baker.'

After Don Gullick left, Deborah decided to go back to her own hotel. 'Jet-lag,' she said to Elise, as the two of them stood at the front door. Connie had vanished again.

'Thanks for coming,' Elise said.

'I had a really good time,' said Deborah. She pointed through the hallway towards the patio. 'This set-up is mad.'

'I know.'

'Where's Con? I should tell her I'm off.'

'I don't know. Did she – say anything to you, about going back to the UK?'

Deborah swayed slightly. 'You really like her, don't you.'

'Why else would I be here?' said Elise, regretting the edge in her voice.

'I didn't mean it like that.' Deborah paused. 'I've known Connie a long time,' she went on.

'What does that mean?'

'She . . . will always do what she wants to do.'

'What are you saying?'

Deborah inhaled the fragrant night air. 'I'm saying this for your own good. The writing's always going to come first. *She's* always going to come first, because she's the writing. And I know she brought you here, and I know you live together – but take it from someone who's seen it so many times before. Make sure you've got your own thing, OK? You're young. Don't forget that.'

'I'm not young.'

'You're *twenty-three*.'

'Jesus. You too?'

Deborah put up her hands in surrender. 'I'm not saying you're fourteen years old and you don't know your arse from your elbow. But – I haven't seen her like this in a long time. Not since *Wax Heart* came out.'

'What do you mean?'

'She's high. She's *up*. She's writing. She looks straight through me. Don't you see her doing it? She's doing it to you as well.'

'How much did you drink tonight, Deborah?'

'Ah,' said Deborah. 'So you *do* know what I'm talking about.'

'Look – I know what it is, to be with someone like her,' said Elise. Deborah laughed with disbelief. 'My eyes are *open*, Deborah.'

'Oh, darling,' said Deborah, turning away and meandering down the garden path. 'They're just not open enough.'

★

Interfering bitch, thought Elise, slamming the front door. She went back to the party and began to drink with renewed focus. She thought she might have embarrassed herself in front of Matt, but she couldn't really remember. There were already blanks in the night. Someone took a group photo with Connie's camera, everyone bunched together by the pool. Elise saw little clumps of people, briefly hunching over, snorting up cocaine. She danced alone to electronic melodies and the erotic disco of Donna Summer, whose liquid voice floated off into the dark sky.

Eventually, Connie appeared. 'Where have you been?' Elise said, her words slurring.

'Hosting a party,' said Connie. 'Oh, my god. You're *wasted*.'

She looked at Elise with such disapproval that Elise thought she might cry. 'My eyes are open!' said Elise.

'What? You're pissed. Go to bed now.'

'Take me. I can't walk.'

'Are you serious? In front of all these people?'

'Fuck these people,' said Elise.

'Right,' said Connie, dragging Elise from under her armpits, shouldering her weight as they staggered to the bedroom.

★

Elise lay back on the bed and Connie peeled off her black dress, putting her head through an oversized I LOVE LOS ANGELES! T-shirt that the production team had bought her for a joke.

'This is a joke that's turned out to be true,' Elise said, prodding her own breasts.

'What?' snapped Connie.

'*You* said this place would eat your brain,' said Elise. 'Don't you remember?'

'It was a friend of mine who said that,' said Connie. 'And it hasn't eaten it so far.'

'I don't want to be here,' Elise slurred. She waved her hand in the direction of the garden. 'All the plants have spines.'

'Come on, El.'

'I don't have a spine,' she said, nuzzling her head onto Connie's shoulder. 'I don't have a spine.'

Connie held her and rubbed her back. 'I can feel a spine,' she said. 'See?'

It felt so good to be held.

'I do like it here,' said Connie. 'I won't lie. I know you don't like it as much as I do.'

'Of course you do, of course you do,' said Elise, her mouth open on the taut fabric of Connie's pantsuit, dampening it. 'It was my *birthday*. It was my *day*.'

'I know. But go to bed now. We'll talk about this in the morning.'

'Fuck you,' said Elise.

'Elise. Lie back down. You're plastered. Go to sleep. I'll check on you in a bit.'

'Stop treating me like a child!'

'Enough. You like it when I do,' said Connie, and she closed the bedroom door.

*

Elise's rage battled with her sorrow and intoxication, and lost. She slid into unconsciousness.

About two hours later she woke up with the need to vomit.

The music had stopped. The bungalow was silent and the night outside was entirely dark. The curtain on the window was still open. Only the pool was illuminated by its own lights, a glow of neon blue. Elise's vision was skewed and she felt extremely sick. *One day*, she thought, as she staggered to the bathroom, *I'm going to have such a sophisticated birthday party. The most sophisticated thing will be not to have a party at all.*

Kiwi and tequila and bits of petal swilled into the toilet bowl. Elise felt rancid, though better for ridding herself of the poison. She didn't look in the mirror, too scared to see a black hole. When she got back to the bed, she realized that she was the only one in it. Connie's side was cold.

'Con?' she croaked. She sat up, looking again through the window towards the pool. Tiptoeing towards it, she saw Barbara behind the wall of cacti, sitting on a sun lounger, silhouetted against the bright shock of water. As slowly and quietly as she could, Elise pulled open the window. The night was cooler than the room and she was grateful for the fresher air. Con was in the pool. She'd submerged herself entirely, and her hair was plastered to the sides of her face. *Has she gone in there in her pantsuit?* Elise wondered.

Con quietly bobbed around in the water, on her back, staring at the stars.

'It's why I didn't have kids,' Barbara was saying.

'She's an absolutist,' Connie said.

'A good thing, until it isn't. But don't forget you were the one who brought her here.'

'She had a choice.'

'*Huh.*'

'OK, *fine*. I shouldn't have brought her,' Connie said. 'I can't look after her and do what I need to do. It's not fair on her. Or me.'

'I think most people would have jumped at the chance to come here,' said Barbara.

Connie put her hands on the side of the pool and pushed herself out. She stood in shadow, but Elise could see she was completely naked, her pale skin dripping water, the outline of her body caught in the blue light reflecting from beneath the pool's surface.

Barbara reached out and stroked Connie's stomach, her fingers trailing down into Connie's pubic hair. Connie tipped her head back. 'Oh, god,' she said.

'Ssh,' said Barbara, removing her hand.

Elise couldn't move a muscle. She tried to process what she was seeing, but it was impossible. She blinked, refocused. The women were now standing apart. 'She doesn't know, does she?' said Barbara, handing Connie a towel.

'No,' said Connie, wrapping herself and taking a seat next to Barbara. 'She thinks I flirt with you. But that's it.'

'Everyone flirts with me.'

'Well, exactly.'

'No one knows how to talk to me properly,' said Barbara.

Connie lifted a hand to Barbara's hair in a liquid, easy motion. 'I do,' she said. 'But you scare everyone else shitless.'

Barbara turned to Connie and Elise saw their faces in profile, the tips of their noses nearly touching.

'She's a good kid, Connie,' said Barbara quietly. 'She's a really, really good kid. She's *lost*, and moody, but I know how that feels.' Barbara put her head in her hands. '*Shit*. I feel like shit. I said it should have only happened once.'

'I *will* tell her.'

'I don't know, Con. I don't know about this. She's – fragile.'

'I don't know about *that*,' said Connie emphatically. 'She just needs to find her own feet—'

Barbara fumbled in her bag and lit a cigarette. She inhaled it deeply, and Elise watched the smoke plume into the air, spreading to nothingness. 'You know yourself,' Barbara said. '*I* know myself, but Elise barely knows her own name. You need to say something. You can't just have her dangling around you for ever.'

'I thought you wanted this kept quiet,' said Connie sharply.

'I do, on my side. I don't even have to come into it. But on your side, you should tell her. It just feels wrong. It feels like we're tricking her.'

'We *are* tricking her. That's why it feels so bloody awful.' Connie sighed, leaning back against the sun lounger. 'But is telling her really for the best? Filming will finish. At some point, we'll go back to London and you'll forget this ever happened. I'm behaving like a crazy person, I know I am. But she can't be hurt if she doesn't know about it. And I don't want her to be hurt.'

'Do you love her?' said Barbara.

'Yes. Can I have a cigarette?'

'Have this one.' Barbara handed over the cigarette and Connie smoked it hungrily. 'Do you want her, Con?'

'What do you mean?'

'You know what I mean,' said Barbara.

'I don't know what to do!'

'Do you *want* her, Connie?'

Connie sighed, stubbing out the end of the cigarette. 'No. I don't.'

Elise clamped her hand over her mouth, and Barbara sighed too, a noise that sounded a million years old. She faced the pool, sitting upright again, like a goddess. Connie leaned towards her and kissed her on the side of her shoulder. Barbara turned, and their mouths met. Elise couldn't move as the two women scooped their arms around each other and sank back onto the sun lounger, their limbs shifting dark against the bright of the pool.

As she turned away and crept back to bed, Elise thought it would be just like Connie to leave their bedroom curtain open.

29

When Elise woke up the next morning, Connie had closed the curtain. Only a slim bar of light fell across the wall. Unable to move, Elise watched it, her heart beating hard. A rush of nausea made her gasp. Her eyes were rocks, so she closed them again, turning on her side and burrowing into the mattress. She couldn't get out of bed because she was stuck by a spell. She could not remember the evening before. And then, in a heat-filled rush, she could.

Elise opened her eyes and peered at the curtain. Behind it, would the pool still be there? Perhaps the women had drunk it in their lust. *I could run into the hole they've left behind*, Elise thought. *Smash my head on the concrete at the bottom. That would serve her right.*

Her mind began to flea-jump. She was going to be sick but she still couldn't move. The bile was rising, and a hammering pain had started in her head, fireflies darting into bullets, exploding until her skull was just a swilling pail of blood where her brain had vanished. Was she going to die here? It was a real possibility. She took a shallow breath, wincing. She was lying like a toad, dying in the half-light of this rented house. She tried to sit up but the pain in her face arched over her skull. She hissed and fell back down.

Elise wiggled her legs: not paralysed. She could run from here if she had to, catch a plane, go home to – where? But her bones were made of jam, spreading into her skin. It didn't matter there was nowhere to run. She patted her collarbone: the necklace from Connie was still there. She thought about wrenching it off, but she didn't have the energy. Never in twenty-three years of living had she felt so terrible.

'Good morning,' said a low voice. 'How are you feeling?'

Elise turned her head very slowly. Connie, fully dressed, was leaning on the door frame. 'Here you go, Lady Lazarus,' she said, coming towards Elise with a glass of fizzing aspirin. 'I thought you were going to sleep for a hundred years. It's nearly two o'clock.'

'What?'

Elise didn't move, so Connie placed the glass on the bedside table. 'Good party, then?' said Connie affectionately, sitting down lightly on the side of the bed.

'You tell me,' said Elise.

'You don't remember it?'

Elise closed her eyes. 'I want to die,' she said. 'Kill me.'

'I'm not going to kill you. Go back to sleep.'

'You always want me to go to sleep,' said Elise, mumbling into the pillow.

30

Matt was standing on the shore with his board stuck in the sand as usual. His wetsuit was rolled down to his waist and he was facing the water with his hands on his hips as if he were ship-wrecked and waiting for rescue.

For a moment, Elise hesitated. Shara was in the beach house behind her. Maybe she was even watching them.

'Matt,' she called.

He turned. 'I came to pick you up last week,' he said. 'Connie said you were still asleep.'

'I was. I got hammered.'

'So you kept your promise to yourself?'

'Yep. In bed for a day. I'm sorry you made that drive.'

'Don't be sorry.' He turned to the water. 'Look how beautiful it is today.'

Elise stared out at the Pacific. The sun was high. It was a beautiful September afternoon. 'Shara's finished the painting,' she said. 'It's over.'

'Do you like it?' said Matt.

'She's got me. I've never seen a painting of myself like that before.' It was true: all those hours spent sitting in the drawing classes at the RCA, and finally, she felt seen.

'Shara does that. Is she going to give it to you?'

'She offered. I said no.'

Matt whistled. 'Wow. Why?'

Elise looked up at him. 'She's already given me so much.'

'What has she given you?'

'And I can't take the painting from her when I'm going to take something else.'

'What do you mean?'

The wind whipped at Elise's short hair and she tried to tuck it behind her ears. Beyond them, a huge pod of pelicans flew by, low to the surface of the ocean. However many times she had seen these birds, they still gave her the shivers. They looked like something prehistoric. 'Have you got your car keys on you?' she said.

'No.'

'Well, go and get them. And let's drive.'

*

They drove along the Pacific coast, with no clear destination, not talking much, still in their wetsuits. When they approached a motel sign, Elise asked him to pull over. By now, she believed it was clear to Matt what she wanted and what was going to happen. It concerned her that Matt didn't ask her why she wanted this, that he wished only to catch this chance on its wing. So she did not know whether he had moral doubts, or any kind of credo – a conscience, say, about his wife's grief for a baby he didn't even know was called Dinah.

And where is my conscience? she asked herself. Buried like treasure at the bottom of a swimming pool. The bright cheer of the sun above their heads was a joke – but it was also necessary to make Elise feel alive in this day. Everything she had hoped for had been eclipsed – and yet she was still here, illuminated. Her arms were brown, the hairs upon them golden. This decision with Matt, she could control. Elise was sure he wanted her

– and it was nice, for once, not to have to fight to be wanted. She had forgotten how that felt. She tried not to think about trouble coming their way.

*

Matt paid for the room, maintaining a bemused expression on his face. He crossed his arms to look casual, but it only made him look defensive.

She unlocked the room door, and stood to the side like a porter. Matt walked in and she shut them away from the sun. The room turned a pale pink through the flimsy curtains as if they were standing in the centre of a shell. 'We shouldn't do this,' he said.

She sat on the end of the bed. 'Why not?'

'We're not being honest.'

'We will be honest. For now, this is just us. Matt, come here.'

She shunted herself further up towards the headboard. He stood at the end of the bed, watching her. 'I do want this,' he said.

'I know you do.'

'I've thought about it.'

Elise opened her legs slightly, still in Shara's neoprene wet-suit. 'Tell me what you've thought.'

'What your skin would feel like to touch.'

'It's soft,' she said. 'Come and see.' She rolled on her front. 'Unzip me.'

Matt knelt beside her on the mattress, running the zip of her wetsuit open to the top of her buttocks. Elise felt him rest a warm palm on the centre of her back and it immediately relaxed her. 'I saw you naked when you were in the studio,' he said.

She rolled over onto her back and began to peel away the arms of the wetsuit. Then she lay back. 'I know you did.'

He put his mouth to her collarbone and kissed it, kissing the battered gold *E* of her necklace, the tops of her breasts – gently at first and then with more urgency. He freed her legs from the neoprene, and she freed his, and they fell back again onto the bed. Elise felt herself unwinding, his hands and mouth releasing her out of her body and into a timeless place where she was floating in pleasure.

'Go into me,' she said, even though she wasn't sure she was completely ready. He eased himself in but it was still a shock, so deep into her that she gasped. 'Oh, *fuck*,' said Matt. 'Elise, I think about you all the time.' He kissed her mouth, and she kissed him back, again and again and again. 'I never thought this would happen,' he murmured.

'Me neither,' said Elise. But as she closed her eyes and let herself go, she knew that she was lying.

2018

31

I'd been so caught up with Connie's manuscript, and with the strange tightrope walk of being two women with both different and familiar lives, and with the question of my mother and who I wanted to be in the world, that when I did pay actual attention to my physical self, I was in for a surprise.

On the 6th of January, Epiphany, I discovered my body again, in Connie's understairs loo, peeing on a stick as she wandered the Heath. My period had been late – but there'd been so much stress. I just thought it was late. I hadn't felt sick, or any different. I'd felt tired, sure, but who by the end of 2017 had not felt tired?

I sat on Connie's lavatory in the black and gold bathroom, urinating on the fibrous stick, and watched it turn pink. And when the two lines appeared on the screen, I did not believe it.

I thought of Joe. I thought of my dad. I thought of Kelly and her online community of instamothers. I imagined telling them. I thought of Elise. I even thought of Christina, dying in her mother's arms – Christina and Margaret, protected by fiction, but penetrating my core as much as my own intangible mother. I thought of Connie.

I thought of all these people, and barely knew what to think of myself.

I went to the kitchen and had a cup of tea, and half an hour later I went back to the loo and did a second test, and the second confirmation forced me to entertain some kind of understanding.

I felt biological. As if my body had passed a test. My ovaries, my womb, my blood, taking things into their own hands. *This is our time now!* they were saying. My imagination was forced to play catch-up.

*

I hid the sticks in my bag, and in a daze I wandered to the front room and sat down on Connie's sofa. Many friends had said to me, *Oh we weren't really trying!* before admitting in the same breath that they'd dispensed with birth control – *just to see.* Just to see what, exactly? If they were viable bodies? If they did, in fact, want to be parents? This was a life we were talking about, not a lifestyle. But I realized now why they had said that. It was because they were trying to embody the paradox of wanting something that they might not want. No one could test out being a parent; have a baby then reasonably hand it back. No one wanted to confess that they didn't know what they were doing. I wish more people did.

Had I, too, wanted to put my body to the test, *just to see*? It made a certain illogical sense.

There was a chance I would not be pregnant in three months' time. It would be healthier not to think of what was inside me as a person who actually existed. And it was easy enough to do. The only person I was thinking about at this point, was myself.

*

Connie was still out, so I used her phone to call my doctors' surgery and got a last-minute appointment for that day (a genuine Christmas miracle). I left a note for Connie saying I'd had to go out, and I walked to the station, feeling like a lightbulb had just switched on in my stomach. Could people see this light shining out of me? It appeared not. I was as invisible as the next person.

In the doctor's consulting room, I told her I thought I was pregnant. 'I've missed a period,' I said. 'I've done two tests that have come up positive. But I want you to tell me for sure.'

She listened to me and nodded, appearing to understand my unwillingness to rely on my own investigations. She was an older woman with grey hair cropped short, and a kindly face. She made me think of Dorothy.

As we waited for the result, I sat looking at the gastroenterology diagram on the wall, at the beauty and intricacy of the gut. I wondered why the doctor had that illustration – and not one of the lungs, for example, or the heart, or the womb. My gaze drifted over the many colours and contours of the gastric system, at the marvel we never know and never see – until it goes wrong, until it turns on us.

The doctor saw me staring and smiled. 'The most extraordinary part of the body, if you ask me. You didn't, but still.'

'Why is it?'

'It's such a sophisticated set of systems and organs. I read recently that researchers believe that ninety-five per cent of the body's serotonin resides in the bowels.'

'Wow.'

'We've dragged up all our emotions into the brain and heart, but doctors since the sixteenth century have thought that the gut exerts the real hold over our feelings.'

'I've probably sat down on mine a little too hard,' I said.

'We all do, at one time or another.'

'So!' I said.

'Yes,' she said. 'The test. OK, Rose. You were right. You're pregnant.'

I stared at my palms, turned upwards on my knees like some act of supplication. It was official. I was in the condition. I was a case. I wasn't alone. A ghost of a person had turned up in the corner of my mind.

We sat quietly.

'Have you told anyone you might be pregnant?' the doctor asked.

'No.'

'If you can share it with people you trust, Rose, that will always help.'

I hesitated, feeling as if I was unburdening my deepest secrets to her. 'I – don't know what to do,' I said.

'What to do? Well, the first thing is to start taking folic—'

'No, I mean—' I stopped, unable to go on, but knowing I had to speak. I felt like I was revealing something sinful, and I hated myself for it. 'I don't know if I can – if I can do it.'

'OK.' She paused. 'That's fine.'

I closed my eyes, bathing in her words with something akin to relief. Just to speak the words was to take the sting out of them. But then I wondered if the doctor really thought that what I was saying was fine. She might only be saying this because as a doctor she had to obey the law. As a woman she would know the grey shades and holistic injustice of having so much going on in just one body, but really only being able to make a stark choice about it – a binary choice of black or white, yes or no.

Hit by the ambiguity of the doctor's reaction, I realized that I'd come here looking to claim some certitude. I still had my eyes closed, waiting for it, when the doctor touched me gently on the arm and passed me a leaflet entitled 'What's Next?'. For a fleeting moment of horror I thought it was some sort of evangelist anti-abortion pamphlet, but it wasn't. It was just a photo-set of all kinds of different things I might be feeling, physically and psychologically. And then, on the other side, my *options*.

'Have you been feeling pregnant – sick, tired?' she asked.

'A bit tired, but I didn't really notice. I've had a lot going on.' I felt so pathetically defensive.

'Of course,' she said.

'The father doesn't know,' I said. 'I might not tell him.' I knew she didn't need to hear all this, but I had to tell someone.

'OK,' she said. 'You're not together?'

'I don't know,' I said, feeling even more pathetic. I was making a nine-year relationship sound like a one-night stand.

'OK.'

'I guess that's life!' I said, and laughed.

Her eyes flicked to the computer screen. 'You don't have to make any decisions today,' she said. 'It's going to be all right.'

'Thank you.'

'Read that pamphlet. There are some telephone numbers on the back for organizations women can consult when they're trying to make a decision.'

'Right.'

She smiled. 'Don't worry, Rose. For now, that's all. Take the folic acid, and if you decide to go another route, I'm here too.'

'OK. Thank you.' I stood up, gripping the pamphlet so hard in my hand that I almost crushed it. 'Happy new year,' I said.

'Yes,' she replied. 'A happy new year.'

I wandered out into the street. It was bitterly cold, and getting dark. I walked. I didn't feel pregnant. I felt alone.

32

Joe and I met up a week later. He came through the door of the cafe where we'd agreed to meet – central, neutral, just off Oxford Street – and I thought, *Here is a man I used to know.*

His beard had grown. I wondered whether this was neglect or intention. It suited him. 'Hello,' I said. 'Happy new year.' A thought almost physically juddered through me of what was inside my body. I pushed it away, smiled. 'Thanks for meeting here,' I said. We hugged, no kiss.

His face was taut, his eyes downcast. 'How are you?' he said, sitting in the chair opposite me.

'I'm well, thank you. Glad all the Christmas stuff is over. How are you?'

'Same. You missed a real fight between Mum and Daisy though. You would have loved it.'

I laughed. 'What was it about?'

'I don't even really know. Dais was pissed off about something.'

'How are her and Radek?'

Joe looked uncomfortable. 'You know what they're like. They'll get through it.'

'Yeah.'

His eyes flicked to my neckline, where to my discomfort I realized I had not removed the *L* necklace Connie had bought me for Christmas. 'What's that?' he said. 'What's the *L* for?'

I grasped it in my fist, my cheeks flushed. 'It's nothing,' I said.

'Nothing?'

'It's just a joke.'

'Did someone give it to you?'

'Yeah. Kelly.'

He looked confused. 'You left the flat, Rosie. You vanished.'

'Actually, you left first.'

'I came back.'

'I'm here now, Joe,' I said, tucking the necklace under my jumper. I felt the instinct to apologize, but I swallowed it down.

'I've been worried about you,' he said.

'You don't need to worry about me,' I said. I placed my words between us with the deliberation of a gypsy come to tell her own fortune.

'Right,' said Joe. He cleared his throat. 'I'm sorry, Rosie. I didn't mean it. What I said.'

'About what?'

He looked at me pointedly. 'About you.'

'That I'm tiring? That I'm a psycho?'

His lips tensed together. 'Yes.'

'I think everyone's a little bit psycho by the end of the year,' I said. 'But thank you.'

Joe hesitated. 'But you have changed.'

I took a light breath. 'How have I changed?'

'You're – more focused. Harder.'

'Harder? I feel the opposite, Joey. I'm soft. I'm letting things in. Maybe for the first time ever.'

He looked worried. 'What are you letting in?'

'Maybe we've both changed,' I said, avoiding an answer. I wasn't sure it was precisely true that Joe had changed. I didn't think he'd changed much in the last few years at all, in fact, but that was because I'd lost all perspective of him. But in this moment I was certain that if he met someone new, then the changes would show. Joe just couldn't change with me.

'Did they like the presents?' I said.

'Yep. Thank you for doing that. I should have done it.'

I waited for a more expansive reply, but none came. 'Are you back at the flat, then?' I said.

'Yeah.' Joe paused. 'And – are you coming back?'

'I don't think so,' I said gently.

'Right. You're not actually *living* with her, are you?'

'Joey, I think you know it's best I don't come back to the flat.'

He was silent for a long while. No one came to take our order, but neither of us could leave the table. 'What are we going to do?' he said eventually.

'I think we need to let each other go,' I said.

He stared at me. He seemed to want to say something, but changed his mind.

'I do love you, Joey,' I said. 'And we could hang on. Stick it out together – for another ten years, another twenty. You'll be fifty-four. Fifty-four and still with me. Is that what you really want?'

I didn't know why I was abasing myself like this, offering myself as a booby prize to Joe in exchange for his dogged commitment, but I knew I had to make him see.

'Everyone has their ups and downs,' he said. 'Mum and Dad – god, sometimes we really thought it was done. But it wasn't. It'll never be done. Mum says it's normal to go through phases.'

So he'd been talking to Dorothy, then. I was impressed that he'd maybe had a meaningful conversation with his mother, for once. I thought she would have liked it. I was good for something, at least. I was also surprised that Dorothy was potentially agitating for us to stay together.

'But we don't have to do that, if we don't want to,' I said. 'Do you really want to? How many ups have there been in the last couple of years – and how many downs?'

Joe looked back up at me. 'I don't want not to know you,' he said.

'That won't happen. We'll always know each other. But we can set each other free.'

'When did you start feeling like this?' he said.

I saw the twenty-five-year-old man I'd met at a party nine years ago, full of ideas and jokes, smoking a cigarette. I thought about how when I saw him, I told myself: *We could be a couple.* He would be a person to do things with. I thought about his warm hands, his attentiveness. His curiosity. His patience that had fizzled, in the end, to nothing. We'd seen each other through a lot.

I knew I owed Joe an answer, but when did I know that our love had changed? Was it at Christmas, wrapping his mother's hand-cream? Was it peeing on those sticks and seeing the path my life might take? Was it before all that, when I walked through Connie's door for the first time? Was it on the beach with my dad? Or had the seed been sown years ago, as happens so many times, when lovers are foolish enough to think everything will stay the same?

I hadn't noticed exactly when my love had begun to slip away. No, that is not entirely true. There had been times when I tasted the staleness. The sense of defeat and affectionate despair. Whenever this happened, I had let that awareness lie untended.

'There's a bit in Connie's first novel,' I said. 'No, wait, Joey – listen – don't roll your eyes. She says that there's you, your partner, and then the relationship itself. Love. You have to look after love, just as you look after yourself. You can't just expect love to sustain itself on its own. We've not been looking after it, Joe. And neither of us have wanted to. And sometimes there's just not an explanation for that.'

'Love isn't a pot plant, Rose.'

'It is a living thing,' I said.

He looked at me. 'Don't cry,' he said. 'You'll make me cry.'

'I think we can cry,' I said.

So we did. Quiet tears, the secret still inside me, on a sodden January day. A beginning of grief. A small goodbye.

*

An electric sense of my skin, my hands and feet. I did not feel triumphant. But I did, in an interesting way, feel more free. To be always waiting and wanting had been my most natural state to be. To be yearning for something, rather than having the guts to make it real. I didn't know how much longer that could last. I got out at Hampstead Heath overground station and headed to Connie's.

By the time I let myself in, I felt composed enough. Connie was sitting in her favourite armchair in the front room with an open bottle of champagne before her, two glasses waiting. A familiar sight, but this time she was beaming at me, and I felt discombobulated by her air of celebration. It was as if I'd walked through the wrong door.

'Hi, Con,' I said.

'There you are! Good news!' she said.

'What?' For a mad moment, I thought she'd divined what was going on inside me.

'Deborah rang. You know that girl she was talking about at the publisher?'

'The editor?'

'Yes. Georgina. The one at Griffin. Deb decided to target her specifically, rather than a general approach to lots of publishers. It *worked*, Laura. Deb sent her *The Mercurial*, and she loves it. She's going to make an offer.'

'Oh, Connie!'

Connie got to her feet. I stood there, half-stunned, whilst she wrapped her arms around me and held me briefly. When she pulled away, her eyes were lit up and she looked about forty years younger. '*Apparently*, "the puritanical tension on the Massachusetts coast was a perfect balance to the anarchy and witchiness of Margaret".'

'Did she actually say "witchiness"?'

'That's what Deb said,' said Connie. 'I like the sound of this Georgina. Would you like a glass?'

'Not for me.'

Connie looked surprised. 'Really? But isn't this what we wanted?'

We. The pronoun glowed. 'Of course it is,' I said. 'I'm delighted. I'm so happy for you. But – it's too early to drink,' I said.

'It's four p.m. and it's *dark*,' Connie replied. 'It's *January*. I'm going to sell a *book*.'

'I know. And it's marvellous. But no, thank you. I'm sorry, Con. It's just – I'm tired.'

'*You're* tired? I'm seventy-three.'

'I'm sorry.'

'Don't worry,' she said, although I could tell she was disappointed. 'I am more than capable of drinking it myself.'

I collapsed into the sofa. '*The Mercurial*'s going to be a hit.'

'Well, I don't know about that,' said Con. 'But the fact that there is a living soul who is still interested in my writing, and she's young enough to be my daughter – well, I can't tell you how it feels, Laura. I'm absolutely delighted. I didn't think I'd feel like this. I thought I'd be indifferent. Isn't it terrible that I'm not? I'm *delighted*. I am.'

I laughed. I'd never seen her this animated. 'And I've got so much to thank you for,' she said.

'No you haven't. You wrote it.'

'But you made it very easy for me, all that typing, all the delicious food. Just your *being here*. You're a bloody godsend.'

I poured her a glass of champagne and she told me that, according to Deborah, Griffin would publish that summer providing the money was enough. If they agreed the contracts, a round of edits would apparently be coming Connie's way, but they were minor; Georgina didn't want to touch it much. 'Do you think that's a good thing?' said Connie. 'Do you think she's scared of me?'

'She hasn't met you. You should meet her. Then she'll be scared of you.'

'I am not a scary person,' Connie said. 'I'm a pussycat.'

I hesitated, remembering what Deborah had told me that evening she'd come round for the pizza – how Connie disliked journalists, how she resisted interpretation. 'Have you thought about what it's going to be like, being published again?' I said. 'Talking to people about your work – do you think you're ready? There'll be questions. Why you haven't written – they'll want an angle.'

Connie was silent for a moment. 'I'll give them an obtuse one,' she said.

'Connie, it's not funny. What are you going to say?'

She swallowed her champagne. 'I'll say I didn't think I had anything worth writing. It's the truth.'

'But why now? Con, why have you written it now?'

Connie snapped her head towards me. 'Why are you always asking me that?'

I felt my cheeks flush. 'I've only asked you twice.'

'That's more than enough.'

'I – just think you need to be prepared.'

'Fine. I wrote it now because it felt right. And I felt ready.'

'Ready . . . for what?'

Connie made a noise of exasperation. 'For god's sake. I don't see why I have to defend myself to you. Is this your attempt at press training me? Can't that wait?' She frowned. 'Or is it something else?'

I closed my eyes. 'I'm fine.'

She snorted. 'Come on. Spit it out.'

'The thing is, Con,' I said. I opened my eyes. I twisted my fingers together, over and over. I couldn't look at her, but I couldn't keep it to myself any longer. I needed her to know, I needed her to make it better. 'Well. The thing is. I went to the doctor—'

Connie put her glass down. 'Oh, god. Laura, are you ill?'

'No,' I said. 'I'm pregnant.'

I dared to look up at her. Her face was a mask of shock, and I was sure, as I continued to wait for her to say something, that my time here as Laura Brown was over. Connie would not tolerate me in her house. The news of this baby would change everything for her. The dynamic between Laura and Connie would implode, I would slink away as Rose, and my mother's story would fall through my fingers, again.

1982

33

Elise would say she was going surfing, and Connie would drive her out to Malibu. Once Connie was gone, Elise and Matt would load up the surfboards onto his car, under the pretence they were visiting other beaches. Instead, they made stop-offs at motels along the Pacific Highway. In whatever hired room they found, varying in ambience and quality, sometimes paid for with Shara's dollars, and other days with Connie's, Elise tried to exorcise her rage on Matt's body.

Connie had no idea what Elise had witnessed between her and Barbara by the pool, but she had begun to comment on Elise's behaviour, asking her why she was so quiet, why was she so angry, why all this surfing, why wouldn't she talk? Elise couldn't bear these interrogations; she couldn't face the conversation that might come. Better to run, better to leave it all behind. Just over a week after their first time together in the motel with the shell-pink light, Elise suggested to Matt that they should leave.

'Leave?' he said. 'But where will we go?' As if there were no such thing as planes or other countries.

Elise swallowed her irritation. He was not as adept as her at this. 'I don't know,' she said, lying back in the mussed bedsheets. 'It'll come to me.'

'How's this going to pan out?'

'Is it that you're scared?'

'I'm not scared,' he said. 'It's just, this is all quite fast.'

'What's happening between us has confirmed something that we already knew, Matt. It's like a pact. We've found each other, a way out, and things can't stay as they are. You're always saying you can't live in that beach house any longer.'

'Yeah, but—'

'And I can't be in the bungalow.'

'Why not?' He sat up, propping himself on the thin pillows. 'Do you think Connie suspects something?'

'It's not that,' said Elise. 'What are we going to do – meet up with our surfboards and pretend we're finding waves until Shara finds us out?'

He thought about it, and then one day quite soon after, they did it: packed a pair of small suitcases and drove to the airport in his car. Elise felt beneath her bare feet the old cola cans Matt never threw away, rolling round in the footwell, the last of their syrup dried in a fine brown line along their lips. As he zoomed along the opposite freeway to the one she'd come in on four months before, Elise ran the arch of her foot over and over one of the cans, and stared out of the passenger window. The world was there, so near – but every time she touched it, it didn't give her what she wanted. She remembered Connie, so excited in her sunglasses. Connie, who'd wanted this trip so much.

It wasn't until they reached the airport and parked in the long-term stay, that Elise chose Mexico City: a short flight to a very different country. Matt agreed to the destination, and Elise felt good that he was saying yes to her big ideas. Being the one who decided things on this magnitude was a novel experience. A border was being crossed and there was a heightened sense of removal: facts which matched Elise's feeling of being a fish out of water in her own life.

'Did you leave Shara a note?' she asked Matt as they queued up at the Aeromexico counter.

'Yeah.'

'What did it say?'

'That I needed to be alone for a while.'

'A while? Is that all you said? You should have said you were with me. How will Connie know where I am?'

'They'll know, Elise.'

'Connie's sleeping with Barbara,' she said.

The woman in front of them in the queue turned round, her expression one of distaste. But Elise wasn't having any of it. She stared at the woman until she looked away.

'What did you say?' said Matt.

'You heard me. Con and Barb.'

'And how long has that been going on?'

'I don't know. A while.'

'Are you OK?' he said.

'Yeah. Course I am.'

*

When they got to the front of the queue, Matt bought them return flights, not one-way tickets. There was something so depressing and prosaic about this decision, but Elise kept her tongue mute, her mouth clamped shut, because what was paramount was that they get out of this city. She supposed Matt was trying to treat this as a sort of holiday, a while, a black hole of time. But even if he couldn't handle the enormity of what they were about to do, she could. She knew she would never set foot in LA again.

On the plane, the quasi-defiance of gravity was a help. Elise felt miraculous: here she was, in all her messiness, and no one was dead! She and Matt had found each other at just the right time. He was not perfect, but he'd got her out of there, hadn't he? He worshipped her body, and she knew now – Connie having brutally confirmed this – that no one was perfect.

Matt seemed to relax, too, as if he had needed to have the ground vanish from beneath his feet for him to come into himself. He held her hand and squeezed it and they looked at each other conspiratorially.

After the plane landed in Mexico City, they caught a taxi to a street of hotels a stone's throw from the span of the Zócalo. Elise lay still in their small clean bed, awake next to Matt's sleeping form, and wondered what Connie was doing now. How long would it take Connie to realize that she'd gone? She fantasized Connie, turning over tables and chairs in search of her, a game of hide and seek. She fantasized Connie's worry and Connie's guilt. It gave her a bleak and petulant pleasure.

By her side Matt tossed and turned, and she wondered how much he thought about Shara. The note he'd written sounded anaemic, and then there was the safety net of the return ticket. It drove Elise crazy that she couldn't eradicate everything before this new beginning, but she reassured herself that with time, erasure would come. She tried not to think about Shara in her studio, the beautiful, careful painting Shara had finished. Shara, telling her to keep the baby, if ever she got pregnant.

The next day, they sat up in bed.

'We could go to the National Palace?' Matt said.

'No. Let's go to the anthropology museum. That'll be much more interesting.'

'OK,' he said, and she felt the thrill again of being obeyed. 'You're probably right.'

*

They spent a long time before the gigantic Aztec stone disc that had been dug out of the city's land during the repairs on the cathedral in the eighteenth century.

'Imagine looking for God and finding that,' said Matt, his eyes like saucers.

It was a monumental artefact. In the middle of the disc was a sun god, Tonatiuh, holding two human hearts in each of his clawed hands, his tongue the shape of a knife. Around the four corners of the deity, carved representations showed different eras of Azteca time. Elise read the information plaque beside it:

> The bottom right square represents _Nahui Atl_,
> which ended when the world was flooded
> and all the humans turned to fish.

It sounded like a poem. Elise imagined herself as someone who measured time in eras of Jaguar, Water, Rain and Wind. She imagined believing that a sun god was holding her and Matt's hearts in his claws, his knife ready for the sacrifice. She was drawn to the warning inside this disc, about the sacrifices one must make, the smallness of a self alongside the enormous universe. She thought she could live in this country that held within its past these viscerally spiritual beliefs, where such treasures were still being pulled out of the ground, where it was a valid fate to be turned into a fish. Even if she couldn't, she already liked it a lot more than Los Angeles.

At night through the windows they heard the sounds of a woman orgasming, but they couldn't locate where her noises were coming from, given the backyard amphitheatre of identical windows and washing lines and collective heat. They lay there, laughing at the sound of it, so detached from them yet so familiar. They couldn't help but listen. It reminded them of their attraction, their bond, and Matt would hold Elise and go inside her from behind, pushing in deep, her face towards their open window. Elise let out her own pleasure with no restraint. The windows, whether they were open or closed, ceased to exist.

*

They didn't stay long in the city, because it wasn't cheap and Matt wanted to be by a beach. He bought another pair of flights, and Elise watched him hand over the dollars. They flew on to the Yucatán peninsula – and when she saw the emerald waters, she thought she could live here too. The sand was like sugar, and what bloomed between them in this new country eroded their sense of responsibility. Matt splashed, fully clothed, into the ocean. Elise thought about ripping up the return ticket, whether he would notice.

She knew they needed to find a shape to their days otherwise he might go back.

'Shall we rent a place?' she said. 'It's cheaper than a hotel.'

He agreed, so they rented an apartment, paying for a fortnight to start with. The floor tiles were beautiful, but they were slightly apprehensive at the lack of air-conditioning or any electric fan. And so it proved. The temperature in and out of the apartment was unbearable. There was no benefit of a cool mountain night or morning in which to steal a few hours' sleep. It was on the top floor of a corner block and its back rooms looked onto three other walls of apartments forming a towering square. Other people's windows before them were endless, open all the time too, with washing hanging and fallen socks splayed on the corrugated-iron roof of the garage that spanned the ground between the buildings. The sound of mopeds at the front and the shouts of children playing in the ground-floor backyards were the only daytime sound they heard. They never saw a face clearly, just bodies moving from room to room, eating at a table, watching TV, having a shower.

They sat in their underwear, playing endless card games, eating strange-flavoured ice popsicles from the street vendor. Elise bought an old-fashioned flamenco fan to cool herself. The backs of their thighs stuck to the plastic furniture to the point of pain when it was time to peel themselves off and fetch another popsicle. It was hard to do anything.

Elise sometimes thought of herself and Matt as felons, with a crime that was going to catch them up. At times, this all felt inevitable. It had all been so easy. You just got in a car and drove. Shara didn't want him. Connie was sleeping with Barbara. They'd done well to remove themselves. *This is the right thing.*

The heat made Elise sleep badly and at night she was visited by the same dream. There was a girl in a house and the roof above her was caving in. The girl climbed out the rafters towards a span of rock pools. In the morning Elise told Matt about it, how it felt perfectly logical that a beach should be on a level with a rooftop. She could still see the light playing in gold flecks on those rock pools, the sea so far out that the sand stretched and gleamed. Matt listened attentively as Elise nestled in the crook of his arm. She loved that he listened to her like this, that he thought it all mattered, but he offered no interpretation. She knew, with a pang in her stomach, that Connie would have spun the next chapter of the story.

*

Two weeks in to renting the apartment, Matt said he would extend the lease, but he thought he should call Shara.

'OK,' said Elise. 'You should.'

'It's going to be awful.'

'It might not be. Maybe she'll understand.'

They didn't have a phone in the apartment, so he went to a public telephone booth with a pile of pesos in his fist. Elise waited outside, leaning against the wall. She was still wearing the necklace Connie had given her, and now she played with it, tugging it against the back of her neck so that the chain dug into her skin. She strained to listen to the conversation going on inside the booth, but couldn't hear much. A stray dog wandered up to her and slumped at her feet. She didn't pat it, worried about rabies. Matt didn't shout: to a passer-by it might look like a perfectly normal scene, a man in a booth making a quick but urgent call, a woman outside, waiting patiently, a tourist resisting the local dogs.

Matt put the receiver back on the hook and opened the door. 'Did she ask you where you were?' she said.

'Yeah.'

'And did you tell her?'

'Approximately.'

'*Approximately*?'

'I said I was by the beach in Mexico. But she'll know it's the Yucatán.'

'Why?'

Matt looked awkward. 'We've . . . been here before.'

'You didn't tell me that.'

'Well, you didn't tell me about Connie and Barbara.'

Elise decided to ignore this. 'How was she?'

'Better than I thought she'd be,' said Matt. 'She was actually quite businesslike. I don't think she wants me to come back.'

Elise could see this had offended and surprised him. She wanted to hit him. 'I've got something to tell you,' she said. 'I think I'm pregnant.'

Matt stared at her. 'What?'

'I think I'm pregnant. I've missed a period.'

'How long?'

Elise pushed herself off the wall and began to walk. Matt ran to join her and the stray dog pushed himself out of the dust and followed them both before giving up in search of shade. 'Since yesterday,' she said.

'Only yesterday? That's not—'

'I'm regular.'

Matt looked terrified. Suddenly, everything about him made sense to her. 'Wait and see,' he said. 'The stress of leaving—'

She stopped in the street. 'Fine. You think what you want. But I *am*.'

Matt looked at Elise as if seeing her for the first time.

Back in their apartment, he took his swimming trunks off the sole dining chair and said he was going for a swim in the sea. Elise lay back on the bed, knowing her period would not come, knowing she was pregnant, and knowing that Matt wanted the water in his life more than he wanted a woman.

34

A month later, Elise was combing the shore, stepping over the membranes of dead jellyfish. She found large pieces of seaweed in the shape of stiff fans, salt-scrubbed driftwood worn away in elegant shapes, crab shells which cracked between her fingers like blown eggs. She looked up, and Connie was coming towards her, as if she had walked ashore from the water, coming from her kingdom in the sea.

Connie stopped. The two women stared at each other. The sky above their heads was dark purifying blue like a whale's back; and deep green, fringed at the horizon with fat, low clouds of grey. Instinctively, as Connie approached, Elise put her arm across her stomach. A storm was on its way, and Elise knew there was no point running. The beach just went on and on, and she had bare feet, so she could not sensibly run into the semi-jungle that fringed the back of the shore.

'What are you doing?' said Connie.

She sounded almost plaintive, but the anger was clear in her face. Elise felt her heart close up again, where it had, without her realizing, opened a tiny crack.

'What do you mean?' she said, looking down at a medusa by her foot, flattened on the sand. She considered picking it up and throwing it at Connie, wondering if she'd get a sting herself.

'He's *married*,' said Connie.

'No hello?'

'Have you any idea how sick Shara is right now?'

'Sick?'

'Her depression's back. She's not getting out of bed—'

'She's not my responsibility,' Elise said.

'Oh, I could slap you. We've been looking everywhere for you.'

'Connie, just go away.'

But Connie stayed exactly where she was. 'Why did you do this?'

'I didn't actively go out of my way to hurt Shara. What me and Matt have – it's not easy to explain.'

Connie hooted with vitriol and stumped her heel into the sand. 'Right.'

'You know what, Con? You're the biggest hypocrite I've ever met. You track me down to lecture me on my behaviour, when you—' Elise stopped herself. To say the words would make them true.

'When I *what*?'

'When you've been with Barbara. For months.'

Connie stared at Elise. 'What are you talking about?'

'Oh, don't start. I *saw* you.'

'What?'

'At my birthday party.'

'Elise, you were off your head.'

'I saw you by the pool. The two of you, after everyone had gone. I heard what you said.'

Elise had never seen her look so furious. 'Is *that* why you're here?' Connie said. 'On this deserted beach? With *Matt Simmons*? All this stupidity because you think I'm sleeping with Barbara?'

'I trusted you,' said Elise, and to her fury, she began to sob.

'I don't know what you think you saw, but I am most

certainly not sleeping with Barbara. Ever since you disappeared—'

'I *saw* you, Connie. I saw you.'

Connie whirled towards the sea in frustration, stomping down to the water's edge to stare out at the water.

'Just admit what you did,' said Elise.

'I didn't do anything,' shouted Connie.

'I heard what she asked you. *"Do you want her, Connie?"* And you said no.'

Connie blanched. 'I wouldn't say that.'

'Don't do this to me,' said Elise, feeling the distress rising in her body. 'It isn't fair. Just admit it.'

Connie still wouldn't turn round. 'It happened just the once. OK?'

Connie burst into tears. Relief at being vindicated for her betrayal flooded Elise's body. She slid to her knees, the sand soft and yielding. 'It was more than once,' she said. 'You've lied to me again.'

Connie turned round, wiping her face, and walked back to where Elise was still kneeling. 'Once.'

They stared at each other. Elise didn't know what to say. 'You're still wearing the necklace,' Connie said.

Instinctively, Elise touched the *E* around her neck. 'I forget it's there.'

'It looks beautiful,' said Connie.

'It's just a necklace.'

Connie hesitated. 'What I did with Barbara. It was a foolish thing,' she said. 'It didn't mean anything. It was a blip. These things . . . happen, El. A one-off. LA's been mad. And Barbara needed someone.'

'I needed someone. I needed you.'

'I know. I'm so sorry. I'm just . . . telling you what happened.

Her ex was a nightmare. I tried to comfort her and before I knew it . . . It's been mad for me—'

'And what about *me*, Con? What about me? Leaving London, following you around—'

'You're in Mexico with my best friend's husband. You left us, Elise.'

'You don't love me. You don't want me. And they don't love each other any more either.'

'What do you know about Shara's feelings?' Connie said. 'You think because they're not having sex it means everything's over?'

Elise stood up and brushed the sand off her kneecaps. 'I understand her.'

'Lucky Shara. Shame no one understands *you*, Elise.'

'I think it's quite clear what's happened. I don't have to have this conversation with you.'

'Actually, you do,' said Connie.

Elise looked out to the horizon. 'Don't try and turn my life into some sordid, unimportant thing that you can just turn up and destroy. What you did with Barbara – why do you think I left in the first place?'

Connie closed her eyes. 'Please. It won't happen again. Come back to LA.'

'I'm never going back there. *Never.*'

Now it was Connie's turn to fall to her knees. She put her arms round Elise's shins. Elise steadied herself and refused to give way. 'I am so sorry,' Connie said. 'It was selfish. But I didn't ever want to hurt you.'

Connie's embrace felt too confident, and Elise shrugged her off. 'We can't go back. You lied to me.'

'Please—'

'No. You don't understand.' Elise clutched her stomach

instinctively. Connie was still kneeling in the sand, looking up at her. '*I* can't go back.'

Connie stared at Elise's hands. 'Are you – is he—'

Elise nodded.

Connie sat back on the sand, her body frozen with shock, a look of horror on her face. 'Are you serious?'

'Yes.'

'You *idiot*,' said Connie. 'My god. You really love to fuck it up.'

'Connie, it doesn't have to—'

'No, Elise. What's happened here? I just don't understand what's happened. You're not *keeping* it, are you?'

'I am.'

'You seriously think keeping this child is a good idea? How selfish are you?'

'I'm not selfish.'

'You are. And naive. You can barely look after yourself, let alone—'

Elise did run, then. She couldn't bear it any longer. The truth of what was growing inside her gave her the strength to run, and the promise – mad and strange, that she'd made to Shara – went round and round in her head. *If you ever find that you're pregnant, have the baby.*

If I ever get pregnant, I will.

2018

35

Connie sat back in her armchair. 'A baby,' she said.

'Well, I hope it's a baby,' I replied, aiming for humour.

Connie leaned forward and poured herself a shot of champagne, and then kept pouring. Her hand was trembling with the weight of it but I knew she didn't want my help. 'Are you scared?' she said.

'Scared of keeping it, or scared of . . . getting rid of it?' I replied.

Shakily, she put the bottle down. 'You're going to get rid of it?' she asked.

'I didn't say that. I don't know, Con – I don't know what I'm going to do. I've – just come back from seeing Joe, in fact. It's over.'

'Oh, bloody hell. Are you all right?'

'I'm OK,' I said. I didn't feel too bad, was the truth. My greater feeling right now was surprise at the ease with which I'd walked out of that building after months of failing to find a single exit.

Connie looked severe and far away. 'Are *you* OK?' I said. 'I know it's not ideal, and I never planned this—'

'Have the baby here,' she said.

'*What?*'

'Live with it here.'

'Connie, be sensible. I can't do that.'

'Why not? Why's it so unlikely? I've got the room. I don't want you to feel you have to stop working for me just because you no longer want the man who impregnated you.'

'Nice way of putting it.'

She narrowed her eyes at me. 'Does Joe know?'

'No.'

'Laura,' said Connie gently. 'Do you want to be a mother?'

'I don't think I'd be a very good one.'

'That's not what I asked.'

I sighed. 'I don't know. I don't want to be with Joe, so I'd be alone. But what if he wanted to be involved? The timing's appalling. And I've just begun to—'

'You wouldn't be alone,' said Connie. She hesitated. 'You'd have me.'

We looked at each other. I wanted to rush towards her and give her a hug, to thank her for being so kind, so understanding, so amazing. I thought she would turf me out, as if I was a fallen woman and she my puritanical landlady, a scene from a kitchen-sink drama. But instead Connie seemed almost keen – for what, exactly, I wasn't sure. She was definitely determined to reassure me. It made my deceptions – my false name, my true purpose here, even the lies I'd told about Joe and his profession – feel even worse.

'Do you – know anything about babies?' I asked.

Connie laughed. 'Not much. I've only known one or two in my life, and that was some time ago.' She looked serious. 'But it isn't just about babies, is it? That baby becomes a child, and then a teenager, a young person with their own agency. And then a fully fledged adult. I don't know much about babies, but I *do* know something about adults, fully fledged or not.'

I found myself putting my hand on top of hers, and holding it there for a good while. We hadn't touched much, and it surprised me how warm her skin was. She took my hand and tried to squeeze it, but her power was not strong.

'Whatever you decide to do, Laura, you can always call this place your home,' she said.

'Thank you,' I replied, my voice barely a whisper. Never in a million years would I have envisaged this: me, in Connie Holden's front room, holding her hand as she offered shelter for me and an unborn baby.

Connie looked up at me, her expression almost bashful. 'You'd be a good mother.'

'I don't have any precedent,' I said.

'What do you mean?'

I looked her in the eyes. The words, and the timing of them: finally, it felt right. 'I never knew my mother,' I said.

Connie stared at me, then frowned. 'What?'

'She left when I was a baby.'

Her eyes widened. 'My god, Laura, I'm sorry.'

'So I guess I don't exactly understand what's involved.'

Connie couldn't stop staring at me. 'But your father?'

'He brought me up.'

She gathered herself, the downward turn of her mouth appearing to push away the weight of my words. 'He did a good job, Laura. Just follow his example.'

I could have laughed. How easy it felt, in the end, to tell her this truth of my life. It was not the whole truth, of course – but it was a beginning. And now, Connie knew – not everything, not yet – but something fairly substantial. She looked thoughtful and I knew I'd sharpened her curiosity. Perhaps now she would be the one to come to me with questions, and I would be the one deciding when to reveal a truth.

'Con, can I – ask you something?' I said. I did not let go of her hand. 'I know you don't like questions.'

She smiled. 'I'll make an exception for the pregnant lady.'

'You can absolutely tell me to shut up. But – was there a reason you didn't have children?'

I regretted my question immediately. I saw her almost brace herself, the question flowing over her like a cold breeze. Her back straightened, her arm reached again for the champagne glass. 'Well,' she said. 'That is quite a question.'

'I'm sorry—'

'Among many factors,' Connie said, ignoring me, 'there was the slight issue of my dislike of sex with men. We didn't have all these options you have nowadays. Either my partner or I would have had to have sex with a man, I suppose.' She made a face, then stared into the unlit fire. 'We wouldn't have been allowed to adopt, either.'

'Did you and your partner – want them?'

Connie turned the glass awkwardly in her hand. I thought the remaining champagne inside it was going to slosh out, but she replaced the glass on the table. 'In the main, no,' she said. 'I only met one or two children that nearly made me change my mind.' She paused, smiling down at the rug as if a child were there, sitting on their small rump, staring up at her. 'But generally, I've always been very much someone who needs to do what she needs to do, answering to as few people as possible,' she went on. 'If you're worrying about being a bad mother, I think I'd have been the perfect candidate, not you. Then again, the amount of fussing and nannying that goes on these days, it's a wonder these children grow up past the age of five. Perhaps my neglectfulness would have been a blessing. But still; I am a neglectful person. I can't, or won't . . . adapt myself.' She sat back in the armchair, her hands resting in her lap. 'I'd spent too long fighting to be the woman I wanted to be, to ever hand her over, to cash in my autonomy.'

I sat down myself, lying against the back of the sofa. I closed my eyes, exhausted.

36

Kel was keen when I suggested a walk on Hampstead Heath. I need to move, she texted. I don't think I've left the house for eighteen days.

I was sitting on a bench when I saw her walking slowly towards me up Parliament Hill, with that unmistakable pregnancy waddle. Behind her, London was virtually invisible. It was late January: the BT Tower was the only landmark you could see in the mist, a vertical smudge of milky grey, a satin pallor of drizzle hanging over the entire city. We could have been anywhere. We could have been up in the atmosphere. Tourists gathered at the view, only to murmur their disappointments before moving off.

'How was Christmas?' I asked her, after we embraced.

Kelly grimaced, holding her sides. 'I've turned into a Christmas pudding.'

'You're lovely.'

'Do you know there are apps now that tell you how your foetus is the size of a cress seed?'

A shot of panic rushed through my body as I thought of the dot inside me. 'A *cress seed*?' I said.

'Then a coffee bean, then a grape. Probably a potato.'

'King Edward or new?' I said, and Kelly laughed. 'Why is a foetus a foodstuff?' I asked.

'I dunno,' said Kelly. 'Recognizable shapes, I guess.'

'Well, for fuck's sake, Kel. When men have bodily growths we say, *It was a lump the size of a golf ball.*'

'*Bodily growths*? Did you just call my baby a bodily growth?'

'Or – *a hole the size of a ten-pence piece*! Sport and money, Kelly. No one wants to eat a dollar or a golf ball. What's with all this cannibalization, of making women seem edible?'

She looked at me. 'You've been with your feminist novelist, haven't you? It's OK. When *you're* up the duff, you can say your baby's the size of a rabbit shit.'

'Ha ha. Chop many logs, did you?' I asked, in an attempt to change the subject.

'Oh boy, did I chop some logs,' Kelly said. She stood away from me and gave me a hard look. 'You look really good, Rosie.'

'You sound surprised.'

She wiped her nose against the cold air. 'I didn't mean it like that.'

'I know. In the end, I did actually do what I wanted for Christmas,' I said as we walked towards the ponds. 'Maybe that's it?'

'You went to France?'

'No. I had a fight with Joe and I stayed with Connie,' I said. My hand moved towards my bare neck; I had left the necklace on the bedside table at Connie's house. I didn't think I could withstand Kelly's nosiness about such a gift; she might not be as willing to let it drop as Joe had been.

'Oh, my god,' said Kelly. 'I was right. You *have* been spending loads of time with her.'

'Yep.'

'And how was that?'

'Pretty wonderful, actually,' I said. 'Revelatory.'

'So you told her who you really are?'

'No.' Kelly rolled her eyes. 'Kel, me and Joe broke up.'

Kelly stopped walking. She turned to me, her face pale, her eyes wide. She put her hands on either side of my arms and held me tight. 'Are you OK?' she said.

'Yes,' I said. 'It was the right thing to do.'

Kelly nodded at me. '*Wow*,' she said.

'Single at nearly thirty-five. What a loser.'

'Er, no. What a hero.' Kelly paused. 'I'm jealous.'

'Oh shut up, you are not jealous.'

'I am. You're *free*.'

'Kel, how am I free?'

'You could go anywhere, do anything – any other bombshells you wanna drop on me?'

I hesitated. Kelly had often said how cool it would be for us to have children at the same time. Suddenly, I saw a vision of myself being interviewed on the @thestellakella page, talking about birth plans. It didn't feel right. What might she think of me if I told her I didn't know what I was going to do? In that moment, I didn't trust our love enough, which was wrong of me. I just didn't want her to think I was a coward. 'No,' I said. 'Just that.'

'How's Joe about it?' she said.

'I don't really know. I mean, I'm not in the flat. But he seemed sad, when it happened. It's scary, really – the way you can just fall away from someone.'

'It's been a long time coming, Rosebud. And women are always like that.'

'What do you mean?'

'Well, all the women I know who've left long-term relation-ships in their thirties checked out of it long before they actually did. They went through all the grief when they were still together with the guy. Played through all the scenarios, processed their feelings – so when the split actually happened, they just felt light and free. Men take it worse. They pretend not to, but they do. They haven't laid any *preparations*.'

'Right. I think it was a shock, Kel. I hope he's OK. I think part of him thought we were going to get back together.'

'He'll be fine, Rosie,' she said gently. 'He was born to be fine. You have to think about yourself right now.'

'I don't hate him.'

'I know you don't. Just – give yourself some time, OK?' She patted my arm. 'There'll be a lot going on, even if it doesn't feel like it. Your mind, your heart, your body – they'll all be dealing with it at different times. Just be gentle.'

I closed my eyes. I didn't want to think about my body today. 'Yes,' I said. 'Thank you.'

She squeezed my hand. 'Come on. Let's get you a hot chocolate.'

'You mean let's get *you* a hot chocolate,' I said.

'Obviously,' said Kelly, and we began to walk.

*

We holed up in a little cafe on the edge of the Heath. 'Mol starts school this September,' said Kelly. 'Can you believe it? I mean, she'll be dating soon and I'm going to have a nervous breakdown about it.'

'Kel, that's at least, I dunno, two years away.'

'Ha ha. But I swear a few weeks ago she was in nappies. You know what she said to me this morning?'

'Go on.'

' "Have a calm and relaxing day with Rosie, Mummy. Enjoy your *you time*." She's four.'

'She's hilarious.'

'I know. I don't think I said things like that when I was four.'

'Kel, what is it actually *like*, being a mother?'

She laughed. 'Oh, Rosie mine. You seriously want me to answer that?'

'Yeah. You write about it every day. Come on. Give me the non-social media exclusive. Tell me.'

Kelly loved challenges like this. She pressed her chin to her chest, then looked back up. 'It's like driving in two lanes at the same time. It's like being the most of everything, and the least of everything. The capacity for feeling shit is so much more than you could ever imagine. Like, fucking *bleak*. I feel . . . *robbed*. And the same applies the other way. Sometimes, I feel God has put his hand on my life and given me this secret experience. This eye-watering joy. I'm so lucky! It feels like a drug! And I know it's silly, 'cos so many people have it. But it feels entirely mine.'

'Thank you,' I said.

'Was that good?'

'Yep.'

'Can I put it online?'

'It's yours.'

She looked suspicious. 'Why are you asking me this? You're not worried that 'cos you broke up with Joe that was your last chance? I promise you, it won't be.'

I opened my mouth to tell her. Part of me – yes, definitely, part of me, *wanted* to tell her – to go forth into that adventure, to speak the child into being. It was a part of myself I had never explored before. I knew Kelly would be there for me, I knew she would help me, and love me, and never let me feel alone.

But this was the problem: the fact that I came in so many parts. I wanted so badly to feel whole.

'Have you ever been to Costa Rica?' I said.

'Eh?'

'I can't remember,' I went on. 'I don't *think* you have.'

'Well, no. I've been to Mexico,' she said.

'I'd love to go to Costa Rica. Home of the jaguar.'

Kelly frowned. 'Are you off on one of your weird things? Mothers, jaguars, I can't keep up.'

I put my arm round her and squeezed her tightly. 'You know me, Kettlebell. I always like to know what's on the other side.'

37

Tentative plans were being put in place by Connie's new publisher to arrange some interviews with her in newspapers and magazines to coincide with the launch of *The Mercurial* – and, if they could swing it, radio and TV. It was all about the Mystery Comeback: *What Kept Constance Holden From Writing For So Long?* According to Deborah, media outlets were very keen to reintroduce Connie to a whole missed generation – or two – of readers. I thought fondly of Zoë, how excited she would be.

But Deborah had been right when she said Connie wasn't keen on interviews. Connie was being very curmudgeonly. 'The publisher wants to do upmarket interviews in classy places, Con,' I said.

'*Classy places?*' I winced as I heard my words spoken back to me. Connie huffed. 'I think I'd rather be asked about my favourite cheese.'

'I could see if *Cheese Weekly* is keen?'

'Is there actually a magazine called *Cheese Weekly*? Don't answer that. Anyway, I'm not interested in all this. I want to know about *you*. Have you thought about what you're going to do?'

A shiver of anxiety ran through me. Three weeks had passed since I'd told Connie I was pregnant. I had thought about the situation constantly, projecting myself forward into a future that was, by turns, both manageable and impossible. Before this discovery, I'd told myself I'd been quite open to the idea of two, maybe three, maybe four years of unfettered living. Conservative, really; no more than four years. Why the lack of scope? Why four? I might have wanted more. It could be ten. Why not twenty? I might have wished to be unencumbered for ever, now I was quite fully a woman. To be unencumbered, and not a girl, and happy. It felt like a configuration long desired, long fought-for by an army of long-dead women. An aloneness that never was lonely. A freedom to do whatever, with whomever, whenever I wanted. Being untethered, eating biscuits in the bath, reading novels till midday. Plane journeys. *That* was what I wanted. It was of utmost importance, heady beyond belief. To feel whole, alone, was a revelation.

But then, on other nights – and some days, too, preparing another dish of tagliatelle for Connie, or walking with Mol in the park – I would think about another small person, a small life that would grow into something unknowable to me but still be tied to me, who might love me, who I would love, whose strange story I would begin, knowing I was not the person who would write their final chapter.

Some days, I just wanted to bury my head. It seemed so brutal, either way. *You raise a child*, I thought, *to teach it how to leave you.* And then I thought: *But my mother got there first.*

Up until now, Connie had been respectful, not asking me anything unless I brought it up myself. But perhaps her limit had been reached. Perhaps, as an employer, she felt she had a right to know.

'I don't know what I'm going to do,' I said to her, feeling helpless.

She looked at me levelly. 'Can I tell you what I think?'

'Go on.'

'I'm not going to tell you what to do, Laura. Only you can decide that. But I think you need to understand that whatever decisions you make in life, there will always be a loss. If you have a child, you will lose something. If you don't have a child, you will also lose something. These losses are both tangible and sometimes completely inexpressible. And it's hard for us humans to know exactly what we're prepared to lose before we've actually lost it. You must be prepared to regret a decision you thought you would never regret – but regret, in my experience, is never permanent.'

'Never?'

She gave me a hard look. 'Something new always comes along to dislodge it. Good or bad. Everything is always changing. So if you can get accustomed to the idea of yourself standing at the forking of two equally but differently enriching paths, two equally *challenging* paths, along both of which you would triumph and fail, then perhaps you can make up your mind.'

I stared at her, unable to think of anything to say.

'What?' she said. 'It's been on my mind, too, Laura. I care about you.'

'Thank you,' I said. 'For everything. For letting me work here. For letting me stay. For being OK about the fact I'm in this state, and—'

Connie put up her hand. 'Anyone would do the same.'

*

She went upstairs to her office and I started the washing-up. I'd barely got going on the second plate when there was a loud rap on the front door, aggressive and determined to be heard. I pulled off the rubber gloves and hurried to the door. I thought, for some mad reason, it might be Joe, but I could see the short shape through the stained glass, the tufty white head. Deborah.

I opened the door, smiling. 'Hi,' I said. 'Connie's just upstairs. She told me the cover—'

Deborah brushed past me. 'You. Kitchen. *Now,*' she hissed.

I followed her down the corridor into the kitchen, my heart thumping hard, my mouth turned dry. I tried to swallow, but I couldn't. Once we were in the kitchen, Deborah closed the door and turned on me. 'You deceitful creep,' she said.

'What—?'

Deborah advanced. 'What the fuck did you think you were playing at?' she said, jabbing the air between us with her finger.

'What are you talking about?' I said, but I already knew.

'Who *are* you?' she said.

Feeling a quiet horror spreading in my stomach, I gripped the side of the kitchen counter. 'I'm Laura Brown,' I said.

'Oh, come on. I very much doubt that's your real name. I'm giving you a chance to be honest.'

'I am being honest. I'm Laura Brown,' I said – and I did, in that moment, believe what I was saying. The hours, days, months I'd spent here with Connie, working with her, talking with her, living with her, absorbing the possibilities of another self, had far outweighed the time I'd been spending as Rose. Laura as she was – as I was – felt real to me. Laura had been liked and trusted; listened to. I was safe here, and Rose was not.

We stared at each other. 'Listen,' Deborah said. 'Either you tell Connie, or I do. It's your choice.'

My panic began to rise. 'Deborah, please,' I said. '*Please.* There's nothing going on. I'm Laura—'

'For fuck's sake! *Connie!*' she called.

I grabbed her arm and she looked at me with disgust. 'I'm *begging* you,' I said. 'Not now. *Please.*'

Deborah shook me off. 'What's your real name?'

It was on the tip of my tongue, but it would not come, not under this roof – not to Deborah, who did not really want to hear it, who only wanted to be vindicated in her suspicions, to prove herself yet again as Connie's knight in shining armour. 'I love Connie,' I said. 'I would never hurt her.'

'Well it's a bit late for that, isn't it, *Laura*?'

'I can explain. It's not what it seems—'

The kitchen door was wrenched open. 'What the hell's going on? Deb?' said Connie, a look of bewilderment on her face. 'What are you doing here and why are you yelling?'

'Con, sit down,' said Deborah. 'You're going to need to be sitting down.'

'No, no,' I said, turning to Connie. 'Please, let me explain. I never meant it to be like this.'

Connie looked fearful. 'Explain what?' she said.

'She's an impostor,' Deborah said.

'I'm not an *impostor*,' I said, becoming angry. This woman did not have the right to take my story away from me.

'Con,' said Deborah. 'For the last time, please, sit *down*.'

This time, Connie did as she was told, and I went to sit next to her. 'Don't you dare,' said Deborah. 'Stay exactly where you are.'

'Deborah, what the hell is this? You're both terrifying me,' said Connie.

'She isn't Laura Brown,' said Deborah, pointing at me. 'She made it up. Laura Brown doesn't exist.'

'Deborah, let me explain—' I said.

'What do you mean, she isn't Laura Brown?' said Connie.

Deborah began to pace the kitchen. '*I'm* going to tell this,' she said, putting up her hands to show she would brook no opposition. 'I was having a conversation with our recruitment agency,' she said, glaring at me. 'And I told them how happy you were with your Laura Brown, this miracle girl they'd found for you.'

I thought I was going to be sick.

'And here's the thing,' said Deborah, with the air of someone who has the last ace up her sleeve. Connie was already looking at her agent with apprehension; and it was true that Deborah in her righteous anger was quite magnetic. 'They didn't know who I was talking about.'

'What?' said Connie.

'They'd never heard of her.'

Connie looked at me. 'But – Rebecca organized the interview.'

'Oh, yes, she did all right. But when I asked Rebecca who it was at the recruitment agency she spoke with about Laura Brown, she couldn't actually say.' Deborah turned to me. 'It turns out that my stupid assistant – who shortly will no longer be my assistant – had one conversation on the phone with a woman whose name she didn't even ask for. Apparently, this woman said she was working from home that day and was using her personal email. The only emails Rebecca could find from this woman were from a Gmail account, in the name McIntyre.' I closed my eyes, but still Deborah drove relentlessly on. '*McIntyre*,' she repeated. 'Ever heard of them, Con?'

When I opened my eyes, Connie was looking up at me, the confusion and worry written over her features. I wanted to reach for her, but I couldn't move. I wanted to say something, but I couldn't speak.

'So I looked this McIntyre agency up,' Deborah went on.

'And it doesn't exist, anywhere. I have to admit, Laura, I was getting a bit baffled. And a little bit pissed off. So what I want to know is this: who the hell are you, where did you come from and what the hell are you doing in my client's house?'

*

For a few moments I simply stood there, staring at the two women – Deborah, incandescent with rage at her lack of control over this situation, and Connie, bemused at hers. And yet – even though Deborah felt she had caught me out, even though I knew there was no escape from this, even though Laura Brown and the protections and freedoms she'd provided me were slipping through my fingers just as I'd half-feared, half-expected they might – none of what I'd been doing seemed ludicrous to me. I still felt justified. I still felt that Laura Brown was as real to me as Rose Simmons.

Laura Brown was rooted to this situation. She was standing here, now, before these women, hoping against hope that they would understand and forgive her. But I knew there was only one throw of the dice left. Rose was going to have to speak too.

'Before I say anything, Con,' I said. 'I want you to know that I never meant to hurt you.'

Connie frowned. 'Have you hurt me? How have you hurt me? Laura, I don't understand.'

'She's not called Laura!' said Deborah.

'Will you just shut up?' I said. Deborah looked as if I'd slapped her. Her nostrils flared, her lips pinched thin and sour.

I turned back to Connie. 'I'm not called Laura,' I said gently. 'I mean, I *am*, here in this house. And Laura is a part of who I am, I suppose. She's come to be.'

'Oh for fuck's sake, get on with it, before I call the police,' said Deborah. 'I knew you were weird. I *knew* it. What woman your age wanders into a house like this, with no family, no career—'

'*Deborah*,' said Connie, with a warning note in her voice. '*Enough*. I want to hear her.'

'Can I sit down?' I said.

'No,' said Deborah.

'Yes,' said Connie.

Deborah huffed. Gratefully, I sat opposite Connie, as I had done almost every day since I first came into her house and offered to make her a cup of tea.

I took a deep breath.

'Deborah's right,' I said. 'I *should* have my shit together. But I don't. Not even a bit. I know I don't. And the thing is, Con, I think in my life there's been a reason for that. But since being here with you, I *have* started to feel like I might know what I'm doing. Like I might know who I am.'

'What are you saying, Laura?'

'You see, my mum—'

I couldn't carry on. I stopped, breathing deeply. 'It's OK,' said Connie, and to both my guilt and relief, she reached across the table and put her gnarled hand over mine.

'Constance,' said Deborah. 'She's tricked you—'

'I only ever wanted to talk to you,' I said to Connie. 'Just to ask—' I stopped again. 'But I couldn't. I didn't know how to. My dad said—'

'Ask what?' said Connie.

'About my mum.' I was struggling. 'My dad. He had your books.'

'What have I got to do with your mum and dad?' said Connie, mystified.

'*Look* at me, Con. Look at me hard.'

Connie did as I asked. I stared deep into her eyes, willing her to understand. 'Can't you see?' I said.

'What are you talking about, darling?' she said. 'Are you all right?'

'I was born in July 1983,' I said. 'In New York.'

At the mention of New York, and the date, I was sure I saw something shift in Connie's face, and I couldn't bear it. I couldn't bear to look. I did not know what I would do if she told me I was wrong. I stared down into the nicks and whorls and crumbs on the kitchen table, and clenched my fists in my lap. 'My dad's name is Matt Simmons,' I said. 'And my mother's name was Elise Morceau.'

*

In the moment of silence that followed in that kitchen, I can't truly express how I felt. I'd waited all my life to say my mother's name out loud, and for it to actually mean something to someone other than my father, so that in turn it could mean something to me. And when I looked up, I saw it, in Connie's face – the way a human being will recognize another person even when they're not in the room, even though they might be on the other side of the world, even though they might be dead. When a person looks at you the way Connie looked at me that afternoon, it's as if you're seeing all their selves, all the ones they keep not just from you, but from themselves – the deep-set, long-buried, unending misunderstandings and experiences of love and joy and hate and sadness that make a life. It was as if I, too, was being seen for the first time. It was like I was seeing my mother.

'Oh, my god,' said Deborah. 'Oh, my *god*.'

Connie closed her eyes. She placed both her shaking hands on the kitchen table, almost as if she was conducting a seance.

Without warning, she let out a juddering sob. 'You're Rose,' she said, and it wasn't a question.

'I am,' I said. 'I'm Rose.'

She kept her eyes closed. 'You're Elise's daughter.'

'I am.'

There was silence in the kitchen again.

'You came to find me,' she said eventually.

'I did. Is it true, then, Con? You really knew her?'

She opened her eyes and looked at me, her gaze roving over my face. 'You lied,' she said.

'I know, but—'

'I let you in here,' she said.

'And I'm so grateful. I was feeling so lost—'

'You probably are her daughter then.'

'Con?'

'I want you to leave,' she said.

'But I thought—'

'You thought I was such a fool?'

'No. Never.'

'So easy to lie to?'

'I hated lying to you. But I didn't have a choice, and I'm not lying now. Connie, I'm begging you. Don't kick me out.'

'You heard her,' said Deborah. 'She doesn't want you here.'

'I don't believe that,' I said. I reached across the table and held both of Connie's hands. She didn't pull away, but they were limp, as if drained of their last dregs of power. 'Con – you care about me,' I said. 'You – wanted me to live here with a child.'

She winced. 'I *am* a fool.'

'You're not. And I care about you. So much. You know I do. Don't do this, please. I was an idiot, we can sort it out—'

Connie slid away from my grasp and pushed back her chair. She walked slowly out of the kitchen, as if she was wading underwater along the narrow corridor towards the front door. I felt pinioned to my chair by shame.

I followed her, but my presence seemed to jolt, even repel her. She staggered slightly, her hands on the walls. 'My dad says you were the last person to see her before she disappeared,' I called. 'Please, Con – what happened?'

'Enough!' shouted Deborah, coming up behind me. 'I'm not having this. My client does not have to put up with this in her own home. Get out.'

At the front door, Connie stopped and turned to me. 'I offered you shelter,' she said.

'I know. And I'm so grateful. But – haven't you liked me being here—?'

'No, no, this can't happen again,' she said, and it sounded less like an order and more like a plea. Her voice was more vulnerable than I'd ever heard it.

'What is it that you don't want to happen again?' I said gently, even though by now I knew my time was up, that this might be the last time I would ever see her. Connie was struggling with her fingers on the lock, but I did not help her. 'You don't understand, Con. How I feel. How I've *felt*. The years I've spent wondering. And then, finally, to find you – a person who knew her.'

'Just stop talking,' said Connie.

'What happened between you and my mum? What happened in New York?'

Deborah thrust my bag and coat into my arms. 'Go.'

'Connie, I know you don't want this,' I said. 'Let me stay.'

Connie had managed to get the front door open. She pulled it and turned to me, her eyes wide. 'I can't,' she said. 'You need to go.'

I stepped onto the porch, and before I'd even turned round, the door closed in my face.

But Connie was still standing on the other side. She wasn't moving. One of her hands was on the glass as if to steady herself, mottled and morphed through the Victorian panes. 'Connie?' I said. 'What happened to Elise Morceau?'

The hand withdrew. The air of the outside cooled my cheeks and made me aware of how heavily I was breathing. Both women receded down the corridor, their figures becoming abstract and willowy, until I could see them no longer.

1983

38

Sometimes, in the crumbling apartment Matt and Elise had rented in New York – Brooklyn, to be exact – Ridgewood to be exacter, on Covert Street at the corner of Wyckoff Avenue – their telephone would ring. It would go on ringing, and neither of them would answer. They never answered the phone. They told each other it couldn't be for them because no one knew where they were. Elise rang no one, Matt sometimes rang his parents; these were long calls, arduous. She could hear him explaining, patient at first, repetitive, reasonable. He was getting a divorce. It was the right thing. Shara understood. He never mentioned to his parents that Elise was pregnant. He never mentioned the fact that it was Shara who forced the divorce. Sometimes he laid the receiver in the cradle quietly, as if Elise might think the call had not actually happened. Other times he slammed it.

They'd left Mexico soon after Connie turned up. Matt looked shell-shocked when Elise told him they'd been found, as if he finally realized he'd burned his bridges. Elise felt the wrench of leaving that place. She was not ready, and had wanted to stay longer amidst the semi-wild jungle foliage, the brightly painted bodegas and the sound of the sea. They'd still been there for the Day of the Dead, and Elise felt her breathing thicken when she saw the families on horse-drawn carts, loaded with a feast and flowers to break bread in the cemetery with all their relatives that had passed. It made Elise think of how Shara had talked about her dead mother with such ease, how fluent Shara seemed in the language of transition and loss, and how inept Elise herself felt with those things. And yet according to Con, Shara was not coping at all well with this latest loss.

Elise didn't want to be bad. She didn't want to be the cause of so much pain.

'Don't you want to be by the ocean?' she said to Matt. 'Let's just stay.'

'We need to be in a city,' he said. 'In your condition. Where we speak the language. We need money. How about London? You were born there, weren't you? I've got a few friends who might let us stay till we find our feet.'

Elise stared down at her real feet, currently entombed in the sand. 'I don't want to go back to London.'

'Why not?' Matt said. He was less pliable these days. 'Don't you have family—'

'I don't want to go back there,' she said, and refused to say any more.

They agreed, for now, on New York.

Another plane, another cheap hotel. Through a contact in LA, Matt found work as a relief writer on a TV network in Manhattan, and they found the place to rent in Brooklyn. Elise wondered where all this would end. She had some meagre savings, but she wanted to work too. For the first three months of the pregnancy she felt terrible, enduring a constant, granular sea-sickness that competed with a primordial exhaustion she almost laughed at. She could wake up on the weekend and go back to sleep for five more hours, and then wake up still tired. All she could think about, staggering from bed to toilet bowl and back again, occasionally veering left into the galley kitchen for a glass of water and some more paper towels to wipe the spray of vomit from the bathroom tiles, was: *Why is this not more publicly known? Why is there not more scientific research into this?*

It seemed insane to her – that women and girls were just expected to take this in their stride and carry on working, eating, sleeping, living. It was a wake-up call to Elise about how the world really worked. Everybody wanted a fecund woman, but Heaven forfend actually helping her out with the day-to-day hell of it. She thought of the women who'd been alive before her – no painkillers, no hygienic gloves, no soft pillows, no lulling television. Those women, Elise concluded, must have been quite strange people, because if they went through what she was going through, and society wasn't helping them, then who would not have turned strange?

They were trying to save money, but they had so little of it to live on. The lifestyles they'd once enjoyed had been funded by Shara and Connie. Matt, it turned out, was not good with their resources, spending too much on food, taking them out to the movies, to restaurants, buying experiences they could not justify, but which lifted them briefly out of their sluggish guilt. Elise was still determined to work, and as she emerged from the first trimester, she found shifts as a waitress, in a diner opposite Goldman Sachs near the tip of the island. It was very different from Seedling – loud and noisy, a theatre of burgers and subs. The regulars quickly came to know Elise by name. They were all ages, from the fresh young twenty-year-olds from Jersey and Queens, to the grizzled sixty-somethings who'd seen it all before. Many of the men there had portable telephones. They would bring them into the diner like *conquistadores* with their latest haul of gold. They wanted Elise to be impressed, and she was, but with the technology, not the man on the end of it.

Conversations between Elise and these men would start up,

orders would be memorized, and she soon became a favourite, earning the biggest tips. She did not know whether they liked her because of her efficiency and responsiveness, because of her British accent, or because of the life inside her, her stomach swelling with the weeks. Wall Street was not a feminine place, and perhaps Elise was a reminder of Nature, its strange curves and unexpected shapes, its persistence, its own rules. Maybe she gave the men a sense of meaning? Harry, the owner, told Elise she was worth her weight in gold, but the raise he gave her was negligible. Elise had regained that status of object which had faded with Connie, but she didn't know any more if she liked it. She wanted to keep her meaning for herself.

*

She didn't tell Matt much about the day to day of the diner, needing something separate from him, in order to want to go to the apartment at the end of the day. She needed distance in order to see the scale of her life. On her day off she left the crack addicts on the corner of Covert Street and walked through Irving Square Park. She rode along the Hudson on a bicycle she'd bought for next to nothing, the weak March sun on her face, going faster as she grew more confident, the buildings whooshing past like Monopoly houses, the pedals liquid under her feet. Despite the cool temperature, after her ride she might go back to the local park and sit on a bench, eating a hot dog from a corner cart. One day, she saw a plaque on a bench dedicated to a woman called Betty, who'd loved the park and the people in it. Elise ran the tip of her finger over the cold and clouded metal and thought of Betty, long dead, born in the age of jazz, fifteen years old when the Depression hit. Not Betty Sheinkovitz, for sure. Betty Sheinkovitz was alive and well in Los Angeles.

Back home in their tiny apartment, she was invaded by inconsolable thoughts about the baby, who was sitting in a deep pool inside her, its shape mutating. Was she going to lose all these moments, the bicycle along the Hudson, the plans to go back to Mexico – all the moments she didn't yet know but which now she felt as both abstract and sharp – with a child? She didn't think it was the baby's fault. It was all her.

If her dreams in Mexico had been vivid, in New York it was as if the foetus was a tab of acid. Elise would fall asleep and find herself back in her early teens, in the years immediately after her mother's death. The river of her hometown glowed like a rainbow and the municipal lime trees seemed to pulse. At night she swore she saw a girl walking round their room, and on her shifts in the diner, as she fed pastrami subs to the men in angular suits, she believed the girl was her unborn daughter. Her face was clear to Elise, and she was alone, and always on the move. She did not mention these visions to Matt.

*

Matt's attitude to the unborn baby was also mixed. He was solicitous about how Elise felt, nervous for her. He focused more on Elise than on the baby, shying from hypotheses about the future – the baby's gender, where they would live, whether it would look more like him or her. He kept wanting to help Elise – but you can't help a person to be sick much more than holding back their hair, and Elise felt this to be very much something she was enduring on her own. She felt a physical boundary between them. What was happening to her was something Matt could never understand. He did what he could, beginning to look for an apartment with two bedrooms, which meant they'd have to move to somewhere even more rundown than where they were living now.

Like many areas in Brooklyn at this time, Ridgewood was falling apart. Once-beautiful buildings were derelict and condemned, their nineteenth-century grandeur long gone. Action was being taken to preserve the old dwellings, built when the area had been booming, but everything was still in a bad state. Elise saw how artists and African-American communities were claiming these vacated spaces in order to stop them falling down, but equally she'd see the crack addicts, the strung-out women left to fend for themselves, kids as young as five or six being sent to buy their parents' drugs. Meanwhile, Wall Street was doing very nicely.

Where will we live? she asked Matt, but he told her not to worry. He made sure she ate well. He built a small bookshelf, ready for small books. She watched him drilling screws into holes, methodically measuring the distance between the shelves, deciding how low to the floor the first shelf should be, for the short arms soon to come.

They never talked about their relationship, nor stopped to question if they even had one. It was as if to question the viability of this union might crack them open at a time when they needed to be watertight. They still slept together, they cooked and ate together, and yet both of them knew that what they had was a completely different creature to their relationships with Shara and Connie. Some days, Elise couldn't believe they'd ended up like this. She grew despondent sometimes. Their story had become less a case of rescuing each other, and more one of deserving each other. An adulterer, a marriage-wrecker. Depending on the time of day, this could easily be their story.

'Do you think Connie told Shara about the baby?' she asked him one evening as they were lying in bed.

'Yeah, I do,' said Matt.

Elise turned on her side to face him. 'Do you feel bad?'

'Yes,' he said. 'Of course.'

'Sometimes, I think we could give her our baby,' she said.

Matt turned his head towards her. 'What?'

'We could give the baby to Shara.'

'Are you serious? "Here, Shar, take a baby I had with another woman – it'll grow up to look like me as a lovely reminder of how shit your life was in '83." Elise, sometimes I wonder what goes on inside your head.'

They lay in silence for a few minutes. 'Elise?' said Matt.

'Yes?'

'Does this mean you've thought about giving it up?'

Elise closed her eyes. Before her death, her mother had always been frank: the addition of a child – the addition of Elise – had not been an extension of what Patricia already had. What she'd had was gone. People were crazy to think otherwise. It was a completely new building and there were weeks, months, years, when you didn't know where you'd put the keys. *An altered life, my love. And it's where I had to live.*

Elise had asked her mother, *Were you happy to live there?* And her mother took her in her arms and said, *Yes.* She said it had taken a while, but eventually, she could not remember what had come before.

The experience of forgetting oneself like that had seemed terrifying to the young Elise, but after her mother's death she had felt as if she was floating in pieces anyway, losing bits of herself. Even now, the act of self-vanishing held an alluring and macabre appeal.

'No,' she said. 'I just thought about giving it to Shara.'

'I don't think Shara's ever going to be your friend again, El,' Matt said heavily. 'Even if you do try and give her your baby. We've made our bed.'

Elise thought again of the dream she'd had, her walking

daughter, the roof of her house caving in. She reached for the chain of her necklace and tugged it absentmindedly, slipping the gold E over her chin and letting it drop back to her chest.

'Things are going to change,' said Matt more gently. 'Even more than they already have. But I've said it before. I'm not going anywhere. I'm here for you.'

'When will you tell your parents about the baby?'

Matt paused. 'They're old-fashioned,' he said.

'What does that mean?'

'We're – not married.'

'So let's get married.'

Matt was quiet. Elise knew there'd been no enthusiasm in her voice, and that such a prospect was unlikely to take place. He began to rub his forehead, pressing his closed eyes as if to push the tension out. 'They loved Shara a lot,' he said.

Elise felt her panic rising. 'That's a cruel thing to say. You make it sound like they could never love me.'

'Hey, hey,' he said, putting his hands on her exposed shoulder. 'Of *course* they could love you. They *will* love you. It's just taking them a while to get used to the fact I'm not with her. I love you. You do believe me, don't you?'

'I believe you.'

Elise didn't tell him that she loved him back. She felt that one of them, at least, needed to be honest.

39

Heavier and heavier, Elise grew. The sickness and bone-dead tiredness abated by the fourth and fifth months of her pregnancy. She had not once taken a day off work at the diner, and had become friends with her new co-worker, Yolanda, a woman in her forties, who was sending money back to Puerto Rico where her elderly parents lived. Yolanda had no children and no husband. She said, '*El tipo está muerto*,' delivered with a shrug. *The guy's dead.* Yoli would bring sweet little cakes for Elise, almondy balls of baked dough, dusted in icing sugar. Yoli was the only person apart from Matt who Elise let pat her belly. Yoli would get to where she guessed the baby's head was and talk to it. '*Hola, mi cariño. Pronto nos vemos.*'

Hello, my darling. We'll see each other soon.

Elise wanted to be near Yoli all the time.

*

One day, a woman came into the diner and sat straight down at a table by the window. She had red hair, like Connie's, and was about the same height. She had a white woman's redhead skin: so pale as to be almost translucent, the telltale freckles over her nose. Elise couldn't stop staring. 'You OK, *mija*?' said Yolanda. 'You look like you seen a ghost.'

After the woman had drunk her coffee, read half of her *New*

York Times and gone, Elise snuck into the staff restrooms and cried. She put her hands ferociously against her face as if to press the tears back in. She missed Connie so much. She missed her like a limb.

That evening, Elise lay alone in the bed in the tiny apartment, watching the street light coming in the window. She imagined if Connie had walked through the diner door today, as she'd once walked through the doors of Seedling. Tall Connie, neat and elegant Connie, wrapped up in a long wool coat. What would Elise have said to her? Their last encounter had been like something out of a Greek tragedy, wailing on a beach, sand everywhere, accusations too. What was Connie doing, right now, this minute?

Matt was still at work. He was often late these days, working on a new show called, of all things, *Mamma and Me*, a sitcom about an Italian-American newly married young couple who are trying hard to establish an independent life for themselves in NYC despite the best attempts of their respective families. 'It's like *The Godfather* meets *Happy Days*,' said Matt.

'Is it funny?' said Elise.

'Bits of it. The bits I write,' he said, grinning.

He'd had a small promotion at the network and was writing several of the episodes. The pilot had been successful, and the first series was due to air soon. He was writing all hours, and now they'd begun filming, he was often at the studio working out last-minute drafts and watching the recordings. He seemed enthused again for life, and bigger bags of groceries were turning up when he came home from work. 'We need to feed you up, good and proper,' he'd say.

*

Eventually, Elise could take the absence of Connie no longer. It pressed on her heart like a dying thing, calling to her, begging her to keep it alive. One day, alone again in the apartment, Elise lifted their telephone receiver to call Connie's house in London. Her hand was sure, her mind was made up. It felt right, it felt important. It was the only number in the world she'd memorized. The telephone did not ring for very long, which caught her by surprise.

'Hello?' said a voice. It was Mary O'Reilly.

Hearing the Irishwoman's tone took Elise straight back to the early days, the sense of languor and excitement that had flooded her daily. She closed her eyes. 'Mary,' she said. 'It's Elise. Is Connie there?'

There was a pause on the line. 'She is not.'

Elise knew that Mary was lying. 'Please let me speak to her.'

'She's not here. Where are you, Elise?'

'I'm in New York. I need to speak to her.'

There was a pause. 'You've done *damage*, Elise,' said Mary.

'*I've* done damage?'

'You'd better not be coming back now,' said Mary. 'You're not coming back, are you?'

'No,' said Elise. 'I'm not coming back.'

'Because it's the last thing she needs.'

'Is she OK?'

There was a scuffling on Mary's end, and Elise couldn't hear what the woman was saying. 'Connie?' Elise called. 'Connie, is that you?'

'I'm sorry, that's a wrong number,' said Mary, and she hung up.

*

Elise sat back against the arm of the sofa. Outside, the traffic flowed and honked. She sat in the dark and listened to the dialling tone, hot tears welling in her eyes, splashing down her cheeks and pooling into the telephone speaker. She didn't move for hours. But when she heard Matt's key in the door, she rose and went to bed and pretended to be fast asleep.

40

The last two months of Elise's pregnancy exhausted her. She felt like her body was eighteen times its normal size. She couldn't sleep for longer than half an hour at a time, because to turn herself over required several manoeuvres. She couldn't see her feet. Parts of herself were literally disappearing before her very eyes whilst one part – her stomach – never seemed to stop growing. She thought that perhaps the baby would never actually come out, but would stay inside getting bigger and bigger until she either levitated or exploded.

She ate a lot. Yolanda brought food back from the diner, where Elise had had to stop working – or sometimes she brought food she'd cooked at her own apartment. Elise met Yoli often, and the two of them would take inching walks round the neighbourhood, the slowest Elise had ever taken in her life, arm in arm round Irving Square Park, pausing on benches, soaking up the sun. It was July, and New York had left behind its pleasant weather, sliding into unbearable humidity and trapped heat. They window-shopped, never going in, until one day they passed a bookshop and Elise stopped outside it, and saw how dark and cool it was, how polished the old floorboards.

When she saw it, she wondered if she'd known it might have been there all along. A pile on a table near the door, under the heading 'New Releases'. Elise waddled over and stood before it like a child at an altar, hardly daring to touch the top cover. It was a green line drawing of rabbit, seemingly morphing into a woman's silhouette. *I'm writing about a green rabbit.* How strange to see Connie's name like that again! She was a far cry from Brixton library. To see the words *Green* and *Rabbit* put together in a new way, thousands of miles from where Con first mentioned them, swinging around on her office chair in London, frowning as she reluctantly alluded to what she was writing. Connie was here again – in words, not a voice on the telephone, or a face on the pillow next to her – but here in the bookshop, nonetheless. Connie had made her presence known again. She too had made a map of herself, and Elise had found her. She caressed the book with something akin to fear.

'What's that?' said Yolanda.

'It's a book my – friend wrote,' said Elise. She put it down and placed a hand on her stomach.

'Your friend wrote that?' Yolanda's eyes widened. 'What's it about? A green rabbit?'

'That's what I'm going to find out,' said Elise.

'Green's a bad-luck colour,' said Yolanda.

'I always thought it was the colour of hope.'

'Jealousy,' said Yolanda. 'Whose rabbit is it?'

Elise flipped open the book and read the synopsis on the inside jacket. 'I think Rabbit is the name of the main character, Yoli.'

Yolanda's eyes twinkled as she glanced at Elise's stomach. '¿Ah si? Se multiplica.'

Elise laughed. 'That's right. She multiplies.'

Elise took the book to the counter and handed over her money.

*

She and Yolanda embraced on the stoop of Elise and Matt's apartment, and Yoli said she would come round tomorrow with some more food. She only lived four blocks away so the walk was easy.

'You don't need to do that, Yoli,' said Elise. 'How will I repay you?'

Yolanda batted the air with her hand. 'You need to eat,' she said. 'The *niña* will be coming.' Yolanda had long been convinced it was a girl.

Elise rested her hand on the top of the huge bump, watching Yolanda make her way down the long street, her denim skirt flapping against the backs of her toned legs, her worn-down mules slap-slapping the hot stone of the sidewalk. Elise had painted her toenails for her, cherry-red, and Yoli had done Elise's. Elise wondered what Yoli would do for the rest of the day, what she herself would do. They'd become close. Loneliness had done it, the trials of the diner, the growing bump. *Stay with me!* Elise wanted to call after the other woman. *Please. I don't know what I'm doing!*

Instead of calling for her, she pulled *Green Rabbit* out of the brown-paper bag the bookseller had wrapped it in. She read the synopsis on the inside jacket again. '*Happy, arrogant and always in charge, Rabbit lives in her own world – until one day she falls in love. Rabbit must learn when to let go and when to hold on – because when you don't know what freedom looks like, it's hard to tell when it's gone. A beautiful, timeless fable of transformation, passion and regret from the bestselling author of* Wax Heart.'

Beneath this were some reviews: '*Constance Holden proves yet again she is the mistress of human emotion.*' '*Sparkling, wise and strange.*' '*A weird tale of a weird woman and how love makes fools of us all.*'

Elise rolled her eyes and lumbered up the stoop, unlocking the front door. She made it up the narrow flight of stairs to the second floor, and moved slowly to the living-room couch, where she lowered herself and opened the book.

For Shara, read the dedication.

Elise read on.

She kept reading until the sun had set behind the rooftops, and the street came alive with the night-goers; the young women of Elise's age, all dressed up and ready to go to a club; the kids on their way to the basketball court, the hard and rhythmic thump of their ball like a heartbeat taken from a body for everyone to hear. The prose of the book was strange – slightly detached, yet more detailed and psychological than any fable ought to be. Rabbit's lover had no name; it was not always possible to intuit whether the lover was a man or a woman, but regardless they wrought havoc inside the large ego of Rabbit's head. The setting had a mystical quality, but it was London all right; Elise just knew. It was quieter than *Wax Heart*, fewer dramatis personae, more interior, almost poetic and bare. The tenderness and brutality of love. Rabbit, skinned alive.

Elise didn't hear Matt come in. He came towards her and leaned over, placing a kiss on the top of her head. Elise felt completely away from him, away from everyone, just a pair of hands clutching a book, when usually her body was weighted with fifty anchors to the seabed of the couch. As she turned the pages, she felt she would never move again, and one day they would discover her, covered in barnacles, if the waters ever took Brooklyn. She felt a desire to be older, *because if I was older*, she read, *I would not feel like I am nothing. I would be as solid as a stone sculpture that has been left on a cliff by a tribe of druids, revered and protected, in the free air, awesome in my lichen-covered skin.*

'What is it?' said Matt.

Elise held up the novel. 'Connie.'

'Oh, fuck,' he said.

★

That night, Elise went into labour. The contractions started at about three in the morning, and by five, she was on all fours, groaning. Matt took her to Wyckoff Hospital. *She's not dilated enough*, they said, *take her home*.

She felt delirious, terrified. *I don't know where that is!* she said. *I really don't know where that is!*

Is your wife all right? the medical staff asked Matt.

I'm not his wife, she said. *Let's go.*

They went back to the apartment and Elise crawled like a drunk up the staircase to the second floor and tried to sleep, as per their advice. Matt sat on the side of the bed and took her hand. 'It's going to be OK,' he said. 'You can do this. Of everyone I know, you can do this.'

She looked at him. He really didn't have a clue what he was asking her to do.

★

Three or so hours later, as the sun was rising, the contractions were coming closer together. 'I have to go back,' she said.

'OK,' he said, and they got a taxi the short way to the labour ward. The baby was pressing down on her.

'Oh, god, oh *god*,' she said. 'I'm scared.'

'I'm so sorry,' he said. 'I wish I could take the pain for you.'

★

Elise demanded relief from the pain. She did not think the pain

353

was a good thing to experience. She did not see why she should, when Matt was just standing there on his hind legs.

*

Again, on all fours. 'Wait, honey,' said a midwife. 'Now, push.'
  'I am pushing!'
  'Push harder, Elise. It's not gonna come on its own.'

*

It felt endless. She turned and looked out of the window. The afternoon had come, the floods to cover Brooklyn would soon come too, and she would still be here, pushing. She had been pushing for a thousand years.

*

Beeping, and people rushing in. Elise had no pain; she could not feel her body: all she had were eyes, on Matt in a blue apron and a blue shower cap. 'Are you going in the water?' she said.
  'Stay with us, honey,' said the midwife.
  'We have to get this baby out,' said someone else.
  Matt, his face so drained of colour. *Is this it*, she thought, *do I go now. Do I go now.*

*

When she came to, Matt was sitting in a chair beside her. He noticed her stir, and leapt up. 'Are you OK? My darling, oh, god. Are you OK?'
  'What happened?'
  'You lost a lot of blood. They had to give you a transfusion.'
  'Where's the baby?'
  'The baby's fine. They had to cut her out.'

'Where is she?'

'Here.'

Matt reached into a plastic tub by her bed. A swaddled baby was in his arms. He placed it gently on Elise's chest. 'I don't know if I'm allowed to do that,' he said. 'But here she is.'

She was very much a baby, Elise thought. After all that! It was odd how normal this felt. Matt was looking at her expectantly. 'How long have I been asleep?' she said, and she stared into the small red face.

'About five hours.'

'She's tiny,' said Elise. 'Look at her fingernails.'

'I know.'

'Look at her nose!'

'I know.'

'Everything is inside her!' said Elise, and Matt nodded, smiling, tired. But she knew he didn't understand. Did he not realize? The tiny lungs, the heart, the stomach, the intestines, the little bones as frail as a chicken's, the brain – and inside that a deep and endless chamber of music that none of them could hear. Elise felt deeply anxious she might break her. 'I don't want to hurt her,' she said.

'You're not going to hurt her,' he replied.

But Elise thought that was wishful thinking.

*

There was a woman in the bed next to her. Stephanie had also had an emergency C-section, and the two of them sometimes talked. It was not easy for either of them to move much, so they turned their faces to each other. 'I gotta look a state,' said Stephanie.

'You don't,' said Elise.

'I've waited years for this,' said Stephanie.

Elise didn't ask her why. Stephanie's husband was a fireman. He wasn't able to come much to the ward, but when he did, he was a big presence, tall and broad with red hair. He was one of seven, Stephanie said. Irish Catholics, his mother having come over in the fifties.

'And she stayed?' said Elise.

Stephanie laughed. 'Oh, yeah. She wasn't about to go back.'

'She must have lots of grandchildren.'

Stephanie grinned. 'So many. This one –' she indicated her little son, Callum, in his own plastic tub – 'he'll probably get lost.'

But the way she said it, Elise knew she didn't mean it. Stephanie was never going to let Callum get lost.

*

The days passed, and Elise lay there in the hospital, itching to leave, staring at the ceiling as Stephanie drifted off. Stephanie's fireman husband had just been and gone, and the two of them seemed so in love. Looking at Stephanie, who was thirty-eight, and finally a mother, Elise felt suddenly ashamed of her youth, which she had so long denied. It all made sense with Stephanie. Stephanie was so comfortable in herself, so warm and witty, and now so rewarded with her baby Callum.

*

Elise stayed in the hospital with the baby for a week. They had wanted to monitor her and the child. She lay in the bed, staring at the ceiling, the baby on her chest or in her bassinet. After seven days had passed, the doctor told Elise she had nothing to worry about. 'You're young and strong,' he said. 'It's time to go home.'

But spiders in Elise's mind were weaving webs. 'Is it going to be OK? Are you sure it's going to be OK?'

'Everything's going to be fine,' said the doctor. 'What's her name?'

They'd thought about calling her Patricia, but Elise wanted a new story. 'Rose,' she said. 'We've called her Rose.'

2018

41

Standing on Connie's doorstep after she closed the door in my face, I realized two things. There was a good chance I'd lost a very important person that day – not just because of Connie's connection to my mother, but because of what, over the previous months, she'd taught me. The space she'd given me. Her example of living was unapologetic and self-knowing, whilst encouraging me to find my own voice, regardless of what name I'd been using. At Connie's side, I'd begun to excavate myself, to question who did I really want to be, and how, and where?

*

I headed to the nearest cafe, and sat down with a coffee. My heart ached. I wondered what Connie was doing right now, whether Deb was going to stay with her, the two of them talking long into the night about old ghosts. I tried to imagine my mother and Connie, back in the eighties. A couple. What had they been like? Demonstrative, balanced? Now, I might never know. However, my most immediate problem was that I had nowhere to live.

I felt there was no way I could go back to Brixton to live in the flat – although Joe would probably let me stay there if I needed, and a lot of my clothes and possessions were still there. I could buy a ticket to Brittany and leave this evening

– but I didn't know the cost of a last-minute journey like that, or if I could face Dad quite yet. Claire might be able to tell something was different about me. I'd lie badly, and then the secret – all the secrets – would come out. And it was too much of an imposition on Kelly and Dan to ask for their spare room, what with Mol, and Kelly's pregnancy. I told myself that these were the reasons I didn't ask Kelly. But truth be told, even though they would welcome me as they always did, I didn't know if I would be able to cope right now in their family unit.

I had other friends, but I'd been neglectful since working with Connie, and it would seem too opportunistic to text them out of the blue. But there was one person who might be willing to put me up, even just for a couple of days. I pulled out my phone and dialled the number.

'Hello?' said a voice, young and light.

'Hi, Zoë. It's Rose. How are you?'

'Rose!' she said, her voice breaking into happiness. 'Oh my god, how are *you*? We miss you at the cafe. Well, maybe not Giles. *I* miss you.'

I laughed. 'I miss you too. I miss our chats. I'm sorry, I've been so shit at being in touch. A lot's gone on. Hey, listen – are you free this afternoon, by any chance? I know it's a long shot—'

'This afternoon? Sure.'

*

Zoë lived in a tiny sub-let council flat in East London with three other people. Every public wall I walked past on the way was flyered with achingly cool low-key club nights, whose bands and aesthetics I couldn't even begin to understand. Elaborate and beautiful graffiti lined the brickwork, and there were coffee shops with square footage the size of a postage stamp and wooden benches outside. I passed a shop that seemed to sell only black socks from Japan, its frontage artfully rough around the edges. The coffees, I noted, were the same price as in Hampstead.

I found Zoë's estate and rang her doorbell. She appeared quickly, dressed in a big baggy blouse and leggings. Tiny gold hoops frilled the curve of her left earlobe. She gave me a hug. 'Come in!'

Her room was a dream. That sheepskin rug and fairy light feel, with postcards from the Tate stuck up with Blu-tack, succulents lining her windowsill, night-lights and slim novellas, a journal and pen-pot on a tiny desk. It felt like a room that held hopes and dreams inside it, and my heart couldn't decide to swell or break.

'You're so kind to let me stay,' I said, and I meant it.

'Oh, not at all. People crash here all the time. I've got you clean sheets. I'm really sorry about you and Joe.'

'Thanks. I'm all right, though. And I promise I won't be here long, I just—'

'Rosie, it's cool, really. Listen, tonight we're having a big vegan lasagne and watching *Clueless*. You wanna join?'

'I'd love to,' I said, feeling about three million years old. I wanted to bottle and sell this heady combination of Zoë's utter youth and sweet maturity.

She gave me the Wi-Fi password, *VirgosRUs* – 'there's three of us here born in September' – and I logged onto the Internet on my phone. No one had emailed me. I went on Joe's @joerritos Instagram account, but he hadn't posted since before Christmas. Kelly had been busy, though – a great photo of all three of them in Christmas pudding onesies. *Tis the season!* she'd typed. *#Puddings #whatdoidowhenineedawee*.

Again I thought about her ferociously chopping logs alone in the frosty field on Christmas morning. I would have loved to have seen Kelly's other self. To see her bright, primary-coloured squares washed in different hues of sage and brown, dark, skeletal trees, a line from an Anne Sexton poem and her selfie with an axe. But I doubt she'd get quite the sponsorship she needed. She knew that too. Since the pudding photo, into the New Year it had been some tasteful interior shots of their home, Dan and Mol's backs, walking along in a park – and yes, Kel's observation on 'what it feels like to be a mother'. She'd remembered what she'd told me practically verbatim. The comments underneath this caption were endless: '*Oh my god, THIS.*'; '*You're so right, sometimes I think it couldn't get any worse and then you turn a corner and all you see is sun!*'

I switched off my phone.

*

That night, I sat round a tiny melamine table and ate a delicious aubergine lasagne, and laughed and listened to Zoë's and her flatmates' conversations. They were all a similar age to Zoë, in their early twenties – and it wasn't until I was with the four of them that I realized quite how different I was. I felt heavier in my mind and in my bones, the effect of the accumulation of time. They liked to talk about themselves, a lot, with little encouragement from me, finding their own anecdotes fascinating and new – but they were generous with each other's stories too, riffing and spinning off into absurd tangents, their moods dogmatic and whimsical by turn. They talked about their work. One was an art student, another was a PA in the City, the third was debating whether to train as a teacher. All of them were in serious debt but this had not dented their ambitions.

I asked the art student, a girl called Lara, what she was making. 'I'm working with plastic, mainly,' she said, free and flowing with her sentences. 'Old plastic. I want to reconfigure it, try and take the blame out of it. All of my processes are low-energy – I use solar energy, natural light, rain water, composted material. I don't buy anything. I feel I can only move forward by bringing with me only what's already here.'

'She does the most beautiful sculptures,' Zoë said, and I knew she thought she had to act as translator for me. 'One of them was bought by a serious dude.'

'A serious dude?'

'The kind of guy you need to buy your work,' Lara said, with no apparent bitterness. 'He's got it in the courtyard of his mews house in Bayswater. I installed it for him.'

'That's amazing,' I said. 'And what do you want to do once you graduate?'

Lara smiled. 'More of the same. But it's not going to be easy. I have a couple of bursaries I rely on at college. They'll dry up.'

'You'll do it,' I said.

Her smile wavered. 'I don't know. You need to know people. Get people's attention. You need followers on the Internet. I've only got, like, six thousand.'

'I doubt a million followers would make you a better artist,' I said.

'I know that,' she replied, a touch defensively, and I thought I'd better not act too much like a big sister.

'Actually,' I said, 'you really remind me of my friend Kelly.'

Lara's face lit up. '*Do* I?' she said. 'Why?'

'She was determined, like you. Still is. She made it work. She needed bursaries too. Have you ever heard of @thestellakella?'

They all looked at me blankly, and I realized that I was asking the wrong crowd. 'Well,' I said. 'She took her passion and she made it work as a living. She didn't worry about what people thought of her. She just got on with it and before long, people were coming to her. It is a gamble though, doing that.'

'Why?' asked Lara, looking baffled.

'Because if you rely on something you love to feed you, pay your bills, put a roof over your head, I think it complicates your relationship with it. That's how it seems with her, anyway. You have to be practical around something that's impulsive, sometimes elusive. If you turn your soul into a business, you have to be ready for that to hurt sometimes.'

Lara looked at me wide-eyed. 'Yeah,' she said. 'You're so right. And the thing is, you can't compartmentalize – but if you don't, you'll pay a price one way or another.'

This was all making me think of Connie. I felt that Connie had paid a price – for what, exactly, I was still unsure. But her reaction to me earlier that day betrayed some deep pain inside her that had never been resolved, and which she had let impact on every aspect of her life, including, I believed, her desire to write.

'Exactly,' I said to the table. 'But you don't have to worry. You're all way ahead of where I was when I was in my twenties.'

'Where were you in your twenties?' asked Gabriella, the PA, who had perfect nails, and bright eyes that still betrayed anxiety.

I took a deep breath. 'I was really lost,' I said. 'Really, really lost.'

I could feel the air in the kitchen condense, their bodies tensing in anticipation of when someone might actually tell a truth. 'People have always disagreed with me when I say this,' I said, looking round the table. 'But I've come to think it's not always a great idea to be spectacular at school. It's hard to keep that going.'

Jacob, the one boy in the room, the one who was thinking of being a teacher, chuckled. I knew I'd touched a sore point. 'Do you remember that ten-year-old, who was made to go and do a physics degree at Cambridge, had a nervous breakdown and never looked at a calculator again?' I said.

'No,' said Zoë.

'Yeah, it was ages ago. Like, the seventies. I mean, my situation wasn't that bad – Zoë will vouch that I'm no physics genius, or any genius in fact. But it can be hard, twenty years on, to have a patchy CV. When everyone thought you would "go to Oxford", or be "living in New York", or running some amazing organization making the world "a better place".'

I had them enraptured. Maybe they didn't know anyone my age? It would make sense. I didn't really know anybody their age. Maybe no one was prepared to talk to them like this? But I realized as I talked on, that I was prepared. Something in me over the past few months had broken open. It felt as if Laura and Rose were joining together, and it felt right, and heady and full of potential. For the first time ever, I felt free to be myself, and to tell my own story. 'It's good to have people believe in you,' I said, looking at Jacob. 'It's better than the opposite. But a lot of it is about them, not you.'

'Fuck,' said Jacob. 'Do you want to tell that to my parents?'

That night, a stolen night slipped from the calendar, I told them my story – these three welcoming strangers and one casual friend. I told them about my missing mother, about how I grew up dreaming fantasies about her. How I felt I didn't have a path, how I slid into this job or that, how I compared myself to others and found myself wanting, how often I ended up the second fiddle in other people's projects – including my boyfriend's. I didn't tell them about Laura Brown, or why I'd decided to be her. Given Zoë's love of

Connie's work, I thought that was a conversation best saved for another time.

'There isn't an endpoint,' I said to them. 'No arrival.' At this, the expressions on their faces ranged from perplexed to despondent. 'But you're all so brilliant, and you've got so much going for you. And if you haven't got to where you wanted to get by the time you're twenty-five, you should probably thank your lucky stars. Seriously. Because if getting there is hard, holding on to your dream is possibly even harder. Nothing ever stays the same.'

They looked at me slightly blankly, and I realized it might be hard to appreciate the idea that all your goals, once achieved, might slip through your fingers. That they might not make you happy.

'So what are you going to do now?' said Jacob.

'I've got an idea or two,' I said. And then I realized it was true.

*

By ten p.m. I was desperate to go to bed. All the talking was exhausting, but being pregnant was draining me immensely. I didn't want them to be disappointed in me, so I stayed up till midnight watching *Clueless*, which I realized Jacob, Gabi, Lara and Zoë were viewing like a museum piece, and I was watching as a comforting return to my adolescence.

My airbed was surprisingly comfy. Zoë loved lavender oil, and had sprinkled some drops on my pillow. When I went to the bathroom, Zoë and Lara were in the kitchen clearing away the last of the washing-up.

'Rose is so cool?' Lara was saying.

'I know,' said Zoë. 'She's real.'

'I want to be like that when I'm older. You know? Like, really knowing yourself?'

Heat emanated in my stomach like a glow. They would never know what hearing those words meant to me. Back on the airbed, I drifted off quite easily, out of my usual life. *But this is my life*, I thought, just before I fell asleep.

42

I stayed with Zoë for a week, rising when she did and making sure I was out of her flat as long as possible in the day. I went to galleries. I walked endlessly along the Embankment, from Cheyne Walk as far as the Tower of London. I thought constantly about two things: Connie, and the pregnancy. I wondered whether I should ring Connie. I began to worry about money. This situation of living with Zoë could not go on. I needed to get a job, a place to live, and soon. I could ask for my job at Clean Bean, I supposed, start making cappuccinos again – but I had begun to feel nauseous so much of the time, and going to the cafe felt like a regression. I wanted to be in Connie's house, making our dinner, working out our next moves. The book was coming soon, and then what? The thought that I might have blown it for ever with Connie was a bit like the pregnancy: not something I was quite fully able to acknowledge. It felt too cataclysmic. Nevertheless, something was holding me back from calling her. When, five days into being with Zoë, my phone rang, I knew what I'd been waiting for.

'Rose?' said a voice.

'Connie,' I replied. It felt so good to hear her voice. 'How – are you?'

There was a pause. 'I'm fine,' she said neutrally. She hesitated again. 'Where are you?'

'I'm leaning against a river wall looking at the Tate Modern.'

There was silence again, but Connie was still on the line. I could almost hear her mind working, the battles at play between her desire to berate me and her need to talk to me. I knew that this time, I couldn't say anything. Connie had to dictate how this went. Connie had to be the one who made this call. One false move and I might lose her for ever. She had to feel like she was in control.

'I'm still angry,' she said. 'You were sly.'

'I'm really sorry, Connie.'

'I told you things I haven't spoken about for years.'

'I know.'

She didn't say anything. *She's going to tell me to come and pick up the rest of my stuff*, I thought. 'I should have told you who I was,' I said. 'But I was scared you wouldn't want anything to do with me.' Again, Connie said nothing and I wondered if I'd hit on an awkward truth. 'I only called your agency in the first place because I just wanted to write to you. But things got out of control. I thought I could make it work.'

'Well you got that wrong, didn't you?'

'I did. But I didn't see any other way. I couldn't – I *still* don't know what happened between you and my mum. You never really wanted to talk about your past.'

'And that's my right!'

'I know it is. Of course. So I didn't know what your reaction would be if I told you who I really was.'

She fell silent again. I didn't know what to do, what to say. I felt old, and tired. I just wanted the story to change, but I felt it couldn't until we'd got through this one. 'My dad's told me hardly anything,' I said.

'Really? I find that extraordinary.'

I stared at the Thames, huge and deep and dangerous, this ancient river I'd lived by my whole life without ever really paying it much attention, still silting up its treasures from centuries past. 'He said you two knew each other. He said that for a while, you were inseparable. He said it ended badly.'

'Did he now?'

Silence again.

'Who's making your sandwiches, Con?' I said.

'No one. I don't need a home help.'

'Of course not.'

'But I do need you to come over.' I felt my heart lift, a sick flutter of excitement in my stomach that wasn't the baby. 'There's something I want you to see.' Connie's voice was expressionless; she wasn't giving anything away.

'Now?'

'Well, it can wait, obviously, but—'

'I'm coming now,' I said.

'Fine,' said Connie, and she put down the phone.

*

Heading towards St Paul's Station, I thought I'd played it as well as I could have. I just had to hope that Connie's natural curiosity and her need to know as much as possible about other people would win out against her pride and pain. She had to be the one to summon me back to her court, and I had to show willing.

As I descended into the station I realized something else: she'd called me Rose as if it were the most normal thing in the world.

*

I walked towards Connie's house, by now such a familiar path for my feet to tread. My phone buzzed with a text from Joe. I'm selling the van, he wrote.

I texted back immediately. Why?

About thirty seconds later, he replied, You know why.

I didn't know what to say to that. I thought of the rusty doors. The way that bits of grated cheese would always get stuck in the join between the old chipped worktop and the interior. Are you OK about it? I wrote.

Well, mum's delighted.

Lol, I typed back, then worried I was being too flippant. I added a van emoji and then a broken heart.

Joe sent three dollar emojis. I'm giving you half, he wrote.

What? No.

You deserve it Rosie.

It's your van. You don't have to do that.

No, I do. When I get the money, I'll put it in your account. Look out for it. X

Joe, this is so generous. Thank you.

He didn't reply. I slipped my phone back into my bag.

*

I still had my key to Connie's house but I didn't use it. I knocked and waited. Nothing happened. It seemed like a dead house, a numb place where no one existed. 'Con?' I called through the letterbox, but no answer came. My skin prickled: what if this was a trap set by Deborah, and the police were going to swoop to arrest me? What if Connie was spread-eagled on the floor, the stress of my revelation proving too much for her heart? What if she'd *killed* herself? I told myself to be reasonable. She had called me a mere hour ago. She had not committed suicide on her carpet. The police were not coming.

I thought about what to do. Call her back? I didn't want to appear too vigilant, too persistent. I knocked again.

I was about to give up when I saw the familiar winnowing

figure through the mottled glass, coming up from the kitchen. Had Connie not heard me the first time? Was she making me wait? Maybe she was testing me, to see how long I was prepared to pine outside her house, to see how much I really wanted what it was she had. Or perhaps she was just moving slower. I realized my mind was jumping too fast and I tried to focus. I'd been waiting on the doorstep for at least ten minutes.

Connie was struggling with the latch, but eventually, she got it open, and pulled the door back to survey me. She was still as imposing as ever, upright and hard – five days were not going to change that – but there was fatigue in her eyes, and a certain wariness. We looked at each other. I really wanted to sit down. 'Hi,' I said.

'I must have been blind,' said Connie.

'I'm sorry?'

'I see it in you now.'

'*It?*'

'Her.'

'Connie,' I said. 'I don't want to upset you.'

'You won't upset me,' she said. 'You've already done your worst. You'd better come in.'

She turned into the house. I stepped gently over the threshold, and Connie shut the world away.

*

We went into the front room. Connie stood in the middle, facing me. 'I don't owe you anything, you know,' she said.

'I know you don't.'

'I paid you for your services. To do a job.'

'I know. And I'm so grateful.'

'Were those questions you were asking me – about why I hadn't written for so long, what happens to Margaret after *The*

Mercurial ends, whether Christina and she were based on people I knew – was all that because you thought you'd find your mother?'

I thought it best to be honest. 'At first, yes. I think I wanted very badly for that to be the case.'

'And what is your conclusion?'

'I didn't find a conclusion. I don't know enough about what really happened to be able to find it in a book.'

She nodded, appearing to be satisfied. 'You coming here and helping me shouldn't mean I have to hand my life over to you, Rose,' she said.

'I know that.'

She sighed and sat down slowly on the edge of her favourite armchair. 'So,' she said. 'Rose Simmons. Does your father know you're here?'

'No.'

'He wouldn't approve. But perhaps you know that. What did he tell you about me?'

I took a deep breath. 'I've told you. Not much.' Connie rolled her eyes. 'Well,' I said. 'He did mention that you were strong and my mother was weak.'

'Did he,' said Connie.

'That there was a woman called Yolanda. She was my mum's friend in New York.'

At the name, Connie visibly flinched.

'He told me that you and Elise were a couple before he got together with her,' I went on. 'He says Elise left him, and took me with her. She was staying at Yolanda's apartment. Then you turned up and she disappeared.' I paused. 'He says you were the last one to be with her before she disappeared.'

At this, Connie closed her eyes. 'And did he tell you whether Elise was alive or dead?'

I swallowed, determined to keep this conversational and free of drama. 'No.'

Connie sat back in her armchair and stared into the distance. 'Did he bring you up OK?'

Tears came into my eyes and I blinked them away. 'Yes,' I said. 'I love him.'

'Apart from your inclination to impersonation, deception and the like,' said Connie.

To my surprise, her eyes seemed to gleam – with amusement, approval or acceptance, I couldn't tell.

'Deborah's furious, you know,' she went on. I feared she was changing the subject.

'I can imagine,' I said. 'But are you?'

Connie ignored this. 'She thinks you're after something.'

'I am. My mother.'

Connie laughed. 'And you thought you'd find her here.'

'It was as good a place as any. My dad didn't elaborate, but the way he talked about you and her—'

'I see,' said Connie, chewing her lip. She seemed to be cogitating on something. 'Come with me,' she said.

'What?'

'I want you to come with me.'

*

We were heading for her bedroom, right up to the attic, her rickety wrists on a narrow balustrade. It was a neat room, a small room. The first thing I saw was a Deco-style dressing table with neat Bakelite handles. Connie's make-up and hairbrush were laid upon it, and a silver frame which held the faded colour photo of a cat. I had not seen this cat in any other photo frame in the house. It was slung like a baby in someone's arms, a handsome animal, tortoiseshell and enormous with a cream belly and green eyes. A slender hand supported its neck, but the focus of this photograph was most definitely the cat.

I followed Connie inside.

The bed was made neatly, the plain pale blue duvet straightened, pillows plumped, a soft-looking shawl scrunched like a woollen nest in the middle. There were two bedside tables both piled with books, but only one had a pair of reading glasses on it, a blister pack of pills and a half-drunk glass of water. There were so many titles it would be hard to tell which one was current. By the dressing table was a row of shelves. A quick glance told me it was filled with nineteenth-century classics in paperback, and collections of Plath and Rich, Keats, Lorca, their spines deeply cracked. Virginia Woolf and Angela Carter had made it, but the rest of Connie's more modern tastes were downstairs in the living room.

'This is what I want you to see,' said Connie. 'Look.'

She was pointing at the wall to the left of the door. It was the only artwork up here – if that's what you would call it, a small painting in a frame, hanging above a chest of drawers. It was the rough outline of a rabbit, expensively framed but executed on cheap notepaper. The paper was yellowed, but the patterns inside the rabbit were a painted chaos in forest green, made up of tiny dots, everywhere. It was not expert nor was it beautiful, but it had a sort of concentration to it that I liked.

'Look,' said Connie.

I moved closer. The two ears were on different levels to each other, the little tail was ludicrous – but such intensity, all in that green. Then I realized that the tiny dots all over the body of the rabbit were made up by the repeated pressure of a miniature fingerprint.

And along the bottom in the corner: *For Connie, love Rose.*

★

I backed away. I had to sit on the bed for a few seconds. Gingerly, Connie lifted the picture frame off the wall, and walked towards me holding it in outstretched palms, like a Wise King bringing the myrrh. 'A green rabbit, for a woman called Rabbit,' Connie said.

I eyed the picture. I couldn't speak.

'You made this,' said Connie. 'Well. Not *strictly* speaking. Your mother did. She took your finger, which was so tiny, because you were such a little baby at that point – and she dipped it in a pot of green paint, and prodded it all over the rabbit.'

A pain came into my eyes, and I couldn't stop what was coming. The idea of my mother holding a tiny finger – my tiny finger – and dotting it carefully, lovingly, unstintingly all over the paper, until this rabbit's entire pelt was covered in the evidence of our joint effort, probably our first and only effort, ripped something apart inside me. I began to cry.

'I want you to have this,' said Connie gently. 'I think you should have it.'

I don't know how long I sat on the edge of Connie's bed, or when I eventually managed to stop crying and take up the picture from where Connie had left it by my side. She sat down next to me and put her hand in mine. 'Oh, Rose,' she said. 'I always wondered if this day might come.'

*

I realized, now everything was out in the open, what I hadn't understood before – that this couldn't all be explained to me in an hour, or two, or even an afternoon. It might take another lifetime. I'd wanted a neat, quick bucketload of information, and I wanted to process it in situ, but life is not like that, no person's story is like that, and Connie knew that better than most.

Instead, she asked me to go downstairs and put the kettle on. She'd be down in a minute, she said. I obeyed, drained of tears and energy, yet charged up with the greatest, most human revelation about my mother I'd ever had. That one day, she'd probably walked to a store to buy a pot of green paint. It was such a tender image – so banal, really – a woman walking down a New York street. But also so touching, because she didn't know that thirty-four years later I'd be thinking of her like that. Had I been with her, in a pram? Or had I been left in the apartment – and with who? I rubbed my index finger, imagining her holding it, guiding it across the paper. In a daze, I put the kettle on, reaching for two of Con's terrible mugs. I dropped teabags in each one, and stared out of the window. I felt a whole new side to myself opening up, and I could do nothing but let it happen now. This is what I had sought.

'Tea's ready,' I called up the stairs.

'Coming,' Connie called back.

I fetched a Penguin bar from her biscuit tin, unwrapped it for her and put it on the table on a small plate. When had Connie framed that painting? Had she always kept it close? Why did she cherish it so much that she would have it on her bedroom wall? Her decision to do that told me something that I didn't dare hope: that I might mean something to her.

*

Connie sat down opposite me. She had come into the kitchen with something in her hand, and she now pushed it across the table. It was a flimsy perspex photo frame containing a picture of about twenty people, grouped haphazardly together in front of a swimming pool, bordered by a wall of cacti. Men and women of different ages, smiling happily. Judging by their hairstyles and clothing, it was from some time in the eighties. I held it close, scanning the faces. There was Connie, so much younger but unmistakable, near the centre of the third row. That sharp nose and fine face, her hair in a wild bob, big earrings, wearing a pantsuit of all things, in a shade of orange. Its loudness was at odds with the woman I knew, but I recognized that upright posture, that confidence. Then more faces, the terrible baggy shirts and hair gel, the double denim, the sequin sheaths and shoulder pads.

'She's in the back row,' said Con. 'In the funeral dress.'

I took a deep breath and looked again. To see her for the first time. It was what I had wanted for so long. A girl, smiling like the others, but with her mouth closed, a hesitancy to her expression. Perhaps she had not been ready for the camera. Her eyes looked determined, almost rageful. Her hair was dark. She looked very young in her black dress, and amidst this group, in their anachronistic markings of fashion, she looked almost timeless. Her face was made for the camera, and even in this amateur snap her unusual beauty was obvious. She was holding on to something round her neck, like a talisman to banish evil spirits.

'That's her,' said Connie. 'That's Elise.'

The truth is, I didn't recognize my mother. For some reason, I thought I would – but now I'd been presented with her, it felt shocking to put a face to the endless idea of her, to the name *Elise*, to the hope and the fear I had poured into her. All I could see was that she was so young. It struck me then, that soon after this photo, she would find herself pregnant with me. I wanted so desperately to know what she might have been thinking about that.

'This was taken before you came along,' said Connie, and it unsettled me to think she was so in tune with my thoughts. 'At her birthday party.'

'Where were you?'

'Los Angeles,' said Connie.

'Los Angeles?'

'She was twenty-three. May I?' She put out her hand in request and I passed the photo over. She stared at it. 'This was the night everything started to go wrong,' she said.

'Go wrong?'

She looked up at me. 'Are you waiting for a happy ending?'

'I don't believe in happy endings, Con.'

Connie smiled. 'Maybe we should.' She sighed, handing me back the picture. 'I've been thinking about you all week,' she said. 'The lengths you've gone to. And I've been thinking about her. I know you want answers, Rose. I've been trying to work out how best to give them to you. What to say, how to say it. And then I realized. I've actually been thinking about this for thirty-odd years.'

I clasped my fingers round my Birdworld mug. 'So have I.'

'It might have been easier not to call you,' said Connie.

'I'm glad you did.'

'I don't hide. I'm not that person. Neither are you.'

I wanted to ask her that if she didn't hide, then what had she been doing these last thirty years? – but I knew that was unwise. As if she sensed the paradox in her statement, Connie turned her attention to me. 'You're strong, Rose. As strong as Laura was—'

'Con, don't—'

'– so I'm going to tell you about your mother. Everything I know. Because you deserve to hear this story.'

1983

43

After the hospital sent her home, the true melting of time began. The apartment *had* no time. Elise felt that whatever time had been before birth, it was now swollen into a solar system beyond her reach, whilst she sat on a tiny mushroom in a giant forest, feeding tiny Rose. And changing her, changing her, changing her, day and night. If there was grace to be found in this repetition, Elise was rapidly too tired to appreciate it. The hours made no sense.

Matt went back to work a week later, because of money. Yoli came round after her shift, her eyes shining as she met the child for the first time.

'So this is Rosa,' she said. '*Bienvenida*, little one.' She held the baby in her hands as if she was weighing her at a market. Rose stared blindly up at Yolanda, her tiny fingers moving slowly. 'She's light.'

'She's fine,' said Elise.

Yolanda shrugged. 'She loud?'

'Not really.'

'That might come.'

Elise resisted the urge to ask Yolanda where exactly she was assuming all this authority, given she'd never had a child herself. She didn't want the exhaustion to get the better of her. Instead, she leaned against the faded couch and closed her eyes.

'Go take a shower, Elise,' said Yolanda. 'Wash off that sweat. I'll hold Rosa.'

Elise let the hot water run over her body, staring down at the empty pouch of her stomach. She came out from the bathroom to see Yolanda sitting framed by the afternoon light from the street coming in through the window, offering a reverential stroke of one finger upon the span of Rose's cheek.

Yolanda and Elise watched the aquatic movements of the child's arms with wonder, as if Rose still wanted to be floating in her mother's waters. 'She's swimming,' said Yolanda. 'She's going to be a good swimmer.' Elise fell asleep with her head on Yoli's shoulder, as the older woman sat up watching TV with Rose in her arms till Matt came home.

*

Two weeks passed in this strange and timeless way, punctuated only by feeding, changing, sleeping in snatches. Elise and the baby had still not left the apartment. When Matt or Yolanda suggested to Elise that she should take the baby out, Elise began to be plagued by visions of catastrophe. Rose, her pram hit by a car. Rose, snatched at a traffic light as Elise rummaged in her bag. But indoors, the visions began too. Rose, poisoned by a misplaced bottle of bleach instead of milk. Rose, left on the floor of the kitchen, a coffee pot flying off the counter to douse her in boiling liquid. Whether they were indoors or out, the act of keeping Rose alive forever began to feel too much to bear.

Elise was paralysed in her attempts to conceptualize a future where she could be a good and strong guardian. She couldn't sleep, dreading the moment when Rose would start to wail for her. Exhausted and grimy from New York's humid summer, she dragged herself to the cot and stared at the creature within it, lifting the tiny beating thing to her breast, her body pummelled by a force she'd not anticipated, her mind assaulted by an experience she was struggling to articulate.

She began to beg Yolanda to stay over, as if Yolanda's presence would keep her from doing something to her baby. She couldn't admit the thoughts inside her; the nightmares that had crept into the day – that she had this power over a helpless baby, and she did not deserve it. That she had a daughter who she could not care for. That she had love – from Matt, and from Yolanda – so much love, and she did not know how to receive it. She could not be relied upon. She could not do this, could not do this. Could not do this. She could not do this.

*

One morning, Elise heard murmurs between Yolanda and Matt coming from the living room. Urgent whispers, Matt's voice pained, saying, *I don't know what to do, but I can't leave my job. We need the money.*

She's not right, Yolanda said. *This isn't right.*

Why are you even here? he said.

Because you're not.

After he'd gone to work and whilst Rose slept, Yolanda practically forced Elise into the bathroom. She peeled off her dirty clothes, guiding her into the bath, pressing down her shoulders until Elise was on her knees, and she washed Elise's sweaty body. Foaming Elise's hair with hot water and shampoo, Yolanda rinsed it clean.

*

On coming in again one mid-morning to find Elise staring out of the window in just her bra and knickers as Rose screamed her head off, Yolanda burst out with frustration, 'Is a child bringing up a child here, Elisa?'

Elise turned to her. 'You tell me.'

'You slept?'

'No,' she said. 'I don't know what the baby wants.'

'She wants *you*,' said Yolanda, softening.

'She doesn't like me,' said Elise.

'That's crazy.'

'She's always quiet with you.'

This was true. Yolanda had a forceful yet tender handling of the child, and she talked to her constantly, walking her round the apartment while Elise tried to sleep. Sometimes, Elise would watch them and think Rose was more Yolanda's baby. Yolanda was playing the part with more aplomb. But then again, Elise thought: it's always easier to love someone from a distance.

*

It was staggering to Elise how much there was for Rose to do, to see, to hear and taste and smell for the first time. And to have to do it again and again and again. 'She has no choice,' Elise said to Matt as they stood by the cot looking down at their daughter. Rose had her knees bent, her tiny feet moving like slow and miniature maracas.

'What do you mean?' said Matt, looking wary. This wariness when he talked with Elise was new, but already becoming familiar to her.

'I've brought her into this situation and she didn't have a choice,' she said. 'Rose is going to have to live in this world.'

'She'll be all right.'

'But there's so far to go,' said Elise. 'And she's only six weeks old.'

Matt tried to embrace her, but she stood there, rigid as a mannequin.

And after all you fight for, Elise went on thinking, after Matt had left – all you do to live a good life – you never remember yourself truly. You think you will know yourself when something big happens: a birth, a death. But you will never remember yourself truly.

There would be Rose's first word. Her first understanding of how her body would be placed in water, that liquid full of bubbles which would distort her brand-new skin. She would find the sea, with pebbles pressing painfully into the soles of her feet. Her first thrill of ice cream. An illustration that might stalk her childhood dreams, to be experienced as oblique longing when she saw a certain colour as an adult. The peril of a dog bark, its bulk a wolf to her small size, its endless reams of fur so different to her own skin. Jewellery, jangling on women with many different faces. Her father's stubble like a strange field he would let her pat, over and over, animal-rough, vanishing one day only to grow back as the days passed through. The warm perfume of a favoured teacher. All sensations and certainties that would happen for the first time, and then be gone.

Maybe that's why people have children, she thought. So that they can remember what once happened to them. It's a recipe for madness, but we just accept it, and go on accepting it, because there's no other option. Well, there is. But I don't want to think about that.

She walked away from the cot slowly. She felt as if she was drowning. She'd never felt like this – never known love or fear like this. Not when she'd seen Connie by the pool with Barbara. Not even when her mother died.

Sometimes, in her exhaustion, Elise thought she'd crossed

over into a different kind of madness. Some days, she could barely move.

*

'You have got to get dressed,' said Yolanda. 'Sunshine, Elisa. I am coming with you,' she added, seeing the fear in the younger woman's eyes.

So Elise did as she was told, taking Rose with her to Irving Square Park. Rose lay on her back in the pram, dwarfed by its size. They walked through the dappled shade created by the full-leaved trees. 'Rosita is healthy. Rosa is all right,' said Yolanda. 'So what is wrong?'

'I don't know,' said Elise. 'Let's have a sorbet.'

Sorbet, *sawbay*, a beach cut in two, just like her mind, slowly fracturing. I could just leave the pram here, Elise thought, as they stood by the sorbet stall. This monumental, unearned power you were given as a parent, that no one talked about. It was almost beyond comprehension! I could just do that to her, and it's horrendous that no law, no test, no procedure can prevent me. If I really wanted.

She gripped the handles and closed her eyes. Yolanda spoke down into the pram – 'Look at the sunshine, Rosita. Can you see how bright it is?'

*

So the days went on. Elise managed to pull herself together in time for Matt to come home, so that he didn't worry too much, but when Yoli was at the diner in the daytime, or when she was unable to be around – they were the hardest times. Rose wouldn't take the breast, so Elise fed her with formula, and saw no one, for hours. 'Why don't we find a mother and baby group?' Matt said one night as they sat together on the sofa. He looked very tired and his face was a frown of concern.

'A what?' she said.

'You know. Where you can go and be with other new mothers.'

'OK,' said Elise.

*

They found her a group in Fort Greene, and she got on the bus and went with Rose in a sling. The women sat on the floor on mats, with their babies next to them, and they played with them, and they talked with each other. Elise felt a lot younger than many of them. They smiled at her. They looked normal. The organizer, a bright, warm woman called Francine, welcomed Elise and Rose. 'Come and sit down,' she said. 'Would you like a juice? A coffee?'

'Water, please,' said Elise. She felt dry-mouthed, shipwrecked.

They started singing songs about farmyard animals. The women scooped up their babies and sang with them, happy to be cows and pigs and roosters and sheep. Elise marvelled at their ventriloquism, their ingenuity, their tired beams of love. The babies were mesmerized. Their small mouths were hung open, their new eyes gauging the big mouths of their mothers. Elise tried to sing too, but no good sound would come. She was out of tune. Croaking, weird. She glanced fearfully at Francine, who she noticed with alarm was already looking at her. Francine smiled encouragingly. Elise could feel a tidal sob inside herself, and wondered how much longer she could keep it in. She felt so useless, so wrong, so out of control. It had been so much easier when it was just her – surfing, walking, modelling, sitting very still with no one who needed her, no one to love. She bowed her head and felt a hand on her shoulder. Francine, speaking gently in her ear. 'Come with me, Elise.'

*

She sat opposite Francine in a small office off the communal hall, Rose on her lap. 'I'm scared,' she heard herself saying. 'I'm scared.'

'What are you scared of?'

'I don't *know*.'

'Elise,' said Francine. 'I think you need to see a doctor. Get your husband to take you to a doctor.'

'OK,' said Elise.

*

No one told her that it was OK to feel like this. That it might pass. Instead, they were always trying to suggest places she should go. Soon after the failed attempt at the baby group in Fort Greene, Elise decided to go deep into Manhattan – to Times Square, because Rose hadn't seen Times Square. She thought it would be good for her to see the inside of someone's head turned out, pictures, flashing lights, people in their thousands; a little bit of madness to touch then flee. She could take her out of the pram and hold her up, show her what this corner of the world was like.

Elise turned the pram into the mass of people, and kept pushing through the crowds. *Good!* she thought. *She's OK with crowds.*

And then she looked up and stopped moving. Above their heads, Barbara Lowden's picture loomed enormously. Barbara's head was nearly twenty times bigger than a normal head, her eyes like plates – beautiful dark, shining plates! – deep and brown and framed by perfect lashes. Her mouth – that mouth – a goddess mouth, slick with red gloss, gleaming; cheekbones lightly bronzed, that overall impression of self-knowledge and power. She didn't look human at all. She was so *big*. Elise thought she was going to be sick.

Thousands of people streamed round them, but only Barbara, up there, felt real.

HEARTLANDS – starring Barbara Lowden and Don Gullick, the poster said. In theaters from September 3. Underneath, someone in the marketing department had come up with the line: A Heart Was Where Her Home Was, which Elise thought Connie would have loathed and laughed at in equal measure.

Don Gullick's face was next to Barbara's. They looked like members of a military organization, shoulder to shoulder, ready to weather the world. It was a sophisticated, challenging image, because even though they were love interests, Barbara and Don weren't looking at each other, gooey-eyed. It was as it should be, because Wax Heart was not a book about married love. It was a bachelorette book, a feminist tract – you could even argue it was a subtextual lesbian paean – but perhaps that little detail had passed Hollywood by.

Really, it should have been a poster of Barbara alone – but even Barbara Lowden in her beauty and power wouldn't swing the box office by herself. Elise remembered Con saying it would never happen. She needed the man beside her.

Connie, Elise thought. Where are you?

She stood there for several minutes, staring at Barbara's face, a grief welling inside her at how the world just never stopped moving on. She wanted to tell Connie she'd seen the poster. She wanted to tell Connie how alone she felt, how sad, how small, how scared. She wanted to tell her she'd called her baby Rose. How Rose was everything, but at the same time how everything had gone.

'Hey lady, you a zombie?' said a voice. Someone was tapping her to get out of the way. Elise jumped, pushed the wheels of the stroller and headed in the direction of the apartment.

44

The doctor was based in rooms six storeys up in a grand old building in Midtown, in an office preceded by an antechamber of dark panelling, heavy magazines and no natural light due to shutters which kept out the sun. The only decoration was a plain white clock. Once in the office, the walls too were white, everything was, and Elise wondered if the decision was deliberate. Here she was, a bug exposed, reluctant and defenceless against all comers.

'Do you know why you're here?' said the doctor, who might have been called Doctor Barrios, but Elise wasn't sure, nor what she was a doctor of. Matt had hurriedly booked her in, the desperation writ across his face.

'Have you read *Green Rabbit*?' Elise countered.

The doctor inclined her head. She glanced at the door, behind which lay the dark and panelled antechamber, and Matt, and little Rose.

'Read what, Elise?'

'*Green Rabbit*.'

'No, I haven't.'

'You should,' said Elise. She wondered if the doctor could see the grease on her scalp. She was not interested in giving answers. She didn't have them. She had *Green Rabbit* in her handbag. She was re-reading it, every day. Matt had seen her reading it and was furious. He thought it was a bad idea for her to read

Connie's words. *It's about me*, she said to him. *It's about Connie losing me.*

'I will,' said the doctor. 'If you think it's a good book.'

'I do.'

The doctor wrote something on a pad. Elise supposed she was about seventy, steel hair in a bob, tortoiseshell glasses. A wedding ring; the stone in the middle old and dark, possibly an onyx. Elise wondered if she was a widow: so many men predeceased their mates. Her pen was an expensive, heavy thing. Her writing, even upside down, was exquisite, Arabic in flourish. Elise watched her lightly liver-spotted hands. *One day, I'll be that old*, she thought. *I hope I'm that elegant.* Imagine being seventy! With an easy disavowal of her own life, and an understanding that she had no clue what the doctor's was really like, Elise wanted it. Outside the traffic honked, but all Elise could see was sky.

'Elise, you hurt yourself,' the doctor said softly, laying down her beautiful pen.

Rude. Provocative. Not the doctor's place to decide. 'I don't need to talk about it,' Elise said, looking into her lap. She felt loosened, calmer. Matt had never commented on the bruises all over her body from when she hurled herself into the Pacific breakers. Connie had. What was the difference now, hurling herself down a flight of stairs?

'The people who love you seem to think you should,' said the doctor. 'Your husband.'

Elise said nothing. She picked at her necklace and slid the *E* back and forth along its chain.

'He's very concerned about you,' said the doctor.

'He's not my husband. And it's a bit late for that.'

'What do you mean?'

'I'm fine. It's been tough with a new baby, but I'm fine.'

'How old is your baby now?'

'She's two months old.'

'Are your own mother or father nearby?'

'I have no contact with my father.'

'And your mom?'

'My mother is dead.'

The doctor laid down her pen. 'I'm sorry to hear that. Do you talk to Matt about that?'

'No. She died of a tumour in her head. He knows that.'

'Right,' said the doctor.

Matt knew that, but Elise had not told him how Patricia had forgotten her words, and how, when she did learn them again, her speech was different, her eyes were different, how it felt as if she'd been replaced with another woman, a changeling mother that Elise couldn't reach. How another tumour grew, like a stubborn vegetable in her mother's head, attached to some eternal stem inside her, growing bulbous, a malignant gourd. Elise closed her eyes. When she opened them again, the doctor was still looking at her. 'How old were you, Elise, when your mother died?'

'I was nine.'

'I see.'

'I'm fine,' said Elise. 'This isn't about my mother.'

'I want you to close your eyes again. Will you do that for me?'

Elise closed her eyes.

'Now breathe slowly. Just be here, in the room. I want you to tell me, if you can: what words come to you when you think about your daughter?'

Elise breathed deeply. She saw Rose, her little eyes peering at the ceiling of the apartment, her small pink paw on the gold necklace of the Madonna around Yolanda's neck. 'Reaching,' Elise said to the doctor. 'Head. Smell. Good.' She flashed her eyes open. 'This is stupid.' She felt a juddering sob and pushed it down.

'Close your eyes again,' said the doctor, still with a soothing voice. 'Just take a little time. Keep breathing. What words come to you when you think about yourself?'

Elise did as she was told, again. She closed her eyes, and listened to the clock on the wall. She tried to think of a word for herself. With Rose it was easy. Rose was *there*, solid and helpless and extraordinary – but she, Elise, she could no more find a word for herself than scale the Eiffel Tower. There was nothing inside her. 'Nothing,' she said. 'Nothing.' Tears were coming now. There was no word for her.

The doctor leaned back in her sprung leather chair. 'All right, Elise. It's all right. Take a tissue. What you tell me in here is between you and me.'

'You'll tell Matt.'

The doctor interlaced her fingers and rested them in her lap. 'I won't. What makes you think I would?'

'Because he needs to understand. That's what he wants. That's why he made me come.'

'*Understand?*'

Elise sighed, and picked again at the necklace, sliding the *E* over her chin. 'That's a lovely necklace,' said the doctor. 'Did Matt give it to you?'

She dropped the necklace back onto her skin. 'No.'

The doctor paused. 'You've been through inexplicable things, Elise,' she said eventually.

'That's a ridiculous exaggeration.'

'Birth is not an easy thing.'

'Millions of women do it.'

'That doesn't mean it's easy. Neither is learning how to be a mother. Or learning how to be a daughter. They don't give you a guide.' The doctor paused. 'Losing your mother like that can't have been easy.'

'Do you have kids?'

'No, I don't.'

'Then you know *shit*.'

The doctor smiled. 'Perhaps. Who have you talked to about how you're feeling?'

'You? I'm fine. I'm just tired. Can I go?'

'I want to give you some medication, Elise. Just for a bit. Will you try it for me?'

'OK,' said Elise.

'And I want you to come back and see me in a week or so.'

'OK,' said Elise, but she knew she wouldn't.

45

Elise decided she did not need to take the pills. She needed to
have her wits about her, to be alert. She did not need to be
drugged. She began to dream of the girl again, trapped in the
house with the collapsing roof, and she woke up with a shock,
convinced Connie was lying by her side. But Matt was by her
side, and Rose was asleep in her cot.

On the 3rd of September, she took herself and Rose in her
sling to a movie theatre on the corner where Nassau Street
met Fulton. The girl behind the glass at the ticket booth stared
at her.

'What?' said Elise.

'Nothing,' said the girl.

'One for *Heartlands*.'

Elise bought her ticket and sat in the dark. She began watching the film wanting to hate Barbara, and she tried but couldn't.
It was a brilliant, career-defining performance. Barbara's entire
body was made for a camera, let alone her face. Her eyes told
stories without the need for words.

It was strange. Barbara didn't look like this in real life. But
when the camera and lights were on her, and a character settled
inside her, the angles on her cheeks and mouth created alarm
and allure. She became someone else. Such was the quality of
the script, the direction and the cinematography, that when
Elise stumbled out into the main corridor of the movie theatre,

staring at the dull pattern of the popcorn-strewn carpet, she wept.

She was not crying for what Connie had done to her with Barbara, nor for what she and Matt had done to Shara and Connie – but for the fact that the film had shown her how flimsy her own life was. The world of the film was beautiful and solid. It felt more like real life. Elise thought New York would give her solidity. It hadn't.

She went on walking the streets around Nassau Street, up Fulton and onto Gold, before wandering back over Brooklyn Bridge. Rose was fast asleep. Elise stood in the middle of the bridge as the traffic thundered beneath her. It was getting dark. She'd been out for hours. Manhattan was blinking its lights on in the dusk. The Hudson was still.

What am I doing? she asked herself. *How did this all happen?* She imagined, suddenly, going straight to JFK and catching a plane to California, then a cab to Malibu – and knocking on Shara's door, her arms extended, Rose resting on her hands. *For you!* she would say. *See? I did it for you. Like you told me to.* And then Shara would take the baby, and everything would be right in the world.

Elise imagined clambering up, right now, onto the iron of the bridge. Who would talk her down? Who would see her jump into the water?

*

It took her two more hours to reach the apartment in Covert Street. By now, Rose was screaming. When she got in, Matt was pacing up and down the living room. He froze when he saw her, looking crazed. 'Jesus Christ,' he said, bounding over to her, taking her by either arm. 'Where the fuck have you been?'

'What?'

'I've been waiting hours. I nearly called the police—'

'I went to the movies.'

Matt crumpled to the sofa. He put his head in his hands, and wept.

'What's wrong?' Elise said, surprised.

'I can't do this,' he said.

'What can't you do?'

He waved maniacally at her, the room, at Rose. 'This is just madness, El. What have we done? I never know where you are, I don't know what state you're going to be in. You won't go to the doctor, you won't take your pills—'

'I'm going to Yoli's,' she said. 'Me and Rose are going to Yoli's.'

He looked up in horror. 'What?'

'I'm going to go and stay with Yoli.'

'Does Yolanda know you're going to do this?'

'It'll be fine.'

He got to his feet, the tears still wet on his face. 'I don't understand. You can't just invite yourself into someone else's – you're in no fit state—'

'I can, Matt. Yoli understands me. She knows how to look after Rose. I need her.'

'But I'm Rose's *father*.'

'It's just for a bit. You can visit of course. I just – can't be in this place any more.'

*

He didn't stop her. She knew he wouldn't. To stop her would be cruel and Matt was not a cruel man. If she wanted to take her new-born baby and stay with her friend, he was going to have to let her. And even if he had forbidden her, she would have slunk away when he was at work. He even helped her pack, disassembling the cot in order to take it over to Yolanda's. Once he'd calmed down, Elise could sense the relief in him; finally something was shifting, she had made a decision.

He walked her to Yolanda's apartment. When Yolanda opened the door to them both, she did not look surprised.

'I can pay rent,' said Elise.

Yolanda batted the air. 'Not now.'

Elise handed Rose over to Yolanda in order to get her suitcase over the threshold. She turned to Matt. In the context of a new apartment, in the outside air, she could see him looking at her as if for the first time in a long time. His face was grey and exhausted. 'It's going to be all right,' she said.

'I hope so,' he replied.

46

For two months, Elise lived under Yolanda's roof. Being with Yolanda definitely felt better than being with Matt. Yolanda was a home cook, and her *mofongo* with fried pork, her deep-fried chicken thighs drenched in lemon, rum and garlic, and her little *alcapurrias* of ground beef and plantain sated the emptiness of Elise's belly. Knowing that Yolanda would come home after her shift at the diner to feed her these delights brought a comfort to Elise that she found hard to understand, let alone verbalize.

Yolanda only had one bed in her apartment, and she had given it to Elise. Every evening Yoli slept on the sofa, and every evening, as Elise sank gratefully onto Yolanda's mattress, spreading her limbs like a star as Rose snuffled in her reassembled cot, she swore she would insist that the next night Yoli could have her bed back. But Yolanda never brought it up, and every night, Elise found the bed impossible to resist.

Matt tried to see them both, but Elise engineered it that Rose was asleep when he came round in the evenings, and that he really couldn't wake her. At weekends, he was harder to avoid. Yolanda, caught in the crossfire, tried to reason with Elise.

'You can't keep hiding for ever,' she said. 'And Rosita needs her *papi*.'

'You don't like me being here,' said Elise. 'You want me to leave.'

'No, no,' said Yolanda, sighing, and Elise felt bad for this cheap manipulation of her friend. These kinds of words and accusations came to her mouth so easily.

'Why won't you go and see the doctor, Eli?' Yolanda begged. 'It's good you're eating, but you don't leave the apartment and I'm worried. You gonna be a woman who lives in a box?'

'Why not? There was a woman who lived in a shoe.'

Yolanda looked at her quizzically. 'How she fit in the shoe?'

Elise laughed. 'It was a big shoe.'

Yolanda seemed uncomfortable. '*Mija*, just tell me. Is it over for ever between you two?'

'Yes,' said Elise, as if she had only just realized. 'Yes. It is.'

*

The days turned into weeks, and the weeks into another month. Eventually, Yolanda, her face looking tired and her movements heavy, sat Elise on the sofa and told her she'd been to see Matt herself to discuss the situation.

Elise was shocked. 'You went to Matt to complain about me?' she said.

'No, Eli,' said Yolanda. 'I am just worried about you. I love you, but you can't live here for ever.'

'What did you tell him?'

'I told him Rosita is OK. Told him you were eating more now. But not going out. Not washing enough.'

Unconsciously, Elise touched her hair. 'Do I smell?'

Yolanda demurred. 'He has called someone,' she said. 'A woman.'

'A woman?'

'Her name is Constance.'

Elise jumped to her feet. 'Yoli, are you joking?'

A look of alarm crossed Yolanda's face. 'No. None of this is a joke. Do you see me laughing?'

'He called *Connie*?'

'She is coming to visit here,' Yolanda said. 'Matt said she was a friend of yours. That you'd be happy to see her.'

'She's coming *here*?'

'Yes.' Yolanda gave her a dark look. 'I've got to clean the apartment.'

'When is she coming?'

Yolanda shifted uncomfortably on the sofa. 'Tomorrow.'

'For *fuck's* sake.'

'You're gonna see her though, yes? Your friend can't fly all the way from London and be turned away.'

*

Yolanda went to her shift at the diner, and Elise got out her vacuum cleaner and mop. She used strong disinfectant to clean the bathroom basin, the taps and floor. She washed the cushion covers in the bath, and while they dried she plumped up their stuffing. She wanted to call Matt and berate him for palming her off onto Connie like this, as if she was a problem child that he was renouncing to a higher power. But if she did that, he would just say Elise was the one who'd left. Matt was such a coward.

She washed her hair – twice – and cut the scraggly ends, tying the fine limp mass of it in a little bun so that it would be wavy for tomorrow. She chucked her sweatpants in the laundry basket. She went out with Rose in the sling and bought fresh flowers – roses, of course – and some lilies, and a pistachio cake from the Turkish baker she frequented, and English-style teabags from a bodega.

Back at Yoli's, she found a black dress in the closet that she thought would suit her, even if might be a little baggy, and she washed it in the bath, praying, like the cushion covers, that it wouldn't still be damp tomorrow. She decided it would be, so she went back out again to take it to the laundrette on the corner.

'Special night?' said the laundry worker.

'Something like that.'

It came out clean and dry and smelling good, and Elise buried her face in the hopeful newness of it. In the thrift shop next door to the laundrette, which she had never bothered to enter because it was dark and weird – even though in her past life it would have been a first port of call – she found a little lampshade, small and satin and pink. Back in the apartment, she screwed it over Yoli's naked bulb where it spread a blush on the wall. Tomorrow, Connie was coming. Connie was coming!

*

When tomorrow came, the wait through the morning and afternoon felt interminable. The covers had dried and Elise dressed the cushions, placing them artfully in a line against the back of the sofa.

Yolanda, having achieved her aim of galvanizing Elise into action, now seemed agitated about the consequences. 'You want me to stay?' she said.

'No, Yoli, it's fine. I have to do this alone.'

'This woman a witch, or what? Look at you. She's got you under a spell.'

'She hasn't,' said Elise. 'I'm fine.'

'Well, you call me at the diner, OK, if you need me, OK? The number's on the phone.'

Yolanda left the apartment, neither of them realizing it would be the last time they would ever see each other. Elise changed the flower water again, so that the roses and lilies were drinking from the freshest liquid possible. She sliced the pistachio cake into perfect eighths. She washed the teacups once more. But all of these actions felt at a distance. She could do nothing until Connie came.

Connie was in Manhattan *right now*. In an attempt to distract herself, Elise ripped a page from the pad that Yolanda used for her grocery list, and dashed off a large rabbit with a felt-tip pen. She sat for a long time with the drawing before her, thinking about Connie. Wasn't life a mystery – that her ex-boyfriend should be the one to bring Connie back? And wasn't it a miracle, that Connie wanted to come? They had so much to talk about, so much to forgive each other.

Elise admitted to herself, finally, that she was excited. She had missed Connie so much. She felt something like love surging through her again. She thought it had died. But it was coming back, and so was Connie.

'Shall we go and get some paint for this rabbit?' she whispered to her daughter.

Tying the baby into her sling, Elise ambled the sidewalk, looking for a place that sold green paint. It was so important to find that paint, to give Connie this present.

Eventually, she found a bodega that had a limited supply of children's paints. She snatched it off the shelf, a little tub of forest green, the poorest quality but the best that Ridgewood was going to offer. The hands on the clock above the clerk's head said nearly two o'clock. *I can't be flustered when she comes*, she thought.

*

Back at Yoli's, she opened the lid of the paint with Rose on her lap and dipped the baby's right index finger lightly on the surface. Rose had no clue what was going on as her mother lifted her over the paper and began to dot the insides of the rabbit with the green paint, guiding Rose's finger until a pointillist effect began to form inside the rabbit's body.

'It looks like measles,' said Elise, but she was happy, because here was a present from Rose, too. Connie would have to acknowledge it. She washed the baby's finger in the bathroom sink and saw a forest green crescent under Rose's nail, the tiniest moon she'd ever seen.

Elise wondered what to write under the drawing. *WELCOME.* No, Connie didn't like fuss. *For Connie, love Rose*, she wrote at the bottom of the paper. The paint wasn't drying quick enough.

She put on the clean black dress and retrieved a lipstick from Yoli's bedside table. She painted her face on like a mask, in as much of a likeness of her old self as she could. She loosened her tight bun and her hair sprang out in waves. She stood before the mirror, eyeing herself. It would have to do. She touched the necklace round her neck, Connie's gift, dulled slightly now, from her endless fiddling.

The buzzer went.

*

Rose was on her back on the small rug in the living room, gently buffing the air with shell-like fists. Elise scooped her up and padded down the short corridor to the front door. She realized then that she had bare legs – no tights, no moisturizer. It was too late to worry. She pressed the downstairs entry and waited, clutching Rose, her back to the wall, heart thumping. There was a knock right by her head, and without hesitation she pulled the door open.

'Connie,' she said. 'Hi.'

Connie's hair was shorter as Elise's had grown. Had she dyed it, to make it deeper, more of what was there in the first place?

She was in a trench coat, with a black Chanel handbag over her shoulder, and large gold orbs clipped to each earlobe.

Connie took a step back at the sight of Elise, as if she wasn't expecting the woman who stood before her. Her eyes flickered to the necklace and over to Rose.

'Elise,' she said. 'Hello. Can I come in?'

47

They didn't touch. Standing aside to let Connie in, Elise saw, suddenly, the shabbiness of Yolanda's apartment despite the attempts with the flowers and the bathroom's sparkle. The place didn't smell of roses, it smelled of cheap bodega bleach. She led Connie down the short corridor to the front room, which overlooked the noisy street.

'Here we are!' she said. The antique lampshade did not look quirky and individual as she thought it might. It looked like stained flesh. She put Rose on the floor and patted herself unconsciously. 'Sit down, please,' she said. 'Tea?'

'Lovely, thank you,' said Connie. She sat against the sofa and instantly depressed the cushions.

Elise went into the kitchen to fill a pan with water. She felt uneasy. They were supposed to have fallen into each other's arms in a hug and forgive it all – everything said, everything done, everything foolish. But they were talking like strangers. *Don't rush*, she told herself. She put the water on the hob and left it to boil.

Connie hadn't moved, but her attention was absorbed by the child on the carpet. She'd made no effort to pick Rose up. 'This is Rose,' said Elise.

'Hello, Rose,' said Connie, as if expecting a response.

'She's done you a drawing,' said Elise, flourishing the piece of paper.

'A green rabbit?' Connie said. 'How clever. Thank you, Rose.'

'You can take it with you,' said Elise, and Connie, realizing what she was supposed to do, took it from Elise's hand. She didn't look at it for long, but she did fold it carefully and place it in her bag. Elise feared the green paint might smear the inside of Connie's Chanel. 'Rose did it with the tip of her finger,' she said, but Connie didn't react.

'How have you been?' Elise went on, her chest tight with unspoken words as she knelt down beside Rose.

'Never mind about me,' said Connie.

'But I want to know.'

Connie hesitated only briefly, then proceeded to tell Elise how *Green Rabbit* had been a critical success back in the UK. Deborah and the publisher were relieved. Here, in the States, *Heartlands* had opened to great acclaim. The mention of *Heartlands* summoned Barbara into the room, and Elise, scrutinizing Connie for signs of discomfort, shame or even pleasure, discerned none. Connie did not allude to herself at all, only to her work. Everything was *successful*, *acclaimed*. The adjectives sounded strange in this dingy apartment, as if they had no place here.

'Are you writing?' said Elise.

'Yes.'

'What are you writing?'

'What I always write,' said Connie. Elise felt constricted.

She was just busy, all the time, Connie said. In London mostly, bar an occasional visit to Shara in California.

Now it was Shara's name that sat unwanted between them. 'I'm pleased it's all going well for you,' said Elise.

'Are you really?' said Connie, laying down a possible gauntlet. 'I don't suppose you think I deserve it to be going well.'

Elise chose not to respond to this. They sat in silence,

looking at Rose, who was on her back, doing nothing. 'I saw the film,' Elise said after a while.

'What did you think?' asked Connie.

'Aren't you surprised I went?'

'A little. I'm pleased.'

Elise placed her hands in her lap and smiled. 'I thought Barbara was excellent.'

'We were lucky to have her,' said Connie. 'I mean – you know what I mean.'

'Yes.'

'There's Oscar buzz,' Connie said. Elise was silent. 'I didn't go to the Catskills,' Connie said suddenly. 'After I saw you in Mexico. I went home. I thought I should tell you that. In fact, apart from the premiere in LA, I haven't seen Barbara since you left.'

'Am I supposed to congratulate you, or say I'm sorry?'

'Neither.'

Outside, a car horn was blasted and a man blasphemed in a thick Italian accent. The apartment was opposite a traffic light and there was always conflict between pedestrians and motorists. 'You were horrible to me,' Elise said. 'On the beach.'

'I know,' said Connie. 'But I was angry.'

Elise waited for an apology to follow, but none did. Jesus, Connie could be arrogant. She could never lose the upper hand, no matter what it cost. Rose gurgled and Elise patted her. 'I read *Green Rabbit*,' she said, feeling foolish saying the words, as if she was yet again trying to prove her worth by consuming all of Connie's creative output.

'I did wonder about the drawing,' said Connie.

Elise picked Rose off the floor, and sat on the hard wooden dining chair at right angles to the sofa. She refused to lubricate the conversation any more. She hadn't invited Connie here – it was Connie and Matt, and Yolanda, who'd plotted this ambush. There was no one on her side. Why should she flatter Connie, why lionize successful, acclaimed Connie, when apparently the whole world was doing that anyway?

She knew what Connie wanted her to say – *The novel was amazing. Is Rabbit you, and the lover me?* – just so Connie could laugh scornfully at her vanity in thinking herself interesting enough to be turned into a story. But Elise had read that book enough times now to know the truth; *Green Rabbit* was about their relationship: of that she had no doubt.

'So?' said Connie lightly. 'What did you think of it?'

Elise stared at her. Here she was, clutching a baby that Connie hadn't even *begun* to acknowledge properly or even enquire about – *how was the birth, what is it like, can I hold her, do you sleep?* – and all she wanted to hear about was her fucking book. 'I thought it was good,' she said.

Connie straightened her back and the cushions got even flatter. 'I see,' she said.

'You dedicated it to Shara.'

'I did. Can I use the loo?'

'Second door down the corridor.'

Elise sat with Rose while she waited. Every minute that was passing was an assault on her composure, and yet she did not want Connie to leave.

Connie returned. Standing by the door frame, she looked so anomalous in this brown room – like one of those extras on the Hollywood lots last year, she was existing out of space and time, a shining centurion in a nineteenth-century hovel.

'Why have you come?' said Elise, feeling her control beginning to break down.

Connie sighed, moving to sit back down on the sofa. 'I'm here to see you, Elise. That's it. Simple. I said to Matt I'd see you.'

'So you're not even here because you want to be here, but because Matt asked you.'

'He's worried.'

'I'm fine, Connie. We're better apart.'

Connie stood up again. 'I'm going to make the tea.'

'I'll make the tea,' said Elise. 'Take her a moment.' She handed Connie the baby.

'Elise—' said Connie, holding Rose at arm's length.

'All you have to do is hold her, Constance. She isn't a bomb.'

*

In the kitchen, Elise attempted some deep breaths. She lifted two slices of the Turkish pistachio cake onto a plate and tried to remind herself that this was her life. It was not Connie's. Connie was in her space. Connie could not narrate her life, nor change it. It was hers.

But it was no good. Connie's physical presence, so potent to Elise, always, was too close. She felt little to no will to defend herself against Con's skin, her pristine clothes, her endless achievements clinging to her almost physically, like perfume. Those gold orbs on her ears, her vixen sleekness and her merciless gaze as she took in the stains on the second-hand sofa.

She put her hands up on the kitchen counter to steady herself. No light came in from the dingy side window, lending the space a subaquatic feeling. She wanted to tell Con about her horror fantasies of abandoning Rose at JFK, with a one-way ticket to Malibu tied around her tiny foot. How she'd almost done it one day, beginning to pack a small bag of nappies before unpacking it again and lying with her face pressed against Yolanda's carpet, waiting for the will to get back up. How she fought with these thoughts and actions on a daily basis, and how she didn't dare tell the doctor the one time she was dragged to that awful room in Manhattan.

She fumbled with the clasp on the necklace, under her newly waved hair. She lifted it off her neck, the reverse of winning a medal. She placed it on the kitchen counter, and went back into the living room with a tray of tea and cake.

'No cake for me, but thanks,' said Connie. She was still holding Rose, which was something, at least. She hadn't dropped her on the floor or out of the window – and just like that, Elise closed her eyes against the ferocious, lifelike vision of Rose flying through the air to meet the sidewalk, the light sick thump as all her bones were broken. She could *hear* Rose's skull popping like a fortune cookie, her brain, the size of an apricot, smashed on the concrete.

All Elise could ever see or hear was bad things happening to this little girl, and she wanted to rip herself in two at how disgusting her mind was.

'Are you OK?' said Connie.

'I'm fine,' said Elise, opening her eyes, kneeling down by the coffee table and off-loading the tea cups. 'But you love sweet things?'

'Do I? Well, I'm trying to cut down on treats.'

'Right.'

'Will you take her?' said Connie, and freed of the child, she reached for the teapot and began to pour.

'It's really a shame you're not eating this cake,' said Elise. 'Don't worry, I didn't make it. It's good.' She broke a large piece off her slice and pushed it deliberately into her mouth, fingers everywhere, crumbs falling from her lips and into her lap and onto Rose's head. 'See?' she said. '*Delicious.*'

'Elise—'

'So if you're not going to eat it, I guess there's more for me.'

'You're agitated.'

'I'm not fucking *agitated*. It only *agitates* me when people tell me I'm agitated. And really, Connie. For the last time. Why are you here?'

Connie narrowed her eyes. 'You're very thin.'

'I'm always thin. Anyway, this is one of Yoli's dresses. She's bigger than me.'

'Are you eating?'

Elise held up the remains of her cake slice. 'What am I doing right now?'

'Exercising?'

Elise thought about her day and night walks that went on for miles, yet took her nowhere. 'Yep.'

Connie sipped from her cup, sat back against the sofa and looked around the room. 'Is Yolanda your girlfriend?'

'She's my friend.'

'But where does she sleep? There's only one bed.'

For a moment, Elise was tempted to toy with Connie, to see if she could make her jealous, seeing as she could not make Con feel anything else. But she was tired, and she didn't want to fight. 'Yolanda lets me sleep in the bed.'

Connie looked like she was going to say something, but she too appeared to hold her tongue. Her effort softened Elise. 'I forgive you,' Elise said.

Connie gazed at her. 'I don't think it's a question of forgiveness,' she said. 'Not any more. Not with a child.'

'That's exactly why it's a question of forgiveness,' said Elise. 'And I want you to forgive me too.'

'We've both made choices,' said Connie, shrugging, sipping from her tea.

'And I made the right one,' said Elise.

'I don't believe you really think that,' said Connie, replacing her cup precisely onto its saucer. She opened her handbag and pulled out a cheque. 'Here,' she said, holding it out towards Elise. 'Take this.'

Elise stared at her in disbelief. 'I don't want your money.'

'It never stopped you before.'

'I beg your pardon?'

Connie made a noise of exasperation and placed the cheque next to the teacup. 'Look at this place, Elise,' she said. 'What happened? One minute you're with me in California, with everything you could possibly dream of. Your life ahead of you, friends, me—'

'That's *your* life you're talking about. I was only in California because of you.'

'Well, you didn't last long,' said Connie. 'And now you're here.' Elise felt a rising fury as Connie continued to regard her with a cool expression. 'Did you know Shara was on suicide watch after hearing about your baby?' she said. 'Or did Matt decline to tell you that?'

'What would have been the point in telling me?' said Elise, but she felt disorientated by this information. She tried to mask her unease. 'I was pregnant, Connie. He was protecting me.'

'From what? You're in a terrible apartment.'

'Don't talk about Yoli's apartment like that.'

'I had to step over needles to get into this place. You're completely lost. And now you've got a baby who's going to leach you for the rest of your life.'

It dawned on Elise, then. All this – the aloof manner, the patronizing cheque – was because Connie could not forgive Elise for leaving. Her departure, possibly unprecedented in Connie's experience of love, had wounded Connie's pride so deeply. Not even writing *Green Rabbit* could expiate this wish of Connie's to come to Brooklyn and humiliate her. No wonder

Connie had looked with such disgust at the baby Elise and Matt had made together. Rose Simmons was a symbol of her failure to keep Elise at a disadvantage.

'You're jealous, aren't you?' she said to Connie. 'You thought I'd never survive without you. That's what all this is. You're jealous.'

'Jealous?' said Connie, laughing. 'You're barely surviving. And that child is your responsibility for the rest of your life. Jealousy is very far off my list of feelings.'

Elise held Rose tight, as if Connie might try and prise the baby from her grasp. Rose placed her head on her mother's shoulder and began to kick her feet. 'Do you think I don't know that she's my responsibility?' said Elise. 'Do you think I don't think about that every single waking moment?'

Connie sighed. 'What happens when the money runs out, Elise. What then?'

'Money isn't everything.'

'It is when you don't have any. How are you going to rescue yourself this time? Are you going to take that child down with you as you try?'

'Shut up.'

Connie leaned forward, speaking quietly. 'You've run away from every responsibility you've ever encountered. You get close and then you run. You ran away from your father, from me, and you ran away from Matt. God knows who else you've run away from in your life. You've never deigned to tell me. And I have a feeling you're going to do it again.'

'Stop telling me what I'm going to do,' said Elise.

Rose began to cry. Connie clasped her handbag, standing up as if to go. 'You're not well,' she said. 'That's obvious. You need serious help, Elise. You can't hide here for ever.'

'Don't turn this on me just because I've made a valid point,' Elise hissed.

At this, something seemed to snap in Connie. She slapped Yolanda's sofa. 'Your friend is sleeping on this piece of shit – for *you*. Matt called me – for *you*. You're a spoiled brat, Elise. We all drop our lives when you decide it.'

The pitch of Rose's scream went higher. Connie winced, walking to the door. She turned back, and her face looked haggard. 'You want to know why I'm here? I'm here to tell you to give Rose up.'

Elise stared at Connie, automatically jigging Rose up and down. Quickly, the child's sobs subsided, but Elise felt stunned. 'Rose is fine,' she stuttered. 'She's clean, she's fine, she's—'

Connie leaned against the doorframe. 'She's underweight. Look at her.'

'You don't just take a child away.'

'You're not a mother,' said Connie.

'What?'

'You don't know what you're doing.'

'No one knows what they're doing.'

'She'd have a better life elsewhere, Elise. You know it.'

'You came all this way, to tell me that?'

Connie came towards her. 'This isn't your life, El,' she said gently. 'It isn't. You've no money. You won't take it when it's offered. You've no support. You're not in a couple—'

'You're so old-fashioned,' said Elise. 'I thought you might want to help me, not throw money at me. You just came here to be sure that the damage had been done.'

'I came here because I want to help. Because I care about you, and that's the truth.'

'Oh, fuck off.'

'Where do you see yourself in five, ten, fifteen years' time?' said Connie. 'Sleeping in another woman's bedroom, serving burgers in a diner? Your life's a broken record.'

Elise felt a white rage run up the core of her body. 'You think your books and your money make you a better person than me. But they don't. No one's going to remember you, Connie. You're not that good. And anyway, no one can bear to stick around long enough. You're an uppity bitch who thinks everyone's beneath her. Thank god you didn't have kids.'

Connie turned away, walking quickly down Yolanda's corridor to the front door, yanking it open. The hallway smell of stale urine wafted in.

Elise ran after her, still clutching Rose. 'Connie—'

Connie whirled round, a mask of fury. She pointed a finger into Rose's tiny face, nearly grazing the tip of her nose. 'I feel sorry for you,' she said to the child.

Elise pushed Connie's hand away and it hit the side of the doorframe. 'Fuck you, Connie.'

'Your mother barely raised you, Elise. And now you're doing the same.'

'Don't talk about my mother.'

'I know you say it was a tumour. But was it that she went too funny in the head to cope?'

'She was sick, Connie. I know you think you're superhuman, but it happens to people.'

Connie's eyes were cold. 'I've often wondered if it might have been you who made her sick.'

Elise felt her knees give way, and slowly, inexorably, still holding Rose, she folded to the floor. 'Shut up,' she whispered into the top of the baby's head. 'It wasn't my fault.'

Connie seemed to sense that she'd regained the upper hand. Elise looked up. Connie's cheeks were flushed, but she composed herself, staring down at Elise. 'With a daughter like you, she probably died of shame. *Patricia*,' she added, lacing the name of Elise's mother with scorn.

'Please, Connie. No more.'

'And this one?' said Connie, looking down at the top of Rose's little head. 'With a mother like yours, it's hopeless, Rose. You're cursed. It's in your blood.'

Connie turned away, disappearing down the stairwell, her heels hard on the concrete. Elise stayed where she was even after she heard the door to the street slam shut. She sat in the semi-darkness, holding Rose, who began to cry and cry, until Elise could bear that particular sound no more.

2018

48

I stared at Connie across the kitchen table. The light from the day had gone. We'd been sitting there – how long? Two hours, maybe three? My sitting bones were numb. No words came to me, but my mind felt more alive than it had in years. I was reeling, trying to understand everything I'd just been told. I'd hoped I might find my mother in Connie's book; I'd never dreamed I might hear of her like this, in such detail, from Connie herself.

'I didn't mean what I said,' said Connie, interpreting my silence as disapproval. Her voice was tired and hoarse from talking so long. 'I am ashamed of myself. Of course I didn't mean it.'

I still couldn't think of anything to say. I'd never envisaged a story so intricate and intense, coiled within her, waiting to come out. My father had been married once before. My mother – vengeful, mercurial, loving and strange – had combed the shores of the Yucatán peninsula for pretty coral amongst the medusas. My mother, loving a woman, loving a man, maybe even loving me. But I knew it wasn't over yet; Connie hadn't got to her ending.

She looked drained, older than her seventy-three years. I felt that perhaps we should stop, but I'd waited too long for this. I tried to imagine my dad telling me all this himself, and I couldn't. I saw, now, how it had been beyond him. He'd never been able to find the words for his own story, let alone those that might help me tell mine. Connie, unsurprisingly, was the only one who could do that.

Seeing that I was unable, or unwilling, to reassure her, Connie carried on. 'It was such a cruel thing to say about her mother,' she said. 'So cruel. I knew I'd hit my target. But I was angry. If I could take those words back, I would. I don't know what I was thinking. I thought I could control the world back then, I suppose. And I did, most of the time. It was my time. I thought I had everything under control—' She stopped, and looked at me in horror. 'It sounds terrible when you tell this story out loud. Perhaps that's why I never did.'

Connie put her shaking hands up to her face, her fingers clutching at her forehead as if to pluck the memory of that dingy Brooklyn corridor from out of it. 'Please, Rose,' she said. 'Please, say something. Will you ever be able to forgive me?'

'Forgive you?'

She dropped her hands. 'Yes.'

'What happened after you left Yolanda's apartment?'

Connie looked distressed. 'I went back to London the next morning.'

'You didn't go back and apologize?'

Connie took a deep breath. 'No. I supposed that Elise wouldn't want me anywhere near her. And I didn't want to be near her, either. I didn't know what was going to unfold. If I had known, I would have stayed. But about a week later, I had a call from your father. Apparently, Yolanda got back from work that afternoon, and Elise had gone. She'd packed a bag, bathed you and put you in a fresh nappy, and left you in the cot with a necklace and a note.'

'Dad never mentioned a necklace or a note.'

'I'd bought her an initial necklace for her birthday.'

'What?' I said, my hands reaching for the *L* still hanging round my neck.

'Yes,' said Connie, eyeing it. We stared at each other, unable in the moment to excavate this creepy symmetry. 'Elise left it behind. If you didn't have it growing up, then maybe your father let Yolanda keep it.'

I wondered if this was true. Perhaps my dad had hidden it somewhere, slipped into an envelope, put in a safe place in order one day to hand it over to me. *No*, I told myself. *No more fantasies.*

'What did the note say?' I asked.

'Just one word. *Sorry.*'

We sat for a long time in silence. I thought of my dad – young, overwhelmed, getting that call from Yolanda, coming to her apartment to find her in tears, me in the cot with this useless note that revealed nothing, and possibly never would. A necklace from Connie he was probably glad to see the back of. I closed my eyes as if to erase the image, but Yolanda's living room – a place I would never see in real life – only came into more focus.

'When my dad called you,' I said, 'did you tell him about your fight with her? What you'd said to her about putting me up for adoption, and the things about her mother? The cheque you left on the coffee table?'

Connie closed her eyes and shifted in her seat. 'I didn't want to take the blame,' she said. Heaving a huge sigh, she bowed her head.

'My dad needed help—'

Her head snapped up. 'Matt had left my best friend's life in tatters. He'd run off with my girlfriend. I didn't want anything to do with him.'

'Yes, but—'

'And I didn't think Elise was really missing at that point! I thought she was just angry, playing games. She'd run away from me once before. When I spoke to him, he had the cheek to suggest that maybe I'd done something to her—'

'But you *had*,' I countered. 'You caused damage when you were supposed to make things better.'

'Why was it my job? Everyone was responsible for the mess we were in.'

'He called you and asked for your help, because he knew how much you meant to my mum. What you just told me this afternoon has made it clear: she loved you. I think you loved her. You were supposed to help her, and instead you pushed her away.' I felt tears coming, and I tried to swallow them down, remaining calm. 'You don't understand, Connie. I've grown up begging my dad to tell me what happened. But he didn't know – and he didn't know, because you didn't tell him the truth.'

'As soon as I found out she was missing, I said I'd come straight back to New York. I wanted to help, Rose. But your father told me I was half the problem. Even so, I did fly back to New York the day after he called me. Deborah came too.'

'And did he know you were there?'

Connie looked away. 'I didn't tell him.'

'Connie—'

'I went everywhere looking for her, making enquiries. I called my bank. She'd cashed the cheque. She'd done it the day of my visit, a branch in Brooklyn, near to Yolanda's apartment. In those days, that money would have been more than enough for a train, a flight to anywhere, and then money for accommodation. It could have lasted her months.'

A flight to anywhere. I put my head in my hands. We were coming to the close of this story, and I sensed the endings were not going to be neat. I pictured my mother with her small suitcase, a wad of hundreds in her coat pocket, staring up at the departures board – where? – JFK, Penn Station, preparing to pick a location as if it were a lucky dip? If there was one thing I had always known about my mother, it was that she was well-practised in the art of escape. What was it inside her that couldn't stay still, unable to remain in one place long enough to nurture even the smallest root?

'I had a breakthrough when I went down to Wall Street,' said Connie, bringing me out of my thoughts. 'I found Yolanda, at the diner they worked in. She thought I was from immigration. It took me hours to persuade her otherwise. She was so distressed. It was obvious that Elise had meant a great deal to her. She blamed herself.' Connie looked at me. 'She wanted to know very badly how you were,' she said. 'She cared about you. I thought the kindest thing to do was lie, so I said you were very well. I'd not seen you, of course.'

'What happened to Yolanda?'

Connie sighed. 'When I met her, she was talking about going back to Puerto Rico. I don't know if she did. I tried to track her down about five years later, when I was in New York again – just to see if she'd heard from Elise. But she didn't work at that diner any more. I went to the apartment, but the building she'd lived in had been bought and jazzed up. So she was gone, too. I don't know where.'

'And after Yolanda, the trail goes dead?'

'Yes. We never found Elise. I stayed in New York for a month and your mother didn't show up. I went to the morgues, the police. They couldn't find records of any Elise Morceau buying a flight at either of the New York airports. She stumped us.

We never found Elise. I took a deep breath. 'Constance. Don't lie to me like you lied to Yolanda. Do you think my mother killed herself?'

Connie stared at me. Then she stood up, walking slowly and painfully to the kitchen window, where she looked out into the darkness. 'I can't deny it's a possibility,' she said. 'But no. I don't think she did.'

'But you can't be sure.'

'No one can be. But for me, it was the bag she packed. She'd thought about it – underwear, socks, shoes. Even taken Yolanda's toothpaste. Your father clung to those details when he called me, and I did too. One thing we did agree on was that a suicidal person might not care about fresh breath.' Connie sighed, as if acknowledging the flimsiness of such a hope. 'And there was the fact she cashed the cheque, of course. And the way she held you, Rose, when I visited. She was always looking to you – kneeling on the floor by you, holding you. Whatever she was going through, she did love you.'

'Don't be idealistic, Connie,' I said, despite the fact this was my greatest hope. 'Don't bait me with a happy ending. It didn't stop her enough to stay with me.'

'But I just know—'

'You told her to give me up!'

'She wasn't well. Perhaps neither was I.'

'I think you're probably right about that. And it wasn't your place to make that choice for her. Why didn't you just persuade her to let my dad have me for a while?'

Connie came back to the table and sat down. 'I'm sorry. But in my opinion he wasn't able to look after you either. He called *me*, for Christ's sake. His sworn enemy. No one knew what to do.'

'She might have got better. In time.'

'If she'd had more support and expertise, yes. But she didn't,' said Connie. 'Nowadays, I expect they'd call it post-natal depression. When I went to Yolanda's bathroom, there was a bottle of lithium tablets on the basin. *Lithium*, Rose. Just give the woman some pills, hope for the best. Yes, perhaps I should have kept away, but at least I was trying to solve the situation.' Connie looked at me with a pleading expression. 'But for what it's worth, Rose – I've never thought your mother killed herself. She left the pills behind, and ran away. It's what she always did.'

'You told her that was what she was going to do, Connie. You showed her you had no faith in her. So maybe she was just doing what she was told.'

'I'm so sorry, Rose. I am. But I didn't force her to leave. Maybe in the end, she thought leaving was for the best.'

'Well, it wasn't,' I said. 'Fucking hell. I need a cup of tea.'

I went to put the kettle on. It felt as if we'd been in the kitchen for a day, a night, and a lifetime.

'You say that,' said Connie. 'But imagine the instability of life with her—'

'Connie. Don't,' I said, my voice breaking despite my best efforts. 'You don't know what my life's been like.'

Connie was silent and the kettle slowly started to hiss with boiling water. I put my hands round it to warm them up, to feel something. 'I'm never going to find her, am I?' I said.

Connie turned round slowly in her chair. 'I don't think you will. I don't know where you'd even start.'

'She's always going to be a ghost,' I said.

Connie appeared to hesitate. 'Forgive me for asking this. But what were you really looking for, Rose?'

I reached for two mugs and dropped in a pair of teabags. 'What do you mean? It's quite simple. This is getting rather repetitive. I was looking for my mother.'

'This was thirty-four years ago, Rose,' said Connie. 'The woman she was then is not the woman she'd be now.' I was still by the kettle, and Connie stood up and came towards me. Her expression was timid. 'Since you've come into my life – and I'm deeply glad that you did, as difficult as this is right now – I've begun to understand why you might be here.'

'I've told you why I was here—'

'Rose. I don't think you have been really looking for her.'

I stepped away. 'I have.'

Connie shook her head. 'I think you've been looking for an idea. I think – you've been looking for yourself.'

I clenched my jaw, willing myself not to cry, reaching for the kettle and pouring out the boiling water, watching the teabags bloat to the surface. 'You don't know what you're saying,' I said. 'You've no *idea*, Connie. Sometimes it feels that I'm *always* looking for her.'

'I know, but—'

'You *don't* know. If there's a knock at the door, there's always a moment when I think to myself, *Is it now? Is she back?*' My voice started to shake, and the tears I'd tried to hold so desperately now fell down my face. I broke down, unable to stop. 'It's never now. She's never back.'

Tentatively, Connie reached out and took me in her arms. With my face on her shoulder, I sobbed like a child.

*

A little afterwards, Connie excused herself and went to the bathroom. Exhausted, drained, I stared blankly through the kitchen window, thinking again about my dad. He'd always been with me. Every school play I was in, no matter how tiny the part. Every craft project. Holidays with him and my grandparents before they died, never leaving England because we couldn't afford air fares or fancy places. Before I became a teenager and started pulling away, he'd always been there.

I thought about how obsessed I'd been with my mother my whole life, and felt traitorous. I'd been so focused on the parent who'd never been there, I hadn't appreciated enough the one who was.

I placed the mugs of tea on the table as Connie returned quietly to the kitchen. She looked almost fearful, as if I wouldn't want her near.

'What happened to the painting Shara made of my mum?' I said.

'I don't know. I wish I'd told her I'd take it. She quite possibly painted over it.'

'Apt.'

Connie gave a small smile, sliding back into her chair and drawing a mug towards her. 'She married someone else in the end. They adopted three children. She's still in California. A grandmother now. She's like a big golden goddess out there. For her, it's like it never really happened. Your father. Elise.'

I felt something familiar inside me: the desire to close down in the face of other people's resilience. I resisted it. 'Well,' I said. 'That's good for her.'

'It is good. Good to know it can all be started over. Just not in the way you think. She deserved some happiness.'

'She did.' I took a sip of my tea and winced. I'd over-brewed it. 'And – did you see Barbara Lowden again?'

'Once, before she died,' said Connie. 'Purely as friends. She was in London a couple of years after all this, for the chat-show circuit after the Oscar win, and another film. We met in her suite at Claridge's.'

'Did you tell her that Elise had gone?'

'No. I probably just said we weren't in touch any more. I didn't like to talk about it. Actually, I think Barbara was a bit embarrassed about her own behaviour during *Heartlands*. Her personal life was in such a mess – I was probably collateral damage. Unfortunately, so was Elise.'

'And what happened to you, Con, when you returned to London?'

Connie hesitated. 'It wasn't great. I sort of – cracked in two.'

'You didn't write another novel,' I said. 'Maybe Elise's insults got to you, too.'

She smiled. 'Maybe they did. We knew how to get under each other's skin. But when it came to writing, I had the feeling that I'd said everything I wanted to say. Everything felt – empty. So I travelled. Rented this place out and lived in Greece for a while. Then down in Sussex. It was a good time, in many ways. I wrote for myself. Had a go at a screenplay, which I shelved. Lived off the rent here, and royalties of the books and the film.'

'But you're an artist. Surely you had to . . . make art.'

'Not necessarily. I couldn't see the point to any of it, Rose. It depressed me. The loss of Elise, and my role in it, was haunting me, I suppose. Her absence was heavy. The lack of physical proof. The memory. I've never accurately been able to describe it.'

'Until now?' I ventured. 'Until *The Mercurial*?'

Connie gave me a wry look. 'Until now. Rose,' she began, then stopped.

'Yes?'

'I think it's possible to free yourself of a ghost. You just have to want to do it.'

I thought of the other ghost inside me, and even though I was so tired – even though I knew I was going to have to make some decisions very soon – I felt released. Lighter. Even free. 'Just one more question,' I said, taking a deep breath.

'Anything,' said Connie.

'Did you really not look at me and wonder? Did you really not look at me and see Elise?'

Connie gazed with weary eyes into my face, and gave me a smile that was almost loving. 'Honest answer?' she said.

'Honest answer.'

'No, I didn't. I looked, Rose. But I saw you.'

49

It was a minimalist, light room, with lots of trailing green plants and successfully inoffensive artwork. Someone had spent a lot of time thinking about this room. It reassured me, especially after having to walk past the placards and people outside. I couldn't tell whether the decor was designed to be businesslike, blithe and blank, indifferent to the emotions emanating from the women who came here – or whether it was in fact chosen to be gentle, to acknowledge the need for a careful, neutral space.

Maybe each woman felt it accordingly.

'You'll be fine,' said the nurse, an older woman with grey hair and round glasses. 'It doesn't take long.'

I didn't know what to say to that. The thought that something like this could be over so quickly, compared to the years that were to follow, blank and unknowable.

For the surgery, I was told to leave all my jewellery at home. I never wore much. In fact, the only thing I had on that day was my L necklace. I stood in Connie's spare room and lifted it off my neck, holding it up to the light coming in through the window. It was such a beautiful, delicate piece of craftsmanship, but I knew that after today I would not wear it again.

At the clinic, I changed into the gown the nurse indicated, wearing nothing underneath, and I got onto the bed. She put cool hands on me, and said she was going to inject the local anaesthetic into my cervix. She was not over-familiar, neither was she cold. She was respectful. I put my knees up and heard the sound of implements clattering gently in trays, the silent hum of concentration at the foot of the bed.

'OK,' she said. 'Just let your legs go a bit, breathe in.'

I breathed in.

'Now breathe out.'

On the out breath, she slid a speculum inside me, and rapidly delivered the injection. I grew quickly numb, and heard the sound of the tube that must have been inserted inside me, sucking and sucking.

Of all things, they call it removal by aspiration.

*

Lying on the bed, I closed my eyes, wishing I'd been offered full anaesthetic, feeling it dreadful to be this conscious, hearing these sounds, even as the site of activity was hidden from my other senses. I felt rage – that I should be put in this position, that I had put myself in this position. That Joe would never be put in this position! Watching with a bird's-eye view, I felt sorrow. Fear – for the images of dark blood gouts, dripping bits of placenta, the vulnerable softness of that place. I felt faint at the thought of having been vacuumed. I felt astonishment at the removal of a story I hadn't asked for. I felt sick, and I felt hopeful.

*

Some days previously, and a few days after Connie told me about my mother, I came to my decision. I made the appointment, had the consultation, the blood tests. I thought about it, again and again and again. I felt relief at having come to a decision – and sorrow, and shame too – that I could experience both these feelings at once, that I could even allow myself them. When I told Connie what I'd decided, she held me tightly for several minutes as I wept, and had been gentle with me ever since. Cups of tea, suggestions for films we could watch on the TV, talking with me when I wanted to talk, leaving me alone when I didn't.

I did not want to be callous. I did not want to be cold. I just wanted to be me. I'd been feeling under such pressure – a pressure I'd found hard to name. Where it came from – from within me or without – I couldn't say. But I just felt like *a bad person*.

'You're not a bad person,' said Connie, as we were sitting in the living room, the evening before my procedure. 'Far from it. You're very brave.'

'Aren't I running away, too?' I said.

We fell to silence, thinking of another woman who had run away. 'No,' said Connie eventually. 'First Joe. Then this. You're facing the truth of yourself, Rose. But,' she added, 'I think there'll be grief, either way.'

'I guess so. I already feel like it's begun.'

'It's good to acknowledge that. Let's not pretend any more.' She leaned forward. 'And I'll be there. When you go in. And when you come out.'

I was grateful to Connie that she did not mention my own mother in all this. She'd made that mistake once before.

*

I had come to Connie looking for my mother, and instead she had given me myself. This was my realization: that I simply could not waste any more time hoping people would love me and respect me. Zoë and her friends had shown me that I'd learned more than I thought, in my thirty-odd years on the planet. Joe had freed me, my father had loved me. I had to stop looking at myself and finding myself wanting. I had to stop facilitating other people's lives at the expense of mine. I had to hold on to Laura Brown's self-confidence, her determination, and make them my own. My life was opening up for me, finally. Being here, in London, with a child; it was not my time. I didn't know when that time might come, or if it ever would, but right now, it was not that time.

It is often said of a woman that she is foolish to consider herself the mistress of her time. Her body has other plans. When it comes to children, people parrot, 'there's never a good time' – but I would counter that with the truth that there can be a bad time, too. When it isn't their own body and life – their own time – under discussion, people blithely generalize, even prioritize the myth of the perfect unborn over more complicated existences already here, now. It's only those who have become mothers who might put their hand on your arm, and tell you, *wait*.

It isn't perfect either way. You might wait, and lose your chance. But now I do not think that rushing will make you win.

What I saw, when I closed my eyes in the bed afterwards, was a woman wandering on a beach. She stopped and I tried to reach out for her. It was my mother, the dark-haired slim little thing in Connie's photo, standing by a Hollywood pool in a black dress. But it wasn't just my mother: it was me. And it was also Margaret Gillespie, waiting in the shallows of the water, without her daughter, waiting to decide if she was going to drown or swim. I wanted to reach out to her, and when I did, to my astonishment, a hand met mine.

Connie was sitting there, by my side. 'It's going to be all right,' she said, holding my hand. She put her other hand gently on my forehead, and held it there for a very long time.

50

There are always women, of course, who don't feel the floor slipping out from under their feet, who see an unwanted pregnancy as a surmountable situation, whether they go through with it or not. They can see the world of difference between being a pregnant human female and becoming a mother. They will not be in thrall to unasked-for biology. They will not have their minds turned in directions they do not want.

I was not quite like that. I know we all mourn what hasn't happened to us; a lover, a child. A different life. But in many ways, my own life had been a phantom to me. I needed to make it more solid if I was ever to build a life for someone else.

After the abortion, I spent the two following days in Connie's house in a quasi form of bed-rest. She had insisted I move back in after my stint at Zoë's, and it was what I really wanted. I felt as if I belonged to myself again. The feelings of exhaustion and nausea vanished, to be replaced with a sense of self-possession and weirdly heightened energy. When the money from the van sale came into my account from Joe soon after Connie and I returned from the clinic, I chose to gloss over the vague irony about the timing of these two events. When I saw the sum he had sent me, my eyes boggled. It was the beginning of February in London; the worst time of the calendar year, without doubt – and this strange gift was like a small candle burning in a window.

I texted Kelly. **Coffee?**

Yessss!!!! I miss you, she wrote. **Where the hell have you been?**

Long story.

After making arrangements with her, I sat on my bed in Connie's spare room and dialled my father's number in France. After a few rings he picked up, which surprised me; usually it was Claire.

'Hello?' he said.

'It's me.'

'*Rosie*. It's good to hear you! I've been thinking about you.'

'Me too, Dad. Are you all right?'

'I'm all right. Are you all right?'

'I'm fine. Actually, Dad.' I paused. 'I'm at Constance Holden's house.'

There was silence on the line. 'You're *what*?'

'It's fine, Dad. It's fine.'

*

I told him everything and he listened in deep silence. I told him about the job I'd got with Connie, and the trust I'd broken between us by pretending to be someone else, and the way she'd forgiven me for this as a means to atone for her own mistakes. I didn't mention Shara. That was for another time – or maybe never. It had been in another lifetime, one that didn't involve me, and one that he'd long ago left behind. But I did tell him the things he didn't know: the final argument between Connie and Elise, Connie's suggestion of my adoption. The cheque she left on the coffee table. The vicious words.

'Daddy?' I said. 'Are you there?'

'I'm here,' he said.

'I know it doesn't sound good. But Connie isn't who you think she is. She's been so good to me. You were the one who gave me her books. Don't hate her.'

He still wasn't saying anything.

'I'm sorry,' my dad said eventually. His voice was low and I could hear he was trying to keep himself together.

I closed my eyes, the tears rising inside. 'I know you are. It's OK.'

I pictured him in the gloomy vestibule of Claire's Breton cottage, amongst the waxed coats and old boots, the wind howling outside. It seemed impossible to me that my dad had once lived on the Californian coast, and surfed the waves in a young man's body.

'So Connie paid Elise to leave,' he said, a hardness in his voice I hadn't heard before.

'I don't think it was that simple,' I said. 'I think Connie was trying to help. She was emotional and it went badly. Maybe Elise was always going to run away?'

'Is that what Connie says?' I could hear the irritation in his voice. I said nothing, because it was exactly what Connie had said.

'Did Yolanda go back to Puerto Rico?' he asked.

'Connie doesn't know for sure. But she couldn't find her when she went back to New York.'

'I can't believe this.'

'Dad. You started this.'

'I know.'

I took a deep breath. 'Dad. You and Connie knew each other once. You could have found her number. You could have made contact—'

'I took you back to England, Rose, and just tried to get on with raising you. Connie was a big star. I couldn't believe how she talked to me after your mum disappeared. You'd think she was the bloody Queen. It was easier not to talk about it.'

'Easier for who?' I said.

There was a pause on the line. 'I just didn't want you to be unhappy.'

'I'm not unhappy, Dad. Not now.'

I heard a heavy sigh and wondered if he might be crying. 'I'm glad to hear that,' he said.

'And in the spirit of better communication, I think I should tell you that I've broken up with Joe.'

'What? On top of – are you OK?'

'I'm fine. I'm really fine.'

'He didn't *do* anything, did he? Another woman?'

I thought of Shara and winced at my father's hypocrisy. 'No. He didn't *do* anything. It was just time for it to happen.'

'When was all this?'

'A little while ago. I've been – working through some stuff.' I closed my eyes and was briefly back in the clinic. 'We're friends. It's fine.'

'So, what now? Are you still working for her? For Connie? I can't believe I'm even saying these words.'

I laughed, looking out of the bedroom window onto Connie's grey and windswept garden, its trees spindly and naked. I thought of the van money. 'I've got a few ideas, Dad. I'll let you know. I've got to go. I'm meeting Kelly.'

'Send her my love.'

'I will. Bye, Dad.'

'Rose—'

'Yes?'

I could sense him rallying himself all those miles away. 'Connie *definitely* doesn't know where your mother is?'

'No, Daddy. She doesn't. Elise has gone.'

He sighed. 'You're right. Of course. She's gone.'

★

Kel was already in the cafe, waiting for me. She was really big now; there was only a month or so to go. 'I know,' she said when she saw my expression. 'I look like I'm going to give birth to a football team. And the football.'

'You OK?' I said.

She smiled. 'I'm really good. Apparently you're always bigger second time round because your abs are fucked. Can you hug me from here, though? I can't be arsed to stand up.'

'Course.'

I embraced her. 'Ooh, you smell nice,' she said. 'New perfume?'

I told her it was Chanel and she gave me a look. 'From the girl who normally wears Impulse body spray,' she said.

'Kelly, fuck off. That was in 1995.'

'So,' said Kelly. 'Radio silence. New perfume. What's his name?'

'No name.'

'Come on. What's new?'

'I've decided to stop looking for my mother,' I said.

Kelly couldn't hide her surprise. 'OK,' she said. 'Well, Rosie, I think that's a good idea. It's a brave idea. I'm proud of you. Well done.'

'*Thank* you, Kel.'

'You seem . . . *lighter*. It's that woman, isn't it? The one you're working for?'

'Yeah,' I said. 'I think it is. I think you'd like her, Kel. You'd be really interested in her story. You should speak to her. She's got a new novel coming out. She's quite . . . a powerful personality.'

Kelly nodded thoughtfully. 'I can see that. I still think she's a witch.'

'Joe sold the van,' I said.

'Whoa,' said Kelly, her eyes wide. 'That *is* big.'

'I know. He gave me half the money, Kel.'

She laughed. 'What'd he give you? £3.50?'

'Two and a half grand.'

'Get out of here.' Kelly beamed and slapped her thigh. 'That is *amazing*.'

I felt a kind of joy bubbling up inside me. 'I know.'

'What a good break-up gift. I'm beginning to respect the guy now. Bit late, but still. What are you gonna do with it?'

'I'm going away for a bit,' I said.

'Oh? Where?'

'I don't quite know yet.'

This was a lie. I knew exactly where I was going: I just wanted to hold the secret of it to myself a little longer. The magic of it, the possibility.

'OK,' said Kelly. 'You are going to be around for the birth though, aren't you?'

'I – don't know, Kel.'

There was a beat. 'Right – no, of course. You do what you've got to do, Rosie. But send me a postcard. If they even *have* postcards where you're going.'

I couldn't believe how much this had unsettled her. 'I am going to come back,' I said.

'Of course. Unless you don't.'

We sat in silence. 'Well,' I said eventually. 'There is always that possibility. But I'd miss you too much.'

She laughed. 'Just tell me an address when you know where you're staying, OK?'

I promised I would. She looked ruminative. 'It's just the hormones,' she said. 'I'm cool.'

'I know.'

Impulsively, I stood up again and went over to her, taking her up in a big hug. 'I love you,' I said.

'I love you too. Rose, you're strangling me.'

'Oh, shit. Sorry,' I said, and let her go.

51

I went to the kitchen, made Con a gin and tonic, and brought it into the living room.

'Thanks,' she said, taking it from me carefully with both hands. Her eyes were bright, her back was ramrod-straight. 'Are we ready?' she said, gazing down at the A4 envelope resting on the coffee table. 'Go on. You open it.'

I did as she said and pulled out the unfolded hardback jacket for *The Mercurial*. It was sublimely beautiful. Two-thirds of it were covered in shades of blue – lapis lazuli, cerulean, royal, Prussian, sky – one upon the other layered like a woodcut, yet with an impressionistic stretch of beach in sunflower yellow running all along the bottom third, over the spine and round the back. The font was in pillar-box red, and had a kinetic, 60s inspired shape to it. The primary colours popped out at you, as did two women – cut, it seemed, from collages of women's magazines, their feet on the sand, but with their skirts at a different angle to their tops, their faces illustrated in fine black pen. The whole thing seemed to have a life of its own.

'Oh, *Connie*,' I said. 'It's incredible.'

'It is,' said Con. 'A lot nicer than the crap they used to come up with.'

'Here,' I said. 'You hold it.'

Delicately, she took it from me as if she was holding the

original Magna Carta. She spent a long time drinking in its colours, its feel.

'Do you like it?' I whispered.

'I love it. Oh, god. It's incredible. Rose, it looks like where you're going.'

We both looked down at the paper beach. 'I think Costa Rica's a bit wilder than that, Con.'

'Take lots of pictures, won't you?' she said. 'I want a full holiday snap situation. Overhead projector in here, the works. When you come home.' She looked up at me.

I came and sat on the arm of her chair. 'I'll be here in time for publication. Don't worry, I promise you I will. There's no way I'm going to miss it. It's still only February.'

She nodded. 'I want you to do this,' she said. 'It's important you do this.'

The air between us thickened with words we couldn't say.

'You know,' I said, 'I don't think I've ever seen a palm tree in the wild.'

Connie smiled. We were quiet. 'Right,' she said, breaking the mood, brisk and businesslike. 'I think it's time to go.'

*

She'd offered to take me to the airport, and although I'd protested I could take public transport, she insisted. I thought about her safety – those hands, particularly – but the truth was, once Connie got behind the wheel, she was pretty confident. She had an old, small sporty car, low to the road. It only fitted two people, and my backpack in the boot. She was a fast driver – too fast, really, but I could see she was enjoying herself as we bombed our way to Heathrow.

'Deborah wants to start interviewing candidates for an

assistant for me,' Connie said as we joined the flow of the motorway. 'I told her no way.'

'I think it would be good to have someone,' I said.

It would; I knew it, Connie knew it. She had come to rely on me as much as I had on her.

'They might make me eat diabetic-people biscuits,' she said.

'They might. But you could hide a few Penguin bars in your bedroom.'

We drove another mile or so in silence. 'Would they – live in with you?' I said.

I saw that familiar small smile on her face. 'No. And the position would be temporary.'

'Right.'

'Until you come back. That's your room, Rose. It's there whenever you want it. OK?'

I felt my throat thicken. I swore I wasn't going to cry. 'Thanks,' I said.

She carried on driving, and I got out my phone to text Kelly. It's Costa Rica, I wrote.

She replied immediately. Noooooooo. And then the emoji of the Costa Rican flag, a wave, a sun and a heart. You're going to see a jaguar! she wrote. So she'd remembered. I texted her the address of the house I was staying in, and told her I'd text again when I got there.

You'd better. Don't go off with a turtle rescuer. For too long.

I placed my phone in my lap and stared out at the motorway's indiscriminate blur of cars and green verge. 'I haven't told my dad what I'm doing,' I said.

Connie absorbed this. 'Give me his number,' she said. 'I'll call him.'

'What?'

'I think it's about time, don't you? We've got something in common again.'

I imagined the dynamite of this; Connie, calling up with all the information on his daughter, Dad realizing he'd been left in the dark again. Except this time, she would be sharing what she knew and he'd be in the dark no longer.

'It'll be fine, I promise,' Connie said. 'I know how to say sorry. We're old now. He loves you.' She paused. 'And so do I.'

*

We were nearing the departures terminal short-stay car-park. 'Do you – think you'll ever write about Elise?' I said.

Connie considered the question. 'Perhaps. What happened. Where she might be. It'd be a good story. But don't think about that now, Rose.'

'I won't.'

She parked the car. 'OK if I come in?'

*

People are turned anonymous, homogeneous inside airports. The air is heavy with the distillation of pain in parting – or the relief in parting and the joy of reunions, all swirling together incoherently. You cannot have a clear mind in an airport. You're halfway to the place you're going, already. No one ever really wants to be here, but it's the price you must pay for getting somewhere. I checked in my backpack, and walked back to where Connie was waiting.

'You take care out there,' she said.

'You take care, too,' I replied.

'I will. Deb's coming round later. We're having dinner.'

'That's good. I put lots of boxes in the freezer. They're all labelled. You just take them out the night before and—'

'Thank you, Rose,' she said. 'I do know how to defrost.'

I could tell she felt awkward, and I was frustrated myself at my inability to say what it was I wanted to say. *Thank you*, in essence. For everything – for the truth, for your shelter, for your trust. Thank you for giving me a chance. 'I'll send you lots of postcards,' I said. 'But they'll probably arrive after I've come back.'

She laughed. 'Thank you for letting me drive you here. I'll be waiting for you when you get back. Just let me know when that is.'

'Of course.'

Connie came towards me, took me in her arms and held me tight. 'Go and find those palm trees,' she said. She took two steps back. 'Go on.'

'Bye, Connie,' I said.

I walked towards the security gates. When I turned round for a final wave, she was still standing there, waiting until I was the first of us to disappear.

When She Left

52

When you pack up and leave, it unsettles other people. They want you to stay where you are, because it's easier for them to understand. Less work. But it's time for you to go. Perhaps a hot place with spots of shade, the astonishing, distant growls of big cats. Fewer layers on your body, your shoulders exposed to the air. The simplifying of days, the letting go.

Always, they think you are escaping, not turning to face your reality. But the reality is this: someone gave you money. The purchase of the ticket, the flight, the being nowhere before arriving somewhere.

But you're not naive any more, to think it's a new beginning. You've entered many houses and left them again. You made your home elsewhere and then realized they'd sold you a story. And it was never quite right – not then, not there, not him, not her – it was never quite your story.

You know, too, that your choices are not made lightly. The sweep of your arm to hand over your passport can feel like you're dragging it through pondweed in murky water, where pike stalk your hip, where your feet sink in brown silt. You can feel weighted daily by the act of trying to stay alive, to keep your head above the surface. But you still want to go on, because this is your story you're making. So imperfect, at times so wrong and unhappy.

And finally, when the beads of light come, and their

apertures open to show orbs as bright as the sun, and a whole planet of happiness bursts into being, and you walk about with it inside your ribs – you realize. How you stood in the darkness for so long, in order for this moment of illumination.

Acknowledgements

My heartfelt thanks to Juliet Mushens, Francesca Main and Kate Green, for their unflagging encouragement, hard work and generous imaginations.

Thank you to the team at Picador, whom I am lucky enough to call my publishers.

My deepest gratitude to the readers, booksellers and librarians of this world.

And thank you, always, Mum and Dad.

Particular thanks to Alice O'Reilly, Amy Cudden, Elizabeth Day, Jean Edelstein, Lorna Beckett, Luke Kernaghan, Maura Wilding, Teasel Scott and Zoe Pilger.

Margot: endless companion, still here.

And Sam: my brightest light and calmest gem. Thank you will never be enough to cover the distance we've come, but it's a start. I love you.

THE CONFESSION:
QUESTIONS FOR BOOK CLUBS

1. Truth and responsibility are at play throughout the novel, 'no one can really say what reality actually is. It's just so slippery.' How do characters in *The Confession* play with the relationship between the two?

2. In *The Confession*, Constance writes that, 'All women deserve the privilege of failure, but very few get it', and Rose observes, 'I could not escape my failing self or the potential selves inside me.' How do characters in *The Confession* move on from failure? What are those failures? Are they things the rest of us judge as failures?

3. 'And did you think I was Rabbit?' asks Connie. 'No. I thought she was fiction,' Laura replies. Jessie Burton has said in interviews that women's writing is frequently, and wrongly, perceived as auto-fiction. How is this played out in *The Confession*? What misconceptions and misunderstandings arise if the reader places too much belief in this? How does this work in novels written by men? What are the differences in the way the books are received?

4. How does Jessie Burton use art (film-making, writing, painting) to explore the relationship between truth and creativity in the book?

Also by Jessie Burton

THE MINIATURIST

The phenomenal number-one bestseller

There is nothing hidden that will not be revealed . . .

On an autumn day in 1686, eighteen-year-old Nella Oortman arrives at a grand house in Amsterdam to begin her new life as the wife of wealthy merchant Johannes Brandt. Though curiously distant, he presents her with an extraordinary wedding gift: a cabinet-sized replica of their home. It is to be furnished by an elusive miniaturist, whose tiny creations ring eerily true.

As Nella uncovers the secrets of her new household she realizes the escalating dangers they face. The miniaturist seems to hold their fate in her hands – but does she plan to save or destroy them?

'Fabulously gripping' *Observer*

'Powerful and richly imagined' *Sunday Times*

'Mesmerising and suspenseful . . . Unmissable' *Psychologies*

'Ripples with undercurrents, secrets, hidden histories and inexplicable mysteries . . . Tantalising, beautifully poised, exquisitely detailed' *Sunday Express*

THE MUSE

The *Sunday Times* number-one bestseller

A picture hides a thousand words . . .

On a hot July day in 1967, Odelle Bastien climbs the stone steps of the Skelton gallery in London, ready for her luck to change. She has been employed as a typist by the glamorous and enigmatic Marjorie Quick, who unlocks a potential Odelle didn't realize she had. When a lost masterpiece arrives at the gallery, Quick seems to know more than she is prepared to reveal and Odelle is determined to unravel the truth.

The painting's secret history lies in 1936 and a large house in rural Spain, where Olive Schloss, the daughter of a renowned art dealer, is harbouring ambitions of her own. Into this fragile paradise come two strangers, who overturn the Schloss family with explosive and devastating consequences . . .

'Tremendous' *Daily Mail*

'Entrancing' *Elle*

'Heart-stopping' *Daily Telegraph*